D0952344

HIDDEN AGENDA

HIDDEN AGENDA

THOM RACINA

A DUTTON BOOK

DUTTON
Published by the Penguin Group
Penguin Putnam Inc., 375 Hudson Street, New York, New York 10014, U.S.A.
Penguin Books Ltd, 27 Wrights Lane, London W8 5TZ, England
Penguin Books Australia Ltd, Ringwood, Victoria, Australia
Penguin Books Canada Ltd, 10 Alcorn Avenue, Toronto, Ontario, Canada M4V 3B2
Penguin Books (N.Z.) Ltd, 182–190 Wairau Road, Auckland 10, New Zealand

Penguin Books Ltd, Registered Offices:
Harmondsworth, Middlesex, England

First published by Dutton, an imprint of Dutton Signet,
a member of Penguin Putnam Inc.

First Printing, October, 1997
1 3 5 7 9 10 8 6 4 2

 REGISTERED TRADEMARK—MARCA REGISTRADA

Library of Congress Cataloging-in-Publication Data.
Racina, Thom
Hidden agenda / Thom Racina.
p.   cm.
ISBN 0-525-94031-6
I. Title.
PS3568.A25H54   1998
813'.54—dc21   97-23039
                                                CIP

Printed in the United States of America
Set in Sabon
Designed by Jesse Cohen

PUBLISHER'S NOTE

For Mark Larson

acknowledgments

To Rick Nusblatt, for the wacky original idea that sparked this.

To Joseph Pittman, for the trust in letting it write itself, and the enthusiasm after it did.

To Jane Dystel, for her support and dedication to this book and to me.

To Susan Feiles, for the continuing partnership that I cherish.

And to all my friends at the TWA Ambassador Clubs and on the planes, for making my commute a little easier.

author's note

This is a work of the imagination depicting events in the future. All of the characters are entirely fictitious, and any resemblance to actual persons, living or dead, is purely coincidental. While I have fictionalized the roles of a few journalists, political figures, news media executives and institutions that are identified by their real names, I have done so only to provide a real-life background to my portrayal of national politics and its coverage by the news media. The incidents and dialogues depicted in this novel, all of which occur in the future, are entirely invented.

Prologue

November 2000

The Marine Band played "Hail to the Chief" as the President and First Lady entered the glittering East Room. Jonelle Patterson glanced around the space she knew so well, filled tonight with familiar Washington faces and important names in the media, and suddenly felt a surge of wonder that she was here for the first time not to cover a story but to *be* the story. It overwhelmed her.

The First Lady handed Jonelle a glass of sparkling champagne. "You deserve Perrier-Jouët, but this is the White House, after all, so it's Napa Valley."

Jonelle smiled and sipped. "It's very nice." Then she asked a question, typical of her reporting style, that honed in on the subtext of Hillary Clinton's words: "Isn't it tough, sometimes? I mean, what if you really want to drive a Lexus?"

The First Lady answered with a question. "Didn't you report on the flack Diana got years ago when she ran around London in a Mercedes?"

"You're saying you're stuck with a Chrysler till the President is out of office?"

"Just two more months." Hillary gave her one of her ingenuous smiles. "I told Bill before the '96 election, you can't run again. He said, 'Why not? Whitewater? Travelgate? Filegate?' I said, no. Cirrus and Stratus."

Jonelle laughed heartily. The First Lady had a sense of humor that few people were privy to. Jonelle wished she could have communicated that side of Hillary's personality to the public. But the Clinton presidency was nearly over; they'd survived, and conquered, ushering in prosperity and balancing the budget in the past four years, as well as accomplishing campaign contribution reform, which everyone had said couldn't be done. And now that Jonelle and Hillary were friends, perhaps Jonelle could one day do a story that softened the opinion—which made that 1996 election so chancy—that this was a ruthless, dishonest woman who was far too driven.

The First Lady lifted her glass and Jonelle gently touched hers to it. Hillary whispered, "Don't tell anyone, but I've got a bottle of Mumm's stashed upstairs. Before we move out of here, we'll have lunch one afternoon, just us girls."

"I'm a reporter, don't forget."

"And the only one I trust." The First Lady looked at Jonelle with genuine gratefulness. "Before this goes into full swing and the speeches start, I want to say thank you again, from my heart. I'll always be indebted to you."

Jonelle whispered, "It was my pleasure."

Hillary Clinton laughed out loud. "Pleasure you almost died for."

The Marine Band played a waltz. Jonelle and her husband, Steven, were introduced to the queen of Norway. They saw friends from broadcasting. Then the vice president—now president-elect—sauntered over and Jonelle told him they'd seen Tipper in the vestibule. Jonelle congratulated him on his victory, for this was the first time she'd seen him since the election two weeks previous. "You're going to make a good one," she told him.

"Wow, that coming from a Republican."

"I'm a realist first."

"I'm just glad it's over. I couldn't have gone to one more brat-wurst festival, you know what I mean?"

Jonelle smiled, glad that he'd unwound. She'd always thought he was the perfect wax museum piece, but this past summer's campaign had really loosened his bolts. Tonight the stiffness was gone; he was wry, warm, and gracious.

It was Jonelle who was suddenly brittle, for as Al Gore segued from his upcoming presidency to the article Arianna Huffington had written about her in the *Los Angeles Times* just a few days ago, Jonelle suddenly and without warning became fast frozen. She'd managed to remain calm when Tipper Gore first brought it up when they ran into her in the vestibule tonight, but coming from this man, who would soon be the leader of the free world, it unnerved her.

The vice president asked how she felt about it, if she took it seriously, but he gave up midsentence, seeing he was losing her, inquiring whether she was all right.

She did not answer, for she was staring at three men who had just arrived to much greeting and fawning across the room. Bumps rose on her flesh.

Steven Patterson saw the three men as well, and immediately looked over to her. Sensing the panic on her face, he smoothly slid between her and the vice president, and, putting an arm around his wife to reassure her everything was going to be okay, steered the conversation away from the three bosses from Network ONE.

A little while later, the ceremony began.

The President spoke in warm tones. "The Presidential Medal of Freedom—the highest civilian honor in our great country—is being bestowed on Jonelle Patterson tonight for two reasons. One is her enormous dedication to reporting the news in America with honesty, integrity, and a sense of ethics that is seldom seen today." He wryly smiled. "If only some members of the White House press corps would take the hint." Sam Donaldson let out a howl. Jonelle's husband touched her hand under the table. The irony of the President's words were not lost on them. "The second reason we honor Jonelle Patterson tonight is a personal and deeply felt one for me. . . ."

Jonelle was aware of the President's voice, but his words weren't registering now as her eyes drifted to one of the Marine honor guard—and stayed there because she saw his face twitch. And as that happened, that seemingly harmless gesture on the face of a random serviceman watched across the room, the hairs on the back of Jonelle's neck stood up.

". . . for Hillary and I will forever be indebted to her for saving the First Lady's life."

Jonelle concentrated on the Marine. She'd seen this man before, she knew him. No, impossible, she didn't know anyone in the military. Maybe he reminded her of someone, but whom? Her husband saw her gazing toward the doorway and looked at her inquisitively, realizing she wasn't even hearing the President praise her.

"And now, ladies and gentlemen, may I present to you our honored guest, the famous, gracious, gifted, and courageous and heroic Jonelle Patterson . . ."

Jonelle realized everyone was staring at her, rising to their feet. She knew she was now supposed to accept the medal. But as she got up, her mind reeled. If she did not actually know the Marine, she knew something about him, had seen him before, had met him. He pushed an uneasy button somewhere deep in her consciousness and it made her blood run cold. As she passed him on the way to the podium, her husband whispered, "What's wrong?"

Smile beaming to cover her sense of curious dread, she muttered the words "I don't know" over the applause.

As the President presented her with the medal, she envisioned the Marine's face different—darker somehow, more hair, a heavier chin . . . no, with a mustache— She found herself shivering, crying out inside, *Could it be him? Was the gold ring under his white glove?* She looked to her husband in a desperate attempt to communicate what only he would understand as well, but his eyes were filled with pride mixed with the frustration of not knowing what was going on inside her mind.

She suddenly found the President hugging her, and she turned to face the gathered throng, trying to put the Marine out of her mind for at least a moment. But as she began her acceptance speech, her eyes wouldn't leave the young man in his dress blues still standing rigid to the right of the doorway. And that's when she realized that his hand had moved. And was moving still.

It wasn't a fast gesture, not one that would cause anyone to notice, nothing to alert the Secret Service or even someone whose eyes were wandering out of ennui, but Jonelle saw it clearly. The handsome Marine's right hand moved from its formal position against the sword hanging at his side and slipped, slow motion, into the front panel of his uniform. His eyes were darting around the room, but no one noticed because the focus was on her. All she kept thinking was the gold ring; if she could pull the white glove from his right hand, she'd find the gold ring. And then another chill: Was this the man she had met on the staircase in Paris? The build was the same, the strong chin, if he had a mustache—

As the Marine moved that gloved hand under his jacket, Jonelle gave her eloquent thanks almost by rote. Still talking, she discerned a bump in his uniform just below his chest bone, which she thought odd, as if there were some kind of growth or tumor there, or he'd wadded up a handkerchief and stuffed it inside. It was only a split second later that, as his fingers began to encircle the object under his uniform, Jonelle was sure what it was, and she managed to scream just as he withdrew the gun. And that's when she knew that she'd been right, that it indeed was *him*.

The first shot had no chance of striking its intended target at the front of the room, for two Secret Service agents pounced in response to her shriek, and the bullet ricocheted, shattering the crystal of one of the East Room chandeliers, raining what looked like rhinestones on the coiffed heads of the panicked people who were now scrambling for cover.

The second, fired from the Marine's prone position on the floor, tore through Helen Thomas's skirt, missing her left thigh only by inches, embedding itself in the wall about two feet from the podium.

The President, vice president, and First Lady had already been evacuated from the room by the time the finger again pressed itself to the trigger, but the foot of a Secret Service agent mashing his shoe there shattered the bones in the Marine's hand, making a third shot utterly impossible.

———

Jonelle and Steven found themselves in the Vermeil Room, se-
questered by the Secret Service along with Clayton Santangelo,
James Martin Findley, and Barney Keller, the three men who ran
Network ONE. It was an unexpected gathering of newspeople as
Cokie Roberts, Sam Donaldson, and two CNN reporters soon were
ushered in to join them, denied the chance to get the story out to
their bureaus. In time, an agent accompanied a very unhappy Helen
Thomas into the room, chagrined to be walking about with a White
House tablecloth pinned inelegantly around her loins, for her skirt,
with bullet holes front and back, had been confiscated as evidence.

The three bosses from Network ONE faced Jonelle and Steven
and expressed their "astonishment." One said it was criminal that
she wasn't allowed to get this out to the wire services. Another wondered aloud who the intended target was: the President? Vice president? First Lady? The third never said a word, just stared at her
with a knowing look, as if to say *I know that you know.* . . .

They were eventually interrogated by the Secret Service and the
FBI. No one, of course, had any idea how a man dressed as a Marine
honor guard could have gained access to the White House East
Room to attempt an assassination in the midst of a Medal of Freedom presentation. It was the most *preposterous*—Helen Thomas's
word—of scenarios. Each person was taken, one by one, to the ad-
joining China Room and interrogated privately by both the Secret
Service and the FBI. Helen went first, partially out of respect for her
humiliation over the tablecloth and safety pin, then Steven Patterson,
then Jonelle.

When Jonelle was questioned, she said exactly what Helen had
said, the same thing her husband had told them, and what Sam,
Cokie, Barney, and the other men would attest to as well: that they
hadn't a clue.

But that was a lie.

Jonelle did know something. She knew a great deal. She knew
that Steven would be waiting for her outside, and that they would
not get into the limousine that brought them, that they would have
to walk, and then, once out of the White House drive, they'd steal
one of the press pool cars and head across the river, never to turn

back, never to go home again. She knew that she was now "on the run," as they said in the movies. She knew her life would never again be the same.

Because she also knew that the bullets that everyone thought had been aimed at the President had really been meant for her.

Part One

chapter 1

O n the evening of December 14, 1996, two well-dressed men sat at a table in the intimate confines of the restaurant in The Inn of Little Washington. "Best food in the country, this place," Barney Keller said, wiping his smiling lips with a linen napkin. "Great food."

The other man seemed more interested in business. "So tell me," Rex Heald asked. "Why her?"

Barney got down to it. "She's completely clean, first of all. No dirt of any kind. The husband as well."

Rex looked antagonistic. "He's a commercial pilot, I understand. That in itself worries me."

"Don't let it. He doesn't fool around."

"I can't have skeletons, no surprises. No Dick Morris here."

Barney laughed. "Keeps it in his pants. Happily married twelve years, kids are postcard perfect, boy and girl, six and eight. Husband's forty-two. She's thirty-eight now, will be forty-nine when we have her in position, just the right age." He nodded to the waiter who brought coffee and continued. "Born in Georgia, outside Atlanta, pretty much to white-trash poverty I'm told, grew up addicted to television news, got a journalism scholarship to Northwestern, switched to Princeton, hooked a job in D.C. after graduation. Government, not media—"

Rex interrupted, impatient. "How'd she meet her husband?"

"In the friendly skies. Commuter plane spun off the runway after landing in a storm at Dulles. He was the pilot, she was the only passenger stupid enough—or driven enough to get a story—to fly that night. He carried her through the mud to the terminal. Rest is history."

Rex searched the recesses of his mind. "Why do I connect him with television as well?"

" 'Cause that's what they had in common. He was a tape editor, worked over at WJLA for a while, mainly did political ads free-lance. He still dabbles on the side; edits some of her pieces, I understand. He's good. But he likes flying more."

"When did they marry?"

"In 85. Bought one of those rotting mansions in a semi-shitty neighborhood on Sixteenth Street, led the gentrification on their block. She was basically fetching coffee for senators at that time, it was going nowhere, switched gears and went into local news, WRC. Got lots of exposure 'cause she's so beautiful. But she was good too, so CNN snapped her up." He reached into his briefcase, which was at his feet, and pulled up a file. "Here's an early review: *She's a hard-hitting, incredibly charismatic young reporter, tough as nails but possessing sensitivity and warmth, much like Oprah, which makes people open up to her. This girl is going places.* Washington Post."

"She's never lived up to that early promise."

Barney smirked. "She hasn't had our help. Nobody's done to her what we aim to do to her. She's got the potential, that's what's important. She's ripe for stardom."

"Finances?"

"Not quite into six figures yet. The husband makes about a hundred K from TWA, however. On the plus side for us, they're up to their eyeballs in debt like all the leftover yuppies. Private schools for the kids, that house has been a money pit, got the summer place to take care of, you know the routine."

Rex grinned. "Sounds a little like me and my wife." He sipped water. "Religion?"

"You'll love it. Not only are they both fine Christians, but the husband's an ordained minister, for Christ's sake."

A scowl. "Barney!"

"I mean that, *for Christ's sake*, like in saving souls and stuff like that."

Rex obviously knew he was joking. "You need to be born again."

"I pray to a different God."

"Yes, I know," Rex said, rolling his eyes, not even considering the possibilities. "Go on. He's a pilot and tape editor *and* a minister? The husband, not God."

"Renaissance man, what can I tell you? Actually, he was ordained by a fringe Baptist sect in Virginia. Don't think he ever practiced. Probably did it for his parents."

"Tell you the truth, I know a lot about his father. I was just testing your research."

"What about his father?"

"You don't know who he is?"

"Should I?"

"Charles Patterson. *Professor* Charles Patterson."

"I know his name, we got that. But who the hell is he?"

Condescendingly, Rex said, "One of the quiet leaders of the Christian movement. Teaches at Regent University."

Barney looked honestly amazed. "Pat Robertson's place? I'll be damned."

"That's for sure."

"It's my goal. So go on."

Rex continued. "Charles Patterson has written several books on—"

"Don't tell me, let me guess: Jesus, God, all that good stuff. I stick to nonfiction myself."

"Very funny."

"So, it's perfect, right?"

Rex seemed hesitant. "Well, this *could* be very good for us."

"That's what I'm telling you. Besides, she's got the highest

Q rating in the television industry for someone not yet in the Sawyer/ Couric league. Remember when they took a poll years back and found that Cronkite—a damned reporter—would beat any presidential candidate if he'd declare? Walters could have done it too. See, America *trusts* this girl. She just needs more prominence. A little push."

Rex relaxed and admitted, "She's my wife's favorite. I like her too." But he had a big decision to make here, and it was not coming easily. There was still some doubt. "But does she have what it takes to . . . to accomplish what we need? To go where we need her to go?"

"She's smart, first of all, top of her class at Princeton. Majored in government there, Woodrow Wilson School. She's got guts and drive, she's covered Europe—at CNN she slogged Christiane Amanpour's cameras through the mud for years—which gives her a working knowledge of foreign affairs. Better yet, she's a Washington insider, yet removed enough so she wouldn't have that stigma. I hear she wants to spread her horizons anyhow. No enemies, is sympathetic to your cause, and she's a Republican. She fits the bill. She once interviewed Mrs. Huffington and Arianna said she was the only reporter ever to ask the right questions."

"The TV audience may trust her, but can *we*?"

Barney suddenly looked closed. "I believe there is no need to share the overall, long-range plan with her at this time, if that's what you mean."

"Of course."

"Things will fall into place naturally. In the meantime, over the years we have to accomplish this, my job is to increase her visibility, to make the people want more of her."

"Starmaker is risky business."

Barney reminded him, "This whole cockamamy idea is risky. That's why I think it could work."

Rex pondered again, looking at the fresh flowers on the table. "Granted, it sounds doable."

Barney smiled and leaned back in his chair. "Then I have the green light?"

"What about the other two Horsemen?"

"They've already given their blessing. I swear on the Bible, Rex, I know this is *right*."

"For a Jew you talk a lot like a Christian."

"Must be you guys rubbing off. By the way, Merry Christmas."

Rex laughed out loud. "Happy Hanukkah."

"Ninety-seven's going to be our year, Rex. She's your girl, I'm positive."

Rex thought for a moment. Then he made his decision. And it was a pronouncement, because what he was giving the green light to was momentous. "Okay, then," he said quietly but assuredly, "make the move. Go get her."

chapter 2

Jonelle heard a voice call her name as she rounded the corner into the main terminal building of Washington's National Airport. It was Barbara Gordon waving a mystery near her pushcart book operation, Books on the Fly. Jonelle hurried over with a grin on her face. "How in the world did you get it this quickly?"

"For you, I'm FedEx," Barbara joked, handing her the book, "and I see you're running—what else is new? I'll put it on the account."

"Thanks, Barb, you're great." Jonelle tucked the hardcover novel into her bag and headed out to the parking lot.

The rain she'd seen from the windows of the plane hadn't stopped, so she popped her fold-up umbrella and Fred Astaired over the puddles until, near her car, someone backed out of a space and splashed her. She opened the back hatch of the Volvo wagon she and Steven had bought just a week ago, tossed in her travel bag and briefcase, and then hurried to the driver's door, eager to duck out of the rain. But she stood frozen for a moment, getting a whole lot wetter, as she stared at the first ding—a bona fide dent, really—in the paint. She hated parking lots for just this reason, and vowed never to leave the car at the airport again.

The sneaking suspicion that God was testing her today was shortly confirmed. The George Washington Parkway was a mess, halting and sporadic, which gave her plenty of time to gaze out through the wet windows at the magnificent beauty of D.C., the city she loved and knew so well. No matter how jaded she sometimes felt with her job, D.C. still held a magic allure for her. Washington was in her blood, of that she was certain, but she wished she could feel the same passion for reporting political news. She'd become restless. It was time for her to move on, do other things, discover the rest of the country, work in Europe again, prowl Asia, seek out a story in South Africa. She was afraid she was beginning to feel like a politician who knew nothing of the world he represented because he lived an insular life in the very comfortable confinement of the District of Columbia.

The 14th Street Bridge was backed up, so she tried Memorial Bridge and succeeded. She considered answering her cellular phone when it rang, but resisted when she saw the number of the caller, one she didn't recognize; she would check her messages when she got home. She'd planned this day to be with her kids, and she was fearing, as usual, that something newsworthy would happen that would mess up those plans. On the Rock Creek Parkway, she told herself she'd give it one more year; if her agent hadn't gotten her a position outside Washington in one year, she'd just quit—fire him, and do it on her own.

She took the Dupont Circle exit in a downpour, braved the traffic in her neighborhood, which seemed peppered with idiots bent on playing demolition derby, and finally came to a halt in front of the big redbrick house on the corner of R and 16th Streets. Hurrying to the side stairs, she noticed Steven's ice skates lying next to the kids' skates on the porch. The rain had only started yesterday; before that it had been freezing, and Steven had probably taken them to the rink. Or, more to the point, Sarah and Wyatt had probably taken *him*, because he was the real kid in the family when it came to things like that. Steven delighted in simple pleasures. That's part of the reason she married him.

She didn't have much time. She hurried through the mail sitting unopened in a pile in the dining room, ran up the back steps, and started stripping as she neared the top, was in the shower in no time. Refreshed and wrapped in a fluffy towel, she looked at the blinking answering machine in the hall, not feeling up to dealing with it but knowing she had to. The messages were the usual mix of work, friends of the kids, Mike at Heishman's Audi asking if she was enjoying her new car, and lovely words from Hugh Downs, thanking her for the birthday flowers. They'd recently fought one another for a story, and he won; he was bigger and more powerful, she was D.C., he was NYC. But it had made news of its own, and the public relations aspect didn't hurt her at all.

She checked MCI One for her cell phone messages, then pulled her laptop out of her briefcase and plugged in her modem to call up her E-mail. Several messages had been posted, all of which could wait, and one from Steven telling her he thought he'd be delayed getting into Dulles later, check with the airline before making the trip. He added that he missed her and loved her, and reminded her that they had promised to take the kids out to dinner tonight at the place of their choice. Jonelle laughed, knowing that meant McDonald's.

Donning jeans and a sweatshirt, she called the studio to set a time for her meeting the next morning, checked on messages there, and learned there were no major crises in D.C. that warranted her attention. She also called Helen, her elderly neighbor who'd become a surrogate grandmother to the kids. "How were they?"

"Angels."

"Tell me another one," Jonelle laughed. She knew Wyatt and Sarah could get away with anything with "Auntie Helen." "How are you feeling?"

"Old," Helen said in her no-nonsense way.

"Me too," Jonelle added. "Gotta go get the kids."

Helen asked, "Will you need me tonight? I marked it down on my calendar."

"Steven's coming in."

"Good. I'm going to bed early, then."

"You rest well. I'll talk to you tomorrow."

"Okay," the old woman said.

"Oh, Helen. Thanks." Jonelle could hear the woman's smile in return over the phone.

Jonelle grabbed her car keys and made her way back out to the car. She wished she hadn't parked on the street because she got drenched again, but the garage door was impossible—they needed a new opener. She looked in the rearview mirror, dabbing on a little lipstick to give the illusion of being alive, and set out to complete her errands before she fetched the kids.

Friday's traffic would have been horrendous even without the rain, but the added annoyance of precipitation made it really ugly. She played the radio loud—news, what else?—and found herself, finally, after listening to a rehash of the crisis in Egypt that she'd been reporting on for the last four days, at Hechinger's at Tenley Circle, where she got the hinges Steven had ordered for the French doors they were putting in between the living and dining rooms. She remembered the garage door opener when she was already halfway out the door, and told herself to forget it. At Fresh Fields, she filled a cart in record time, like some quiz-show winner who had a minute to collect all the groceries she could push. The bill was higher than she felt was morally acceptable for food, but she paid it with her Visa card to get miles (it took the edge off) and was delighted to find only a drizzle greeting her as she piled the bags into the back of the Volvo. But the little dent in the driver's door still pissed her off.

Ten minutes later, she pulled into the parking lot at Saint Alban's on Wisconsin Avenue just as her son, Wyatt, was walking out the door, backpack dragging behind him.

"*Back* pack," Jonelle said, stressing the first word to hint at where it goes, as he climbed into the car. "And it's all wet."

"Hi, Mom." He pecked her on the cheek.

She tousled his blond cowlick. "Wyatt," she said, looking at the ratty bookbag, "we just bought that a month ago. It's supposed to go over your shoulders, not pull it like a flight attendant."

"Dad drags his."

"His has wheels."

He noticed that she turned right instead of left. "Where we going?"

"Your sister is in a recital."

The boy turned green. "Oh God, not—"

Jonelle cut him off. "Not a word," she warned.

"Potomac will go for me."

"No, he won't. You're sitting through every last arpeggio."

"What's that?"

"Some kind of finger action on high notes, I think."

"Nooooo," he groaned as if suddenly stricken with pain.

"Sarah sat through your baseball games all summer, mister. The least you can do is spend one hour in the auditorium, calmly enjoying the music."

"They stink."

"They're young."

"You say I stink when I play bad baseball."

"These are Philharmonic musicians in the making."

"Making noise."

"Come on, Wyatt, be a sport."

He crossed his arms in submission. But added, "Yuck."

She figured the way to his heart was through his cholesterol level. "You get to pick where we're having dinner."

His eyes lit up. "McDonald's!"

She turned left and rolled hers. "Figured."

"Ma?"

"Yes?"

"You look pretty today."

She beamed. Leave it to her kid to know just what to say.

They picked up Sarah, two years Wyatt's senior, and the direct opposite with her dark locks and secretive brown eyes, at her school, Sidwell Friends, and then they drove to the Levine School of Music, where a handsome instructor named Victor Gallindo introduced his students. Sarah was the last one, probably because she was the best. But that meant that Jonelle and Wyatt had to endure all the others, and it was trying. There were a few honestly excruciating moments, ones that tear mothers' hopes apart; one little boy was so nervous that he peed in his pants and had to stop while they wiped up the floor under the piano bench. Twice Jonelle had to grab Wyatt's arm to keep him from bolting. When Sarah finally appeared, she played Bach's "Musette," and very well.

After the lights came up, while partaking of tea and cookies, Mr. Gallindo congratulated Sarah on her performance, and told Jonelle it was clear she really had talent. "She's come a long way since the last recital."

Jonelle grinned. "For seventy-five dollars an hour, she'd better."

He laughed as well.

Wyatt said, "Can we get out of here?"

"Hey, buddy," the piano teacher said to Wyatt, "when are we going to start your lessons?"

"Potomac says it's for girls."

"Who's Potomac?" Mr. Gallindo asked.

Jonelle jumped in. "His . . . uh, friend. We'd better go. It was a beautiful recital, Mr. Gallindo. Thanks so much."

Wyatt pulled his baseball cap from his belt and popped it on his head. "Yuck," he muttered.

And Sarah smacked him.

While Jonelle took Wisconsin Avenue to Georgetown, she let Sarah call TWA on her cell phone; they learned Steven was going to be on time. In Georgetown, Jonelle ran in to see her seamstress, Rosita, who had taken in a gown she'd loved but felt uncomfortable wearing. "You lose the weight, look very good," Rosita said to her.

"I feel better." And she did. Her on-screen image had never meant much to her, and she cared less if she put on a pound or two. During the pregnancies, it mattered nothing to her when the ice cream and Kron chocolate added some heft to her figure; she wanted healthy kids and she was going to eat for them. But lately she'd started to feel like a sludge, and she'd suddenly joined a gym—she'd never been able to find the time on the road, but in Washington it was practical, no excuses—and it had made a difference in how she felt, as well as how she looked on camera. Her ratings had gone up slightly just because she was more attractive. Which pissed her off as much as the dent in her car, but she knew it would take years yet before women were less the sex objects and more equal with men.

On the Key Bridge, going toward Interstate 66 on the way to Dulles, fighting the still-awful traffic, Jonelle asked the kids about the coming weekend, how much homework they had to do, whether they wanted to stay home or go to the house in Bucks County now that their father was joining them. It merely set off an argument between them. At the Ballston exit, Jonelle had to slam on the brakes to avoid hitting the car in front of her, which had no taillights. Jonelle reminded the kids that their grandmother Patterson's birthday was coming up, suggesting they might want to make their own birthday cards for her.

"She's not a very happy lady, is she?" Wyatt asked.

Jonelle knew exactly what he meant. "She's very reserved, Wyatt. They're like that down south."

"She hardly talked much at Christmas time."

"She's a very quiet person." Jonelle felt she was running out of excuses for Steven's mother's seeming lack of interest in anything. Jonelle on occasion had secretly referred to her as "the Corpse."

"Is Grandma Lighter a quiet person?" Sarah asked. Never having met her other grandparent, it was an honest question.

Jonelle just laughed out loud. "Quite the opposite, honey, she's loud and brassy."

"Why don't we go see her this weekend?" Wyatt suggested.

Jonelle changed the subject. "Look at that accident." The kids peered out the right window at a car that was lying on its side.

"Wow!" Sarah exclaimed.

"Potomac's dad was in an accident."

"Really?" Jonelle said, with a tone of skepticism in her voice.

"You didn't tell us!" Sarah said.

So Wyatt did. In detail (on a country road, no one was hurt), for the next twenty minutes.

When they got to the airport parking lot, she aimed the car for the empty spaces way over in the corner and parked over the line between two of them. "That's not very courteous, Mom," Sarah said.

"It wasn't very courteous of someone to smack my door," she replied.

"Can't wait to see Dad," Wyatt just said.

There was a thrill Jonelle always felt when she saw her husband striding toward her dressed in his captain's uniform, and today was no exception. Perhaps it was a throwback to the time she first met him, but it was never something she took for granted. Today was no different. As the kids ran to Steven Patterson with shouts of "Daddy, Daddy!" as he stepped off the jetway inside the terminal, Jonelle thought he looked handsome, suave, and younger than any pilot she'd ever known. They were all supposed to be about sixty and have silver hair. Hers could have doubled for a model. At forty-two, Steven Patterson had the dark, ruddy good looks of someone ten years younger. He lifted up his sunglasses and kissed her on the lips. Then he turned to the kids again. "Where we eating?"

"McDonald's," they said in unison.

Steven rubbed his stomach and said, "Mmmm, yummy."

Jonelle groaned.

But McDonald's it was.

She almost nodded off between the french fries and coffee. She'd gotten little sleep in the last four days. She'd been covering the Washington side of the tense situation in the Middle East, and had gone to New York to interview Madeleine Albright. Shortly before she and Jonelle were due to arrive back at the secretary of state–elect's apartment, a bomb had been discovered in the building's lobby; it was detonated with no injury or loss of life. However, the message was clear: Terrorism was now firmly planted in American soil. Jonelle, for CNN, had been lucky to scoop everyone, for she was with Albright when the former ambassador was informed of the incident.

Steven, who was just as tired as she was, but for other, easier, reasons, hurried the kids along, and they were home by seven. "There is a blessing to all that grease in fast food," he said with a smile. "It makes you sleepy." Sure enough, by 7:15 he was reading to the kids in the king-sized master bed. By 7:30, Jonelle had changed into a stunning dress, kissed them all good-night, and was out the door.

The glittering black tie preinaugural affair thrown by The Phillips Collection was held (oddly, she thought) at the French embassy, a building Jonelle hated because it reminded her of her high school gymnasium with its cold marble and glass walls. For the French to build such a place shocked her the first time she saw it, but then again, as Steven reminded her, just look at the horror of the Parisian suburbs built in the 1980s. She sighed as she drove through the gates, thinking that for the same money they could have constructed a Loire Valley chateau. She almost got her wish, for tonight the whole place was transformed.

She stepped from her car onto the flower-covered bank of the Seine, where boatmen in their wide-collared striped shirts who were also tonight's waiters graciously handed out champagne and truffle-oiled toasts as the guests arrived. Memories of the earlier McDonald's feast were immediately erased.

Mrs. Robert "Oatsie" Charles, grande dame of Washington's Old Guard, warmly grasped Jonelle's hand in the receiving line, and said, "Lovely to see you, and thank God you're the last."

Jonelle loved this generous and humorous woman who, despite being one of the richest people in America, always made her feel she was just one of the boys. "Been doing this long?"

"Seems like all day. What I wouldn't give for a cocktail."

Jonelle offered a sip of her champagne.

Oatsie shook her head. "Vodka. I've earned it." She took Jonelle's arm. "Let's find you a chair and me a stretcher and we can chat all night."

Jonelle laughed as Oatsie took her arm. They crossed the gorgeous, elegant room. Jonelle told her she was impressed. "I was expecting red, white, and blue bunting. This is pretty wonderful. The flowers alone . . ."

"Thank *him*," Oatsie said, grabbing the hand of a tall, lanky, striking young man walking the other way. "He redid this place tonight. Jonelle, meet Mark."

Mark happily shook her hand. "Your interview with Arafat was amazing."

"I think your transformation of this airport hangar is what's amazing."

"Thanks. They wanted to keep it French."

Oatsie interjected, "Celebrate giving us the Statue of Liberty, huh?" while nodding to a replica of the statue.

"Something like that," Mark admitted.

"It's a relief from all the inaugural stars and stripes you see around town," Jonelle said. "But," she grinned and sighed, looking at Mark, "what I really want to know is where were you when I planned my wedding?"

Oatsie and Mark drifted off to replenish their drinks, and Jonelle made her way through the crowd, where most people who recognized her expected her to be followed by lights and a minicam. She was not here, however, to cover the party. She was here to attend it. What the public never understood was that besides being a Washington reporter, she also lived there, and she loved it, the city beyond the federal buildings and political life. She loved the culture, the ambience, the glorious concerts and plays and museums, the Phillips especially, of which she and Steven had been supporters for years. Lynne Flexner, Jonelle's sometime tennis partner and the board member who'd put this evening together, walked up from behind and hugged Jonelle, joking, "You in your civvies tonight or is this all on the record?"

Jonelle said, "Night off."

"Hey, we could use the publicity."

"What I'd like to do right now is a good serial killer profile. Something to break the mold."

"I'm thinking of murdering a few waiters," Lynne said, and they both laughed.

Katharine Graham joined them, and after the usual It's-Inaugural-Time-Again niceties, Jonelle got into a spirited discussion with the matriarch of the *Washington Post* about the annual

SuperSale benefit Kay sponsored a few months back to benefit the Nina Hyde Breast Cancer Research Center at the Lombardi Clinic. Jonelle's mother had lost a breast to cancer just three months before, and even though they were estranged, this was a cause she wanted to be part of. She planned to do three in-depth pieces on it on the news. If they'd let her. She was finding little artistic freedom at CNN these days. And for the next two weeks all they wanted her to report on was the inauguration. Ugh. Restless had become her middle name.

Jonelle enjoyed her dinner companions, a table around which sat younger, hipper people than one might think the staid Phillips into its seventieth year would draw, and danced with now-fellow reporter George Stephanopoulos when they found themselves the only two wallflowers left staring over the blue hydrangeas and red roses. They were old pals, a few skirmishes in reporting Clinton news notwithstanding. She chided him that he should be practicing his Macarena for the Inaugural Ball. He laughed and whispered, "Confidentially, here's an exclusive: The reason I'm departing the administration is I can't dance it."

At midnight, Jonelle had her car brought round and drove home tired and eager to curl up in Steven's arms.

She was precisely in that position when the phone rang. She'd just gotten comfortable against Steven's chest, just turned the lights off. She didn't want to speak to anyone, and Steven certainly agreed. But when she heard the machine pick up down the hall and it was clear to her the voice was one she didn't know personally but was shocked to hear, she grabbed the extension next to the bed. "I'm here . . ."

She was talking to Barney Keller, a man she knew only by reputation, and an incredible one at that. He was the current God of Television Programming, and had made headlines for the last few months because he, along with two other men, had just started a fourth national network and were busy robbing the others of their best talent. "Sorry to call so late, but I hear newspeople never sleep."

"This one does."

"I've been an admirer of yours for a long time," he said, ignoring the insinuation that he woke her up.

"And I of you. But you called to tell me that in the middle of the night?"

"Can you come to New York in the morning?"

"I just flew in from Kennedy *this* morning."

"Planes go the other way as well."

"How about later in the week?"

"Not good."

She looked at her husband, who motioned her to hang up the phone. "Can I ask what the urgency is?"

"I can't say over the phone."

"Well, then I can't say it's worth flying back tomorrow for. I'll call you the next time I'm there."

"Jonelle—"

"Good night." She said it pleasantly, but firmly, and hung up.

Just when she'd snuggled against Steven's hairy chest and felt his protective arms around her again, the phone rang once more. She groaned, he groaned, unlocked her, turned the other way, and she grabbed it before the machine again did. "You don't give up easily, do you?"

"Huh? Jonelle, it's Dick."

"Dick?" It was her agent. "You suddenly a night person like Barney Keller?"

"He call?" Dick sounded urgent, impressed.

"Yes."

"Did you *say* yes?"

"To what?"

"Meeting with him."

"No."

"What?"

"I'm not going back to New York tomorrow, not on Saturday. I haven't had time with my family since—"

"Are you nuts?"

"Dick, what's going on?"

"Jonelle," the voice said with urgency, "I've never steered you wrong before. Well, maybe once with CBS, but never again. Do as I say: Call him back right away. Don't hesitate, don't take a breath, write this number down—" He rattled it off, and she did as told. "Just make sure you do it now, call him immediately and tell him you'll be there, first thing in the morning."

She took a deep breath, her curiosity really teased. "Okay, Richard, tell me what this is all about."

"This, my darling, is all about what you've been saying you've wanted for a very long time now. To break free of Washington, get out and soar, blah blah blah. This is also about the fortune I'm going to make off you when you become the kind of star that only Barney Keller can make you."

"Dick, come on—"

"Jonelle, 'Killer Keller,' the most powerful man in the business today, plans to offer you the job of a lifetime."

chapter 3

Jonelle was ushered into the most lavish office she'd ever seen. It felt more like a private gentlemen's club in London than a high-rise in New York City, all polished dark cherry wood and leather, humidor holding Havana's finest, Cragganmore Scotch and Waterford crystal positioned on a polished silver tray on a marble sideboard. Books lined all four walls, and—odd for one of the most powerful men in television—there wasn't a monitor in sight. The tall, balding but good-looking man rose from behind an exquisite antique desk, the focal point of the room. "Jonelle, how nice to finally meet you. I'm—"

"I know who you are," she said softly, "everyone knows who you are."

Barney Keller graciously took her hand and motioned to one of the comfortable wing chairs near the window. She walked over, sat in one, and he did the same, facing her. "How is it we've been in this business for so long and we've never met?"

She smiled politely. "You've been here a lot longer than I."

"I just turned fifty. Don't rub it in."

She smiled. "I think it's because you're in a different world from mine. I'm still a cub reporter in the trenches."

"Not if I can help it."

"How do you mean?"

He crossed his legs. "Forgive me. Coffee? Water? Soft drink?"

"No, thank you. Your secretary asked when I arrived. I would like that desk, however."

"Desk?"

She peered over his shoulder at the desk from which he'd imperiously risen. "My granddaddy had one like that, all pine too, in his office when I was growing up."

"Ah. What kind of work did he do?"

"Dry cleaner. My father as well. They said my great-grandfather made that desk himself and brought it down to Georgia from Pennsylvania when the family resettled."

"Make an interesting piece: 'Death Knell for the American Craftsman.' "

"I'll do it." She got up and walked to it. "May I?"

"Be my guest."

She ran her fingers over the wood, the carved curves of the corners. "It's not as old as it looks, but well crafted," Barney said.

"The depth of the finish is remarkable."

"No stain, just wax, waxed to a gleam."

She admired it for another moment, then turned back to join him. "Are you interested in antiques?"

"I appreciate things of value. Articles that shine, sparkle. Finely crafted pieces that appreciate with time."

She sat again. "We have a house in Bucks County because I love antique country."

"I'm not talking about furniture. I'm talking about you."

"I've been called a lot of things, but never an antique—at least not yet."

He smiled warmly. "We want to make you a star. We feel you have what it takes."

She stifled her gasp. "I'm flattered. But what do you mean by 'a star'?"

"You're going to be the domestic Christiane Amanpour."

"Chris is my mentor. I can't leave CNN."

"Then what are you doing here?"

She swallowed hard. He had a point.

"Jonelle. Listen to me. We're a new network, you've read every-thing there is to read about us, you've even heard the inside gossip, there's nothing I can tell you that is going to be news. But I want you to hear this from the source: We're hungry for talent, we're going to be the biggest and the best, and in a very short time. We're going for names, but we're also going to *create* names—fast. You sign with us, I promise you an Emmy in the first year."

"No one can promise that."

His eyes fixed on hers. His gaze was like a laser of sincerity. "I *promise* you an Emmy. Guaranteed. Or double your first year's sal-ary as a bonus."

She laughed out loud. "Are you for real?"

He only returned a sly smile, then reached into a briefcase that had been strategically placed near the chairs and pulled out a con-tract that looked to Jonelle as if it was the original manuscript of *War and Peace.* "Have Dick look this over, get back to us, we want to close this right away."

She felt the weight of the pages in her lap. "When—?"

"Immediately."

"But . . . I can't just—"

"Yes you can. We'll see to it."

"How—?"

"We'll sever your contract with CNN effective tomorrow. We'll pay the costs of that broken agreement. You'll start as a featured reporter."

"I'm already that at CNN."

"That's just the beginning here. With your talent for sniffing out the toughest story, combined with your beauty and on-screen charm—off-screen as well, I must say I'm happy to see—you'll go on to anchor the network news."

"Oh no. I'm not Connie Chung, don't set me up for failure. Anchoring the big news has never worked for a woman."

"Alone. No Rather or Reasoner to steal your thunder."

"That's not what I want, chained to a desk in New York."

"You'll do it from Washington."

"The only thing I want right now is to be out there getting stories. I've got the nose for it. I'm still going to live there, but I'm tired of Washington coverage. I don't want to be Cokie Roberts at the end of my career."

"Washington is in your blood, you know the players, you have respect. But, no, frankly, we don't see you parked forever on the White House lawn. The plan is this: We'll give you your own featured story every night for three months—on the network news, any subject you choose—to get the public to demand more and more of you, then—"

"You're so sure?"

He just grinned. "Then we'll give them what they want. Your own hour-long, prime-time news specials—one a month starting in June '97, then we go weekly when we feel the audience is there, probably a year. Which is where you're going to get your Emmy."

Jokingly, she said, "How about my Peabody? My Pulitzer?"

"In time, even Nobel won't be out of the question."

"No reporter has ever won the Nobel Peace Prize."

"Let's make that your goal then."

"Yeah, sure." She let out a nervous laugh and got up, walked around the chair, looked out the window at countless Manhattan spires, and felt giddy, like a kid who'd just gotten off a carnival ride. *The Nobel Prize?* She turned to the man in the chair, the carnival barker who'd drawn her inside the tent, studied him, but he seemed as serious as a bank manager. He *wasn't* kidding. He actually believed what he was saying. He had to be nuts.

Then she stopped herself, remembered that this man was a brilliant programmer, he'd been called a visionary, a genius. He ruled in the power game. At thirty, he'd sold his own cable company to become almost as rich as David Geffen. He'd gone on to retool FOX after Barry Diller left, create their cable news network, and went to Viacom to single-handedly sharpen their competitive edge in the rapidly expanding cable and interactive worlds. This was someone a reporter dreamed her whole professional life to meet, someone you would give anything to work for, have on your side. And here he was, offering Jonelle, one-on-one, face-to-face, the career of a life-time.

It seemed too good to be true, too easy. So she asked, "What's the downside?"

He thought for a moment. Then looked up at her and smiled. "We'll own you."

"Meaning?"

"You sell us your soul. You'll do nothing for anyone else. Nothing, not even charity. And we get you for ten years."

"Ten years?" she gasped.

"Five to start, we can drop you at each year's interval, pick you up at year five for five more, but you don't have the right to leave. And we'll expect a great deal." He didn't take a breath. "Of course, we'll also pay you a great deal."

Somewhat defensively, she said, "Can I ask what that is?"

"Half a million for the first year, a million dollars the second, a million more each year for the next three. If we renew our option, seven million dollars in the sixth year and so on."

She could not allow him to see her shaking, nor could she bear to let him hear her heart pounding, and she figured she was going to faint face-first to the floor if she stayed standing, so she turned gracefully around and slid back into the chair and deadpanned, "Don't suppose there's any chance of putting in some overtime, huh?"

Barney, not a man who was easily amused, actually laughed out loud.

Jonelle walked into the living room and tossed her purse on the sofa, where she joined it in a flop. Steven came in from the kitchen, knife in his hand, where he'd been chopping onions. "Good flight? I picked up some swordfish, making mango and onion salsa to put—" His voice stopped when he saw the numbed expression on her face. "What happened? It didn't go well?"

"Well? I'm numb. I think I was just offered the sweetest deal since ABC renewed Ted Koppel."

Steven wiped his hands on the apron he was wearing and sat next to her. "That's great."

She grabbed his hands in hers.

He pulled them away. "Don't touch me. I stink."

"I don't care. I have to hang on to something."

"What's wrong?"

"You mean what's right. It's . . . well, it's greater than you think."

He finally got it. "How much?"

"Millions."

"Millions?"

"Millions."

He grabbed the telephone.

"Who are you calling?"

"TWA. Retiring."

She howled and hugged him. "No, no joke," he kidded joyously, "I'm giving notice and writing that book I always talked about."

She kicked him playfully. "You never talked about writing a book."

He set the receiver down. "I never talked about retiring either. They're nice new thoughts. Just think, a man of leisure, living off his wife's paycheck. I'll get myself a nice new Audi A4 and go fishing."

"You hate to fish. And you'll get bored."

"I'll edit free-lance. Buy my own plane. Maybe start a restaurant . . ."

"Don't count the horses. I didn't sign anything yet."

"On second thought, I'll work a few more years for my own pension."

She laughed. "We're invited to dinner next week with the three men who run the network. They're coming here to 'get to know us better.' "

"You played *that* hard to get?"

Jonelle squeezed his leg. "Millions," she whispered, as if the action represented pinching herself.

"You're already on TV," bright-green-eyed Wyatt said, stabbing his mashed potatoes again and again with a spoon.

"So I'll be on TV more." Jonelle grabbed his hand and gently forced it down beside his plate. "But a different station."

Sarah said, "MTV?"

Jonelle laughed. "I'm too old."

"And they don't have enough money," Steven added.

They changed the subject as they ate, talking as they usually did each evening about how the kids did in school that day, how much homework they were facing, what their plans were for the next day. But through it all there was an underlying giddiness and delight that really surfaced once the kids had gone to sleep and Jonelle and Steven were sequestered in the privacy of their own bedroom. They felt like two kids themselves, adolescents who'd suddenly been welcomed into an adult playland of future success and accomplishment, the world at their feet, good fortune easily at hand, security attained.

They had a pillow fight, which they'd not done since their honeymoon, Jonelle bouncing on the bed on both feet shouting, "I love it, love it, love it!" until Steven pulled her down to him, kissed her, and told her it was she who he loved. And then they made love that was romantic and caring, but wild and passionate at the same time. It was the start of a new chapter in their lives.

The dinner took place a week later at the Occidental Grille on Pennsylvania Avenue, one of the most popular restaurants in the Washington power structure. Barney Keller took the shuttle in from NYC, and the other two owners of Network ONE—James Martin Findley, the old-school money man, formerly second-in-command under Paley for over twenty-five years, and Clayton Santangelo, a video whiz kid not yet thirty who leaped to the top of the TV heap with unbridled enthusiasm and a brilliant publicity-minded psyche— flew a private Jetstream from California. The food was fabulous, and the purpose of the meeting was an easy one, and it should have gone smoothly. But not at first.

At first things were tense. For all the "we already feel like family" banter, Jonelle felt on trial before three men she didn't know at all. Their Hermès ties began to loosen as the fine wine kicked in and Jonelle warmed them with fascinating anecdotes about her career and life, in which they seemed rapt. As the dinner progressed, there seemed about the group a united drive to succeed at something new, unchartered, going directly against the odds.

But Steven played devil's advocate. "Who in the world needs another network?" was his bold question, designed not to cost his wife the potential job but rather to understand where these guys were coming from, and why they'd spend more money than God to make it work. Besides, suspicion was in his makeup.

Clay, by far the most gregarious and at ease, answered. "No one. There are too many already. Then why do it? Because none of the others are any good. Oh, some have strengths: Roone Arledge keeps ABC News on the cutting edge, NBC owns sitcoms, Lifetime has the women locked up, CBS's got daytime and nothing much else, MTV and Nick have the kids, and so on."

Barney interjected, "CNN's got hard-core newsies."

Clay continued. "What we aim to do is have it all. We'll be number one with news, number one with sitcoms—intelligent, smart, human situation comedies—a daytime lineup that's the antithesis of creaking soaps and the garbage talk shows that still linger on, children's programming at its finest, and at night, a touch of drama in the old *Playhouse 90* tradition that transcends television as we know it."

Steven said, "That's what they all say." He looked a little embarrassed because it came out so firmly.

Barney replied just as firmly. "Yes. But only we will do it."

"I tried to tell Paley this," Findley said with a kind of dead-end frustration. "If he'd have listened, CBS wouldn't be in the toilet. And I guess I'd still be there." He smiled. "Not that I don't like working with you guys." Everyone laughed. "We have one major difference from the others, however," he continued, "that's going to give us the edge."

"What's that?" Jonelle asked.

"We have deeper pockets."

Steven bluntly probed, "Where's all this money coming from?"

Barney stood up and patted his pants pockets. When he sat down again, he said, "We're very rich men. We're just doing what Spielberg and Geffen did, putting our money where our mouths are along with our investors. And we don't plan to lose a cent, we plan to make a great deal. So you can see our commitment."

"More wine?" Clay asked, devilishly.

By the time dessert arrived, the talk had turned from the logistics of making this network a success to the politics of succeeding where they were all out for a common goal: a better, cutting-edge, ethical network, and Jonelle was going to lead the parade.

Clay asked about her own political feelings. She admitted she was a Republican, that she leaned slightly to the right of that center, that she had hoped last fall's presidential election would produce the right candidate, but Bob Dole obviously wasn't it, and that she didn't see anyone exciting on the horizon.

"Because Gore has it in a lock?" Clay asked.

"Not necessarily, though I think you're right about that. It's a bigger issue, a deeper one. We don't know the difference today between celebrities and heroes. Where are the heroes? I want my kids to grow up believing in leadership. It's frustrating on a very disturbing level."

"You're very passionate about this," James Findley commented.

Steven chimed in, "She's a closet senator. I've told her for years she'd stir 'em up something good."

Barney looked quizzical. "Run for office?"

Clay was about to say something, but Jonelle anticipated his thought and cut them off at the pass. "I'm a reporter. I've covered those crooks for years, I wouldn't be caught dead in Congress." The men laughed. "I'm taking this job because I've had enough of Washington."

Barney Keller agreed. "Are we out of our minds? Do we really want to lose her to politics?" He stood and lifted his glass. "Here's to our new star." They all joined in the toast.

After he sat down and they talked about it being late and time to go, James Findley, who was more soft-spoken and thus seemed more thoughtful than the others, said quietly to Steven, "Don't discount the idea completely, put it away for a few years. Leadership is hard to find, and she's already got a built-in following."

Steven nodded politely, humoring him.

"I mean," Findley said, "after we make her a star, she could have any office she wants."

Playing along, Steven replied, "I wouldn't let her run for anything less than president."

"You'd get my vote," Clay joked.

Findley lifted his glass again, humorously toasting. "To the first female president of the United States, then."

Then Findley glanced at Barney Keller, who eyeballed Clay Santangelo, and there was a fleeting moment of contact as if firming up a pact, the look the Mafia godfather shares with his lieutenants to the exclusivity of everyone else in the restaurant, something unsaid that speaks volumes and is decisive and still innocent, yet somehow patently dangerous.

But Jonelle and Steven missed it altogether.

They were supposed to.

chapter 4

"Wipe your feet!" Jonelle called to the kids as they started in through the back door of the stone house in Bucks County. "I just washed the floor."

"Mommy," Sarah said, kicking the snow from her boots against the doorframe, "we made a big snowman. Didn't we, Wyatt?"

Wyatt was rubbing his feet on the mat just outside the door. "You messed it up with that face you made."

"I wanted to make it an alien," Sarah commented, shaking one of her boots in his direction.

A wad of muddy snow smacked Wyatt on the forehead, and he in turn smacked Sarah, and Jonelle pulled them apart, kicked the door shut, and talked them into some hot cocoa. It was March, and winter showed no sign of abating. But here, in pastoral Bucks County where the Pattersons had owned their country house for six years now, one didn't care, for the snow was magical no matter how long it lasted. Alien snowmen notwithstanding.

As the kids sat at the old butcher-block kitchen counter sipping their chocolate, Jonelle turned on the TV and pulled a steaming, golden apple pie from the oven. She was being Martha Stewart this long weekend, her first vacation since signing with Network ONE, and she was loving every moment of it. Even including scrubbing the tile floor on her hands and knees. She was loving playing with the kids, helping them with homework, watching videos with them. No matter how busy she ever was, she would never slight her children. But times like this were special and magical, when they became her entire world.

Sarah looked up at the TV screen where *FirstNews Tonight*, ONE's six o'clock telecast, was playing. "Mommy, why aren't you on?"

" 'Cause I'm here."

Wyatt disputed that. "Dad said you're on even so."

"I've got a pretaped spot coming up."

Sarah frowned at the woman subbing for her in the "Capitol One" spot. "I don't like her."

"Neither do I," Jonelle admitted. "But I hope the majority of people do." She looked up at the auburn-haired former model, who was doing her best to sound like she cared about the surgeon general's newest report on obesity, and sighed. Part of her really wanted this woman to get better ratings; maybe that way Barney Keller would give Jonelle what he promised: more work outside Washington. So far, the reports had been few and far—

The excited voices of both kids stopped her train of thought. Jonelle looked up and saw her spot beginning, and she turned up the sound. It was a story she'd pursued for weeks, and she'd been worried about how it turned out. It was on the old controversial topic of abortion, but this was something new. An abortion clinic in suburban Virginia had been bombed two weeks before, badly injuring a woman who'd just driven up to the building. Jonelle had interviewed the doctor who founded the clinic, who seemed distraught. She'd even had words with her husband about that interview. Steven, who was opposed to abortion of any kind, felt her handling of the doctor almost put her on the pro side of the issue.

However, when she tracked down the doctor's partner, another doctor in the midst of a divorce and large debt problems, Jonelle found that their stories about what happened didn't match. Jonelle had unknowingly uncovered a possible conspiracy between the two owners to bomb the building themselves, taking the insurance money and giving their cause sympathetic publicity. The police had intervened after her report, but the investigation seemed to go no-where until Jonelle visited the injured woman in the hospital, got a few painful words from her on camera, and then, hours later, the woman succumbed.

Her death thrust the story into headlines that could not be ig-nored. The grand jury subsequently indicted, and the report running tonight was on how the men defrauded the public by trying to blame the attack on antiabortion sympathizers and using a volatile issue for their own gain. Standing at the grave of the woman who died, Jonelle gave an impassioned summary on the tragedy of two sides —pro- and antiabortion here—not being able to come to an un-derstanding, having to resort to violence—violence that in this case took the life of an innocent bystander. "Gloria Gramaho, the woman who died, was coming to the clinic to apply for a job as a cleaning person. She was Catholic, the mother of three herself. This is Jonelle Patterson . . . reporting from Virginia."

"What's abortion exactly?" Sarah asked.

"You're dumb," Wyatt said.

"I'm not dumb. I'm just little."

"Abortion is what Grandfather Patterson says is a sin," Wyatt added in a grown-up voice.

"Among other things," Jonelle commented softly. "Okay," she added, taking their mugs, "go change. We're leaving to get Dad in about an hour." Steven was flying an MD80 from Saint Louis to Newark, and they were picking him up there. "We'll have some pie before we leave if you guys get ready fast enough."

The kids ran from the room.

Jonelle turned off the set, poured herself a cup of coffee, and sat down. She made a list of things to remember—*Get Steve's April schedule, birthday card to Barney Keller, dish drainer for DC, Call Larry King and Peter Jennings back!!*—and then pinched a hunk of crust from the pie and sampled it. She thought it was a little too salty, but against the sweetness of the apples it would probably taste fine. With a little frozen vanilla yogurt.

She got up and walked to the small window seat in the corner of the eating area, her favorite spot in the house. In fact, they'd bought it because of this very room. What had once been a parlor and tiny dining room and even smaller kitchen and pantry they transformed into one large, luxurious, unpretentious family area. The big rock fireplace took the chill out of every corner, and when that heat wasn't enough, the warmth radiating from the massive Viking professional range—their one concession to pretension—did the trick. They'd replaced the casement windows with double-paned antique French glass, and constructed the window seat by knocking out a bookcase the former owners had haphazardly constructed. This is where Jonelle came to veg out.

As she sat there this early evening, looking out onto the last shadow as night fell over the melting, lopsided white alien on the snowy lawn, she felt blessed. Her life had never been so good. Yes, it had been good ever since she decided to get away from Atlanta and make a life for herself, ever since she married Steven, ever since God had given them two adorable, healthy kids. But now it was perfect, for her career was finally working as well as everything else was. All that struggling as a kid, all the horror, the fights, the blocking out, the pain, the determination to live through it and get out and never look back, it had come directly to this moment.

When she used to sit on the rickety back porch at twelve, listening to the rain on the Nehi Cola sign that served as a roof drown out the shouting of her father, she dreamed of this day, this cup of coffee, this window seat, this house that was hers, the sound of little—calmer now—voices upstairs, the anticipation of picking up her husband at the airport as he walked off the plane looking so striking in his uniform. She dreamed all this and here it was, in her hand.

She dreamed she was a TV star back then, but never Elizabeth Montgomery or Mary Tyler Moore; Jonelle fantasized that she would one day be Barbara Walters. Now Barbara was her friend, and even a fan (or so it was reported in a recent print interview). She was slowly climbing the ladder to success, but success that was not just based on her beauty or even her brains. This was success that came from her drive, her zeal, her desperate attempt to *com-*

municate. This from a girl who had barely been able to get words out as a child, who longed for communication of any kind in the first sixteen years of her life.

The phone rang. It was Barney. "Did you see the piece?"

"Yes. What did you think?"

"Sensational. I'm sending you to the Philippines."

It caught her by surprise. "Ramos threw in the towel?"

"Yes. And Imelda is wearing it."

"She's not going to talk to us. Chris Amanpour couldn't even get to her. She's bitter about the U.S."

"So bitter that she asked for you."

Captain Steven Patterson was holding Sarah's hand and carrying Wyatt piggyback through the terminal building when Jonelle told him she would be going to a gate rather than the car. "What?"

"Mom's flying to Vanilla," Wyatt said.

"Manila," Jonelle corrected him. "I'm taking the red-eye to Seattle, connecting to the Philippines in the morning."

"Well," Steven said to the kids in an ebullient tone, trying to diminish their disappointment at her departure, "that means I get these two all to myself."

"Don't spoil him too much," Jonelle warned the children. She looked at the monitor and saw that her flight was boarding. "I'd better get going."

Steven asked, "What's the story?"

"Barney says Imelda Marcos wants to sing for me."

The Honorable Imelda Romualdez Marcos, congresswoman from the province of Leyte, rises regally from her seat in the Batasang Pambansa, the Philippine house of representatives, crosses the floor parting the air in front of her—like sweeping through the jungle with a machete—with a silk monogrammed handkerchief. She knows the camera is trained on her, and she performs in classic Imelda style: the smile, the glances to friend and foe alike in the chamber, stopping to kiss the wind over a shoulder here, a nod there, but everywhere completely the star, totally in control, a pro.

She greets Jonelle with a glowing grin, her eyes examining her from head to foot. "You must tell me now, where did you get such a beautiful dress?"

And so it begins.

The interview is shot over three days, per Imelda's request, for she can't take precious time away from "guiding" the country. Part One takes place in and around the halls of congress, a world she fairly dominates these days. The presidential election of 1998 is coming soon. Will she or won't she run? Jonelle asks her point-blank. There is that winning smile again, as if she's going to burst into song. She reaches down and rubs her heel that she's dropped a white pump from. She says only, "I would like you to come visit my home."

Part Two takes place at the Pacific Plaza apartment in Makati where Mme. Marcos lives with her past. Photographs of her and Ferdinand with every world leader and famous person once in their aura line the walls. She shares feelings of that time, the glory, then the banishment, a world turned on them. The bitterness is still alive when speaking of Cory Aquino not allowing Marcos to come home to rest. Jonelle asks her if it will be her first proclamation as president. Coy, smartly, Imelda says, "If I were to run, and if I were to win, that would be up to the people."

Part Three takes place at the Manila Hotel's Lobby Lounge, dark and clubby, regal and yet comfortable, scene of some of Imelda's greatest hits. Here she speaks of the glory of Manila, the development, the investments, the crown jewel in the Asian tiara. She pulls out a tattered copy of Condé Nast Traveler *from 1996, shows Jonelle an article by Luisita Lopez Torregrosa called "Asia on Speed," pointing out her own photograph, the highlighted printed words that flatter her: "proud, energetic, a leader." Jonelle presses. A candidate? Imelda skirts the issue. Jonelle gets down to being Jonelle: Where's all the money hidden? How do you account for the debacle you left behind? Imelda is smooth, insisting she knows nothing of such injustice, citing her own version of the Fifth Amendment: "I'm just a provincial girl."*

While Imelda spends half an hour on her cell phone to congress, Jonelle reads the Traveler *piece. And there it is. "You can only un-*

derstand me if you understand the provinces. Come with me to Leyte." And I understand what she's saying—that the Philippines is not in Manila or in the resorts and the beaches, but out there where she was born and grew up, in the dirt barrios and barangays, in the places where the dust gets in your hair and the mud splatters on your feet and the children hang on your skirt; and in those places, in many of them, Imelda Marcos is still the Philippines. *Jonelle makes a note to get the rights to quote the article; it is impeccably right on.*

Part Three continues with a walk through the bustling throngs in Rizal Park. It is there, with the clatter of machinery and boats and the future in the South Port making sound bites difficult, that Imelda Marcos gives Jonelle Patterson the scoop of a lifetime: "I will be a candidate for the presidency of my beloved country."

Jonelle has it exclusively; there are no other reporters tagging along the well-trod yellow brick road that the widow Marcos has paved for herself. No one, least of all Jonelle, anticipated this revelation. Then, as she asks Imelda why she chose to declare on an American television program that is being taped for later airing, Mme. Marcos tells her it is because she can trust Jonelle. "Doris— my dear late friend, Doris Duke—told me no reporter was ever so honest as you are."

Then, suddenly, as Jonelle begins to say thank you, reaching her hand to Imelda's ringed one, with the cameras still rolling, there is a sound like pop pop pop but it does not come from the South Port, this is not the echo of a loading crane tapping against the barnacled side of a steamer on the South China Sea, this is the sound people have become used to since Jack Ruby introduced assassination to live television—

Shots ring out. Pandemonium. Imelda Marcos falls against Jonelle, sending them both to the ground. The bodyguards pile on top of them, others give chase, passersby scream in terror and everyone recalls Cory Aquino's husband being killed in the exact same way when running for president, but this time there is no Marcos alive to be behind it, this time it's too shocking and jarring and unimaginable that this comeback queen of the shoes and karaoke microphones and George Hamilton dancing legends, this Eva Duarte of the archipelago of the Philippines, would be cut down in a hail of bullets in Manila's famous park at a time when she is again respected, or is it—as she boasts—loved?

Jonelle's tape goes to Network ONE exclusively as word breaks over the world. There is no tape of the incident but ONE's. Everyone replays the moment again and again, the hands clutching, the bullets popping, Imelda's blood defacing the light green Donna Karan dress she complimented Jonelle on wearing. There is commentary alluding to suspects: the Islamic terrorists who have made the Philippines a stronghold, mountain outlaws, former Marcos opponents, current other declared and undeclared candidates, even, ridiculously, the faded Cory Aquino herself. The would-be assassin disappears, and there is no clue to his whereabouts.

But Imelda Marcos survives. Jonelle brings flowers to the hospital and there is a heartfelt kiss from the patient/candidate, along with genuine tears from both of them, knowing how close they came, how God provided them with protection. Perhaps it means Imelda's path is assured; the sympathy vote will surely now be overwhelming. A martyr for her beloved land.

And Jonelle Patterson? When she gets off the plane in Washington and speaks to Barney directly for the first time after getting what was surely one of the great news stories of the year, at great personal risk, she asks what he thought. She's asking his personal opinion on what happened, how he feels.

Barney only says, "The overnights went through the roof, honey. Through the roof."

chapter 5

"*That* was his reaction? Not even a question about that poor woman, or how much danger *you* were in? Those bullets could have hit you just as easily as her." Steven and Jonelle were sitting on the floor in front of the fireplace in the house on 16th Street. He was astonished at the callousness of Barney Keller.

"He's a news producer," Jonelle tried in his defense. "All they care about are the ratings."

"And you certainly delivered on that account, didn't you?"

"Did you see what we aired tonight?"

Steven nodded. "It's like that old sixties film, *Blow-Up*. The gun in the bushes on tape, magnify it a thousand times and you get—"

"In this case, nothing. A hand. Caucasian. But nothing identifiable."

He ran his fingers down her arm, lingering on her hand. Then he lifted it and kissed it. "This one I can identify."

"I think it was a nut. There are a lot of them down there. America doesn't hold a patent on crazies who shoot public figures."

"Probably right." He moved closer to her, putting her fingers lightly on his lips now, biting on them slightly.

"The kids—"

"Are asleep."

"Shouldn't we go to the—"

"Let's be daring. I like the fire."

"You're starting one in me."

"Corny line." He kissed her passionately. "But it works."

They moved to the floor, stretching out in one another's arms as the logs turned to glowing embers. Steven pulled his shirt off and leaned on one elbow, teasing her with his index finger, running it over her chin, down between her breasts, up through her hair. She moaned slightly as he brought his lips to her earlobe and nibbled there. She felt him press his body against the side of hers, felt the hardness between his legs. She let her hand touch his thigh, let it rest there, driving him crazy. Then he took a deep breath, leaned on his elbow again, and said, "You're getting the cover of *Newsweek* I hear."

"So they say."

"The photo of you and Imelda on the ground? The one that was flashed everywhere?"

"I guess so."

"God, I'm glad you're okay."

"I went through worse in Sarajevo."

"You never got the cover of *Newsweek* out of Sarajevo."

"I think Chris did."

"Aren't you thrilled?"

"It could have been any one of us. It's what we do. I was just—I hate to use this word in this context—lucky."

He kissed her passionately, rolled on top of her. She brought both hands up to his buttocks, firmly clasping them with her palms, kneading slightly, drawing him toward her. He moved his head back and looked into her soft green eyes. "Come on . . ."

"What?"

"This ingenuous act. You love it. Tell me you love it."

"What? Making love to you?"

"The publicity, the fame."

She admitted, "Well, a little."

He laughed and then kissed her again. "But be careful. Anchoring isn't dangerous. Waltzing through Manila with Imelda Marcos is. I know that's what you have always wanted, but I don't want to lose you."

"You won't."

"I just want to be proud of you."

"You will be. I promise."

"I already am."

And then she brought her face up to his chin, licked at the hardness there, felt the stubble of his beard grate against her soft wet skin, and he found her lips and opened them with his, and slid his tongue over her lips. She drew down his shorts with her hands and felt him move between her legs, gasping as a tingling sensation ran the length of her body. She felt weightless suddenly, sensational, every nerve in her body was floating, crying out for connection to his strong, hard body. And when he pressed himself down upon her, she was pulled down from her orbit, the kite drawn in from the wind, drawn tightly to the only man in the world she felt safe with.

And then they made love.

In New York City, at the corporate headquarters of Network ONE, centerpiece of the new Times Square, Barney Keller, Clayton Santangelo, and James Martin Findley uncorked a bottle of Merlot that Clay's grandfather had brought over from Italy almost sixty years before. He had been saving it for a "momentous" occasion.

Tonight they had put together a show that would air against *20/20* that Friday, fairly confident they would knock it "out of the water." Over at ABC, Hugh Downs had, in fact, that very morning, told Roone Arledge that "we should go with a rerun because the world is going to be on ONE."

The show was the first of the planned specials called *Jonelle Patterson Reporting . . .* , but two of the three segments planned and already taped for the program were scrapped; the entire hour would be devoted to the Marcos story. A crew had shot filler—comments from friends of Imelda, the word from the police, the view from the streets in the provinces that Imelda had boasted were "hers." Most effective was a candlelight vigil kept around the clock by the people of Leyte, with much weeping and gnashing of angry teeth against the "assassin," and great wringing of hands over the fear that this incident would scare their Evita into throwing in her towel. "Or her shoes," Findley couldn't resist. All this had brought Mme. Marcos from passé to hip again.

But the star of the show was Jonelle, for this was not entirely a news program, this was designed—even without the good fortune of having Imelda Marcos nearly murdered on camera—to showcase Jonelle, not her guests. There she was, talking to the camera in her nonchalant style, drawing you in, making you feel you actually cared about the joke that Imelda Marcos had become to Americans, making you believe you gave a damn about the shady elections on those distant islands where hurricanes raged and old Marcos cronies in white gauze shirts milked the poor and got richer still. Jonelle created a certain sympathy for Imelda even before the bullet tore into her shoulder; she made you feel something for this somewhat pathetic, somewhat dizzy, somewhat fragile but resourceful human being. She gave Imelda Marcos the vulnerability Judy Garland had, that Marilyn Monroe projected. She portrayed Imelda Marcos as a person, able to laugh at herself, to love her grandchildren, and to, after the shooting, fight fear and danger and win yet again. Another comeback. Judy lives. Ah, that was Clay's touch, and it worked brilliantly. He even put a track of "Over the Rainbow" over a foggy Manila morning sweep that ended the program as Jonelle said, "This is Jonelle Patterson Reporting . . . from Manila."

As anticipated, or rather as planned, the show was the highest rated single hour of the week. Barney got his overnights. The price for advertising dollars had been tripled for the hour, and Findley got every penny he asked for. Tied in with the cover of *Newsweek* and the enormous coverage in every facet of media the world over, Jonelle Patterson had indeed arrived.

The next summer, Clay would win an Emmy for producing and directing the program, as would Jonelle, fulfilling Barney's promise/ prediction.

But on this night in New York, over the finest merlot that had ever graced their palates, the three owners of Network ONE knew they couldn't wait that long. The momentum was starting. They were on a roll. But tomorrow the big story would be Jeff Greenfield's, or Ted Koppel's, or something *Meet the Press* would dig up on Sunday. They needed staying power in the fierce competitive game called news. "We need—putting it bluntly, gentlemen—another Imelda," Barney said with a sort of leering enthusiasm.

A month later, they got their wish.

Jonelle is doing a story she has to be forced into doing, because it's too "soft." Barney and Clay feel, however, it will provide balance against a hard-hitting exposé on the tobacco industry's push into Third World countries, and another look at corruption still festering in the post-Peña FAA since David Hinson was forced to resign in the wake—tidal wave?—of the public's outcry for safety following the ValuJet/TWA 800 crashes. She's in Santa Clara, California, at the opening of an enlarged Olympics training facility. She's doing a piece on the youthful, hopeful enthusiasm of teenage athletes. She likes it more once she gets into it.

After interviewing a dazzling seventeen-year-old diver named Molly Binenfeld, she kicks off her shoes, yanks her jeans up, and sits with legs dangling in the huge Olympic pool, awaiting Molly's attempt at her toughest dive, one she's only accomplished three times. Jonelle does soft commentary about how, in her black swimsuit with her jet black hair, Molly looks like some kind of precious black swan, and the grace of her moves belie the technical precision necessary to carrying them off.

But then, as Molly begins her run to the tip of the board, she slips, spins actually—memories of Greg Louganis striking his head on the board ring suddenly in memory—and like a projectile fired from a cannon, careens through the air with no control whatsoever, gravity forcing her body down, not swanlike now but more as if a gentle bird were unsuspectingly caught in a twister—splatting onto the water just inches from the concrete, as if being delivered by all the force that a tornado can muster.

Jonelle finds herself gasping in horror, as is everyone in the building. Two custodians are on the other side of the pool, Jonelle's crew is behind her, taping, but no other swimmers are here, no one in the water. Jonelle doesn't have time to think. She's doing the breaststroke suddenly, finding the weight of the girl less than she'd even have guessed, pulling her toward the side where she sees hands reaching out.

When they get Molly to the pool decking, Jonelle goes under, for a second blacking out from her own panic and sense that this is not happening. The water is pink with blood; she remembers Imelda. She comes up, hands grab at her, she hears sirens, Molly's eyes are suddenly facing hers, she's alive, she's lucid though in shock, and Jonelle, in an effort to provide some kind of comfort, touches the girl's foot, which spasms. Jonelle feels grease on her sole. It is all caught on tape.

After the girl is rushed to the hospital, Jonelle tells the custodians what she felt. The men check the board. Indeed, someone has put what later is identified as hydrogenated cooking oil on the far two feet of the board. Three days later, the mother of another girl Molly has been swimming against for three years is arrested and charged with the deed. The motive: to eliminate her daughter's nemesis from competition. It's the aquatic version of the Cheerleader Mom. It's a ratings grabber, and the Movie-of-the-Week rights are snapped up in a second.

"So, who will play you?" Barney jokingly asks Jonelle, who is not laughing.

"The movie's going to be on this network, so why not let me play myself?" she says without humor.

His eyes sparkle. "That could be arranged."

What troubles her is that she knows he means it.

chapter 6

Jonelle didn't play herself or anyone else in any TV movie. She was a newswoman, not Oprah Winfrey, and she was glad Barney Keller never again mentioned, even kiddingly, the possibility of her attempting stardom in another facet of the media. She was, everyone agreed, a big enough star as it was.

At the end of her first year with Network ONE, Jonelle and Steven were more than pleased with how things were turning out. Any deep-seated fears of "selling one's soul to the devil" had been dashed by the professional treatment Jonelle received on every level. She had been given free rein—in fact, encouraged—to go after those stories that grabbed her at some gut level, and as always, those stories were the kinds of reports people wanted to see. Barney, Clay, and James offered their suggestions and comments, sometimes inspiring Jonelle in a new direction, sometimes leading her completely astray; she was, however, always smart enough to rely on her own instincts first. The three owners of the network trusted their individual producers, in this case Alicia Maris, who'd been a *Nightline* producer for years and had been lured to ONE by an enormous salary and the promise of artistic freedom. The men kept their prom-

ise; Alicia and Jonelle both remained autonomous, and that trans-
lated into profitability for the network.

Steven bought himself that spanking new aluminum silver
Audi A4 that he'd wanted, and Jonelle won the promised Emmy in
1998, the summer after she began working for ONE for the *Jonelle
Patterson Reporting . . . from Manila* segment. She returned to the
Philippines shortly before that to accept a distinguished heroism
award from President Imelda Marcos, which made news all on its
own. *Jonelle Patterson Reporting . . .* aired only three times before
it was put on the regular nighttime schedule, and became the third-
highest-rated news magazine show after *60 Minutes* and *20/20* out
of the gate.

In December of 1997, Jonelle had begun anchoring *FirstNews
Tonight*—alone, as promised. The ratings, which had been dismal,
rose overnight to "put it in the running," as Barney Keller boasted.
It turned out that he was more prophetic than optimistic; by August
of 1998, less than a year later, on the very day Jonelle won her
Emmy, her presence had catapulted *FirstNews Tonight* into second
place after Peter Jennings with the *ABC World News*. It had given
her star status.

But now she wanted out.

It came as no surprise to Barney Keller, who knew she'd never
desired an anchor position in the first place. She did her stint in
the chair as a trooper would, dedicated, resourceful, eager. It was,
as Barney had predicted, like the old days when Walter Cronkite
was warmly welcomed into the homes and hearts of Americans with
the CBS nightly report. He was everyone's father or grandfather,
and you trusted what he was telling you, even if sometimes what he
was telling you were lies. Jonelle was everyone's daughter, wife,
friend. Her beauty and bubbly optimism combined with professional
no-nonsense reporting made for irresistible television.

She was good copy too. CBS, in a decision that shocked many
in the industry, decided to profile her on *60 Minutes*. It was a calculated risk, giving even more publicity and play to their strongest
female competitor ever, yet at the same time they knew the ratings
for the segment would be a blockbuster. Jonelle was interviewed by
Morley Safer as an old friend, which was the truth, and the piece

was critical (the stardom issue) and appreciative (she is an "excellent newswoman," CBS's Amanpour herself said) at the same time. But the surprise of the segment was the delightful portrayal of Jonelle's family. Morley followed Jonelle and the kids flying TWA (coach!) with Steven to San Juan for a three-day vacation, caught up with them again in Bucks County, celebrated Sarah's ninth birthday with a party in the house on 16th Street, and then accompanied the family for a walk down that block to the White House, just to watch in pride as the lights came on inside the portico of a building that represented continuity and solidity. It was clear that the Pattersons were teaching their children values and what being an American really meant. It was the best public relations spot ONE could hope for, and it came from a rival network.

Yet, on camera, Jonelle told Morley she had told ONE's owners that she had no interest in continuing the nightly news anchoring position past a year, and time had definitely run out. Safer, who, like others, thought it was in ONE's best interests to keep her there for the rest of her natural life, was surprised she stated it, and even more surprised when ONE announced that Jonelle would anchor the news only twice a week, leaving three days for her to do what she loved best, hard reporting in the trenches. Keller and the others were taking the calculated risk that the audience loved Jonelle so much that they would continue to tune in each evening in the knowledge that she would be on in some role, whether that be as anchor or reporter.

And it paid off. Ratings dipped slightly at first, but when Jonelle brought in a big news story and continued her report over a three-day period, the audience returned, and never left.

"How were the overnights?" Clay asked Barney as he took a seat in his office.

"Mediocre."

"What do you expect? She didn't have a big story last night."

"We need a nice assassination attempt, another World Trade Center bombing, maybe a plane crash on Michigan Avenue."

"Careful, God might be listening."

Barney got up and looked out the window. "Times Square," he

muttered. "Who'd have thought this would happen? Insurance towers where the greatest porn used to be. I used to jerk off in those booths on my lunch hour when I was an intern at ABC."

Clay was startled. "I really don't want to know."

"I wonder, you think Rex does the same thing?"

"Rex Heald? He's got a wife and kids."

"Most of the guys in those places have wives and kids."

"He's deeply religious."

"Used to see a priest in there regularly. Hell, I'll bet Rex does. What do you think? Down in Nashville or Tulsa, wherever he's peddling that Christian crap?"

"How would I know what Rex does?"

"I hear you're close."

"We're friends. But I don't ask about his sexual habits."

Barney looked out the glass panel again and scowled. "Hypocrites, all of them. In church with their families, repentant on their knees, wife beaters, cocksuckers, masturbators, child abusers, drunks, adulterers the lot of them. They'll all burn in hell, and they know it too. What a crock they spout."

"Why are you so down on Christians all of a sudden?"

"I'm down on anyone who presents a false image."

Clay almost fell out of his chair. "Hey, man, let me remind you just what your public image is, and what it is you really do."

"My public image is that I'm a power-hungry monster, and privately that's about right on. No hypocrisy there."

"Jesus."

"Yeah, just who I was thinking about."

"Why?"

"Jesus. And a big old busful of faithful followers, the sheep."

Clay shook his head. "What kind of drugs are you on?"

Barney pushed a button on the sleek but complicated control pad on his desk. "She at the studio in Washington?"

"Who?"

"Our girl."

"Jonelle?"

"Patterson there?" Barney barked when someone in the control room answered. "Barney Keller."

They both heard her voice on the speaker a moment later. "Barney? I'm just about to go live—"

"Want you to head down south tomorrow."

"Where?"

"Atlanta."

There was no response.

"Careful. That chill will freeze the line. Don't worry, you won't have to see your old lady."

"That's none of your concern," she said sharply. Then, in a professional tone, she asked, "What's the story?"

"Religion. Hypocrisy. Good stuff."

"I'll call you at home tonight. I'm on the air." She hung up on her last word.

Clay stared at him. "You wanna let me in on this one?"

Barney laughed out loud, leaning back in his chair. "Just my natural instinct for the big story."

The story starts out as an entertaining and controversial piece, and then becomes bigger than anyone ever dreamed. Jonelle goes home to Atlanta, not to see her dysfunctional mother from whom she's been estranged since she ran away at seventeen, but to do a piece on a faith healer who is sweeping the South with his tent shows, causing havoc in every rural area he visits. For three years now, the Rev. Billie Bob Hatfield, descended from the original Hatfields who famously battled their neighbors, the McCoys, has covered the territory from Savannah to El Paso, and back again, blazing a trail that leaves believers and skeptics, supporters and haters in its wake. Local headlines like LIBRARIAN WALKS AGAIN *are balanced by threats of arrest for child molestation (from the mother of a seventeen-year-old girl whom the Rev. "cured" of bulimia after a few hours in a motel room). A sheriff throws him into jail for three days for drunkenness and indecent exposure, while another town gives him a parade. When his revival tent blows over after a freak storm outside Little Rock, the Rev. Billie drags the whole show over to one of the local dance halls, where many believers refuse to even enter because their religion forbids the drinking of liquor.*

Billie's religion or religious affiliation is never really clear—an amalgam of Southern Baptist, Holy Roller, Church of Christ, and Church of Hard Knocks; Billie had been arrested and jailed twenty-two times in six states by the time he was ordained in Alabama. Seventeen children, all from different mothers, claim him as their father. His claim: He is sterile. Four hundred plus people say they owed the remission of their cancer to his touch, three hundred boast he's healed their infirmities, and another hundred or so claim that he's given them "eternal life," but no one has lived long enough to prove the truth of that one. Hundreds more call him a liar, thief, pervert, and fraud. The Rev. Billie Bob is, if nothing else, a colorful, flamboyant, and controversial personality, and Jonelle dreams of getting her hooks into him. And maybe some truth—sham, ham, or, as he bills himself, Gifted Apostle?

Ham he is for sure. Jonelle finds his arrogance appealing in an outrageous way, and while she objects personally to his sense of being above the law and laughing at the charges that have been documented against him, he is the kind of dynamite interview a reporter loves to get—wild, unpredictable, interesting. Sham? She's sure of that too; when she confronts him with pages of charges in which he is accused of fraud in his "healing" of hundreds of sick people (only to find their illnesses return once the "magic" of the revival wears off), he dismisses the accusations as "the power of Satan" here on earth. Gifted Apostle? His faith seems real when Jonelle speaks with him, yet she feels it important to report the crimes he's been charged with, presenting a real dichotomy of a man to the viewer.

All that, in itself, makes for good story. But the day Jonelle finishes interviewing him, something happens that turns the story into bigger news. This night is the last of the Rev. Billie Bob's scheduled healing revivals. He says he needs a rest; the authorities say he's about to be busted. At around four in the afternoon, a bus filled with Christians making the journey to the revival goes off the road on a hairpin curve when trying to avoid slamming into a semitrailer that has jackknifed and overturned just moments before. All fifty-four passengers from Augusta, Georgia, where the bus had begun its journey, including the bus driver and a well-known New York writer who was doing a positive book on the Christian Right, are killed. Jonelle, along with local reporters, rushes to the scene and within minutes is reporting live through the local affiliate feed. In the drizzle, she manages to get close enough to the wreckage to interview a weeping fireman who has been unsuccessful in extricating a three-year-old girl from the mangled mass of steel alive. His tears, his unbearable hopelessness, touches the hearts of viewers everywhere.

It also propels Jonelle into what she does best: investigating. She doesn't know what it is about the accident that makes her feel there is a story untapped, that something more is behind this hideous and pointless loss of life. She smells something, as she did with the abortion clinic story, as she had with the diver, Molly Binenfeld. Something is fishy, she thinks, when she hears an eyewitness tell his story of how the truck jackknifed. The driver was steering erratically, the man who was following the truck states, driving too fast for the road and certainly too fast for conditions. It was almost as if, the eyewitness says, the "truck driver was looking to wreck his rig."

Jonelle tries to interview the driver of the overturned truck, but to no avail. His wife won't even open the door to a reporter, and statements from the police don't help much until, days later, the sheriff whose jurisdiction the area of the accident was under issues a warrant for the man's arrest, charging him with involuntary manslaughter, and adding a charge that has been kept secret—for some reason—until now: driving under the influence of alcohol.

That should end the story, but in Jonelle's mind it is far from closed. Why didn't the authorities release the information that the man was drunk until five days following the accident? Why was the man's blood-alcohol count never mentioned in the early reports, when that test had to have been administered within an hour of the crash? Jonelle returns to the driver who'd witnessed the accident, speaks with him again, this time in more depth. She notices a reluctance to say something that he's been keeping secret, a pause in his words whenever he talks about the bus, a hesitation she finds puzzling and telling. Finally, after coaxing in a way only she had the patent on, the man admits that he felt there had been plenty of time for the bus to stop. Indeed, it had been traveling very slowly because of the light rain, and though the curve was an extreme one, there was clear visual indication of the truck blocking both lanes in time to apply the brakes. Yet the official report on the condition of the bus mentions nothing about mechanical failure of any kind. Jonelle smells something again and refuses to return to Washington, wanting to pursue the truth of the story.

She gets it. The brakes on the bus were acting up, she learns, and that was one of the reasons the driver was obviously taking the curves so slowly. A mechanic who inspected the bus just before it set out on the trip admits he was "a little worried about the brakes," but thought nothing more of it because the school bus was nearly brand-new, and there "couldn't possibly have been any real problem." Jonelle finds that a "few pages of relevant material" from the inspection on the bus following the accident had been "misplaced," and that, indeed, the brakes on the bus had been tampered with prior to the journey. "There is clear indication," the report says, "that the brake linings had been impaired mechanically, making sure braking unlikely in the case of a panic stop." Jonelle has uncovered sabotage, but who did it?

The Rev. Billie Bob Hatfield blames it on his detractors. But who would want to kill a busful of handicapped or dying men, women, and children and their families because they hated the Reverend? What possible effect would that have on the controversial Billie Bob and his laying on of hands? If he'd been on the bus, that would have made some kind of warped sense.

A better bet, and one immediately put forth by Jonelle's own father-in-law, Prof. Charles Patterson, is that the deed was carried out by an opponent of the Christian Right. One of the passengers killed on the bus was one of the most vocal and vociferous of Ralph Reed's comrades. He was accompanying his wife, who had emphysema, to the healing revival. There are many camps who would want the man silenced. Coupled with the fact that the writer who died was compiling a book everyone knew to be pro-Christian, it seems a good bet that some anti-Christian zealot out to destroy the movement had tampered with the brakes. Luck was on his side when the truck jackknifed.

There is nothing more Jonelle can dig up; the rest is up to the authorities. Rex Heald, head of the Christian Alliance, the even-more-powerful successor to the Christian Coalition, takes every op-

portunity to condemn the backlash against the Christian Right that has been evident, certainly in less severe ways, since the Coalition fell apart following the 1996 election, with its decimation of the Republican leadership.

After a few weeks, the incident drifts into old news status and is forgotten by most people. Except Jonelle. Something nags at her still, something she can't put her finger on, something that tells her there is still more to this story.

On a visit down to Virginia Beach, to Steven's parents' house for Wyatt's birthday, Jonelle talked about the bus accident with the professor. Charles Patterson had been so vocal in pinning the "terrorist action" on some anti-Christian faction because he knew several people on the bus and felt the loss deeply. He had traveled to Tampa to attend, with Ralph Reed and Rex Heald, the funeral of the man who had been an important mover and shaker in the field. "I wish you'd do a piece," he said to Jonelle as they walked along the riverbank on their property, "about all the terrorist actions against Christians down here."

"The church fires?"

"That and more."

"There's more?"

Charles leaned forward and said, "Christians in 1998 are like the blacks just before Kennedy and Johnson made a difference in the late sixties. There's great hatred in the land. Great animosity. It has to stop."

Jonelle found it hard to fathom. "I just don't see many instances where it's clear that Christians are being persecuted. Jews still seem to get the worst treatment."

"Favored treatment," he corrected her, sharply. "There is an entire liberal, white, northern army working toward stopping the Christian movement."

"Now, Dad, you sound like General Lee."

He laughed a little. "Guess I do. Mother has said that of me several times."

His wife said nothing, did not even nod in agreement. She was looking out the window, watching Wyatt playing some kind of ball game with Steven and Sarah on the lawn of the house. She simply sat in her chair, fanning herself. Then she commented, "Wyatt's gonna look like you, Charles, when he grows up."

Jonelle said, "I hope so." She meant it, for Charles Patterson was a distinguished-looking man. So was her husband. "He's a Patterson, that's for sure."

Charles inquired, "He doing well in Sunday school?"

"Fine. May even start piano lessons, though I can't push him."

"Good, good. Happy with your job?"

"Yes."

Charles turned to her, touched her shoulder tenderly. "You say that without the enthusiasm I'd think you'd muster for someone so famous and honored."

"Sometimes . . ."

He prodded when she looked up into the clouds. "Sometimes what?"

"Sometimes it just seems too easy. It's like these stories come to me instead of me having to go to them."

"You're just good, that's the answer."

"But some of them are so tragic."

"That's the Christian love in you responding," he assured her in perfect paternal fashion. "God has a reason for these things, no matter that we can't see it. He has a purpose for you too, and it just might be one you can't understand as yet."

She shrugged. "Yes, well, thanks, Dad."

"So, can you stay a few extra days? Sure like having the kids around."

"Unfortunately, we promised a friend in Richmond we'd spend a night with her. Great lady, met her a year ago when we were shopping down in The Fan."

"Best part of Richmond, Mother really likes it too." He always called his wife "Mother," and Jonelle and the kids had taken to calling her "Grandmother Patterson," even though her name was Alma.

"Good antiques there," Alma whispered.

"Kathleen sells them. Paints too. Artistic, very creative."

"Christian?"

Jonelle gave him a teasing smile. "Would it really make a difference if she weren't?"

He changed the subject. "Football?"

"I'm game!" And she ran off, with the professor chasing her out the door and across the lawn.

The kids loved visiting Kathleen Holm because she had a tree house in the backyard. This time, Wyatt and Sarah decided that they would give a "tea" in the structure, and the grown-ups attended, even dressed for the four o'clock reception. Climbing up a rickety ladder in heels was something Kathleen had not been expecting to do, but it made her laugh, and from there on almost everything seemed funny. Sarah had made "tea" with a mix of Crystal Light powder, cranapple juice, and Diet Rite. Wyatt had slapped peanut butter on Ritz crackers, then topped them with raspberries. It was ghastly, and wonderful.

"Flying a lot?" Kathleen asked Steven as they all sat on the floor of the tree house.

"Less in the past six months. Seniority lets me get better routes, more time with the kids."

"What a life," Kathleen joked. "I'm envious."

"Me too," Jonelle said. She'd been working nonstop. She looked tired. "I should have been a pilot."

"Yeah," Kathleen said wryly, "I could just hear you on the loudspeaker: This is your pilot, Captain Jonelle Patterson, hoping you are enjoying the flight, and I just wanted to point out that the investigation into the sinking of that cruise ship off San Juan, Puerto Rico, last week is heating up. Authorities say . . ."

Jonelle howled. "Ever the newscaster."

"Leave the piloting to me, honey," Steven added with a grin.

Jonelle shrugged. "It's all I ever wanted to do with my life. I had pictures of Harry Reasoner on my wall, for God's sake. Other girls had Paul Newman."

"Wyatt," Kathleen asked, "who do you most want to be like when you grow up?"

"Potomac."

Sarah sighed.

"Why?" Kathleen asked.

" 'Cause he's smart."

Kathleen nodded. "How about you, Sarah?"

Without hesitation, without feeling she had to answer this way, Sarah said, "Mom."

Kathleen asked, "Why?"

Sarah looked at her mother. "Because she's the kind of person a girl is supposed to grow up to be."

Steven mocked hurt and humiliation. "No one wants to be like me?"

Jonelle socked him in the arm. "Oh, go fly a plane."

The banquet at the Russian embassy was thrown by CNN. Jonelle met several former coworkers she'd not seen since jumping ship and defecting to Network ONE. It was a good reunion, but it soured when she was approached by Rex Heald.

She had met him before, of course, several times when he was Ralph Reed's second-in-command. Now that he was heir to the Christian throne, he seemed taller, more sure of himself, though she found him as humorless as she had remembered. She commented that he'd been keeping her busy by making his Christian Alliance so powerful so fast. He smiled, then brought up the bus accident and thanked her for her hard work on that. "Charles told me how deeply concerned you were."

"He was very affected by the loss."

"Without you, I don't think the truth would have come out."

"That's what reporters are here for."

He smirked. "Sometimes."

"Have they learned anything more?"

"Not that I know. What worries me now are the church fires. Not like the black churches that were burned a couple of years ago, these are white middle-class Christian churches being torched."

"We reported the most recent up in Oregon just yesterday." She studied him. "Know something I don't?"

"Only that there's a conspiracy in this country to destroy the Christian movement."

"You sound like my father-in-law." A hostess came by with a tray of canapés and Jonelle helped herself to a cucumber and caviar thing. Then she poured herself a shot from one of the Stoli bottles sitting in urns carved from ice.

Rex said, "I'm shocked you drink."

"Why?"

"Same reason I don't."

"I think," she said politely but firmly, "God doesn't consider me any less close to him because I down a vodka now and then."

He went back to the previous subject. "It's true and you know it. The signs are there, conspiracy is creeping up all over."

"Mr. Heald, I only—"

"Rex."

"I only report the news, Rex. I can't have opinions."

"Off the record?"

She grinned slightly, finishing the little cuke cake. "I'm a Christian myself. I detest violence. I care about the world my kids are going to inherit."

"The Christian Right got the bad rap of intolerance, especially in the last election, especially from women. Now it's the target of just that very thing."

"I think we need to plead for a world in which tolerance is at the core, differences don't matter as long as people are good, kind, honest. It matters not what God we worship, but that we do. There is room within the framework of good Christian ideals for everyone."

"Antiabortionists?"

"Everyone."

"Perverts?"

"I don't know what you mean by that word." She did, but she wanted to remind him the word was offensive.

"Homosexuals."

"Everyone."

"For a Christian Republican, you're very liberal."

"You asked for an off-the-record discussion."

"I thought you were more conservative at the core."

"I began that way. But as time goes on, you become less rigid, less frightened I think of those ghosts and goblins you were told were going to get you one day. I think experience tells us that all God's children are the same, truly the same. The differences on the surface don't really matter."

"Heresy, I could say."

She didn't know if he was serious or not. So she answered, "Ralph Reed did it. His message grew more open and loving and tolerant as time went on."

"That's why he's gone."

Ah, yes, so he was that rigid. And she knew nothing more she could say to this man that would change his mind. After all, this was the most vociferous Christian leader to come along the pike in a long while, and one of the most charming too, which gave him his power.

Jonelle saw Steven motioning to her from their table. It was time to be seated for the dinner. Just in time, for she was growing uncomfortable with Heald's third degree. "Time to join my husband," she said softly.

"Has he swung to the left as well?"

"I don't know that I've 'swung' any which way, Mr. Heald."

"Rex."

"Mr. Heald." She made her point. "No, you'll be happy to know, Steven is just as rabid a far-righter as you are. He would have voted for Pat Buchanan in '96 if he'd made the ticket."

"Smart man," he said with a nod. "I hope you'll come back one day."

"Come back? I don't think I've wandered," she said pointedly. Then she added, "Excuse me now," and drifted across the room to her husband's table as the waiters began to serve the first course.

The only person not to take his seat for dinner in the ballroom at the embassy was Rex Heald. He was on his cell phone at the end of the bar, trying to keep his voice down, but emphatic. "I want a meeting. Tomorrow." He paused, listened, then his voice got louder. "I don't care where you are flying to, Barney, tomorrow. I just spoke with our girl. What she said and where she's going distresses me. I'm thinking of calling the whole thing off." He fidgeted as he listened. "No, I am calm, I am thinking clearly. I'm very, very worried about this plan. If this doesn't suit—"

He stopped and listened again, turning to see Jonelle enjoying her dinner across the room, speaking with the other guests at the table, charming them with her celebrity, passion, zest for life. And he looked not so much worried anymore as frustrated, as if something were slipping through his fingers that he wanted so badly to keep in the palm of his hand. "All right," he finally said into the telephone, "I'll come to New York. Who are you flying? I'll meet you in the British lounge. Get the other Horsemen there as well. And tell them this to encourage them: Our entire plan may be dead unless we do something about our girl real fast."

Rex paced back and forth in the British Airways First Class Lounge at Kennedy Airport. He kept staring at a sign that blinked the time, then 24 AUGUST 1998. His blood pressure was up. He thought it would be 1999 by the time they got there. Finally, Barney and Clay walked in.

"Where's Findley?" Rex snapped.

"Not well," Barney responded. "Ulcer."

Rex said, "I hear he's got prostate trouble."

Barney was amused. "Don't we all?"

Clay looked impatient. "What's this about, Rex? I've got a busy day. Let's get down to business."

Rex motioned for them to sit down. They chose chairs in a corner for privacy. "It's about our girl."

"What about her?" Clay asked.

"She's talking like a liberal Democrat these days."

Barney laughed, "You mean like me."

Rex looked incensed. "I'm not joking here!"

Barney loosened his tie and turned to Clay to fill him in. "Clay, Rex called me from some do in D.C. yesterday to tell me he had a private discussion with Jonelle in which she didn't preach the company line."

"How so?"

"She's leaning toward abortion and gay rights, she's talking tolerance for everyone, she's moving to the left and I won't have it."

Clay said, "All reporters are liberal, it's their nature."

Rex became even more incensed. "This one can't! Have you forgotten what's really going on here?"

Clay didn't like being made out to be a moron. "Come on, Rex, I think you're overreacting—"

Rex shouted, "Like hell I am!"

Clay was shocked. "Did I hear that word come out of your mouth?"

Barney took over. His voice was calm. "Rex, in less than three years we've positioned her where you wanted her in four or five. There's no problem here."

"No problem? She's talking like a liberal Democrat. I've funded this entire thing, thrown blank checks your way, never asked just how you were going about doing your part, never really wanting to know. But if she's not going to uphold the values of the—"

"Rex, come on. You're jumping to conclusions."

"No," Barney said, cautioning Clay, "I think he's got a point. I'd worry too. This has cost him a fortune. And will cost him a lot more by the time she's where he wants her."

Rex agreed. But he went further. "The risk is too high. I'm considering cutting my losses."

Barney didn't believe it. "No you're not. You know she's the one, the only one. You just want our reassurance."

Rex ran his hand through his hair. He was sweating, deeply concerned. "I'm scared to death. After what we're doing—the downside here is enormous, not just the Christian money, but the law— we have to know she's going to carry our flag."

Barney reached out and touched Rex's shoulder, as if petting a dog who was agitated. "Rex, Rex, understand something. She's got a real taste of fame now. Once they get it in their blood, they only get hungrier, like a vampire that needs more blood to survive. She wants it all, and when she learns what she can have with us, the possibility that exists here, she's going to say anything we want her to say, trust me. So she had a liberal moment, everyone's entitled."

Clay jumped on the bandwagon. "Barney's right, Rex. This is now a woman hungry for power."

Rex thought it through, got up, and looked out the window at a 777 just taking off, soaring effortlessly into the blue. When the plane was out of sight, he finally turned and said, "Just make sure she knows who owns her."

Part Two

chapter 7

As 1998 became 1999, and particularly throughout the rest of that year, Jonelle became certain who owned her; she felt her creative parameters increasingly narrowed. Alicia chalked it up to a kind of conservative paranoia on the part of ONE's owners, but Jonelle felt there was something more to it that she couldn't get a handle on, an agenda she didn't understand. Subtle changes were implemented in her magazine show, and, as a result, she seemed less risky and more even keeled. The ratings stayed on top of the nighttime heap, however, even increasing market share in places, but the artistic freedom was less than she'd started with. Safer issues, more fluff pieces, more political stuff—increasingly urging her own political viewpoint, as if she were suddenly one of the participants on *Crossfire*.

"Getting a little gray," Lynne Flexner told her one day on the tennis court in the summer of 1999.

"What?"

"Your show. Where's the juice?"

"Safety is TV's middle name."

Lynne served. "You used to be different. People watched you because you were different. You never toed the company line."

"Your serve.

"Better tell them to do something hot when you go back on the air this fall."

"You really think it's been dull lately?"

"I'm gonna change the channel."

Jonelle missed the ball.

Lynne was right. And nothing changed that September when she returned to the ONE lineup. A distinct change had occurred, but did it matter? Or was the fact that Jonelle's show had taken on a more middle-of-the-road stance that had captured an even larger audience? Who was right? The ratings were what a show was judged by, not its content. *Jonelle Patterson Reporting . . .* was number two, just behind *60 Minutes.*

Outside television, in the public arena, however, she was becoming even more popular. She was touted and promoted by the network in magazines like *Good Housekeeping, Redbook, McCalls, Martha Stewart's Living, Family Circle,* as well as a host of Christian publications. The Patterson family was everywhere, living, working, eating, playing, praying. At one point they were voted, in a *USA Today* poll, the family America most admired.

"Don't even open the papers," Steven warned as he stomped snow off his boots one bitter cold Sunday morning in January of 2000. The millennium had arrived with an icy blast from the Arctic. Chilling way, Jonelle said on her show, to start another thousand years.

Jonelle and the kids turned to him from the kitchen table, where they were just sitting down to breakfast after returning from Sunday school. Wyatt, taller now at ten years of age, guessed it. "We're in there again?"

"Some girls at school made fun of me last week," Sarah admitted.

Steven took off his parka and joined them. Jonelle poured him steaming coffee. "What did they say?" Steven probed.

"Stuff about the perfect family. Stupid stuff."

"Ignore them," Jonelle said.

"Punch 'em," Wyatt said.

"Enough of that," Steven warned his son. "Has it been tough?" he asked Sarah.

"It's okay."

Jonelle knew she was lying. "I talked to her teacher the other day," she said to Steven.

"You what?" Sarah exclaimed, surprised.

"Mrs. Gittelman called me. She asked me to encourage you in English, thinks you have a real future in writing."

"She wants everyone to be a writer," Sarah said.

"She told me that when Chelsea Clinton went to Sidwell, the same thing happened to her. A few jealous girls made cracks about her fame and where she lived, some were particularly hard on her about her mother—"

"Fellow Republican offspring no doubt," Steven muttered, sipping the strong brew, reading the first section of the *Washington Post*.

"—and she just let it roll off her back. It happens to anyone with parents in the limelight, these girls are just envious and don't know how to express it."

Wyatt pulled out *Parade* magazine as he was looking for the funnies. "Wow. The cover."

Indeed, there they were, coming out of church, all four holding hands like the perfect American family in a Rockwell painting. The story was by a Reverend S. Rovig, whom they had never heard of, gushing on how they were the epitome of the ideals of the Christian family in this new millennium. "Oh, God," Jonelle moaned.

"What do you expect?" Steven asked. "You're the most famous newswoman in the country."

"The world," Wyatt said, never looking up from the comic strips. He must have felt them staring at him. "Said so on TV last week."

"The world," Steven repeated with an ironic tone. "It's what you wanted."

"I only wanted to be successful. I wasn't looking for this kind of fame. Not when it hurts my family."

"I don't mind," Wyatt said. "It's sorta cool."

Steven smiled and gave Jonelle a hug. "We'll survive."

Even Sarah told Jonelle it was fine, that she was proud of her, and that they liked it better than if it hadn't come to pass; this way no one was ever worried about money, there were certain places where the kids were treated like royalty, certain perks that were exciting. Their lives were richer by far from the experience, they'd traveled more than they'd ever dreamed, and to more exotic places— even the kids had been to London, Paris, Sydney, Bangkok in the past few years—and they'd met people one would never hope to meet in a lifetime. It really wasn't so bad.

Kathleen Holm called from Richmond. "Did you see it?"

"Sure have. How are you?"

"Fine, fine," Kathleen said. "Boy, you guys are all over the place. Pretty soon you'll be so famous you won't know us little people."

"This isn't changing me."

"I believe you," her friend said. "So, I got myself a laptop."

"Good for you."

"You were right, it helps with business. And now I can E-mail you."

"J-O-N-E-P-A-T at dci dot com."

"Goodness, wait, I've got to write that down."

Jonelle laughed. "Just type it right into the computer."

That afternoon, Jonelle and Sarah were walking to Results, her gym on Florida Avenue where she loved the light and space, when they recognized a man coming out of the building at 1915, on 16th Street where they lived. It was Mr. Gallindo, Sarah's piano teacher of several years now. "Hello, Mr. Gallindo," Sarah said.

"Well, hi, Sarah." He took her hand and then nodded toward Jonelle. "Mrs. Patterson."

"What are you doing in our neighborhood?" Jonelle asked.

"Live here." He saw how they were dressed. "Going to Results? Great gym, cool music."

Jonelle smiled. "You work out there too?"

Victor nodded. "Mornings, right after a few private lessons here."

Jonelle said, "I stood out here one particularly stressful afternoon, just staring at the peonies and listening to Mozart, I think it was, coming from the window. That was you?"

"Probably."

"How long have you lived here?"

"Six years now."

"We're just down the street, corner of R."

"I know, from your checks," the man said.

"You should have said something," Jonelle urged.

"That would have been unprofessional."

"Are you kidding? I could have just sent Sarah up the street for lessons."

"Cost you more," he said with a twinkle in his eye.

She'd always given him a bad time regarding the amount of Sarah's lessons. "Worth it," she now said. "She's really getting good, isn't she?"

"Mom!" Sarah blushed.

"She is."

"Mrs. Patterson, Sarah told me some English teacher wants her to—"

"Mrs. Gittelman," Sarah said to Jonelle, reminding her.

"Oh, become a writer," Jonelle recalled.

"Fine," the piano teacher said, "but don't let her talk Sarah out of piano. I think she could well have a career in music."

Sarah glowed.

Jonelle did too. "It's in the genes. My mother played the piano. In church. Quite well, as I recall."

"Well, it's cold, and I'm late for a concert. Maybe I'll catch you two at the gym sometime. Nice seeing you again, Mrs. Patterson."

"Jonelle."

"Jonelle. Call me Victor."

Jonelle smiled, but gave Sarah a stern glare. "But he's still Mr. Gallindo to you."

"Oh, Mom."

He said to Sarah, "We'll sneak a few first names behind her back."

Jonelle started walking away, then looked back to Victor. "I think Wyatt is weakening. Told us his pal, Potomac, is going for lessons. Means he's next."

Victor walked up to them. "Somebody really named their kid Potomac?"

"No," Sarah replied, "Wyatt made it up."

"It's his imaginary friend," Jonelle added, "which, at his age, is starting to worry me."

"Don't discourage him," Victor urged. "I think it shows a lot of creativity. And send him over when he decides he wants to follow in Potomac's shoes. But he's got a hard act to follow in Sarah."

Sarah blushed again and continued up the street with Jonelle.

In their bedroom that night, Steven sat on the comfy chaise to take off his shoes while Jonelle slipped out of her slacks and sweater. "Sarah said her piano teacher lives a few blocks up."

"Yes. At 1915."

"Good year."

She sat down on the bed facing him. There was a sudden change of mood as something struck her. "That was our address in Atlanta when we moved into the city for a while. 1915 Magnolia Court."

"Sounds pretty."

"That's all that was pretty about it."

"That was, what, husband number three for your mom?"

"Four, but who was counting? He was the one who was supposed to take us away from the squalor. Hah."

"She called."

It hit her so hard she almost gasped the response. "Who called?"

"Esther."

"My mother ca . . . called here?"

He nodded.

"When?" Her voice was lightened by astonishment.

"About a week ago."

"Why did you wait till now to tell me?"

He shrugged. "The last time she spoke to you—when was that, a year back?—you hung up on her."

"She was drunk."

"She was begging for your help. She wanted to stop, she told you that, she needed your support. Jone, you never even spoke to her when she had the breast removed."

"I don't want to go . . . go through all that again, Steven."

"Then don't ask why I didn't tell you this time."

"What did she want?"

"I thought you're not interested. You're the one who returns her letters with *deceased* written over your name."

"That's when she was asking for money."

"She sounds pretty together right now. Tough as nails, still, but together."

"She wasn't drunk?"

"No."

"I don't trust it."

"I do. She told me she divorced again."

She shook her head in amazement. "Fifth time."

"Told me she was real proud of all that's happened to you. Said she was trying to become 'worthy' of you. But she's pretty bitter about your not being there for her."

"*She's* bitter?"

"Give her a chance, Jone."

"She never gave me one."

"Are you really still that angry?"

She softened, got into her flannel nightgown; it was going to be a very cold night, no matter how high they turned the heating blanket under the duvet. Then she said, "She still have the farm?"

"Yes. Living alone now. Asked if someday we'd bring the grandchildren down—"

Jonelle cut him off, raising her voice. "*Now* she's interested in seeing her grandkids? *Now* she's ready to make peace? Why, so she can brag to her church group about her famous girl and all the fancy celebrities she knows?"

"You are so hard on her."

"She left a lot of scars."

"It's not Christian, honey."

"What isn't?"

"This hatred you carry." He got up, slipped off his pants and shirt, and climbed into bed in his boxer shorts. "Ah, you turned the blanket on early, I love it."

She joined him under the covers. "I don't hate her."

"I don't hear any love in your voice."

"It is very difficult, you know the stories, you know what happened."

"Forgiveness is a great virtue. I think it brings you closer to God."

"Why?"

"Because it's one of the hardest things to do."

She turned off the light, saying nothing.

But he knew she was listening. "I think you have to understand that your mother married too young, wasn't educated when she was suddenly living like an adult with the responsibilities of adulthood, that she made mistakes."

"There are things even you don't know."

"You said that many times. I wish you'd trust me enough to tell me."

"It isn't trust. I just don't want to rehash what was my problem, not yours. It's ancient history, and belongs in obscure books with the Boer War."

"I think we should listen to her when she says she's trying now."

Jonelle shrugged. "Why this time? Why should I believe her this time?"

"She sounds—I don't know—different." There was a long pause while he contemplated telling her the rest. He decided to go for it. "Jone, I've had conversations with her all along."

She turned the light back on and stared at him.

"I don't mean to betray you."

"You kept that from me?" she said in astonishment.

"You've kept a lot from me regarding her. I kept it from you because there was no point in talking about it. But this time I feel she's really trying to change."

"You've been talking to her behind my back!"

"Yes."

"Steven!"

"Honey, come on, it couldn't have been any other way. If you two would only—"

"It's too late."

"I think the cancer scared her into sobriety."

"She in AA? Some kind of program?"

His eyes lit up. "Now, that's progress."

"What is?"

"This is the first time you've let your guard down. You really do care after all, don't you?"

"Listen," she said, trying to cover, turning out the light again, "I've never not cared. I've just let the pain warn me not to be vulnerable there again."

"You two may have a chance yet," he whispered, putting his arm around her, snuggling.

"Don't jump to conclusions."

He grinned and patted her under the covers. "Let me live with my fantasies."

But Steven couldn't sleep. He tossed and turned, got up, and tiptoed down to the kitchen, where he made himself some hot chocolate, but the caffeine in that only wired him more. He went down to his workroom and turned on his computer. In moments, a photograph appeared on the screen. A photograph of a hand. A hand he'd been staring at on and off for almost three years now. The hand in the shooting in the Philippines.

He had a theory and that theory was a preposterous one, but he would not rest until he proved himself wrong—or right. Perhaps that's why he couldn't sleep, he thought. He stared at frame after frame of more shots of Imelda Marcos than one needed to see in a lifetime, and then switched to Jonelle's piece on Molly Binenfeld, the swimmer. He froze on frames where the pool custodians stood in the background, where they rushed, along with Jonelle, to help the bloodied swimmer. He kept zooming in, closer and closer, enlarging frame after frame, until he had the men's hands on the screen. And then he studied them, moving back and forth between them and the Imelda shooter, and finally, his eyesight blurring, he turned off the equipment.

But not his mind.

For he was more troubled than before.

chapter 8

The next evening, Steven was in the same spot when Jonelle entered and set a cup of coffee beside him. He'd been down there for hours after dinner, and he was again intent on his editing screen. "I read to Sarah till she finally fell asleep, a whole thirty pages I think."

"She never sleeps well when she has a cold," Steven said, somewhat distractedly.

"Kathleen E-mailed me. Pretty funny. She's both fascinated and frustrated as she becomes computer literate."

No response. He peered forward, studying the frame on the screen, then punched the computer keyboard and the image magnified again and again, until he was studying a tiny portion of the original picture, but on the entire screen. He reached for the mug, sipped without even looking at it, said, "Mmm, Verona?" and went on enlarging the image. "Get to Starbucks this afternoon?"

"Martha called from Mystery Books, got a thriller in that I want to read, so as long as I was on Connecticut, I ducked across the street for coffee, made a hair appointment with George at Axis—"

Distractedly, he said, "Why don't you just have your hair cut at the studio?"

"Let them cut yours and then answer the same question. Anyhow, I picked up two caramel éclairs at Sutton Gourmet, which were going to be dessert, but the kids ate them when I wasn't looking." She waited for a reaction. When there was none, she said, "I mention éclairs, those gooey things you'd die for, and you don't react? What in the world are you working on?"

She didn't need an answer; she looked at the screen and saw for herself. "The Philippines tape?" She realized he was studying the blowup of the hand of the gunman who had shot Imelda. He'd done this many times after the incident, but when no law enforcement agency either in the Philippines or United States could state anything more than the fact that the hand pictured was a male Caucasian between the ages of twenty-five and thirty-five, Jonelle thought that he'd dropped any interest in it. But here it was again. And he was still not answering.

She tried again. "Steven?" Still nothing, as he zoomed into another picture that now filled the screen, another hand, not holding a gun this time but wearing a ring that looked very much like the one on the Philippines tape. She began to grow curious, pulled a chair up next to him, and drank his coffee. "Okay, Columbo, what's going on?"

"Well," Steven intoned, pointing to the ring on the hand, "it's a wedding band, or like a simple gold wedding band, but there's a mark on the gold, a scratch, a striation, that seems oddly like the one on the hand that shot Imelda. Look . . ." He switched screens and pointed out the little line in the gold of the ring, then went back to the previous one, the one with the gun in the hand, and sure enough, they looked alike. Then he pointed to the fleshy part of the ring finger. "See here? He's a slim guy, you can tell by his hands, they're not pudgy at all."

"Yeah, and so what?"

"His ring is too tight for his hand. It's a little swollen under it. See?"

"Yes. So?"

"I think these match—look at the Philippines frame again." He put it on the screen. "See, it looks like the ring is tight there too."

"Once again: so?"

"So I think these are photos of the same hand."

"Right. But where is this other one from?"

"From this . . ." He tapped the keys and the screen went blank, then blinked, and then filled with the image of another moment Jonelle recalled so well, the incident involving Molly Binenfeld. It took her a moment to get the thought out. "You mean . . . the same person was there?"

"Looks that way, doesn't it? Watch again." He pulled up the Philippines tape and froze the hand. Then he switched to the tape of the pool in the Olympic training center. The hand looked remarkably like the one in Manila. "I don't know what it means yet, whether they are really the same or they just look alike, but it's interesting as hell, isn't it?"

She moved away, facing him from her chair. "I don't understand."

"I don't know. Pictures don't lie, that's all."

"Same guy? Both places? Is that what you're saying?"

"It's a possibility."

"That's crazy."

"I think it says something about conspiracy."

She nearly choked on the word. "Conspiracy? By whom?"

"I'm not sure," he admitted.

She shook her head. "What's a teenage Olympics hopeful in Santa Clara got to do with presidential elections in the Philippines?"

"Nothing, far as I can see. Except you."

She was startled. "Me?"

"You're the connection. You were both places."

"But—"

"That's all I'm saying."

"I don't understand."

"I don't either."

They stared at one another for a moment. Then Steven said, "Listen, last week, I was just playing around with tape, putting together some stuff for your reel, and the gold ring jumped out at me when I was blocking to edit. I thought for a moment I was looking at the Imelda tape again, then realized no, it was the swimmer, but it just wouldn't leave my mind that the hands looked so much alike."

"So . . . what now?"

"I'm going to pull up every story you've done and see if I don't find more gold rings."

"Most people wear gold rings."

"Too tightly?"

"Some do. Lots do."

"Then I can check fingernails, shape of the fingers, you can almost get a print from the new enhancement technology."

She jumped to her feet. "Oh, Steven, come on. You sound like one of those guys ranting about the Kennedy assassination. The Cubans! No, the Mafia! No, the CIA! Oswald alone!"

"Jone, I'm serious about this."

"Just get off it already, Steven," she said with her own seriousness.

He was wounded by that. "Come on, Jonelle, I need your support here."

She shook her head and left, unable to give it.

The Pattersons spent the 2000 Easter holiday with Steven's parents. On the surface, they had a wonderful time, but the tension that had taken hold like a virus that night in the basement was just under the surface. The kids loved dyeing eggs, participating in an egg hunt at the elder Patterson's church, where the sermon was preached by one Reverend S. Rovig, whose first name turned out to be Stefan, they learned, the same man who'd written about them a year before in such glowing terms. "I should have guessed your dad was behind it," Jonelle whispered to Steven, "a puff piece like that."

"Didn't do us any harm."

It surprised them when the Reverend Rovig and his family were invited to Easter dinner, for they'd never before had any indication that these were close friends. Jonelle felt it odd that Charles, who spoke to both Steven and her every few days, had never mentioned this man, who suddenly seemed to be a dear and trusted colleague.

The talk at the table was pleasant enough—Rovig's children, though slightly older than Sarah and Wyatt, got along with them very well—and the adults crammed their faces full of ham and sweet potato pie while discussing, mainly, politics.

This year's presidential election was on everyone's minds, for primary season had just begun. Everyone knew that Al Gore, despite a few challengers who couldn't be taken seriously, was a sure bet for the Democratic ticket, but of the Republican lineup they disagreed. Jonelle thought Quayle would come up in the polls to capture the nomination, but Rovig (not very happily) insisted that George Bush Jr. would be the candidate. Alma Patterson said she rather liked Jack Kemp, but realized no one else seemed to, while Charles said he hoped Buchanan would win it, and Steven echoed that sentiment, "Just because he's so darned committed to his opinions."

Jonelle said, "That's the danger."

It was at that table, at that dinner on that Easter Sunday in 2000, that someone first proposed, seriously, that Jonelle become a candidate for office of some sort in the year 2004. It was laughed at by Steven and Jonelle, but no one else. The professor and Grandmother Patterson, though taken by surprise, thought it an "intelligent" idea. Rovig's wife, a severe-looking woman with sharp, Nordic features, encouraged Jonelle to listen to her husband because "we really need someone like you in the House."

Wyatt ate it up. "Didja know that Potomac's mom was a senator?"

"When?"

"Before she had Potomac. She was real good. No scandals."

Everyone chuckled. The Reverend Rovig asked, "Who is Potomac?"

Lots of eyes rolled, but there was no answer.

Sarah said she wasn't sure about the idea, that she would have to "think about it."

Jonelle wrote it off as silly banter. But later, in the privacy of their upstairs guest room in the house where Steven grew up, a stone's throw from the campus of Regent University, the Pat Robertson/Christian Broadcasting Network's pride and joy where

Charles Patterson toiled in the name of the Lord, Steven assured her that they weren't joking. "Bullshit," Jonelle said, clasping her hand over her mouth the moment it came out because she was sure no word like it had ever been uttered under that roof.

"Bullshit to the idea?" Steven asked. "Or bullshit to the fact that they were serious?"

"To all of it, bullshit."

Ten minutes later, in the darkness of night with Steven's butt up against hers, she turned to him. "What office?"

"Huh?" he said, half asleep already.

"They said I should be a candidate. But what for? House of Representatives?"

Steven shrugged. "Who cares?"

"Right." And she moved back to her original position. But she knew what office he'd really meant. A different House, up Mall from the Capitol. And it made her laugh.

For the next few weeks, every night after dinner, Steven disappeared to his workroom. Jonelle didn't venture down there because his obsession with some kind of conspiracy theory about her newscasts was really beginning to bother her. Every time he'd bring it up, she'd demand to know one simple thing: *why*. "Why would someone do that?"

Steven could only say he didn't have a clue.

And Jonelle felt enormous distance from him for the first time in their marriage.

One afternoon while the kids were still at school, Jonelle and Steven went to Results together. They each did half an hour on the treadmill, then worked on butt, abs, arms, and finally legs. When Jonelle finished a set on a leg extension machine, Steven didn't take over. He was leaning against one of the big yellow pillars on the floor gym, lost in thought. "Steven? Hello?" she said.

"I keep trying to put the pieces together," he suddenly burst out in frustration. "The missing link in my brain that would finally answer the hows and whys and whens and make some sense of this thing!"

She was astonished. And angry. "Oh, Lord, again?" she said. "The way to make sense of it is to give it a rest." She walked over to the huge safe that now served as the towel cabinet and grabbed herself a fresh one. She was sweating more out of frustration now than workout exhilaration.

Steven followed her. "Jone, listen, I know I sounds nuts, and it's all still pretty much a jumbled paranoid fear. But the same guy is in several news incidents you reported on."

"Maybe he's in some with Katie Couric or John Stossel as well."

"Honey, stop living in denial."

She blew up. "Denial? I'm supposed to say you're right? I'm supposed to say someone's creating the news? That's what you're suggesting, aren't you?"

"I didn't say that."

"Well, then what are you saying?" Her eyes burned red and she knew she was shouting but she didn't care. "Maybe what's happening here has more to do with you, Steve." She rarely called him Steve. She knew he hated it.

"How so?"

"Maybe you're just jealous."

"Of what?"

She hesitated, but she said it just as it came into her head for the first time. "I'm making more money than you are now. You say you want to be the house husband but I wonder if you're not resenting having so little to do."

"That's crap and you know it!"

"I don't know it, I don't know anything! I don't think I even know *you* anymore!"

Everyone was looking at them, they suddenly realized. They were actually shouting above the cool dance music, which was always set at a fairly high decibel level. Doug, the owner and a trainer Jonelle knew, was watching them, looking concerned. He walked over and politely said, "Is everything okay?"

"Fuck you," Steven snapped at him, and hurried down the stairs to the men's changing area.

The classical music playing down there was soothing. He stripped his gym clothes off, grabbed a towel, and walked to the center stall of a line of three showers and pulled the curtain. The icy spray was meant to clear his head, then he switched to hot to relax him. But his anger and frustration remained.

While Steven had his eyes closed, someone stepped into the stall on his right. Steven wasn't aware he had company until he opened his eyes and his peripheral vision registered a hand visible in the open space between the stalls' partition fabric and the tile wall. The hand pressing the soap dispenser there sported a gold ring on a stubby finger.

Without thinking, Steven grabbed the guy's hand, twisting it backward toward him, practically pulling the man through the partition. The bather shouted out in fright, and almost instantaneously Steven realized the ring was not the same as the ones in the incidents. But by the time he released the hand and tried to apologize, the damage was done. The frightened bather looked at Steven as if he were dangerous. And Steven felt ridiculous.

As he slid into his pants at his locker, he speculated whether or not Jonelle was right. This obsession was getting to him. He'd practically attacked a guy in the showers, for God's sake, an innocent man. There were a lot of guys with slender fingers wearing tight gold rings; Jonelle had said that. He *was* becoming like one of those assassination diehards. He would put it out of his mind forever. The man whose hand he grabbed now walked past him in a towel, keeping his distance. "Sorry again," Steven explained. "I'm just really jumpy."

"I'll say." The man hurried away.

But Steven knew that wasn't it. He wasn't jumpy. He was frightened. For Jonelle. And for his marriage. This was really getting to them both. And he knew that all the talking to himself wouldn't ease the feeling deep in his soul that there was something to this. He grabbed his gym bag and headed out.

Jonelle hadn't even gone to the women's locker room. Steven found her sitting in one of the black leather chairs on the gym floor. Lost in thought while he was showering, hating herself for the things she'd said, she finally faced something she'd not wanted to admit since the day Steven had first suggested his suspicion: that she had some herself.

But she didn't tell him that.

Her unspoken and denied fear didn't actually take root in her until a few days later, when Alicia Maris innocently told Jonelle some gossip she'd heard the previous night at a party. The late Pamela Harriman, while ambassador to France, the story went, turned off the heat in the American embassy in Paris so the pipes in the attic would freeze, thereby causing a flood that damaged furniture and artwork so that she could have the place redecorated to her taste. When Jonelle left Alicia, she got the creepiest feeling, one she couldn't quite explain. Something about creating a situation so you could come out more comfortable and pleased.

A few days later, she reported on a shocking ending to a story she'd covered for months: The rare plague that had ravaged a certain African country had actually been injected into people in a hospital there under the orders of the country's president, a dictator who cried out for the world's help. Aid had come in the way of money from the United States, Great Britain, France, and Germany, which bought medicine from a huge pharmaceutical company in Switzerland. A reporter, sensing a feeling Jonelle understood, a gut feeling that there was something more to uncover here, learned that the largest single shareholder of the company was the dictator himself, and searched out proof that he'd created the health crisis to fill his own Swiss bank account and make himself more famous.

She shivered when she let her brain take this seemingly unconnected story into her own life.

She couldn't even fathom the thoughts she was having.

But she was scared to death.

Steven and Jonelle were on their knees in the garden of the Bucks County house, planting the little dry seeds that, they hoped, would become luscious summer vegetables. They watched the kids doing the same at the side of the house. "Sarah's going to have great sweet peas again this year," Jonelle said, faking enthusiasm for something she wasn't concentrating on at all.

"Yes. And Wyatt's pumpkins will win a prize."

"Where?"

"Four F or whatever that is."

"He's no farmer."

Steven suddenly dropped the pretense. The tension that had bubbled over that day in the gym was still there. "Are we ever going to talk about it again?" Steven asked.

She nodded. "Go ahead."

"I don't want to argue. I hate when we fight."

"We won't fight," she promised, and she knew that was true. For she wanted this discussion herself.

"All these incredible incidents you've covered," Steven began, "do you . . . how do I say this? Have you ever felt there are just too many of them?"

She tried to look puzzled.

"Too many big ones, stuff that's just fallen into your lap."

"You saying I'm no good and it's all luck?" Her attempt at humor didn't work. It sounded dead serious.

Steven got up, brushed his hands free of dirt. "I told you I don't want to fight. And that's where we're headed." He lifted the basket of flower seeds and took them into the house.

Jonelle followed him. In the kitchen, he washed his hands in the sink, dried them on a towel. "I was sitting there in church on Sunday and the minister was talking about God's plan for everyone, how things happen, fall into place for some, and for others it seems that nothing works right, life is a mess, he was saying it's all in God's vision." He opened the refrigerator, tossed a handful of ice cubes into a glass, and poured himself some milk.

"How can you put ice into milk? I've never understood that."

"Subzero doesn't keep it at zero. I like it like you get it in a diner, freezing."

She braved communication. "So what's that story about church got to do with me? 'Cause it sounded like something your father has said?"

"No, but that's when I started thinking, is this all God's plan to make you the best, the most famous reporter in the world? Or is it someone else's?"

"Whose?"

He shrugged. "I can't imagine. The whole thing is just preposterous."

"If that's true, why don't you just drop it?"

"I can't." He moved closer to her, enthused now that he saw she was really listening. "Jone, have you ever wondered about it being so coincidental that you're right there? On the scene when it happens? You must have."

She would have answered, but Wyatt appeared, covered with mud. "Corky dragged me into the creek." Corky was Janet Edwards's dog, and while she was a great neighbor, the dog was not. Jonelle was thrilled because now she didn't have to answer, a German shepherd had stopped this line of thought dead in its tracks.

"Wyatt, you're a mess," Steven said, turning the water back on in the sink. "Want me to take a shot at this or should we just put you through the car wash?"

"Why don't we have a dog, Mom?" Wyatt asked, approaching his father.

Jonelle said, "Look in a mirror. That's why."

Steven rinsed his mud-caked hair and face and then tossed him a towel. Wyatt noticed the batch of chocolate chip cookies Jonelle had made. "Can I have one?"

"Just one, mister," Jonelle warned. "But only after you shower."

Steven poured Wyatt a glass of milk. "Ice in your milk, squirt?"

"Sure, Dad."

Jonelle laughed. "Get 'em while they're young," she sang, and went back out into the yard.

Once there, her expression changed and she shivered. She was petrified that he was right.

Steven found her there later. She was staring at the setting sun, which cast a bluish gold tint to the new leaves on the trees. "It goes so fast, you almost have to grasp at spring to savor it . . ."

"Jonelle, we can't ignore this."

The friendly discussion from earlier did not repeat itself. She was defensive again. "But what can we do about it? How do you pursue a theory you yourself call preposterous?"

"Well, we have to—"

"No," she said firmly. It was too hard for her to admit to herself that so many things, so many big stories that she'd reported, had been a sham. "I'm a good reporter, the best there is. I don't need anyone helping me, offering up stories, making them happen for me. I'm not some kind of fraud."

"I never suggested you were."

"That's what it feels like if I . . . if I give in to this notion, this insanity."

He suddenly realized why she was so brittle at the gym, why she accused him of being jealous of her success. This theory of his destroyed her confidence, her belief in herself. "Jone—"

She got up. "I'm making dinner and this is the last we're going to talk about this."

Steven shut up. He knew not to push her any farther.

But he knew he would push himself as far as he could. Nothing would stop him from finding out the truth.

The next day, Jonelle was on edge at the studio. What Steven had concluded disarmed her. Barney Keller was in Washington, wanted to lunch with her, but as she was about to say yes, word came in that Muslim leader Farrakhan's plane had crashed in Libya, killing many aboard, but that he and four others had miraculously survived.

She spent four days in Tripoli, covering the story, which concluded that weather had been the cause, but talk was rife with rumors of CIA intervention in Farrakhan's ever-closer ties with Libya. Jonelle gained access to Col. Mu'ammar Gadhafi, the only journalist he allowed to interview him. In other words, he chose Jonelle over Barbara Walters. It said a great deal. He claimed a conspiracy on behalf of the American government to rid themselves of Farrakhan. And the ratings soared.

Back in D.C., Jonelle took twenty minutes out of the editing room where she and Alicia were putting together a *Jonelle Patterson*

Reporting . . . from Libya segment, to grab a salad and Diet Pepsi, and found Barney sliding in next to her in the lunchroom. "You were superb over there, just amazing," he said, beaming. "We knocked the others out of the water. The overnights were great."

"Thanks. But boy, the colonel is a real sleazeball."

"Like some TV people I know."

"I'll bet," she said, edgy.

"So, how's it going?"

"Getting back to the mundane stuff. Clay called this morning. You guys really want me to speak at that fund-raiser next week? It's Republican."

"We'll give the Democrats equal time."

"No, I'm serious," she said emphatically. "I thought we don't take sides."

"You're not going as a Republican, you're the guest of honor, the most famous newswoman in the country."

"It makes me nervous, this partisan thing."

"You'll get over it. Besides, you *are* a Republican."

"I'm a journalist first, and we don't take political sides."

"You're going to give the speech of your life on the effect of TV on family values, how science and technology are not at odds with the intellectuals and humanity, stuff like that." He said it too much like an order. Softening the pitch, he added, "They'll love you."

"I'm not running for anything."

"Not yet."

"What do you mean?"

"Remember we once joked about losing you to politics?"

"No."

"In the beginning, that first dinner."

"Oh. I guess, something like that."

"Today's another time. You're big, influential, you could win."

"What? PTA chairman? Neighborhood Watch captain?"

"Anything you like. Everyone would vote for you. You could run for president. We've come a long way since Geraldine Ferraro."

"You're sounding a lot like Steven's father and my rabid fan,

S. Rovig. And my son, come to think of it. If anyone should run for office it's Madeline Albright, or Dianne Feinstein."

"She may be Gore's running mate."

"Make a nice debate with Chris Whitman."

"She'll be on the ticket with Bush or Quayle, and that'll kill her political career. It's time for a woman to go for the Oval Office. On her own."

She thought this was a waste of time, so she changed the subject. "I may have a real story brewing."

"What about?"

"Conspiracy of some sort. A killer, assassin, following a reporter around."

He rubbed his chin. "Who's the reporter?"

"Me."

"Give me more."

"There is no more. At least, not yet. Steven's the one who started uncovering this, he's working on it."

"Uncovering what? I'm lost."

She told him. "Remember the famous hand blowup from the Philippines tape?"

"Cover of *Time*, how could I forget?"

"Steven thinks he found the same hand in the tape of the Molly Binenfeld incident."

Barney sputtered, "Who the hell's Molly Binenfeld?"

"The Olympic swimmer who almost died from the fall off the board."

"Sounds far-fetched."

"It sure is. I think it's crazy."

"So forget it."

"Forget it? I thought you'd eat this up. Talk about a story! Besides, I may be in some kind of danger."

"Come on, Steve's gotta be wrong."

"I agree. I told him as much. Just wanted to know what you thought."

"I think you'd better get back to editing. We have another chance to win the week with *Reporting*."

"We will. There's stuff you haven't even seen." She squirted the packet of nonfat blue cheese dressing over her lettuce. And the entire table. Some of it struck Barney's right hand. She laughed, wiped it with her napkin, and in doing so noticed the garnet ring on the middle finger. Like the ring in the blowups, it was too tight, it made the flesh bulge out above and beneath it. It gave her confidence that Barney was right and Steven wrong, that millions of people wore rings that were too tight, and what Steven had discovered was simply a coincidence. But she only said to Barney, "You'd better have that ring sized. It's going to cut off the circulation."

"Yeah, 'cause then I wouldn't be able to give producers the finger." Barney picked up his briefcase and left with a smile.

"And that, gentlemen," Barney said, "is all I know at this point." Barney, Clay, and James Findley sat in Barney's minimalist living room in his TriBeCa loft. No one responded.

"Well?" Barney asked.

"Put some sofas in this place, for Christ's sake," Findley said, his ass hurting on the hard chair.

"She said nothing more?" Clay inquired.

"Nothing. Just that Steven 'uncovered it' and is 'working on it.'"

Clay wrote it off. "Speculation. There's just no way that he can tie the two incidents together."

Barney wasn't as sure. "James, can he?"

James snorted. "No. Trust me, Saint Paul knows what he's doing."

"Who the hell is Saint Paul?" Barney asked.

"Code for the shooter."

Clay groaned. "Saint Paul, Jesus."

"You prefer Jesus, we can call him that too." James withdrew a prescription bottle from his pants pocket. "This is all much ado over nothing. They aren't onto a thing." He swallowed a few tablets with bourbon.

"What are those?" Clay asked.

"Ulcer stuff."

"Bullshit," Barney said.

Clay added, "Come on, James, we've heard the rumors. Why don't you feel you can trust us?"

"We're your partners," Barney reminded him.

"All right," the old man said. "Cancer."

"Cancer?" Barney repeated.

"Prostate cancer. They're not going to operate, could make it worse. Old men like me, doctors kinda like to let it go, spread slowly. That's supposed to be a consolation."

"I'm sorry, James," Clay said.

James grunted.

Barney asked, "How long have you known?"

Clay said, "You just find out?"

"Hell," James replied, looking at them as if they were naive or crazy. "You think I'd have taken this on for any other reason? You think I'm totally mad?"

"Without morals," Barney said, "as most everyone in television is, but not mad."

"I did this because I have a big family I want taken care of when I go. I haven't been able to buy more insurance for four years. This is the only way."

Barney said, "You may need those policies if Steven Patterson goes the route here and traces your 'Saint Paul' to other incidents."

"Impossible. We are clean." Clay was adamant.

"Nixon probably said that to Mitchell and Haldeman at one point," Barney muttered with little apparent humor. "Pretend he does trace him to us. What then?"

James was cold as steel. "He's a TWA pilot. Flight 800 could happen again."

Barney almost fell out of his chair. "Are you stark raving mad?"

James retorted, "How is that any different from what's already happened?"

"He's her husband," Clay reminded him. "Kill him and you might kill everything. Who knows what would happen to her if she were widowed! She may not want it anymore, grief may destroy her, she might just pack it all up and head for Atlanta from whence she came."

Barney said, "No chance. She hasn't seen her mother in twenty years, doesn't go near Atlanta. But she's an investigative reporter. She'd seek the truth if it meant chasing it down for the rest of her life. And she'd get us too."

James smiled. "I'll be dead."

Clay snapped, "You'll be dead a lot sooner—and not 'cause of your asshole—if you don't warn your Saint Paul to be careful."

Barney sipped his Black Label. He was thoughtful. Then he said, "So. We have to be careful. So here's the word: I'm putting on the brakes. No more incidents for a while."

James was aghast. "Wait a minute! Rome took a year to set up, it's ready to go."

Clay agreed with him. Looking at Barney he said, "The Pope's ready to croak. They say any day now."

"He can croak without us."

James was fired. "But knocking off—"

"No," Barney said firmly.

James continued. "It'll be the scoop of the century!"

Clay was jazzed as well. "He's right, Barn. It'll blow the papal funeral right off the airwaves. Jonelle will own the coverage."

Barney was calm now. "She'll cover the Pontiff's shiva. And that's all the news I want to hear from Rome." Barney slammed his glass down on the thick glass of the coffee table and rose to his feet. He towered over them. "Capisci?"

In the elevator, James looked at Clay. "What would Rex say?"

Clay shrugged. "I think he'd go for it."

James smiled. "Then fuck Barney Keller. That's what we're gonna do."

chapter 9

*J*onelle and two other reporters take their assigned places on oversized velvet chairs in a small study nestled inside the Vatican's North American College. Young priests in cassocks show up with trays of coffee, tea, pastries. An old nun rushes in, all flushed, patting a pillow she reverently sets on the biggest chair, apparently readying it for Riccio's bottom, which, as he enters, Jonelle realizes is substantial. The man sits pompously, regally, as if he already is Pope, nodding and waving his ringed hand in a way that makes Jonelle think not so much of things papal, but more of Mafioso godfathers. Or at least Mario Puzo's depiction of them.

Then he begins to speak.

And then he drops dead.

He simply stops talking and, it seems, breathing. He topples forward before Jonelle and the others realize exactly what is happening, and even though all three rush to help him, there is nothing they can do. The priests try to prop him up—all three hundred pounds of him—to no avail, then decide to put him prone on the floor, which makes him look like he's already lying in state in Saint Peter's, which causes the old nun to have what is assumed is a heart attack

*of her own, and Jonelle finds herself fanning the woman until a
doctor rushes in. . . .*

Il Observato *the next day calls it a "massive heart attack," and
it overshadows the death of John Paul, which comes quietly three
days later. The entire funeral, period of mourning, and meeting of
the College of Cardinals to select the new Pope is relegated to
second-story status by the sensational charge, generated by the Italian faction, that Riccio was poisoned. It brings back the theory that
John Paul I, whose reign as Pope had been so short-lived, had also
suffered a similar fate, and headlines scream of plots, counterplots,
rebirth of the Borgias, and countless cries of corruption from Catholics, Methodists, Buddhists, and atheists combined. It is not a good
day for the Church.*

And, in the end, an Italian is elected Pope anyway.

"It was sensational stuff, the Riccio saga," Alicia said to Jonelle
at dinner at Nora's restaurant the night she returned to Washington.
"You did a smashing job."

"Wyatt started piano lessons today."

"Come again?"

"Said he'd never play, was beneath him, girl's stuff."

"Jonelle, we're talking about Italy."

"I changed the subject."

"I noticed. Any reason?"

"It isn't Italy, exactly, that I don't want to talk about."

"What exactly is it that you don't want to talk about?"

"These coincidences. All this stuff that happens when a camera
and I are nearby."

"Connie Chung would have given up Maury for that!" Alicia
said. "You should be proud."

"I am. Of what I do. But this repetition of—" She stopped talking, cutting herself off, unwilling to go there.

Alicia dug deeper. "No, you're not getting away with that, you
can't just stop midsentence. What do you mean?"

"Nothing."

"Want to talk about your kid's piano lessons again, is that it?"

"Remember when you told me that gossip about Pam Harriman?

How she manipulated the refurbishment of the Paris embassy building?"

"What's that got to do with you?"

"What if someone were—" Her voice cracked and she held it in. Instead she only said, "I get a creepy feeling sometimes, that's all."

Alicia smiled and sipped her wine. "You get all the creepy feelings you want. I get great satisfaction from the ratings your creepy feelings bring."

"Alicia, Riccio was poisoned. I don't think it happened to get rid of him. It happened to give me a great story."

Alicia sat in stunned silence.

"Yes. Steven thinks some lunatic is running around setting up the news for me."

Alicia gave her that you've-been-working-too-hard look. "Honey."

"I know, I know."

"Maybe *you* need piano lessons. They're calming."

Jonelle tried to shove her "creepy feelings" to the back of her brain, into the subconscious, but Steven wouldn't let her. He got all the tape he could find of Cardinal Riccio's death, but nowhere on any frame could he find a ring that matched the other two. He felt it was preposterous that whoever was doing this could have gotten into the Vatican anyway. He and Jonelle, after months of digging, felt reasonably sure that the incident wasn't connected to her.

But they felt no more at ease.

The next day, Alicia handed Jonelle an envelope.

"What's this?"

"Tape. From the Vatican."

"I thought I had it all."

"I found this in editing. Stuff you haven't seen. I haven't seen. Thought you'd like to . . . well, thought it might help."

Jonelle nodded. "Thanks, Alicia."

"Just to help you get this out of your mind."

Late that night, once again in his workroom in the basement, Steven found himself painstakingly studying the newly found tape of the Vatican incident. He blew up frame after frame, obsessed the way he once had been with the Philippines tape, the Santa Clara tape, all the rest. At 3:18 A.M. he hit what he thought was pay dirt: a gold band, barely distinguishable to the naked eye, on the hand of one of the young priests in the room.

Steven couldn't be sure, so he chose not to tell Jonelle as yet. There was no point in worrying her more.

But in his gut, he was positive that the hands matched.

He wished they didn't.

For it meant his suspicions were right.

chapter 10

At five the next morning, Jonelle rushed out to cover a breaking story on a yacht that had capsized on the Potomac. Two congressmen and their wives had been partying on it the night before, and so far they were unaccounted for. It was hard news, the kind Jonelle ate up. By afternoon, the story was wrapped up—all four passengers had left the yacht hours before, and a crew member who had been drinking took it out to show off for his buddies, with disastrous results. But in the short time the story was in the forefront, Jonelle was brilliant.

When she returned to the house at 6:00 P.M. however, she found Helen there instead of Steven. "No one informed him his bid for a flight to Rome was accepted and he had to rush out."

"Rome," Jonelle said, feeling a twinge up her spine.

Helen laughed. "He thought he'd be flying to Albuquerque tomorrow."

Wyatt walked in on that. "What's Alba Kerkee?"

"A city," Jonelle said, as he walked over and kissed her cheek. "In New Mexico."

"Sounds funny."

Wyatt pondered it. "Can we go there sometime?"

"Yeah, when I retire," Jonelle said, taking the cup of coffee Helen had just poured for her. "Which may be sooner than anyone thinks."

Helen folded her arms over her apron. "What is going on with you?" she asked firmly, motherly. "You haven't been yourself lately."

Jonelle shrugged. "That's the point. I'm not quite sure just who I really am lately. Reporter, or puppet."

Jonelle ate dinner with Helen and the kids, then packed Wyatt off to his piano lesson just up the street. Helen watched TV with them for a while, then went home to her apartment next door. Jonelle and Sarah were working on a crossword together when Alicia called, wanting to know if Jonelle was still interested in doing a piece on Jared Tucker. It was a gig Jonelle had been lobbying for for a long time now, and she was thrilled to hear Alicia coming around.

Jonelle had met Jared Tucker—a writer whose book, *Epiphany*, was making controversial news on both sides of the Atlantic—years ago in Seattle when she was with CNN. Only twenty at the time, he'd been talked about because of his controversial and disturbing lyrics for a band called Stinking Rose, and though most critics agreed that the group did, indeed, stink, Tucker himself got rave notices for his poetry, his voice, and the passion with which he sang. When the band broke up, Jared moved to New York City, where he sang with Patti Smith for a while, then took up living with Courtney Love. But as her movie career soared, their relationship diminished. Close to *Rolling Stone* editor and founder Jann Wenner, he seemed to experience the same *Epiphany* that Wenner had had just a few years before, because, when he landed in Paris, living the life of the young hip expatriot, he created a kind of Gertrude Stein salon with his own Alice B. Toklas: his new love, Alain Christofle, a decorator and charmer—and very much male.

Jared Tucker interested Jonelle for obvious reasons, but there was another motivation in wanting to interview him: He had become the leader of gay rights in France, where his name was now synonymous with the movement. He'd recently led the fight against child pornography after a case in which a husband and wife in Belgium had been prosecuted for the murder of four little French boys. Jonelle was eager to learn what made Jared Tucker, a straight stud musician on the fringe of the Heavy Metal movement most of his life, come out as a gay man at thirty and lead the cause for equality in a country that wasn't even his.

Jonelle felt there was an opportunity here to deeply probe a controversial mind. What really caused this life change? Why was he so zealous? Why did he feel it a "moral requirement" that homosexuals admit their orientation the world over? Had he felt he was gay from the start but hid it from the world and himself until he could no longer stand it? She knew little about sexual political issues and had never really delved into the mind of a man who had been straight and was now gay, and she wanted badly to learn for herself. Her own passion for education was her best motivating force; she knew it would be a dynamite piece. She told Alicia she wanted to do a segment on him.

"Hmmm," Alicia had said, always the savvy producer. "I didn't read the book, but it sure as hell has polarized a lot of people. I agree with you, he'd be a hot piece."

But Barney nixed it.

" 'Absolutely not,' " Alicia told Jonelle he'd said. "When he saw the list of upcoming segments, he purposely called to kill it."

"Why?"

"Too controversial, he claims."

"That's why it should air."

"Maybe he's got his moral limit," Alicia had suggested.

Jonelle said, "Are you kidding? He'd sell his mother for ratings."

"And throw in his dad for good measure." But Alicia already knew Jonelle was going to do it. "You don't care, do you? You're going to do it anyway."

"I want to talk to this guy! I remember Tucker seeming sweet and too smart for his age, like there was all this brilliance just building steam inside, not knowing how to vent it—"

"That was ten years ago."

"He's got to be bursting by now."

Alicia had warned her, "I'm gonna get in trouble for this."

"Come on, let's risk it."

"He could refuse to run it."

"Not after he's seen it, I promise you."

Barney got wind of it before she left for Paris. And he blew his top. "You're not going to waste time and money on that fag."

"Since when are you a bigot? You've got gay boys working for you in every department. Some say you are yourself."

"Please."

"It would at least explain your vehemence."

"Tucker would have named me. He got everyone else."

"Look at the sparks he produces. Controversy! Isn't that what we want? Or would you rather I do a piece on Elizabeth and Bob Dole's recent divorce?"

"Look, Jonelle," he said, letting down his guard. "I have— how to say it—certain people to answer to. Certain interests to protect."

"Who? What interests?"

"The money behind this network. There are people I have to answer to."

"I still don't get it."

"There are some good Christians involved. Shit, Tucker's an atheist on top of it all. They'd find this very offensive."

"I find censorship offensive."

"Jonelle, if the people on the board at NBC hate something personally, NBC might have to think twice about airing it, I promise you."

"I'm doing it," she said with her most alluring tease, "and you will just have to ram it down those good Christian throats."

And she left him.

She spoke with Steven in Rome every night, after he'd chatted with the kids. She knew that he was staying there so long for a reason that had nothing to do with TWA. "I'm doing a little checking, that's all."

"What?" she probed. "You said the gold ring wasn't in the Vatican incident."

He hadn't told her what he found on the tape Alicia had given her. And he didn't want to do it over the phone. "Honey, don't worry."

She was frustrated, and replied flippantly. "Okay, I'll just put it out of my mind."

"What are you up to?"

"I'm going to Paris."

"Paris? Let's meet for coffee in Vienna."

"I'm interviewing Jared Tucker."

"Finally, huh? Listen, stay at the Hotel Jeanne d'Arc."

"Okay."

"Honey?"

"Are you going to tell me to be careful?"

"No. Just wanted to say I love you."

Paris's Hotel Jeanne d'Arc sits on a quiet corner in the heart of the Marais, just off the rue de Turenne. Jonelle is impressed how the staff remembers her husband. She is greeted with warm, open arms, and given a large room on the top floor with windows on two walls, overlooking the rooftops of the old part of the city and the place de Vosges, the square she loves so much. She sips tea and consumes a luscious, buttery croissant while she dials Jared. Alain informs her that Jared is out and gives her directions to meet them at their favorite restaurant for dinner. She is thrilled when he suggests Bofinger, because she's never dined there and has always wondered what it is like, this famous, oldest restaurant in the city.

It doesn't disappoint. The food is glorious, the decor something akin to the stage set for the Harmonia Gardens in Hello, Dolly!, *and the company is fascinating and fun. Alain has a poise and wit that delights Jonelle, and Jared is more relaxed and less guarded than she remembers or would have thought from speaking to him on the phone, less the pressure cooker now, more a man who seems to have the confidence of someone who has finally found himself, who is certain of what he is all about. And they seem, she is sure, very much in love.*

They discuss everything but Jared's book, for that is the purpose of tomorrow's interview and forbidden territory without the camera

*running; talk tonight of the getting-to-know-one-another variety,
feeling comfortable with each other. Jonelle drinks too much wine,
eats too much crusty bread, talks spiritedly and nonstop about politics, sex, music, France, children, and decorating. She falls into an
exhausted sleep back at the hotel and doesn't wake till eleven the
next morning.*

She rises and walks briskly to a boulangerie *where she has a café
au lait and a gooey, sinful chocolate roll. She crosses the pont Marie
and shops on the Île St-Louis, picking up souvenirs and chocolates
for the kids. She crosses the pont St-Louis to the Île de la Cité where
she stops for a moment to gaze up at the splendor of Notre Dame,
which never ceases to amaze her, and says a prayer inside for the
blessings she has been given.*

Then she goes to work.

*Gathering her gear, she calls the video crew and is down on the
street waiting when they fetch her in a Peugeot van. Arriving at
Jared and Alain's building in the 17th arrondissement, she goes inside while the crew unloads the equipment. A maintenance man
standing at the elevator is posting a sign that indicates it is out of
order, so she slings her bag over her shoulder and braves the stairs.*

*She is almost to the second landing when a man, bounding down
the steps, rounds the corner and slams right into her. She feels she's
been hit by a truck, loses her footing, and grasps the railing with
both hands to keep from falling. Her bag drops to the step under
her feet. She looks up at the man, who is rising after being knocked
on his butt by the collision, and she immediately notices three things:
He has a mustache, he is handsome, he is obviously very upset.
There is no apology; indeed, he rattles on in unintelligible French,
and she can only guess that he is blaming her for being in his way.
Then he seems to leap right over her and continues on down the
staircase, slower this time. She now notices he is wearing running
clothes; she figures he's late for some marathon he is sure he's going
to win.*

*She picks up her bag and makes her way to the third floor. When
she rings the bell at number 320, she fluffs her hair a little, feeling
slightly disheveled after the run-in with the man on the stairs, wanting to look fresh and bright. She anticipates Jared opening the door*

and chiding her for drinking so much last night; yes, she has a hangover. But the door does not open. No one, in fact, even answers the bell.

The crew arrives, cursing French buildings for their faulty elevators, only to find Jonelle still standing there. After another try, knocking, ringing, calling, they assume no one is there—which Jonelle finds very strange—and a worried neighbor shows up in the hall, calls down to the concierge, who ascends the stairs with keys in hand, and after much consternation and with great concern, for the concierge is as fond of her two renters as Jonelle is, they open the door of the apartment. Jonelle follows the woman inside, and when the concierge turns toward the bedroom, calling for Monsieur Tucker, Jonelle instinctively looks toward the kitchen. That's when she sees Jared Tucker's legs.

He is lying on the floor, facedown, naked, dead. Drug paraphernalia sits on the countertop. There is a plastic bag with what looks like heroin on the floor, and on his blue arm is a tight rubber tourniquet. Overdose?

Suicide, says the media in scandalous tones.

But not Jonelle. She and Alain, who arrived shortly after the body was discovered, know that Jared's murder was made to look like he took his own life. The fact of his death is the biggest news Paris has chewed on in months; the controversy over whether this was murder or not makes it even bigger. Jonelle is in the center of the storm, not only the single eyewitness to the possible assailant but dispassionately reporting the story on ONE's camera, passionately defending Jared's honor when speaking as his friend. She's really only known him one day, but it feels like a lifetime. And of this she is sure: He loved life and had no apparent reason to take his. Drugs, Alain insists, were part of his past in music, not his life in Paris. He was murdered. And framed.

Jonelle peers at hundreds of mug shots over a period of days, but she cannot pick out the man she'd seen face-to-face on the staircase. He was not a resident of the building. He has disappeared. The press calls him "M. No Name." But he does have a name, she is sure of that, and she is also sure that if she were to see him again, she would recognize him. More details come alive: a strong, prominent chin, fluffy dark hair, that distinctive mustache, and besides his being handsome, he is youthful, stocky, strong. She would know him in a minute. But she is quite sure she will never see him again.

Barney Keller acted as if the trip to Paris had been his idea. He took credit for "sending" Jonelle to do this very controversial piece, and even went so far as to put up some of the reward money for information leading to the truth of Jared Tucker's death. It was great PR for Network ONE. And once again Jonelle had scooped the world.

But she was anything but thrilled or proud.

"What's the matter, honey?" Alicia asked over the table in the lunchroom. Jonelle wasn't eating at all. "Tucker?"

"Yes."

"You really were taken with that guy."

"I was, but that's not it."

"Want a shoulder?"

"I want Steven. He's still in Europe."

"Try *me*."

Jonelle felt herself ready to burst. She needed to share her fear with someone, this unsettling sensation that she'd felt from the moment she saw the legs lying on that cold kitchen floor. So she shared with Alicia the feeling she couldn't shake, what she didn't want to look at, what she wanted to deny, and had been denying for a long time now: that too many coincidences peppered her professional path at Network ONE. "Someone is making these things happen."

Alicia didn't take it seriously. "You mentioned something like this before. I think you're just a magnet of some kind."

Jonelle said, "No. Steven was onto something. He was right."

"Honey, it's just too—what's the word?"

"Preposterous."

"Thank you."

"I'm scared."

"Don't be. It's silly. You're jumping to conclusions that are simply unbelievable, and you can't do this to yourself."

Jonelle shrugged. "Maybe so. Still, it makes you wonder."

It made Alicia wonder as well, and she wondered out loud to Barney Keller that very evening. He asked what was wrong with Jonelle, she seemed edgy on camera lately. She told him what Jonelle had told her that afternoon, and how "preposterous" it was, and how Alicia thought she was a little "paranoid" about the amazing events that she'd been so close to. Alicia said, "She thinks some sick admirer wants to boost her career."

"Who'd that be?"

Alicia laughed. "Don't look at me!"

He teased her. "You want ratings."

"The ratings more directly affect you."

"Well, I confess. I murdered the Pope."

"Now *that's* a story I'd like to see Jonelle do," Alicia said, and left for the day.

Clay and Barney were at Madison Square Garden, taking a break from the Ice Capades. Barney was in pain. "What are we doing this for? Sitting here watching has-been figure skaters make more money than we do."

"For James. You saw his grandkids loving it. We're supposed to be happy to be part of his birthday celebration. Hell, he may not have long to live."

"I'd like to kill him myself."

" 'Cause of Tucker?"

"He should have been shot for Rome alone. Taking matters into his own hands. I expressly forbade doing any more."

"Rex overruled you."

"Little prick. And then Tucker. Christ, Clay, the hit man smacks into her on the stairs, real genius Findley hired."

"He got away. She didn't get a close look. He changes his face every time anyhow." Clay tried to reason with him. "Look, Barn, it frankly doesn't take a rocket scientist to figure out she's had like really good karma when it comes to finding a story. Suspicion is natural."

"The husband worries me. Remember how he tried to help with that blowup of the tape in the Philippines? How obsessed he was with that hand?"

"Forget it. We lay low awhile, it'll be fine."

"I hope we haven't gone too far already."

Clay bought himself a hot dog. "Rex is worried about something else."

"What?"

"Her mother. She could prove a bit of an embarrassment. Quite a character, been married as much as Liz Taylor, a lush too, it's chancy."

"Remember Clinton's old lady?"

Clay smiled. "Actually, she was kind of endearing, wasn't she?" He bit into his hot dog. "Want some?"

"Is it kosher?"

Clay just grinned. "So, when do we make the big move?"

"Hillary? It's April, the election's not till November. We wait for their suspicions to die down and Gore's campaign to heat up before we attempt that. I want that incident to overshadow the election, almost wipe it off the front page."

"And till then?"

"Give her time to let her suspicions die."

"We still do Regent U. in June?"

"I'll make that decision when the time comes."

"What about Alicia Maris?"

"Don't worry about her."

"*Don't worry about her?* You're the one who told me on the phone that she's dancing on a powder keg."

"I'm on top of it."

Clay tossed the wrapper in the trash. "Let's get back to the ice. Findley's gonna wonder what's going on."

"Hey," Barney said in a lighter tone, "Rex and Marjorie had a new baby. It true that you're gonna be godfather?"

"They asked me, yes."

"You guys pretty close?"

"I'm close to the whole family."

"I mean Rex. I hear you two are like brothers."

"You might say that."

"Well, see if you can't use him to get through to James. Nothing more till May. And nothing sloppy when he does it."

"You've got my word."

As they entered the stadium, Barney said, "Rumor says Rex's a fag." He watched Clay's reaction.

"That's the single most ridiculous thing I've ever heard."

Jonelle ran across the parking lot when she saw Steven coming. She'd driven all the way to Baltimore to pick him up. This was the only time she'd greeted him after a flight that she wasn't struck by the sight of his uniform; indeed, her mind was on nothing but her growing feeling—fear?—that he had been right.

"Honey," he said, pulling her tightly to him in a supportive embrace. "It's okay, okay."

She clung to him, shivering. She had not seen him since before she went to Paris. Now, in his arms, all her fears came to the surface. "Did he do this? Did he kill Tucker?"

"Who?"

"The guy who shot Imelda, who tried to kill Molly!"

He put a hand firmly on her shoulder, pulled his bag with the other, and told her, "It's going to be fine. We are going to really study this and see what our options are. We're going to be levelheaded about it."

"Levelheaded? I'm a wreck. I'm agreeing with you, Steven. Wherever I go, people die."

They reached the car. "They usually go to a story that's already happened, it doesn't find them."

Driving out of the lot, Jonelle asked him, "What did you find that night in your workroom? Before you went to Rome? That's why you stayed in Italy all this time, isn't it?"

"I saw the ring—I'll show you at home. I worked with Vatican officials to try to figure out who the priest was who had the ring on his hand."

"Right there? He was in the room with us?"

Steven nodded. "And it seems that the Vatican is crawling with guys in cassocks and there was a lot of confusion that day. This priest spoke perfect Italian and told the old nun they'd just run him over from some other job in the North American College to help assist at the press conference."

"The Vatican. They got into the Vatican." She shook her head. "That's a story in itself." She grasped his right hand when he rested it on the shift lever. "Steven, I honestly believe Jared Tucker was killed just to give me a story."

He drove a half mile before he responded. "I do too," he finally said. "But there's no tape on that one."

Once home, they had dinner with the kids and put on their best family faces. Wyatt and Sarah had no clue how terrorized their mother felt, for Jonelle covered brilliantly. Pasta and sauce and a big leafy salad helped too, and when it was over, four spoons dug into a quart of butter pecan ice cream. Wyatt decided he was going to practice the piano (he'd become the young Van Cliburn of late) and Sarah was going to a girlfriend's for a sleep-over. Jonelle had to wait till the friend's mother picked her up, but once she'd seen Sarah safely off and Wyatt had said his prayers and was tucked into bed, she joined Steven in his workroom. She locked the door. It made her feel more secure.

Steven brought the suspect frames of tape to the screen of his computer. He showed her the gold ring in the Manila frame, the gold ring in Santa Clara, and then the glimpse of gold ring on the hand of the priest. There wasn't enough gold visible in that photo to determine conclusively if it was the same one or not, but the puffiness of the fingers matched. They then blew up the man's entire image, face included. And then Steven asked the hard question: Could this have been the same person Jonelle ran into on the staircase in Paris, the infamous "M. No Name"?

"No." She felt the man on the stairs was stockier, more handsome—or was that just the mustache?—and his hair was curly, completely different from this young, but balding, priest. "No, Steven, that's not him."

She was relieved. But also disappointed.

Steven felt the same. "I was hoping we'd get some kind of identification. We need a face."

"We need a reason."

"We'll find that out later. It doesn't really matter right now. I mean, I could give you several reasons, some nut who is obsessed with you and wants to see your career soar, somebody at the network who wants ratings, somebody who one day wants to tell the truth to discredit everything you've ever done."

She looked stunned.

"Whatever—whoever—it is, we need proof. Tape, documents, we need to know if this insane plot we're cooking up is true or not."

"Can't we go to the police?"

"With what?"

She nodded; he had a point. This was only a theory, and one that could not be substantiated. And one that would sound, they were certain, a little crazed.

"We need help."

"I'll say." Then she thought a moment. "I think I know how to get it."

"How?"

"I talked to someone else about this."

His reaction was sharp. "Jone! We can't trust anyone!"

"I trust Alicia."

"You told her?"

"Yes. Steven, we got the Vatican tape from her, without that we'd have been—"

"How much?"

"How much what?"

"How much did you share with her?"

"Some."

"How *much*, Jone?"

"That we were worried. That you had suspected that the same person had done Manila and Santa Clara. And I suspected Tucker as well."

"What was her reaction?"

"She thought I was nuts. Why are you third-degreeing me about Alicia?"

"She's the perfect suspect. She's got access, knows everything on the inside, has a reason—they're her ratings too."

"Nonsense."

"You sure?"

"She'd do anything for me. She's been my producer for years. I'd trust her with my life."

"You positive of that?"

"She's on our side, Steven."

He sat in silence for a long time. He was wrestling with two sides of the coin. Heads: Alicia Maris had orchestrated this. Tails: She was one of the few people who could really help them, because she had access to everything they needed. He made the call: tails. "All right, we'll trust your instincts because we can't do this alone." He picked up the phone and handed it to her.

"What?"

"Call her and tell her to come over here. Now."

chapter 11

Alicia Maris arrived late at New York's Aquavit Restaurant, one of Barney Keller's favorite haunts. Barney was already seated at a quiet table in the most private corner. "Alicia," he said, offering his hand over the table, standing slightly.

"Barney," she said, touching his fingertips for a moment, then settling into the chair across from him.

"Vodka rocks for the lady," he told the waiter, adding, "Belevedere. And bring her the bottle."

"Yes, Mr. Keller," the man said as if answering his commanding officer, and hurried off.

"Bring me the bottle?"

" 'Cause it's a work of art. Belevedere's the name of the Polish presidential palace. Bottle's frosted glass, painted with a birch forest, and you look through the trees, through the only clear part, and you see, through the vodka on the back of the bottle, the line drawing of the building."

The waiter showed up with the bottle, and Alicia saw what Barney had described as the waiter poured the clear liquid over the ice cubes. "It's exquisite," she pronounced of the bottle, then sipped, and nodded that the adjective fit the contents as well.

Barney sucked down a shot himself. And poured himself more. "So, Alicia, what's on your mind?"

"Have another drink first," she said. "We have all the time in the world."

"I'd rather talk."

"I'd rather we relax."

"You didn't fly here to make sure I get smashed. Cut the bull-shit."

Alicia decided to listen to the man. She went for the kill. "I know what you've been doing."

"Pardon me?"

"*You* cut the bullshit. Jonelle isn't quite there yet, but she's close, she's at the point I was at a few months ago. Riccio pushed me from considering to believing. Pretty amazing. Got to hand it to you guys."

"I don't know what you're talking about." He stuck his finger in the glass and stirred the ice, trying to look unflustered.

"Yeah."

"No BS, baby."

"Really? Then let's talk about the peripatetic Saint Paul."

He was pouring more Belevedere as she said it, and some of it splashed over the edge of his glass.

"Nervous?"

"Why would I be? Who is this you refer to?"

"Don't play coy."

"Coy is not in my blood."

"Blood?" She sipped the drink. "More like ice water."

"Get to your point."

"There's a bookkeeping entry for a plane ticket to Rome."

"Whose ticket to Rome?"

"Santa Paulo. His first name is Leopold, I understand. Same guy who went to Memphis just before that bus crash. And guess what else? He was in Santa Clara the day of the swimmer's accident." She smiled a smug smile; she was nailing him to the cross and he was starting to squirm.

"You're talking nonsense."

"He happened to be in Paris the afternoon Tucker OD'ed as well."

"So what?"

"Sounds mighty suspicious. Oh, you're right, maybe he's just a fan of Jonelle's and follows her around like those diehards still do Michael Jackson or Madonna."

"I don't know what you're talking about."

"Findley would."

"Findley's private life is not my business."

"Not mine either, but what's fascinating is that a failed screenwriter so dull and boring has such fascinating friends."

"Alicia, come on, stop playing games."

She did. Her voice even changed. She was hard now, as tough as she could ever be as a producer. "Findley knows a character up in Montreal by the name of Leo St. Pere."

"So what?"

"He went to Findley's son's bar mitzvah."

He felt rage surging through his eighty-proof blood. But on the outside he stayed calm. "I couldn't care less."

"Leo St. Pere is sometimes called 'Saint Paul' by people who know him well. Apparently he's got that kind of ego."

Barney replenished her glass. And poured himself another. "Bottle's almost empty." He spied the obedient waiter at a nearby table. "Waiter! Another bottle." He held it up till the man nodded and scurried off once again.

"Good idea," Alicia said. "You're going to need it."

"I'm curious. Who is this Leo guy?"

"Some no-talent scriptwriter Findley felt sorry for. Old family friend or something."

"That so."

"I actually think you *didn't* know that. I believe you trusted that 'St. Paul' was untraceable." She let out a hearty bellow, almost laughing in Barney's face. "Turns out he's a buddy of Findley's. Talk about the gang who couldn't shoot straight!"

"You're making this up."

"There are photos of the two of them together over the years. Family album stuff."

Barney couldn't keep up the facade. He started sinking. "Stupid bastard. I swear to God—"

"God and Saint Paul both."

Then a look of admiration appeared on his face. Even though she was the enemy, he could appreciate excellence. He hated when CBS or ABC won the overnights, but he had to hand it to them if the programming deserved it. He gave her that much now: "You're thorough."

"A good producer."

"You're also a cunt."

She lifted her glass and licked the rim. "Why is it," she asked softly, "that men only pull out that word when they are completely threatened?"

He glared at her. "Findley could learn a few things from you."

"Findley is a mess, like some of the morons we do stories on."

He let that sink in while the waiter produced a new bottle of Belevedere. Then he looked her in the eye. "What do you want?"

"Justice."

"That's rich."

"What's Jonelle being paid this year?"

"A lot of money."

"Good. You can make out matching checks."

"She's talent. A star. You're well paid for what you do."

"Same amount, or I'll destroy you."

"You'll break me."

"The Christian Alliance has very deep pockets."

A look of complete astonishment came over his face. "You know that too?"

"You forget I'm the one who blew the whistle on the SEC a few years back? Don't be naive."

"Alicia, come on, that kind of money—"

"Seeing that I could put you away for—at the very least—conspiracy to murder several times over, I would say I'm being generous." She pushed her glass toward him. "Can I have more, please?"

"You fucking bitch."

She helped herself to the vodka. "I prefer 'enterprising business-woman.' "

"Greeks. You're worse than us Jews."

She sipped, crossed her legs, relaxed in a confident manner. "Barney Keller, sweating bullets. That's worth the price of admission alone."

He had to ask it. "How much do they know?"

"Jonelle and Steven? Not as much as I do."

He breathed a sigh of relief.

"But enough for you to worry."

He drank some more. "You know, you are possibly even more slimy than I am. They are your friends, and you're selling them out for pieces of silver."

"Gold."

"Fucking female Judas."

"I'm helping them and I'm helping you, and getting something for my services," she corrected him. "I promised them I'd help, and I'm doing that. If I can put an end to the stuff that's been happening, I'll have done what they want."

"And they'll never have to know the truth?"

"Not if you meet my price. I could go to the highest bidder, who'd probably be the FCC or the FBI, but seeing that you're already writing my paychecks, I've come to you first."

"This is unbelievable."

"Finish your bottle and get used to it." She detested this man now more than ever. She stared at him over the table, this admired figure of strength who was shaking in his boots, and almost felt sorry for him. "My God, all for the overnights? Jesus, Barney, what kind of power plant are you plugged into? What do you hope to gain?"

"You wouldn't believe me if I told you."

"Fine. But Jonelle's onto you, so you'd better cease and desist or your plan is going to fly right up your ass."

"We have only two more—how to put this?—scheduled 'incidents.' "

"I'd cancel them both. And send Saint Paul back to the catacombs."

"I have others to answer to."

She laughed. "Seems to me I remember reading *Barney Keller answers to no one.*"

"Not in this case."

"Then convince them," she said darkly.

There was a long pause as he considered this. Then he said, "And what do you do for me?"

Alicia was expecting the question. "Convince Jonelle that she's on the wrong track. I'll even go so far as to offer up a patsy."

"How so?"

"I can make her believe it was some nutso cameraman who was out to boost her stardom."

"Like some stalker."

"Exactly. I can create a fake person with doctored personnel records, make her think the guy just quit."

Barney shook his head. "Jonelle's smart. She's been with us for three years now. She knows her cameramen."

"Only the guys in the news division."

"You've got to do me something better!" he barked.

She was sharp. "I don't think you're in the position to make demands of me."

"Steer Jonelle and the pilot away from this! We need just a little more time. She's almost where they want her."

"How do you mean?"

"You just do it. You'll see how this plays out one day. And baby, I promise you, the results are gonna be worth it."

She looked at him for a long time. Then she picked up her menu and said, "Shall we order?"

Barney finished explaining to Clay about Alicia Maris. The Metroliner car was sparsely occupied. It gave them a chance to discuss this in private, without hurry. "What do you think?"

Clay shook his head. "I don't like it at all."

"Whether we like it or not, we have to make a choice. Either we give in to blackmail. Or risk Jonelle's continuing suspicions."

"Doing something about Alicia Maris certainly will raise Jonelle's suspicions."

"Not if that's the last incident."

Clay looked shocked. "Forgo Regent University? Hillary?"

"I know, I know," Barney admitted, loosening his tie. "I don't like this either. God, I think of the ratings we won't be getting . . ."

"It's Findley's fault."

"I'd like to kill the bastard with my own hands."

"God is taking care of that for you."

"Not fast enough for my taste." He unbuttoned his shirt collar. "Of all the stupid things, hiring a guy who can be traced to him."

"I should have handled that." Clay looked out the train window. They were passing a simple farm. "My pa farmed grapes in Napa. Maybe I should have gone into the business." Then he looked straight at Barney. "You want me to get rid of Alicia?"

"Before we get rash, consider that Alicia might be useful."

"How?"

"Just what she proposed. She could send Jonelle in another direction, possibly keep her from ever knowing that part of the truth."

"Get real. Jonelle's a very intelligent woman. You think she won't figure this out one day?" Clay turned to Barney and lowered his voice. "You want to know what I think? I think we should continue as planned. We're past the point of no return."

Barney said, "Shit, Clay, she's the highest rated newsperson in the country! She doesn't need more manipulation."

"Fame is fleeting. Overnights are good for one night only. Besides, she's six or seven years away from what Rex wants her to do, good reason to go on. The next two events will put her over the top."

"And put us in prison."

Clay refused to believe it. "I used to admire you. Nothing could dent your determination. We'll stop Maris. Everything will be okay."

"You're starting to sound like Findley. He's got carcinoma crawling up his butt, I can understand it affects his rational thinking. But you—"

"When was any of this rational?"

Barney knew he had a point. And he didn't like being perceived as weak. He succumbed. "So what would you do?"

"Knowledge outside the Four Horsemen is dangerous. I know how to stop Jonelle's suspicions *and* get rid of Maris. First, you have to find out everything Maris is telling them about this fictitious cameraman, so we can go from there. Then we ice her."

"Where'd you get that word 'ice'?"

"I watch TV."

"It'll rot your brain."

chapter 12

Three days later, Jonelle and Alicia were on a plane bound for Toronto, on their way to do a story on the breakdown of trade unions in Canada. The autoworkers had started it in 1999, and it spread across the land like a brushfire, a phenomenon never seen before in any country; Jonelle was particularly interested because there had been rumblings that the United States would follow suit.

But Jonelle's mind wasn't on her story, it was on the information she and Steven had trusted Alicia with. "It's been days," she reminded Alicia when the plane took off. "What did you find out?"

"It's not Barney," Alicia said emphatically.

"How can you be sure?"

"I've worked on this, honey."

"And?"

"It's going to take some time, but my hunch is that it's someone on the inside who finds your career his life's obsession."

"Wonderful. What did you tell Barney?"

"Pretty much what I suspected."

"I could have done that! You trust his denial?"

"Trusting him is like saying you trust that pretty python not to bite. The guy's a monster, we both know that, but I honestly don't think he'd go this far, he's got too much to lose if it came out."

"We've got to find out who it is. Got to stop him before it happens again."

"It's going to take time."

"Why?"

" 'Cause we can't scare him off. We can't start accusing without proof. All we know is someone's been helping your ascent to stardom. Someone inside, that's for sure, someone who knows where you are going next."

"Someone in the news division."

"I checked out everyone at least on the surface, and no one looks suspicious. Except for one."

"Who?"

"A guy who left a few weeks ago. Quit suddenly."

"Did I know him?"

"Second-string cameraman, don't think so. John Talkington."

"Never heard that name. Did he know me?"

"Silly question."

"I guess so." Jonelle looked out the window of the 737, down at the expanse of crisscrossing squares of farmland framing the shores of Lake Ontario. She wanted to feel better after hearing Alicia's opinion, but she felt strangely empty, and in a way even more afraid.

"I'll get the network's internal security on him," Alicia said. "And Barney told me he'd help in any way he can. In fact, he said you had mentioned something to him about it already."

"Yes," Jonelle hesitantly voiced. But she said no more because something inside her, a little voice deep in her soul, told her to keep her mouth shut. It was the newsperson coming out in her, the same instinctual voice that told her there was a story to be had in the most average of stories, the voice that compelled her to search and to dig and to excavate. Something about Alicia's pat answers to her questions didn't ring true. There was more there, more that wasn't being said, or possibly wasn't even known at this time. But there was more, of that she was sure.

"We'll be landing soon," Jonelle finally said, changing the direction of the discussion. "You think there's a baggage handler's union left at the airport?"

Alicia laughed. Jonelle was pleased. For that was the intended effect.

Pulling up in a cab outside the InterContinental Hotel on Bloor Street in the heart of Toronto, Jonelle said, "I'm almost afraid to do this story."

"Why?"

"Reason I'm afraid to do any story. I think if I turn my head, someone's going to get shot, a building's going to fall on people, a plane's going to crash. Just for me."

"You have to put it out of your mind." With that advice, Alicia allowed the doorman, a perky fellow in a dark green uniform, help her from the backseat. He held a huge umbrella over her head. "Thank God for the hotel workers' union," she laughed, as Jonelle joined her under the protective canopy, and together they let the man guide them toward the revolving doors.

Jonelle spent the afternoon interviewing workers in industries all around Toronto. She spoke with autoworkers, truck drivers, men who worked on fishing boats, women who sewed garments, baggage handlers at the airport, and ticket takers at movie theaters. But her mind was on Alicia and what she'd said on the plane. The fact that she'd gone to Barney with the information, the fact that she seemed to trust him. Was that only because she was sure about this John Talkington? Jonelle found workers restless and upset; she felt much the same herself.

It wasn't her best day in front of the camera.

Alicia and Jonelle pored over the tape at a studio on the lake, feeling as they watched the day unfold again on camera that they'd gotten some good footage, and agreed that one particular interview Jonelle had done with a striking parking lot worker was worth the trip in itself.

Back at the hotel, Alicia was curled up in a robe in her room, glass of white wine at her side, when Jonelle walked in dressed in sweats, announcing they were going upstairs to the health club to work out. Alicia fought it all the way, kicking and screaming, bitching and moaning, as she donned exercise clothes and accompanied her to the eighth floor.

They were the only two in the place. They grabbed big white fluffy towels, cranked up the temperature control for the sauna, and headed for the fitness room. Jonelle hit the StairMaster, while Alicia tackled a treadmill, though fairly slowly because the wine was making her dizzy. Half an hour later, they took turns doing butt exercises and crunches, but Alicia soon said, "I'm sick of this shit."

In the long, luxurious lap pool on the roof, they watched twilight disappear and the stars come out above the glass roof. They talked of everything but Jonelle's stalker, and Jonelle was glad, for she'd not shed the strangely unsettled feeling she'd gotten from discussing the problem on the plane; she wanted to wait to get Steven's opinion on whether or not she was simply being paranoid.

The women went to the sauna finally, which had already shut itself off. Jonelle cranked up the heat once again, and they sat sweating and gossiping until they heard the sound of the health club door opening and closing out in the vestibule, thinking someone would be joining them any moment. But no one appeared. "Probably a guy," Alicia said. Then she added, "Going to the men's sauna. Taking his clothes off. Sitting there naked, all alone . . ."

Jonelle giggled. "And maybe he's cute."

"God, what am I doing here?"

Jonelle said, "Me too."

"You're married," Alicia reminded her.

"A girl can dream, can't she?"

Now Alicia laughed.

They spent the next five minutes asking one another where they should go to dinner. After the usual list of suspects, which included most of the pricey, trendy places in town, Alicia said, "I remember a place Diane Stead used to take me. Know her? Terrific singer, good writer too."

"No."

"Jesus, what's the name of it?"

"What kind of food?" Jonelle asked.

"Russian. No, Polish. Maybe both. Anyway, the greatest pierogi in the world. It's right on Bloor, near Spadina, we can walk it. And they have this terrific bakery with gooey cakes and pies, fabulous, and cheap as shit. Cafeteria style."

"Polish steam table?" Jonelle did her best to sound horrified.

"You'll love it." Alicia got up. "I'm gonna take another dip to cool off," she said, exiting, "and maybe check out Mr. Wonderful who may be swimming off his sweat right at this very moment in those tight Speedo trunks you see in the Olympics."

"Can I ask a very personal girlfriend question?" Jonelle inquired.

"Sure."

"When's the last time you got laid?"

"Last week, but I forget fast. Could use a refresher course."

"Good luck. I'll be roasted in about ten minutes. If I'm not out by the time you get back, stick a meat thermometer in me and serve well done."

Alicia laughed and left.

Twenty minutes later, she'd not returned. Jonelle was still in the sauna, and felt it was time to cool down. If Alicia was still in the pool, she'd join her. She grabbed her towel and went through the doors to the main entrance of the club, and then up the white tile stairs to the pool room. Inside the room, the tile floor glistened with water, and there was an eerie, empty silence. Thinking Alicia wasn't there after all, she turned to go back down the stairs, guessing she was back in the exercise room—or had she really met a man and disappeared into the men's changing area? Jonelle wouldn't put it past her.

But as she was walking down the steps, something caught her eye. She stopped and turned back.

In the corner of the pool, the far corner from where she stood, something bobbed in the water. It was a person, facedown. It was Alicia Maris. And she was dead.

The next hours seemed like days to Jonelle, an eternity of nightmares. Screams echoing in the pool room, the call to the hotel operator, slipping on the water on the tile floor, hotel employees and paramedics rushing about, a corpse not wanting to exit the pool easily, as if attempting to remain forever in the calm sweetness of the water, an ambulance and police and questions and phone calls, terror infecting every cell of Jonelle's body, and overpowering it all the desire to get out of Canada, get the hell away from the line of fire, run from them, whoever they were who did this, who'd done the other things, who would one day do the same, she was sure, to her. . . .

When the Royal Canadian Police finally allowed Jonelle to return to her hotel room, she did so only long enough to gather her things and get out. She was home in Washington in exactly six hours to the minute she'd discovered Alicia's body, and in the protection of Steven's arms. "He killed her," she cried, "he killed her."

"Who? Who killed her?"

"John Talkington."

"*Who?*"

"John Talkington. That's who Alicia said she thought did it. But I didn't believe it, didn't buy it. Something told me it was too easy, too pat. John Talkington may have done it, but John Talkington is all of them, lots of them, it's Barney and maybe Clay and Findley and who knows who else? It's everyone who decided they were going to make me a star. It's who Alicia talked to, and who then killed her because she knew too much."

"My God," Steven only muttered.

She pressed her face to his. "Steve," she whispered, something she'd rarely called him, but at this moment it seemed right, endearing, as if crawling inside his heart, under his skin, "am I crazy? Am I dreaming all of this?"

He wished he could say yes. Instead he just held her and ran his hands through her hair, providing comfort and love that spoke louder than any good words might have.

She was hardly comforted, however. The terror that they were inside something that was getting bigger and badder with each day paralyzed her. All she could whisper was, "What are we going to do now?"

chapter 13

B arney called Jonelle that night. He expressed his shock and sympathy, his concern that Jonelle was "emotionally all right" after what she had gone through. His voice was as sincere as any Jonelle had heard. He said he couldn't "believe" what happened to Alicia. Jonelle said neither could she.

She spoke to him in short bursts of words loaded with anger and shock, fear and distrust. He promised help in learning whether or not foul play had been committed, for she'd told the Toronto press all about the sound of a door opening, how they guessed someone had entered the health club while they were in the sauna, and how they did not hear the person leave.

When she told Barney that she was tired and grieving and that she wanted to be left alone, he said he understood but encouraged her to find the story here—he knew she smelled one, this kind of thing was what she did best—and they of all people had to be the ones to uncover "the truth."

"Just what is the truth, Barney?"

"Whatever it is, it's going to do numbers," he replied.

"That truth, someone knows it, someone just has to say." She felt bile rising—did he understand what she was alluding to? "You might know more about that truth than I do."

"I know that Alicia was a good swimmer. Hell, she swam in the health club across the street for years. Makes no sense, unless someone had a reason to do her in."

Yes, she thought, *yes!* "Why?"

"Who knows? Revenge over a broken love affair, money, madness? Why do people kill?"

"To silence people," she replied pointedly.

"That's true. Sometimes."

"Because they know too much."

Barney didn't respond to Jonelle's accusatory tone; he seemed, in fact, to miss it completely. "Alicia never knew too much. That's what made her good in a newsroom, always wanted to know more."

"Barney, cut through the crap. She told you what Steven and I believe."

"Some guy in the news division, we were sure of it." Then it seemed to register. "My God, you think he did *this*?"

"I don't know. Yes."

"Why? Wait, you just said, to silence her. Jesus, Jonelle, I don't know. I'll help you uncover every stone."

"Stone? How about mirrors?"

"What?"

It was maddening. Was he just dense or was he the ultimate liar? "Barney, what's going on?"

"I wish I knew, Jonelle. I wish I knew."

In the morning, the papers on the front stoop—the *Washington Post, New York Times,* and *The Wall Street Journal*—all screamed front-page stories on the untimely death of *Jonelle Patterson Reporting . . .* producer Alicia Maris. Pending further investigation by the Canadian authorities, the death was being called an accidental drowning. But the police were trying to find the person who'd entered the health club while Maris and Jonelle Patterson were in the sauna. It had been the lead story on all the news programs the evening before, and CNN was even more aggressive than ONE in its pursuit of Jonelle's comment to the press gathered outside the InterContinental as she left the hotel the previous day that "there was more to this" than the simple misfortune of drowning. They'd pursued Jonelle all night, wanting to know why, who would have killed her, who would have wanted to kill her; Steven had protected her. On this morning's E-mail, there were countless messages asking for more information.

The kids were in a sad mood at breakfast, for they'd known Alicia Maris and had liked her. They also sensed Jonelle's despair and panic, and took it as shock and mourning. That their father had canceled flights for the next few days also worried them, for he'd never done such a thing before. In other words, something was up. Jonelle and Steven did their best to soothe their young fears.

Wyatt told them a story of how Potomac's mom's good friend had died in a "boating accident" and how difficult it had been for the family. But, he assured them by comparison, Potomac's family wasn't as close as theirs was, they didn't share things as much, so he believed that "things are gonna get better." It was his way of expressing his optimism and belief in his family.

But Sarah wasn't so sure. She was older, and more attuned to what had been going on in the past few months. "Mom, you're scared, aren't you?"

"It's shaken me."

"If that person you heard killed Alicia, would he—?"

Jonelle stopped her question. "We don't really know if someone killed Alicia."

"Mom. I read the papers too."

"Sorry, honey."

"You thought someone killed that guy in Paris too."

"I'm sure of it."

"Is someone going to hurt you?"

Steven said, "No one is going to hurt her, or any of us." But he could see that Sarah remained unconvinced. The fears of the last weeks were apparent to the kids on a visceral level; you could breathe it in the air.

Jonelle's cell phone rang. It was Barney, asking how they were, again expressing concern, assuring her that he'd already begun his own "investigation" into what happened, how he "wouldn't sleep" till this whole issue—of someone having a hand in creating news for Jonelle to report—was resolved.

When the kids had gone off to school, Jonelle and Steven faced one another. She shrugged, "Well?"

He knew what she meant. She was referring to what she said last night: *What do we do now?* "I've not stopped thinking about it for a minute. We need help."

"That's why we went to Alicia."

Her words caused a silence that lasted a long time. Steven finally said, "If I knew someone in the police department, someone I could talk to without having them look at me as if I'm nuts when I tell them this plot."

"Which we aren't entirely sure of."

He nodded. "Yeah, and for which we don't have any hard evidence tying these incidents to Barney—"

"I tried to think of someone on the Hill," she offered. "Someone who would believe us, no questions asked."

"I'm blank."

"Clueless." Suddenly a name came to her. "How about Barbara McMillan at the FCC?"

He brightened too. "You know her?"

"Not really. Met her once at a party."

He shrugged. "Forget it."

She pondered a moment. "Why? That's what I don't get. Why would they do this? What reason other than ratings?"

"Ratings translate into money for everyone involved. The star gets to renegotiate a higher salary, the producer's fee goes up, the executives in charge get fat bonuses, advertising space can be sold at a much higher rate, profits rise for the network, the owners . . . so on and so forth, right down the food chain."

"That's a lot of suspects."

"Do you think," he asked one last time, as if to put to rest the nagging doubts that they may be on the wrong track, "that what Alicia said was true?"

"About it being a cameraman?"

"Yes. And he was onto the fact that she knew it was him, and killed her?"

Jonelle had to admit it was possible. "It could be. I mean, we can't rule that out. I just don't believe it myself."

"What we believe doesn't matter. Only truth matters."

"What's that?"

The bell rang. "*Who's* that?"

He looked out the kitchen window, which faced R Street. "Police car."

"Really?"

"Maybe we don't have to seek help. Maybe help has come to us."

Detective Matthew Snyder, a man in his early thirties who looked more like a bodybuilder than a police officer, sat in the front parlor with Jonelle and Steven and explained that he was investigating the death of Alicia Maris for two reasons: Jonelle's statement and "feeling" that it was foul play and not an accident, and because Barney Keller personally asked him to. They were glad for the first reason and distrusted the second. Steven asked the detective if he and Barney were personal friends. No, the man replied, they'd never met until this morning. But he was impressed with the passion of Mr. Keller's appeal for him to get to the bottom of it. That's why he was here, to understand everything Jonelle felt and thought and saw and recalled.

Jonelle said little, apprehensive about the fact that Barney had already been in touch with the man. But she did offer up everything Alicia had told her about John Talkington.

Steven wanted to trust this, wanted to believe Alicia's story, wanted to know that this cop was going to start digging and resolve everything in a way that made perfect sense.

The husky detective said, "I'm going to check out this Talkington guy right away. Now, who else would Maris have talked to?"

"No one that I know of," Jonelle said immediately. "She was a very private person."

Immediately after the detective left, Jonelle said, "I lied."

"How so?"

She told him that although Alicia had kept an apartment in D.C., her permanent home was in Manhattan, just around the corner from her mother. Alicia did keep things close to home, but "home" was Mrs. Maris; they were constantly embroiled in a love/hate scenario that was passionate, vocal, loving, and yet explosive. Jonelle had never met Mrs. Maris, but she'd spoken to her on the phone, and remembered the woman's voice was very demanding, yet filled with pride when speaking of her daughter.

"So why didn't you tell him that?"

"I want to talk to her first." She picked up the phone and dialed information, and in a few seconds heard the ghostlike voice of a woman who'd just lost everything she lived for.

They spoke for almost an hour. Mrs. Maris seemed to want to hold on to Jonelle's voice forever, as if it were a way to still touch her daughter. She wanted to know, as the detective had, what happened, moment by moment, detail by detail. Jonelle told her the story, hoping it would help put closure to her suffering, and then she shared the story of John Talkington, as Alicia had related it to her. Mrs. Maris knew nothing of it.

But she did know "something was up" with Alicia for the past few weeks. She described her as being "agitated, terse, more terse than usual with me, which was plenty." Alicia's mother sounded gritty and without nonsense, Jonelle felt, one of those New York City women who'd lived most of her life in the war zone and wasn't afraid of anyone. She envied Alicia just the fact that she'd had a mother there to bicker with, argue with, get advice from, love. Mrs. Maris told Jonelle that Alicia had shared with her a notion that something was up at the studio. "She never said what it was exactly, but that it had to do with you."

"Nothing specific?"

"Her big chance."

"Pardon me?"

The woman repeated it. "Her big chance," she barked. "She said her big chance had come up and she wasn't going to blow it."

"How did she mean?" Jonelle asked. "A promotion, a story?"

"Money. She felt she was on the verge of finally making some big bucks."

"But she made a good salary," Jonelle offered.

"It wasn't enough."

"Almost three hundred thousand a year?"

Alicia's mother said, "Who can live on that?"

Jonelle smiled, and understood.

They talked more about the name Talkington, about Alicia's belief that some single nut case had helped create news events, but that Jonelle and Steven were more inclined to the conspiracy theory, though they didn't know who was behind it. Mrs. Maris was savvy: "So you think whoever participated in these news events killed my daughter to shut her up?"

"Yes."

The woman suddenly burst into tears.

Jonelle told her they'd talked long enough, she apologized for being more of a burden than sympathetic, and promised she would be in touch with her again soon.

"I'll let you know if I learn anything that might help," the woman softly said, blowing her nose. "And, dear, thank you. This call meant a lot."

"I loved her," Jonelle offered.

"You're very sweet." And she hung up the phone.

Alicia was cremated in New York City, and memorial services were held both in New York and Washington. Jonelle and Steven attended both, and met the formidable Mrs. Maris at the one in Manhattan. Alicia's mother was a tiny though strong-willed figure with jet black hair severely pulled into a bun, Jackie Onassis sunglasses, and she used a cane almost as a teacher with a pointer, jabbing the air in front of her to accent what she was saying. After the service, Mrs. Maris told Jonelle she'd learned nothing more than she already knew, although she came across a scratch pad near one of Alicia's phones where she'd written the name—doodled, actually—*John Talkington* several times.

A week later, at the Washington service, Alicia's mother told her she recalled something her daughter had said when she spoke with her shortly before her death. Mrs. Maris had been out shopping, and stopped at her daughter's apartment on the way to her own to drop off some feta she'd bought but knew she couldn't eat all of. "My eyes are always bigger than my stomach," she said to Jonelle, "especially when Helen takes me to Price Club in New Jersey." When she got to Alicia's apartment, the living-room floor looked like a cyclone had hit a Xerox machine, papers everywhere. The exchange, as Mrs. Maris reported, went like this:

"What are you working on?" Mrs. Maris asked.

"A story. Ma, I'm busy. I don't have time."

"You have time for your mother."

"Ma, please, no guilt, not today."

"I brought you some feta. Fresh."

"Feta by nature isn't fresh. It's cheese. Cheese takes time."

"You're not funny."

"I don't aim to be." Alicia looked at the page in her hands, lost in it. "It's the Four Horsemen. I'm sure of it."

"The what?"

"Never mind," Alicia said, putting the paper down, getting up to take the bag from her mom.

"Four Horsemen? You doing a show on riding?"

"Ma."

"Or something on the Christian Bible?"

"Ma, forget it. Come on, I'll put up coffee, I've got bagels, we'll have lox and a schmear."

"I want feta and kalamata olives. You forget your roots?"

Jonelle listened to the story and while she was curious what story Alicia had been working on—she didn't recall anything that would have required tons of paper—she didn't know what "Four Horsemen" referred to in this context, and doubted after all that it had anything to do with her.

Several times during the following week, Jonelle saw Detective Snyder hanging around the studio, the newsroom in particular. Barney kept Jonelle informed that the cop was doing everything he could to help them, and Jonelle played grateful while secretly still scared to death. With each event she covered, she feared another incident would fall into her lap. Covering a conference of international leaders, she was sure a gun or bomb would go off behind her, giving her the exclusive. On a trip to Oregon to report on a volatile environmental issue, she held her breath when a logger whom she'd just interviewed suddenly cried out in pain and died a few moments later. But his death was the natural result of a history of heart disease. Even on a trip to Israel to cover the violent overthrow of the Likud government and Netanyahu's subsequent resignation, she worried that something would happen for her cameras alone, but nothing came to pass. She'd hoped that it was finally over. She felt more secure.

She felt even more secure when Detective Snyder told her and Steven that he'd tracked down John Talkington, and gave them the details of how the man had been employed at ONE's newsroom as an assistant cameraman, how he had a history of mental problems, how he had seemed to disappear, that even his family in Ohio had no clue as to where he was. What helped convince both Jonelle and Steven that what Alicia had said was the truth came when Snyder showed them proof from Canadian Immigration that Talkington had been in Canada—he flew to Montreal—the day before Alicia Maris's death.

But what really convinced Jonelle and Steven was the fact that in a picture of Talkington, one produced by the detective who said he'd gotten it from Talkington's family, there was the stubby hand sporting a gold band. Steven hurried down to his workroom and produced photos of that same hand. Without having to enlarge the picture, Steven could see the hand matched.

Jonelle commented that she, however, found it curious that a man with such a skinny face and seemingly slight body would have fingers so sausagelike. Snyder held up his own hand. While his body was well developed with muscles and he had a fairly well-rounded face, his fingers were as slim as cigarettes; he had the hands of a surgeon, proving hand size had little to do with the rest of one's body.

No, the detective said, Talkington was their man, and he was now wanted for questioning in the death of Alicia Maris both in Canada and the United States. He promised it was only a matter of time.

Steven and Jonelle breathed slightly easier. They would give the man some time. In that time, they would hope that they'd been wrong and Alicia right.

What Jonelle didn't know was that very night, however, Steven called another pilot he knew, a man who had been his mentor when he arrived at TWA, a vastly experienced now-retired captain named Randy Kramer, who was well connected. He'd been influential behind the scenes of the crash of Flight 800, working closely with the authorities on behalf of the airline and the pilots' union. "Randy," Steven said, "I need your help."

"Want a little more vacation time, huh?" the man joked.

"I need to talk with someone in the FBI."

chapter 14

"We were studying about Russia," Sarah told her mother. "Our teacher said they've been at war for two years because the country is a mess."

"That's probably true. Turn." Jonelle was brushing Sarah's hair. She'd taken to letting it grow long of late, though Jonelle warned her she'd hate it during the coming hot summer months. "There have been civil wars in Russia ever since the Soviet Union collapsed."

"Auntie Helen told me about May Day. They did these big parades and all the soldiers marched. They paid people to come and watch. I'd like to be paid to watch a parade."

"We do things differently." Jonelle ran her hands through her daughter's mane. It was soft and springy. She wished hers was like it.

"Auntie Helen said when she was a girl, May Day was a big celebration here too. She said they'd dress up pretty and give presents and things."

"I think Catholics celebrate it as a kind of holy holiday."

"Why?"

"In the Catholic religion, the Blessed Virgin is revered. May was always Mary's month."

"Why?"

Jonelle shrugged. "I don't really know. Maybe today is her birthday. You have to ask someone Catholic."

"I don't know anyone Catholic."

"How about Mr. Gallindo?"

Sarah's eyes brightened. "Maybe."

Jonelle brought the girl's soft hair together in her hands and fastened it with a neon blue clip. "I think perhaps you have a crush on your piano teacher."

"Mom!" Sarah jumped up. "Come on."

"He's cute."

"He's an old man."

"He's in his thirties," Jonelle reminded her.

"That's what I mean," Sarah explained, making a face.

Wyatt walked in, catcher's mitt on one hand. "Tommy can't pitch," he muttered.

"Neither can you," Sarah replied.

"That's why I catch. Mom, can Tommy come have lunch with us?"

"Sure." Jonelle pulled silky hairs from the brush. "But what time's your piano lesson?"

"Three."

"No problem then." She threw the hairs into the trash can in the powder room off near the front door. In it she saw a business card. She lifted it up and read it—Detective Snyder's name and phone number—then moved back to the parlor. "Anyone know about this?"

When she waved it, Wyatt remembered. "Oh, that guy was here this morning when you were at work."

"He left his card? Why'd you throw it away?"

He shrugged, looking a little guilty. " 'Cause I thought I'd remember."

"Did he say anything?"

"Yeah," Wyatt said.

"Well, what?"

"That he wanted to talk to you, but no big deal, no hurry."

"Thanks a million."

She called the District police and got Snyder on the first try. He told her he stopped by just to inform her that they'd tracked Talkington to Hawaii, where, they learned, he'd been employed by a firm who made island tourist videos. But when they got close, he seemed to vanish again. They found that he'd flown to Hong Kong. While they missed him, they were sure now that he was running from them, and it was only a matter of time.

But he'd said that before.

Jonelle called Steven at the Adam's Mark hotel in Saint Louis, where he was spending the day between flights. He said he was pleased to hear it, but Jonelle thought he sounded oddly unconvinced.

When she hung up after speaking to Steven, the phone immediately rang. It was Charles Patterson, and he had exciting news for her. "Regent University has selected you to receive an honorary degree next month."

"Really?" She was taken aback.

"I'm so very proud."

"Dad, how much did you have to do with this?"

"Nothing, honestly. It's the board of regents. They just wanted to give me the opportunity to tell you."

"I'm very honored."

"We'll be beaming with pride."

"They want a speech?"

"It's customary."

"Anything I want to say?"

"Well, nothing too liberal," he tried to joke, but it came out dead serious.

"How's Mom?"

"Fine, fine, Mother is fine. Honey, congratulations."

"Thanks, Dad. Oh, when is it?"

"June fourth."

"We'll make plans right away, the kids will be thrilled. Thank everyone for me. It's the first degree I didn't have to study night and day to get."

"You deserve it."

But on the day that Jonelle received her honorary Master of Fine Arts degree from Regent University at the school's 2000 commencement ceremonies, there was chaos at the school.

Three weeks before, around the tenth of May, the campus became a hotbed of political unrest. During an interchange on his TV show with Christian students from the school, Pat Robertson found himself being challenged by a young man by the name of Jacob Hughes. Jake's charge was "manipulation of the mind" by professors at the school. Robertson defended that the university was in fact created to produce journalists, lawyers, businessmen who would serve God first, country second, and the common good third. That meant that all curricula adhere to "solid Christian principles." Jake likened the censorship to Nazi Germany, teaching hatred of those who were not Aryan and blond. He accused Robertson of creating Regent University for one reason alone: keep the Christian coffers full of cash in the coming years.

The next day, Jake found he had followers among the student body. Not a great number, of course, but there were those who felt overwhelmed by the perceived lack of freedom to think for themselves, those who believed their basic First Amendment rights were being violated, those who simply agreed that the school was too restrictive in its policies. It made for controversial news, for unlike most detractors of the Christian Alliance, these were kids for whom the Christian Right was their passion; this was coming from within.

Pat Robertson, Ralph Reed, and Rex Heald had all been pummeled by the press since the protests and marches on campus began, and Jonelle had interviewed all three before she traveled to Virginia Beach for the commencement ceremony. All three had maintained the status quo, suggesting the protests had been the work of one person—Jacob Hughes—and the only reason he'd been successful was that he had charisma. "Would have made a great preacher," Pat Robertson said sadly. "A shame."

The unrest was remarkable in that it couldn't be contained. It seemed to grow on other campuses as well, especially those run by churches. Students everywhere seemed to be reverting to the protest marches, sit-ins, demonstrations, and rhetoric of the 1960s and '70s, though this was not about integration and free love, this was about the role of religion in colleges today. The old arguments of church versus state, long thought buried since Kennedy won the White House and the Pope hadn't even come to dinner, much less rule America, were revived with a vengeance. It made hot news, and by the time Jonelle showed up at Regent, the place was an armed camp of journalists, like she remembered it being in Bosnia with Chris Amanpour, waiting to see what would happen next.

It happened during her speech to the crowd, which in its own way was as controversial as Jake Hughes's original argument with Robertson. She talked of freedom of speech, our guaranteed right, which was the essence of and ruled the ethics of her work as a newswoman. But she also spoke of freedom of the mind, freedom of spirit, freedom to express oneself in a contrary manner, which, in history, always led to the betterment and enlightenment of mankind. It was the kind of speech she knew Rex Heald, seated in the front row alongside Robertson and Charles Patterson, would hate. She watched them both squirm. And she rather liked that.

But she never got to the closing lines, for a firebomb flew through one of the huge windows, sending a storm of glass shards raining over part of the gathered crowd of graduates and their families, and then there was the crash of a bottle and the smell of kerosene and fire spreading out from that Molotov cocktail—again, reverberations of the '60s—as people ran, screaming, for the doors.

Jonelle ran for the story. Already in front of the network cameras as the bomb went off, all she had to do was segue from honored recipient in cap and gown to hotshot reporter, and she stayed with the story all afternoon. Jake Hughes, who had been in front of the school with protesters, had taken off when the incident happened, and could not be found. CNN, ABC, NBC, CBS, FOX, and MSNBC all did a thorough job of reporting the incident and fallout, but Jonelle captured the audience for ONE because this had been about her to begin with.

It was about four that afternoon, when she signed off from live reporting, that it hit her. The controversy had been brewing for weeks, commencing shortly after Charles Patterson had informed her of the honorary degree. That meant the conferring of the degree would be guaranteed news. Had there been no unrest on campus, no one would have covered a newswoman getting an honorary degree; it happened every year at various schools. The firebomb flew through the window during her own speech, and ONE was watched by most everyone in America as the news broke. It was too perfect. Too pat. Just like the others. It had been made to look almost random, but she was sure this happened only because of her. And her ratings.

Later that evening, in the safety of the Patterson house, Charles hurried in, joining the gathered family. He was beside himself with grief because he'd learned that one of the people hit by the firebomb had died in the hospital only minutes ago. Jake Hughes was a murderer, he proclaimed, and bowed his head in prayer for the man's soul.

Jonelle asked her mother-in-law to feed the kids while she pulled Steven to their upstairs guest room. He anticipated everything she was going to say, for he believed the very same thing. Jake Hughes didn't do this, John Talkington—whoever he was—did. But how could they be sure? Could they prove it? Was there a cameraman outside covering the demonstrators while the ceremony was in full swing? Was there a gold ring on anyone's tape or in someone's lucky photo? How did they begin to find out?

As they shared their fears, they heard the phone ring a few times, then get answered downstairs. Jonelle begged Steven to find someone they could honestly trust, someone who would really help them. Steven admitted he'd already called Randy Kramer, and the pilot had given him James K. Kallstrom's number, the FBI assistant director who'd headed up the investigation into the TWA crash in 1996. But Kallstrom was in Bangkok on a case and would return Steven's phone call when he returned, but that would not be for several weeks.

"We don't have that much time," Jonelle said. She was about to say more, but there was a knock at the door.

"Jonelle, phone call for you."

Steven pulled open the door. "She won't talk to anyone."

"It's—" Charles Patterson looked as if he were about to kill, the anger in his eyes showing red fury. "It's him. It's Jacob Hughes. He will speak only to Jonelle."

Jonelle picked up the extension. "Jonelle Patterson."

"I didn't do it." The voice was young and full of fire the same way Charles Patterson's eyes were burning. She recalled seeing Jake several times on TV and wished that she'd had the opportunity to interview him rather than his Christian Right opponents. He would make a fascinating guest. And now he made a fascinating phone conversationalist as he said, "It wasn't me, it wasn't any of those who support me. It was a man we have all seen before, he's been around the CBN, he's been around Heald. No one knows his name but we've seen him—"

"Wait," she cautioned, "who's we?"

"The people hiding me, the kids who march, the students who want free speech. I've seen this guy. I could identify him."

"I talked to several spectators who witnessed it. They described you."

"I never swear," the passionate student said, "but I'm going to swear now: bullshit! They were paid to say that, everyone you talked to is on Regent's side."

"I talked to several who believe in you and your cause."

"Did *they* see who did it?"

"No. But they stated it wasn't you."

"Not good enough, is it?"

"Jake, you're getting into more trouble running. There's a warrant out. Come in and tell your story."

"Who will believe me?"

"I will."

With that the line went dead.

And it went dead to the third party listening as well.

Within hours, Jake Hughes was captured, in the very shack on Witch Dutch Creek from which he'd made the call to Jonelle. He was charged the next morning with murder and conspiracy, and it wasn't until the following day that Jonelle was allowed to meet with him.

He swore on the Bible they allowed him in his cell that he did not throw the bomb, that it was a setup, it was manufactured for the right moment and the right time to shut him up for good. That the Christian Right would go that far, to him, was "unthinkable," for he was, at heart, a devout Christian.

But to Jonelle, another devout Christian, it was not "unthinkable." Extremism was something she'd always objected to. Rex Heald's zealousness had always bothered her. The fact that Ralph Reed's followers had tried to choreograph the 1996 election after the big congressional win in 1994 rubbed her the wrong way. Even Charles Patterson's rigidity in believing that the only way to save America was through religion met with opposition in her mind. These people were fanatical, she believed. They would stop at nothing to see their cause forwarded.

But murder?

She tried to apply it to her own situation. What if it were not the network, what if it were not Barney Keller (a Jew, after all) or the other men who ran the network, what if it had been the Christian Right all along? Again, her thinking hit a brick wall: *for what reason?* She could answer that: *none.*

As she thought this, she was standing outside the university library, unobtrusive as students passed, the campus silent of protest now that Hughes was locked up, strangely Disneyesque once again. Then another revelation hit her: Her conversation with Hughes from the Patterson house had to have been tapped. That's how they found him, that's how they had arrested him. She was sure of it. She wanted to rush to her father-in-law and inform him that someone was listening in on his conversations, but something stopped her from moving. She realized she was standing next to a metal sculpture. Three men on horses have already ridden out of a wall in the background, and all but the last flank of the fourth horse has emerged. He is a pale steed, representing Death. The men are the Four Horsemen of the Apocalypse. Mrs. Maris's words rang out like clarion bells in her head: *"Alicia said, 'It's the Four Horsemen. I'm sure of it.'"*

Jonelle suddenly felt sick.

chapter 15

Jonelle told Steven what she'd been thinking, and how the Four Horsemen had suddenly appeared behind her. He said he understood that the coincidence was unsettling, that he had already spoken with his father about the fact that someone had tapped the phone, and that Charles was trying to learn who. But he'd told his father something else as well. "I said we were in trouble. I told him that the firebombing might have been exactly what it seemed, but then again it might not. I told him that Hughes actually might be innocent. I told him this is bigger than we are, and we need help."

She looked cautious. "What did he say?"

"He said he'd do anything if we were in danger. I asked him if he knew someone in the FBI. Someone we could get to faster."

"Today."

Steven pulled out a piece of paper on which he'd written a name and phone number. This is someone my father knows. And trusts. He's at Quantico. We could easily meet with him as soon as we get back."

She looked at the card. *Agent Sam Druey.* "Does your dad

really know this man? It's not a name he just heard in passing, is it?"

"He went to school with him. The guy's been with the FBI as long as Dad's been teaching."

She looked hesitant.

"Look," Steven said, taking her hands in his, "I know what you're thinking. I have even more reason to distrust because I know that our Detective Snyder lied to us."

She looked shaken. "He lied? About what?"

"The photo of Talkington. Hey, the man's name may be Talkington, I'm not doubting that, but he's not the same man as we have in our blowups of the hand."

"But you said the hands matched."

"They did, but those hands didn't match the body. Remember how thin the guy was? Even you thought that."

"Thin face, fat hands, that could be."

"As soon as he produced the photograph, I knew the picture had been altered. The hands were a paste-on. I saw the lines—only a professional would catch it—where they were doctored."

"We did a story years ago about some celebrity's face on a different body. Rosanne or Cher I think it was, in the *Enquirer*."

"The hand with the gold band wasn't the hand of the man that Snyder showed us."

She was even more shaken. "So Snyder wasn't a cop after all?"

"He was, and probably still is, one of those District good ole boys who will say anything for money."

"But how could they have gotten to him?"

"He came to us," Steven reminded her. "Someone had 'gotten to him' before he ever showed up at our door."

"Barney."

"We're not sure of that."

She practically shouted, "Barney sent him! His first words were something about Barney Keller having asked the police to investigate."

"I remember."

She took a deep breath, trying to compose herself. "So if Barney could get to a real cop, why can't he get to the FBI?"

"I've asked myself that as well," Steven agreed. "My only answer is we can trust my father."

She looked at the card again. "I think we should talk to Charles once more before we call. Just to be sure."

"Okay. It pays to be cautious."

"I'm scared now."

He almost smiled. "I've been scared for months."

That night, after dinner, and after Grandmother Patterson and the kids had gone to bed, Steven and Jonelle talked openly to Charles Patterson about Agent Sam Druey. "I have a picture of us together," Charles said, digging through albums on the bottom of one of the library shelves, "taken in Honolulu after the war." He found it and handed it to them. "We were still kids, but we'd been through a lot together."

"Steven said you went to school together," Jonelle said, not trying to point up a discrepancy in the story, rather looking for more information.

But Charles took it as an accusation. "Well, we did both. We met in the service in the South Pacific, then we both went to Duke and were roommates all four years. Friends from the day we met. Always in touch. Lost his wife to cancer about a year ago, heard from him then, poor fellow. Really loved her. They were never able to have children."

Jonelle and Steven stared at a photo of a nondescript man standing on the beach at Waikiki holding onto a prop surfboard, while a younger and skinnier Charles Patterson stood balancing coconuts in his hands. Leis around their necks, surfer trunks hugging their hips. Girls giggling in the background. Two GIs goofing around. "When did he become an agent?" Jonelle asked.

"Right out of college. In fact, before. He wanted to do FBI work from the day I met him. He was always talking about espionage and such, Tokyo Rose fascinated him, he—"

Steven cut him off. "Sounds more like CIA material."

"Tried them first, but they were full up. FBI was his second choice. Never wanted to be a cop, always interested in something bigger, deeper, cases that would really affect the country. He's a patriot. Real patriot."

"This isn't national security," Jonelle reminded him. "Will he be interested?"

"Sam's been teaching agents for years now. Was one himself, I mean actively for years and years, but when he married—and he married late, only twelve years ago—Rose, his wife, wanted him close to home. So he took up as an instructor, and is one of the best. Won't ever retire, he'll die in the saddle, as they say."

"We need someone we can trust," Jonelle asserted.

"That's why I gave Steve Sam's number. Trust him with my life."

Steven bristled at being called "Steve" by someone who knew better, though his father had done it for years when he was a kid, before he came to the conclusion he hated it, and by then the pattern had been set. His mother never slipped, it was always "Steven" to her, but Dad was another story. So he let it pass. "We'll call him in the morning."

"Want me to do it?" Charles asked. "Be happy to make the initial call."

"We'd be grateful," Jonelle said.

"Who do you believe is doing these things?" Charles now asked them. "Steven said you were led to believe it was someone named Talkington, but that now seems unlikely."

"I think the name's made up," Steven replied.

"We believe that was manufactured to throw us off the trail."

"Who then?" Charles persisted.

"We don't know," Steven said, "but we suspect the man—or the men—who run Network ONE."

"Barney Keller himself?" Charles exclaimed. "That's mighty hard to believe."

"We agree," Jonelle said.

"Barney Keller?" Charles repeated. "Well, he's a powerful man. Like that Eisner guy, or that man who was the big agent, what's his name?"

"Mike Ovitz," Jonelle offered.

Charles nodded. "I know they accomplish great things, but I worry that men like that need to find Jesus."

"Jesus?" Steven blurted. "Right now I hope Keller finds a nice cold prison sentence."

"Steven! That isn't very Christian of you."

"Father, right now, with all due respect, being forgiving to the guys who have been doing these things 'for' Jonelle—murdering innocent people, hurting others by firebombing, planned accidents, shootings—being Christian is the last thing they deserve."

"God teaches forgiveness," Charles said softly, a gentle reminder.

"Not these guys. I'm never going to forgive these guys."

Charles said no more.

In the morning, Charles Patterson made the call to the FBI Center in Quantico, Virginia. He was told Sam Druey was in a meeting at the Hoover Building in Washington and would return the call.

Three hours later, Sam Druey did just that. After a short greeting between the two men, Charles told him that his son was involved in something that looked like real trouble, and there were reasons he needed the FBI. Charles put Steven on the phone, and he talked with Sam Druey for no more than three minutes, but in those three minutes he felt that everything his father had said was true: This was a likable man whom he and Jonelle could trust. They arranged to meet the day after next, and Druey asked them to suggest a place that would seem not at all unusual, a place they often frequented. Jonelle suggested Mystery Books on Connecticut Avenue, because the staff knew her and the store would provide relative privacy while seeming completely the opposite of clandestine. Jonelle couldn't help but chuckle at the irony, however: a surreptitious meeting with the FBI in a place called Mystery Books.

Before they left Virginia Beach the next day, Jonelle phoned Jake Hughes, who was still being held pending the outcome of the investigation. She promised she would do everything she could to help him, telling him she felt he was the scapegoat in something that was bigger than he—or she—even realized. She felt that she herself was the object of a sinister plot and that she bore some responsibility for his incarceration. He didn't understand that at all, and she didn't expect him to. But she made it clear she felt for him.

The kids were ornery on the plane. June 2000 weather was breaking heat records, the South was stifling, and with humidity at 87 percent, the airplane felt like ductwork leading to a steam bath. The kids argued, Steven had a sinus headache, and Jonelle was a basket of nerves, for she would soon have to face Barney Keller again. She didn't know how she would act, for the anger was brimming inside her and showed every sign of blowing the lid off. But was it really him? Were they 100 percent right? Would the FBI really be able to help?

Before they landed, she E-mailed John Wallace, the manager of Mystery Books, asking for a little time, a sofa and two chairs, and some privacy the next afternoon. When they got to the house, John had already posted his response:

Granted (and very intriguing). JW.

But there was a message from Barney Keller as well:

Hope you and your family are all right. Need you back at work soon. You handled that story down in V.B. brilliantly. Do a segment of J.P. reporting on that guy Jake, he's fascinating. Nail him if he's lying, absolve him if he's not, it's still a good story. Clay Santangelo himself is going to take Alicia's place as your producer. Knew you'd have no objection. Best to you and Steven as well. B.K.

"Clay Santangelo? Taking Alicia's place?" She was aghast. Clay had no experience in news, much less producing. She looked at Steven.

"Makes perfect sense. Keep better watch on you."

She slumped into a chair. "Why? I keep asking myself, why?"

"Maybe the FBI will figure that out."

It looked like business as usual at Mystery Books near Dupont Circle. Martha moved a small sofa to face the corner of the book-lined back part of the store, and then sat two chairs at either side of it. She dragged over a display of books they were pushing for the summer, which aided privacy. "But it's a slow day, and a good time in that slow day," she assured Jonelle and Steven.

Erin, the pretty young girl at the front desk, said, "If you want anything, coffee, iced tea, just say so."

"We'll be fine. I can't thank you all enough."

John came down the stairs. "Tina should be working today, she'd get a real kick out of this."

Martha laughed. "This is really one for the books, pun intended." Then she handed them some. "Here, a few props to make it look real."

Jonelle hugged her. They'd been buddies for years, and Jonelle knew she could trust her. She also knew that she was loving this, because a good mystery pumped her blood. "Maybe," Jonelle suggested to her, "you can tell Roderick Anscombe to use it in a new novel."

"Hey," Martha said, "let me see how it plays out first. Maybe I'll take up writing myself."

And then a customer walked in. No one would have guessed he was anything but a nicely dressed grandfather with soft features and a head full of gray hair. But Jonelle and Steven had seen the photograph of this man when he was younger and knew him right away. To break the ice, Steven said, "Didn't recognize you with clothes on." The man looked at him strangely, and for a moment Steven and Jonelle feared they had the wrong guy.

But when Steven explained, Agent Sam Druey extended his hand, and a few moments later they were laughing as though they were old friends.

They spent two hours together at the back of the bookstore, pretending to discuss the tomes in their laps. They interrupted their discussion only once, when a man entered and walked up to Martha, who was near the rear of the store stocking shelves, and asked, "Martha, you have another copy of *Snow Angel* for me?"

"Sure, Mike," she said, "back by the counter," turning him in the other direction when she saw Jonelle and Druey react.

"Mike Deaver," Jonelle said softly when Martha had secured him near the counter, "and he would have wanted to talk."

"He'd know me too," Druey said, "old friends."

Mike was soon off with book under arm, and they resumed. Erin brought Sam coffee every half hour, and Jonelle and Steven had iced tea, but let the cubes melt, for they talked nonstop. They told the man everything, every detail they remembered, and when he asked questions, they tried to remember more—and did. Steven showed him the still photos he'd taken off his computer and invited him to view the tapes himself. Druey said he'd be happy to put them through the FBI lab to see if they could come up with more than Steven had. "We've got some pretty sophisticated equipment there these days," Sam said, and Steven didn't doubt it.

He listened to the facts as they knew them, he made notes for himself on a leather notebook he withdrew from his black Coach briefcase, writing in an elegant style. Jonelle was amazed at the sophistication of the man. The finely tailored suit, the perfectly knotted tie: none of it fit the slovenly, chain-smoking image of the FBI as she knew it. The fact that the man appeared to have just walked out of Britches of Georgetown somehow made her trust him all the more. Yes, she felt, Charles Patterson would be lifelong friends with this man, for he was of the same level, educated and refined. She felt her fears lessening with every minute.

Sam Druey gave them his card with more phone numbers on it, a personal cell phone, the office fax as well as a home one, an E-mail address, though he warned them to be discreet and only use their initials, as well as a code number they would have to use to get him in an emergency through a number that was to be dialed only in the most dire circumstances. He warned them not to talk to anyone about the case again, including even Charles Patterson.

He told Jonelle to go about her business as usual, doing everything she could not to let Keller think she was afraid of him or even suspicious any longer. When she worried that an abrupt about-face would cause more curiosity than acceptance on Barney's part, Sam agreed and augmented his order to a gradual diminishing of suspicion, letting Keller feel, over a period of weeks, that she was abandoning her position that he'd had anything to do with creating the news.

As for the question of why, Sam said, "That's the stumper, I agree. But we'll learn it. We always do."

He shook their hands warmly, thanked the staff for being so kind, and even bought a book when he left the store.

The next morning, precisely at 8:00, the doorbell rang and a messenger accepted Steven's package—wrapped hurriedly the night before, addressed to *Graf's Auto Body*, as Sam had instructed— which contained copies of the tapes of the incidents in which Steven had identified the gold ring.

chapter 16

For the rest of that hot June, and part of an equally roasting July, Jonelle kept the status quo as Sam Druey had instructed. Her public gradual lessening of contempt for Barney Keller seemed to be working, and the fact that she was now working closely with Clay Santangelo (who was proving her assessment as a totally inept producer right) all seemed to create the "happy family" once again. She gave the impression that she'd believed the story about Talkington, and even said that to Detective Snyder, who had the nerve to show up at the studio one day to say he was still doing his best "to find the man."

Druey met Jonelle weekly at Mystery Books, where he sometimes simply posed as a customer, talking for a moment about a new novel he'd read or one Martha had just recommended—he was indeed a fan of mysteries—and at other times asking for privacy upstairs in John's loft office, where they went over facts and suspicions and data. Steven was flying less and less so that he could meet with Druey as well. There was little to go on, other than the fact that the man agreed with them that the same person had committed the crimes and that the gold band was indeed so tightly bound to the finger it decorated that it was impossible to remove; thus, they might see that very hand again. He told them that he was investigating, with the help of the FCC, the backers of Network ONE, searching for the missing motive. But he didn't rule out the fact that it might be someone completely removed from the network bosses, "a 'Talkington,' if you will," he had put it, but when he did find that out, he promised a motive. Alicia Maris's death was a homicide, he was sure of it, as his investigation found witnesses who had seen a man enter the health club while the girls were in the sauna, just as Jonelle and Alicia had heard, and a kitchen worker saw a man dash out one of the alley doors about the time Jonelle found the body. But who was he?

Down in Virginia Beach, against the rantings of Pat Robertson, who didn't want to see him ever again breathe free air, Jake Hughes was finally released for lack of hard evidence. The firebombing had not been his doing. Jonelle had kept her promise, and he called to thank her. She wanted to do that segment of *Jonelle Patterson Reporting . . .* on him, which Clay encouraged, but Druey felt it would not aid them to publicize any aspect of the case this soon. They needed patience, and time. Barney accepted Jonelle's reasoning that Jake was "old news" but professed to be on Clay's side, believing the segment would "grab some numbers." But Jonelle refused.

As for what Alicia knew, they could not discover. Her mother had been questioned repeatedly in New York City, and knew nothing. No notes were found in Alicia's apartment, and nothing on any of her computers. They'd even searched the hard disks in hopes of finding something that had been deleted; it was a waste of time. They had also tracked every male with the last name of Talkington in the country, ruling them all out. One of them with the first name of John worked, in fact, as a landscape architect for the White House.

They seemed to be at dead ends, but with Sam Druey's enthusiasm they felt encouraged—at least someone was helping them! So Jonelle and Steven began to feel they were now beyond danger. Perhaps it wasn't only Sam who instilled that feeling of invincibility, of protection; perhaps it was also the fact that they had set the problem into the hands of the law where it belonged. They slept better at night and had no fears that it would happen again. Of that, they were sure; whoever was behind it, they must now be scared. They must now sense that the law was involved. They now have to know that they're being watched, playing with fire, and it was just a matter of time before they would be arrested. Jonelle knew in her heart that Barney knew this, and probably Clay and Findley as well. She found herself almost gloating when she was with them. She would come out the winner.

But the gloating stopped the day Alicia's mother called Jonelle's cellular phone. Collect. "I'm in a pay phone outside Zabar's," she said loudly. "I need to see you."

"What is it?" Jonelle asked.

"Something you should know."

"What?"

"You think I'd use this disgusting dirty phone for fun?" She suddenly shouted, "Go away, I'm using the phone!" Then, back into the receiver, "Little bastards, no respect." She seemed to growl. Then she said, "I have documents."

"Documents? What kind?"

"What Alicia was working on that night."

"The night you brought the feta?" Jonelle asked. "The night she said 'the Four Horsemen'?"

"Come to Manhattan. We shouldn't talk anymore."

"Why are you afraid?"

"When the FBI grills you about these things, you get a funny feeling."

"I'm on the next plane."

Jonelle showed up with dinner. She wanted to do something to get Mrs. Maris to warm up to her, and she recalled Alicia telling her how much her mom hated to cook. So she found a Greek restaurant and had them box up their best salad and *mezedakia*, tomatoes stuffed with orzo and wild mushrooms. Mrs. Maris sniffed it, pronounced it "not like my mother's," but deemed it fit to serve in any case. She poured them each a glass of retsina, which Jonelle hated, and then strong coffee. But it wasn't food Jonelle had come for, and they got down to business.

"Alicia said she wanted to help you," the woman explained.

"When?"

"A while ago. Before that night I found her with the documents."

"Mrs. Maris, did she say—?"

"Eliki. We're friends now. Those little brats on the street, they should learn respect for the aged. You don't have to do that."

"Eliki," Jonelle said warmly, "did Alicia tell you why?"

"No. In fact, I paid no attention. Hell, wasn't my business. But a mother cares, you know what I mean? No matter what happens, no matter the problems, a mother loves."

Jonelle closed her eyes, thinking of her own mother. A surge of guilt ran through her blood, but she put it out of her mind when she realized Eliki was still talking.

"And I listen, I'm a good listener. I play my cards close to my chest, and I listen. I heard that there was some trouble, heard that she needed to find out who someone was a 'saint,' I remember her saying once on the phone when I wasn't supposed to hear."

"Saint? Like in Saint Michael, Saint Anthony?"

"I'm Greek Orthodox, how would I know?"

"How about a place, like Saint Petersburg or Saint Paul?"

"I don't know. It might be in the documents."

"Tell me about these documents."

"This is good *orektikia*. Where'd you get this?"

"A place called Rakos."

"Andy Rakos. Yeah, he's okay. You picked good."

"Eliki, what about the documents? How did you get them? The last time we talked, you didn't know anything."

"They went through her apartment after she died. I thought it was the police or the FBI, I guess that wouldn't have been unusual in a murder case. But it wasn't them."

"How do you know?"

"The doorman, he's been here longer than you and I have been on earth. Zorba—I call him—tells me some men were in Alicia's apartment, and he describes one of them, handsome, balding, he's seen him on TV, says he's famous, claims he went to the apartment—how he snuck by the old man, I don't know—to see me, pretended he didn't know I lived around the block."

"Keller," Jonelle whispered.

"He comes to New York and doesn't even knock on my door to express his condolences? That's when I hated him. Never did like the guy—never paid Alicia enough, you ask me—but now I hate him. He went through it all, didn't leave a thing untouched."

"Why didn't he find the documents?" Jonelle asked.

" 'Cause Alicia had given them to me. In a locked briefcase, telling me to hold them for her while she was in Washington, and then Toronto."

"How do you know they'll help me?"

" 'Cause they have your name written all over them." And with that, Eliki Maris produced the briefcase, the gorgeous Cross leather bag that had had the brass lock brutally decapitated. "I only had a bread knife," she said in explanation.

Jonelle looked inside, at the folders and pages inside those folders. She didn't have the time now to read through them all, nor did she have the stomach for it, for she knew somewhere in these pages was the proof she needed, what they waited for all along, what Alicia had found that had gotten her killed.

"Should I have given them to that FBI guy last week?"

"Sam Druey? Did he speak to you?"

"Nice man. Lost his wife last year. I'd go out with him if I thought he had money."

"Pretty snazzy dresser."

"Too showy. Those agents are paupers, don't have a pot. But I liked him. Not like that cop who came here."

"Snyder?"

"Asshole. And dumber than a stump."

"You read him right. He was working for the enemy."

Jonelle noticed her name in two places as she flipped through the sheets, then stuffed them into her own bag. "But you could have trusted Sam Druey. He's on our side, and he's going to be thrilled with this."

"Pardon me for being selfish. I mean I don't know what kind of trouble you're in and I'm real sorry for that. But I hope this does one thing and one thing alone."

"It won't bring Alicia back," Jonelle said, sensing what she meant, "but it will bring to justice whoever killed her."

"Then I can die," Eliki said, "in peace." Then she bit into another piece of the delicious *orektika*. "In maybe, say, twenty years."

Jonelle smiled and zipped her briefcase shut.

At the door, Eliki Maris took her hand. "I'm gonna ask you something personal. You okay with your mom?"

Jonelle was taken aback. Could the woman have read her mind when she resisted the pang of guilt. "How do you mean?"

"I mean, do you love each other? Do you do things together? Do you talk? Fight? Are you distant?"

Jonelle was honest. "I haven't spoken to my mother in years."

"She alive?"

"Of course."

"Then why not? Oh, you don't have to tell me, just ask yourself that. And think how she—what's her name?"

"Esther. Esther Lighter."

"Think how she'd feel if what happened to my Alicia happened to you."

She thought only of her mother and Eliki Maris's words until she got on the train. The Metroliner won over an airplane because it gave her more time to read. She chose a seat at the rear of the first coach, and piled newspapers, magazines, her bag, and even her shoes on the next seat so anyone even thinking of sitting there would get the message. Then she put Esther out of her mind, and for almost three uninterrupted hours, she read, again and again, the pages that Eliki Maris had given her.

It wasn't quite as clear as Alicia had laid it out for Barney when she confronted him, but most of it was there: dates coinciding with all the news incidents, a record of plane tickets issued in the name of "St. Paul, L." The name Talkington appeared nowhere in the documents, but "Paul/Pere" was listed many times, and so was Findley—but Jonelle didn't see how they tied together, nor what Pere meant. But as she read on, poring over Alicia's determination that Barney Keller and his cohorts were the real John Talkington, she knew for sure that Alicia had lied to her about Talkington, and came to the conclusion she'd made him up to throw her and Steven off the track. Who was on whose side here?

It seemed more and more clear to her that Alicia had found out the truth—a truth that still wasn't clear from reading this—and then had confronted Barney with it, probably blackmailed him, and then was murdered after she tried to steer Jonelle in another direction. Jonelle felt the sting of betrayal and an overall emptiness that seemed to be growing larger and larger.

All of that surprised her, but there was only one page that truly shocked her, truly made her hair stand on end. When she read it, she gasped out loud, and had to apologize to the man sitting across the aisle from her, who feared she was having a heart attack or trouble breathing. She read it again and again and again, still holding it in her hand when she got off the train at Union Station.

In the cab, she gripped it tightly, so enveloped in fear that she gave the driver the wrong address, and ended up getting out of the taxi in front of the piano teacher's building. She knew Wyatt had his lesson today; the address must have been on her mind. Victor Gallindo was just about to climb the front steps with groceries in hand when he saw her, called out to her, but she ignored him and walked down the street zombielike, not even realizing he'd said her name.

At home, she sat drinking iced coffee for hours until the kids had fed themselves and gone to bed, thinking she was in a trance of some sort. They'd never seen her like that, and Sarah even called TWA to be sure her father's plane would arrive on schedule, in time to save Mom. "She's freaked out about something," Wyatt said. "Totally."

When Steven finally did arrive home, he found his wife sound asleep in her clothes, her head down on the island in the middle of the kitchen, now-warm iced coffee at her side. He tenderly touched her shoulder, but she didn't move. Next to her was a document of some kind, a list of names that looked like it had been pulled off someone's computer. He scanned it and saw the names of people—representing incidents—that Jonelle had reported on: Imelda Marcos, Molly Binenfeld, Rev. Billy Hatfield, Jared Tucker, Cardinal Riccio, Jacob Hughes. His eyes moved to another column, where the familiar names of Barney Keller, James Michael Findley, and Clayton Santangelo caught his eye. Farther down the list, he saw Rex Heald, and then a name that jumped from the page and seared his brain much in the same way it had Jonelle's when she first discovered it on the train: Charles Patterson.

Charles Patterson.

Charles Patterson.

Charles Patterson.

It repeatedly echoed in his skull like he was some schoolboy who had to write his punishment on the blackboard twenty-five times.

Charles Patterson.

His very own father.

chapter 17

They sat cross-legged like kids on their bed, feeling secure in the privacy of their own bedroom. It was well near dawn and Jonelle was wide awake now. Steven was dead tired, but running on adrenaline. "I kept saying to myself: *What's your father's name doing here?*" Jonelle explained. "When I studied everything Alicia had gathered, it became clear."

Steven had been reading through the pages for hours, digesting what was clear and pondering what was not. What he understood was that they had been right: Barney, Clay, and James Findley were behind the plot to raise Jonelle's ratings with shocking news events that only she would report, or at least be the first on the scene to cover. Someone code-named "Saint Paul" was at all the events and probably was the one who shot Imelda, who greased the diving board, who cut the brake linings, who threw the firebomb, who poisoned the Pope-hopeful, who injected the heroin into Jared Tucker's veins. Alicia had noted plane tickets bought in his name with company funds, a fact that astonished Jonelle and Steven. She'd also drawn circles around the entry "Paul/Pere" and Findley, connecting them several times. Under one of the circles, she'd written *BAR*

MITZVAH, CLOSE FAMILY FRIEND. At the bottom of the same page she'd doodled: *SLOPPY SLOPPY SLOPPY.* Jonelle and Steven didn't know who "Pere" was, and wondered if that was another name for Paul the Saint. Saint Pere? In what language? French, she assumed.

The truly chilling part of the gathered pages was the repetition of the name Rex Heald, and several references to the Christian Alliance. What had that to do with ONE? With creating the news? Yes, in the case of the Regent University firebombing, it was all about that. And to a lesser extent, the bus accident taking the faithful to the Reverend Billy Bob Hatfield's revival was in the same vein, for there were those who believed it had been caused by anti-Christian forces. What the document seemed to say was that the Christian Alliance had a hand in all this, that they worked with ONE. How? Why? What was the connection? What could higher ratings do for *them*?

And then there was Charles Patterson's name. They did everything to justify it being there, going over and over again the fact that it could have no connection at all other than the fact that Patterson was a teacher in a Christian university. But they recalled that it was Patterson who had phoned Jonelle, offering her the honorary degree. If the whole thing had been set up by ONE and Rex Heald, if the firebombing was a neatly choreographed news event, the culmination of the unrest that had proceeded it for weeks before, was Charles Patterson aware of it? *In* on it?

Steven made a good point in his father's favor: Charles called only because he wanted the thrill of telling Jonelle himself. The board of regents had made the decision, and Rex Heald sat on that board. Perhaps, then, Charles Patterson was innocent. Yet wasn't his phone tapped? Did he know that? For that matter, was Jake Hughes no more rebel than anyone else? Was he a plant as well? Did he create a volatile situation to simply pave the way to the moment when Jonelle would stop her speech and take up reporting a shocking and horrifying moment? Was he to be trusted?

And—it suddenly occurred to Steven—what of Agent Sam Druey? Who had recommended him? Who had made the initial call? Was the man another Detective Snyder, on the take, bought and paid for by the bad guys—in this case, it seemed, ONE and perhaps a faction of the extreme Christian Right?

They watched the sun come up, had breakfast with the kids, went for a walk with them on what looked to be a bright, sunny August day, all the way down 16th Street to the White House. It reminded Jonelle that she was supposed to cover a gala in San Francisco the day after tomorrow. A fund-raiser for the Juvenile Diabetes Foundation; the First Lady was going to be the guest of honor. She'd completely forgotten.

The kids walked on ahead of them, enjoying the oppressive heat. Jonelle and Steven pondered what to do next. And then a thought came to him. "What time is it?"

She looked at her watch. "Eight-thirty."

He pulled a card from his wallet. "You have your cell phone?"

"In my bag," she said, reaching for it. "Who are you calling?"

"Sam Druey."

"Why?" She sounded frightened.

"I wonder about something . . ." He dialed the usual number, the one on the top of the list.

The usual woman's voice said, "Federal Bureau of Investigation, Agent Druey's office."

"This is Steven Patterson."

"Mr. Patterson, he's at the Hoover Building. Can I have him return your call?"

Steven's eyes flashed at Jonelle. "Can I reach him there?"

"I'm sorry, sir, he's in a meeting and is impossible to reach."

"Thank you," Steven said, and hung up. His mind was speeding. "Every time we call, that's what we get. My dad too, first time he called, remember?"

She nodded. "Do you think he—?"

Steven cut her off. "Here, take the phone. I want you to find the general number for Quantico, try to get through to the woman I just talked to without using the number on the card." He began to move away.

"Where are you going?"

"To that pay phone across the street."

"Why?"

"To call the Hoover Building." Then he shouted at the kids who were, by this time, a whole block away. "Wyatt! Sarah, whoa! Wait up!" He dashed across the street, dodging cars.

MCI connected Jonelle to the FBI Quantico number when they found it for her. She asked politely for Agent Druey's office. The woman immediately asked what department, and Jonelle said he was an instructor there, and the voice said hold the line. A moment later, she asked the man's full name and spelling. Jonelle gave it to her. She made Jonelle wait another thirty seconds, then came back on the line to say she was very sorry, but there was no agent there by that name. Jonelle said that's impossible, she just spoke with his secretary . . .

But as she was mouthing the words, she saw Steven hanging up the phone on the wall across the street, a look of triumph crossing his face as he hurried back to the curb, waited for a limousine to pass, and then ran back to her. She had just pushed the off button on the cellular when Steven yelled, "Bingo. No Agent Druey at the Hoover Building, never heard of him!"

"I got the same thing," Jonelle added.

"I knew you would." He grabbed the cell phone from her hands and dialed the number on the card once more.

"Federal Bureau of Investigation, Agent Druey's office," the voice sang.

He hung up. He dialed one of the emergency numbers on the card, the cell phone number. He got the same woman. One of the other numbers elicited a recording, again the same woman's voice. The pager number only beeped. He turned the phone off.

Jonelle said, "This is pretty elaborate. Printed business cards and all those phone numbers, paying some woman to sit at a desk and answer to cover."

"Desk? We're probably getting the guy's kitchen in Trenton, wife answering the way she's trained to," Steven said. "He's no agent, never was an agent, and he isn't helping us."

"That day at the bookstore," Jonelle remembered, "Mike Deaver wouldn't have recognized him."

Steven agreed. "He just acted that way to make himself appear more believable."

Then it hit Jonelle, the overwhelming and suddenly uncompli-
cated truth: Charles Patterson was in on it.

"I know what you're thinking," Steven said. "But Dad could
have been duped too. I mean Druey could have lied to him as well
about being with the FBI."

"For forty years?"

Steven said nothing more. They walked a few blocks, stopped
in with the kids at the Safeway on 17th to pick up a few things they
needed, and as they were waiting in the checkout line, Steven said,
"I'm going to Virginia Beach. I'm going to see my father."

"Me too."

"No. You go on with work like nothing is up, we don't want
to give Barney a hint that we're onto this."

"You will when you speak to your dad."

"We'll see. I don't know how I'll handle it yet. But make sure
you just keep working, go to San Francisco tomorrow, cover the
First Lady, do what you need to do."

Outside, Jonelle asked, "What do we say when 'Agent' Druey
calls back?"

"Tell him we just wanted an update, but don't meet him at the
bookstore. Let him know you're going out of town."

"Sarah, wait at the curb!" Jonelle called out to her rambunctious
daughter. "Steven, when are you going?"

"Today."

"But you have a flight tomorrow."

"I'll play sick. Heck, I don't care if they fire me. This is what's
important now."

"Be careful."

"I'll say."

"Son! What a surprise," Mrs. Patterson said, kissing Steven on
the cheek. "Come in, come in. What in the world brings you down
unannounced? Where's Jonelle, the children?"

"I flew down alone, Mom," Steven answered. "Rented a car. I
need to see Dad."

"Well, he's teaching, of course. Dinner isn't ready yet. You look
tired."

"I am." He chose not to tell her he'd flown in last night. Instead he simply said, "Didn't sleep well."

"Come with me. Just baked my final peach pie, last fruit of the summer," and she led the way to the kitchen, where the air smelled of burnt sugar and cinnamon.

Steven ate heartily and drank a big glass of milk, into which his mother had remembered to drop several ice cubes. They chatted about nothing important, about the kids starting school again soon, where in the world had the summer gone, what kind of planes Steven had been flying. Then he told her he was going to take a walk, he'd see Dad on campus, or he'd be back in time for dinner.

"It'll be wonderful," the old woman said.

"I don't think so," Steven muttered under his breath as he walked away.

Steven wandered aimlessly, nervously around the campus, the same questions whirling around inside his head. The campus was nearly deserted, for summer school attracted fewer students. He found himself chatting with two girls whose school books looked too heavy for their arms, and who were impressed to learn he was Dr. Patterson's son and, even more so, Jonelle Patterson's husband. When they walked away, he realized he was standing under the Four Horsemen statue. And he felt sick.

His father strode across the lawn with brisk steps, much the way Steven walked. He'd always thought he looked like his dad, but in the past twenty-four hours he'd begun to believe he wasn't like him at all. "Steve!" the elder Patterson exclaimed when he was sure.

"Dad."

"What in God's name—?"

"Dad, I—"

"Lord, is something wrong? Jonelle? The kids? Someone ill? Has something happened?"

"Don't worry, they're fine. I'm fine."

"Then what is it, why are you here?"

"Dad, I don't know quite how to start this. I've been practicing all night, but nothing I planned is going to work."

"What in the world are you trying to say?"

"Dad, I think we should go somewhere."

"Home. Mother will have supper on soon. We'll talk over food."

"No. Someplace we can be alone."

"Well, all right, son. But I'd best call Mother and let her know."

"Fine. So, where shall we go?"

Charles thought for a moment. "How about my office here?"

"That's fine."

"All right. Let me drop these papers at the administration office, and we'll be on our way."

Charles Patterson listened carefully to his son for over an hour after they called home to say they might not make dinner. He listened without giving any emotion away, patiently allowing Steven to go into the history, every detail, every thought and nuance; if he had any prior knowledge of the incredible story Steven was telling him, he didn't give it away. Steven wondered if it was because he honestly didn't have a clue, or out of respect for his son to get the whole story out before he would comment.

Steven hardly took a breath, determined at any cost to communicate to his father the terror and fear that he and Jonelle had been living with all this time. For if his dad did know something about this, he wanted him to truly understand the anguish they'd been put through.

But Charles only continued to listen without reaction.

What amazed Steven was that it was like talking to a wall. He'd never seen his father like this, for the more he talked, the more Charles Patterson seemed to lose his humanity.

When Steven finished his story, he took a deep breath. Sweat was brimming on his forehead, and he felt exhausted. All through it, he'd hoped for some give-and-take, some input, some indication at least that his father was comprehending what he was saying, some sign that it was penetrating. His accusations were strong against the institution his father stood for, the world of Rex Heald and the religious right, but he stood his ground for what he believed was an incredible misuse of the actual Christian principles by which he had been taught to abide. "Dad," he finally said, "say something. Anything."

Charles Patterson coughed. Then he removed his sport jacket and rolled up his shirt sleeves as if to say they were going to hunker in for the whole night. Steven was starving, for it was now about 8:00 P.M., but he thought his father looked as if he were brimming with energy. Finally, he spoke. "Son, why would you think any of this absurd story has anything to do with me?"

Steven reached into his pocket and produced a copy of the page that Alicia's mother had given Jonelle. "Because your name is here." That was one of two parts that Steven had left out.

Charles studied it, dismissed it with a scowl.

Steven gave him more. "You were the one who called Jonelle to tell her she would be receiving the degree. You got her down here."

"I did. That doesn't make me guilty of anything."

"No," Steven agreed, "I'm on your side there. And your name on some list doesn't mean much either. I mean, they could put my name on a list of child molesters but it doesn't mean I am one."

"Precisely," Charles nodded.

"But there is one thing that rolls over and over again in my mind," Steven added, "the one thing that I can't make sense of, the one thing that can't be explained or justified."

"And what's that?"

"Number two: Sam Druey, while perhaps really your friend, is not and never has been an FBI agent."

This time, Charles Patterson went white.

Steven stared at him for what seemed an eternity. In that wrenching lifetime he felt his stomach turning and his heart sinking, for there was no explanation coming, no words of protest, no denial, no, "Son, how could you think this of me!" to make him feel guilty, to try to turn the onus on him. He sat in front of a man who looked defeated, caught red-handed, indefensible.

On the other hand, there was no confession forthcoming either.

"Damn it, Dad!" Steven shouted suddenly.

"Watch that language with me, boy," Charles sternly warned him, the strength returning.

"You're worrying about my language? My *language*? You know

people are being killed, murdered, framed, hurt, injured, lives are being ruined in the name of God, and you have the gall to warn me about my language?"

"I don't know anything about murder or any of the other evil deeds you've been talking here tonight. What someone or many people did to make Jonelle famous is not my responsibility, nor is it even my business."

"Then why is your name here? What have you to do with this?" Steven was practically begging him. "Explain what I don't know."

Charles thought for a moment, then slid open one of his desk drawers and withdrew a jar of salted peanuts. Steven watched as he opened the jar and dumped the contents into a pile on his desk. In the nuts, he found a key, and then got up and walked to a framed photograph of himself with Pat Buchanan, Ralph Reed, Rex Heald, Pat Robertson, Ben Kinchow, and Terry Meeuwsen when they all appeared on an anniversary segment of the *700 Club*. He lifted it from the wall, revealing, as in old British detective movies, a wall safe. He fitted the key into the lock, and the opened door revealed that the safe was filled with papers. He withdrew several folders, looked through them, found a file, and then handed it to Steven.

Steven said nothing as he looked inside the folder. There was one document there, a letter. On the top of it was a stamp that warned CONFIDENTIAL—TOP SECRET. He looked up at his father.

Charles had an anticipatory grin on his face.

Steven just stared.

"Read it," Charles said.

"What is it?"

"You will see. It's the way to make you understand what I know this to be about."

Steven looked down at a piece of Rex Heald's personal stationery, at a letter from 1996, and started reading:

11 November 1996
Dear Charles,
    Last night I had the good opportunity to attend a wake for the Republican chances after Bob Dole set us back a thousand

years. No, I'm just kidding. It was a dinner party I attended—along with such diverse and interesting Republican movers and shakers as George Will, Paul Gigot, Kay Bailey Hutchinson, Trent Lott, Dick Cheney, Bill Kristol, Christine Whitman, and others—at the Huffington Mansion in Washington. It was a going-away party of sorts, and we all probed what Arianna's plans were regarding her upcoming move back to California, would she run for office, and which one? Arianna was the perfect host, but this was more than grilled lamb and sorbet, this was a think tank, and it was a spirited evening.

Much discussed was the Republican Party's future after Dole's defeat, what the GOP can do to recapture the voters. They carped on about the wrong candidate stressing the wrong issues, the lock Gore has on 2000 (great disagreement on that, though I personally think he's a shoo-in), how Kemp lacked luster and there's no one sparkling sitting in the wings. Pretty typical stuff, no different from *Newsweek*. Bill asked, "Where's the new Ronald Reagan?" Dick replied, "Where's the *old* Ron Reagan?" and everyone laughed.

Steven looked up at his father, who was now eating the peanuts he'd dumped on the desk. "What am I reading this for? What does this have to do with Jonelle and the news?"

"I'm not sure it has to do with the news, but it has everything to do with Jonelle. Peanut?"

Steven continued:

George said, jokingly, they should have run *Elizabeth* Dole. Kay said hear hear, a little bit about Liddy's own possible attempt next time around, and Gov. Whitman smiled when Arianna said now they were getting it, run a woman! The men were ready to laugh her out of the room, of course, but Arianna, who has a fine sense of humor and is always cracking jokes, told them firmly but graciously that she was dead serious. "The only chance we have left is the contrarian one," she said. I remember her words exactly. "We must be bold, we have to startle. Let's yank ourselves out of the doldrums of the ancient times we're still clinging to. I sound like I'm giving a speech. What I want to say is let's get with the program already!"

Well, they all jumped on the bandwagon and claimed that was their motto, Chris had some warm words about Susan Molinari's chances in the future, and of course everyone thinks Chris will be the VP candidate in 2000 (possibly battling Dianne Feinstein as Gore's running mate, though I think the nod will go to John Kerry) so that was discussed, and they went on and on about including women voters this time, no more the party of exclusion, blah blah. But nothing anyone said hit me as much as these words from Arianna: "If we blow it again in 2000, the only hope the GOP has of recapturing the White House in 2008 is with a woman."

Steven stopped chewing as it hit his stomach first, the realization, the feeling coming over him like a virus making its insidious way through his bloodstream, to his guts, to his head, where the enormity of the concept wouldn't fit. He looked at his father and said, "You don't possibly mean to say . . ."

"I say nothing. It's what *Rex* is saying. Please, Steven, continue reading."

He did:

Now, Charles, I don't think this little think tank was particularly successful, because the Republican strongmen in conservative shirts will ignore Arianna's brilliant vision and things will pretty much go on as usual, and yes, the Democrats will win again in 2000 (and probably 2004 as well) and Christ will take a back seat once again.

What has this specifically to do with us, you ask? Well, look at the past. Ralph couldn't lead the Christian Coalition up the White House steps, the backlash has affected us all, and we don't have a candidate anyone will accept into their hearts. In fact, if a candidate associates himself with the Christian Right today, chances are that will do him in. Just last night at the party, I was pretty much ignored; I was there more as a listener than a participant. No one really asked my advice. I have millions of good Christian voters behind me, but I'm powerless without political muscle. Chris Whitman particularly gave me cold stares when I spoke, probably because we differ so completely on the abortion issue. So, we must be subtle, Charles, and to be subtle we must be clever. We must put God in the White House, but the way to do it is on the coattails (or is that skirt hem?) of a woman.

Did you just laugh? Think about it. We find the perfect good Christian Republican woman who we can promote, groom, publicize until someone else in the GOP—not us!—drafts her to run. We will never be associated directly with her, she will never be "the candidate of the Christian Right," but we will own her and through her we will gain the power necessary to save this country from sin and the evil direction in which it is headed.

Steven took a break, looked up at his father, who handed him a glass of water, anticipating that he'd need it. "I'm beginning to get the picture," Steven said.

"And it's a thrilling one, isn't it?" Charles Patterson replied, almost starstruck.

Steven did not answer, but he kept reading:

We created Network ONE the same way, secretly funding what will one day fill every sinner's home with programming that will enlighten them and bring the word of Jesus. We can use ONE to promote our candidate, we have ten years to do it in, and I'm already inquiring as to who that might be. I also want to throw this out to the other Christian leaders, and see what the reaction is. (Can you imagine?)

When I left the Huffington residence, I told Arianna that the evening had been "enlightening and thought-provoking." I hated being so coy, but I didn't dare give a hint that her suggestion made an impression on me. Me, of all people! The Christian Right wanting to run a woman for president? Heresy! I just realize now that no one would believe it anyway, which makes me think Robertson and the others will laugh *me* out of the room. But do you know what? I actually think a woman in the White House is a good idea. If she can bring Christian peace to the land, God bless us all. No man has ever been able to do that.

I need your support on this, Charles. I'll call you soon.

Respectfully, I remain,

Yours,

Rex

Rex Heald

Steven's mouth actually hung open. "So Rex set out to find the perfect Christian girl with the perfect Christian husband—"

"You're an ordained *minister*," Charles said proudly, and defensively.

"—and the perfect Christian family, the perfect Christian package for the White House in 2008." It was so crazy, so off the wall, so unbelievable, that he started to laugh. "This can't be possible. This is a joke, you're playing a joke on me."

"Rex and I met, discussed, as he says there, and then we proposed the plan—above board, to run a woman—to other leaders, to get their opinions. Rex was right, they laughed him out of the room. Reed hated it, but it didn't matter because by then he was pretty well washed up. Buchanan howled, Jerry Falwell thought it was nuts, and he too asked who would it be? The whole thing was dropped. After all, none of them know of our involvement in ONE, and we have to be careful.

"But Rex and I sat down and went over names, political names of course, and none of them would work. Then I told Rex—without being totally serious, I think—that the perfect candidate would be my son's wife."

Steven was stunned. "*You* started this?"

"The simple wish of a proud father-in-law."

"But how did—?"

"Barney Keller really sold Rex on Jonelle."

Steven was hit by a thunderbolt. "At that first meeting, a dinner we had with those three guys, they joked about Jonelle being president someday."

"The Christian Broadcasting Network was suffering a backlash, so Network ONE was created to carry the Christian word without the word Christian in the title."

"ONE's deep pockets, it's money you guys rake in from those hillbillies who send their week's wages to the *700 Club*."

"Steven."

"Come on, Dad, it's all about money, and that's all it's ever been about. Religion equals cash. What's the Pope worth? Check out the Vatican bank balance. Look at Robertson's house down the slope from here, that ostentatious fortress with underground tunnels and more security than the Pentagon—"

"Paid for with his book royalties!" Charles shouted.

"And that hotel with the Monet in the lobby, the Cadillacs, the minks, the trips, the greed! All funded by the faithful, the ignorant believers keeping the coffers full."

"I won't have this. I won't speak to you if you're going to take this tone."

"Tone? You're telling me my wife is the choice of you Good Christian Soldiers to be the presidential candidate in 2008 and you've killed people to make her a star and I'm supposed to keep a decent tone? Dad, are you insane?"

Charles caught his breath, relaxed. "I know this is hard for you to swallow."

"I'm dying, Dad. I feel like I'm choking on my own vomit, because that's what I want to do, I want to puke."

"I had nothing to do with the methods ONE's owners used to make Jonelle famous, *nothing*. I wash my hands."

"Guilty! You're as guilty as anyone in this. My own father, Jesus! And don't tell me not to take the Lord's name in vain." Steven got up and walked from wall to wall, socking one of the books that lined the mahogany shelves. "I'm going fucking crazy! How could you let them do this?"

Charles waited until Steven had calmed a bit. "I know nothing of what Barney Keller did, how he did it, who did it for him, nothing. Clayton and James Findley I know even less about. Rex told me only that they had sold him on the fact that Jonelle would be the perfect choice, that she was electable. But first they had to really give her prominence."

Steven sarcastically muttered, "The new Cronkite, the new Walters, loved by the masses."

"President-elect," Charles intoned, loftily.

Steven moaned, "Dad, please."

"The forty-fourth president of the United States of America."

"Stop saying that."

"Think of it, Steven. Think of the glory, think of what it means, think of what it will mean to Wyatt and Sarah, think of the *possibilities*."

"The only possibility I am sure of today is that you will go to jail with the rest of them."

"Steven!"

"And—God forgive me for saying this—I'll be glad."

Steven returned to his parents' house only to retrieve the bag he'd left when he arrived. His mother didn't understand why it was so late when they got there, why he didn't want to eat, why there was so much unspoken tension between him and his father. "Did something happen?" she asked her husband.

"Nothing, nothing," he said, dismissing her. "It's none of your concern."

"Why don't you tell her, Dad?" Steven said combatively. "Tell her your plan for Jonelle. Doesn't she have a right to know? Hell, this way she can start shopping for a gown for the inauguration!"

"What inauguration?" Alma Patterson asked.

"Jonelle's going to be president one day, didn't Dad tell you? Didn't he share with you the good Christian plan, the zealous plot, the excitement and joy that it was working just the way he and his cronies wanted?"

Alma Patterson hadn't a clue. "Dear, I don't understand."

"None of your concern, Mother," Charles repeated, more as an order to Steven to shut up.

"Why don't you tell her if you're so proud of it?" Steven challenged his father. Then he shook his head, trying to comprehend. "I don't get it. What did you think we'd do? Become so enamored of the possibility of being the First Family that we'd overlook what had been done?"

Softly, the elder Patterson said, "You were never supposed to know."

"Not supposed to know?" Steven howled. "People are dying left and right—on camera yet—and we're *not supposed to know*?"

"I told you I don't know about that."

"You're an accessory to these crimes!"

"I'm not a violent man. I condone nothing, I simply look the other way. Turn the other cheek, the Lord teaches. If you have a problem with what they did, take it up with Barney Keller."

"Barney Keller?" Steven's mother asked, bewildered.

Steven said, "Who are the Four Horsemen?"

Charles cleared his throat. "Rex Heald and the three of them, I assume. I don't know everything."

"These monsters use a biblical name? It's kinda like the Mafia calling themselves the Knights of Columbus. Hell, they probably are."

Charles was sputtering, his face red. "I only know the order was to make her the most famous newsperson in the country. That is all I take responsibility for."

Steven closed his eyes. "The moral issue, Dad, how can you close your eyes to that? It's what's at the core of this. The means never justifies the end."

"I could quote scripture right now," Charles said, "but I imagine it would do no good."

"It would do more harm, if that is possible."

"Can't you two be more civil to one another?" Steven's bewildered mother asked. "I've never seen you like this, Steven."

"I've never . . . never felt like this, Mom." Steven's eyes brimmed with tears suddenly. He didn't expect them, and he didn't know where they came from. But they were there, rising from some dark place of pain in his soul, erupting down his cheeks as he stood in the bright kitchen looking at a man he suddenly didn't know at all. "I've never felt like this in my life." He wiped his eyes with the back of his left hand and grabbed his overnight bag with his right.

"Steven, don't go, it's late and—"

"Mom, I'm sorry, but I've got to get out of here."

"You'll be back soon?"

"I won't ever be back." He directed the words to his father. And then he started to the door.

"Steve!" his father said sharply. "You talk to Jonelle about this. You discuss this, you tell her everything I told you. This is her decision too, you hear me? We have spent years and more money than you could count on this project."

"Project? We're a *project*?" He felt rage coming out of his pores. He could barely say the words: "I thought, Father, that we were a family."

"Steven, tomorrow the emotion will lessen, you'll calm down and you'll see this objectively."

"Go fuck yourself," Steven said, and literally bashed his way out the back door.

"Steven!" he could hear his mother say behind him, probably in shock at hearing that word in her house, he was sure for the first—and last—time. Then he heard the telephone ringing, and he hurried away.

He got to the little rented car, tossed his bag into the backseat, then jumped in and started the engine. He saw his father in shadows in the porch light, but he didn't look at him, and he wouldn't stop. The man was waving frantically, chasing Steven down the drive, trying to tell him something, but Steven had had enough. When he hit the road, he headed for D.C. and hoped his rage would diminish as he drove through the night.

Rather than diminish, it changed to terror. For, as he drove wildly with frustration bursting from every pore, he suddenly realized something: Why did he think the incidents had stopped? Just because he now knew the plot, would they cease creating the news? No. They were sick enough to continue the events right till the day Jonelle took the oath of office.

And then he thought about where she was tonight. San Francisco. At an important function that would be televised to millions of homes. The perfect setting for . . . ?

A chill ran up his spine, and he shuddered, hoping against hope that he was completely wrong.

chapter 18

When Steven had set out to confront his father in Virginia, and the kids were safely with Helen, Jonelle boarded a plane for the West Coast. She tried to psych herself for the event she was covering, but it wasn't easy; all she could do was wonder what was happening down in Virginia Beach. The metal statue of the Four Horsemen invaded her mind. She saw it, blazing in the center of the campus, but riding the horses were Barney Keller, Clay Santangelo, old James Martin Findley, and—who was the last one, who was riding out of the wall—Rex Heald? No, someone more familiar, Charles Patterson, her own father-in-law. She shook her head, drawing her eyes tightly closed, and put the thought from her mind. She prayed that they'd been wrong. But she knew in her heart that they hadn't.

Jonelle's room at the Stanford Court was luscious, but she could just as well have been in a Rodeway Inn; amenities and pleasures were lost on her. She met with the ONE crew and planned their strategy for the evening's event, then she took a short nap in which she slept a fitful sleep, waiting for Steven to call. He did not.

She called the kids and talked for twenty minutes. Yes, they were being good. No, Dad hadn't called. They were planning to watch the news tonight because she told them she was covering one of the biggest parties ever. She was dreading every moment of it.

After dinner, back at the hotel, MCI One chased her down— ironic, she thought, the name of the phone service—and she retrieved a message from "Agent" Sam Druey asking if everything was all right and, if not, please don't hesitate to call at any hour. Another from Clay, telling her he'd arrived in "Frisco," as he called it, was in the same hotel, he'd see her at 4:00 P.M. for a run-through. Nothing from Steven.

But it didn't worry her. She trusted that he was going to come away from his father with the truth about all this. And that would take time.

Jonelle met Clay and the crew at the Cowell Theater in San Francisco's Fort Mason Center. The place was a blizzard of last-minute chaos, caterers and decorators and security, plus the just plain curious lining up to get a glimpse at the glitterati who would be joining the First Lady for the gala. It was the event of the year for Golden Gate society, and already the photographers were snapping shots of those famous enough to sell. Jonelle, a reporter herself, was photographed several times.

They got down to work. Clay started out the run-through, but as usually happened, Jonelle took over, and the crew ignored him once they got into it. He may have been a genius behind a desk, and he had great hip style and energy, but he was a loser in the production department. Tonight he'd be no better, for at most parties he ran around, a celebrity in his own right, schmoozing. Jonelle found it hard to even look at him, for the hair on the back of her neck stood up every time he got close. He may have killed people, she knew. Killed people to boost her popularity. God almighty, she wanted to strangle him herself.

She put it out of her head, the anger and bitterness and festering frustration. She tried to feel like the good Christian she was. She had a job to do, and she was going to do it well. She was into it now, the blood was rushing. And she was looking forward to seeing Hillary again. It had been months—when Jonelle had reported on a conference the First Lady attended in Hamburg—since their paths had crossed. She thought this might turn out to be a good gig after all.

She could return to the fear and loathing later.

At 5:00 P.M., Jonelle put on her black Todd Oldman sheath and returned to the Fort Mason Center. She was almost glad of it, for work would drown out her worry. She jumped in with both feet.

Jonelle had decided to take the viewers, both of tonight's news and the subsequent segment of *Jonelle Patterson Reporting* . . . , through the gala as if they were honored guests themselves. *Cameras catch her as she arrives in a corridor filled with the bold and dissonant sounds and scents of Chinatown, where humble guides in traditional silk garb bow respectfully and lead her down a hallway, through enormous arches framed in futuristic steel, the entryway to the future, another world. Jonelle becomes a time traveler, and signs in on the wall there, along with Ann and Gordon Getty and their sons in front of her, and coffee heiress Ines Folger and Gap founders Don and Doris Fisher just behind her, under moving projected images of the brawling, honky-tonk San Francisco of the Gold Rush days. . . .*

Jonelle, the time traveler, introduces her audience to a feast of delights in a vibrant street scene teeming with shops, bars, food stalls, complete with a Chinese New Year's celebration. Champagne flows. She interviews Amy Silver and Karen Friedman, planners of the event. All the guests, the in names of Bay Area society, are presented with a gift to commemorate the visit, a red silk box containing a prediction for their future in a Lucite fortune cookie. Jonelle's reads: THE OFFER MAY OVERWHELM, BUT ONLY THE FOOL ANSWERS IN HASTE. *She shudders to think what it means.*

The sound of a gong dramatically summons the rising of a temple from the mist, the Divine Emperor's Palace. The guests are led to the mysterious building by ushers guiding them with Chinese lanterns on poles. Once the guests are seated inside the palace theater, the lanterns softly bathe the room in a reddish glow. Suddenly, the stage is alive with color and sound, presenting not the Emperor of the Sun but something more appropriate for the evening: the Juvenile Diabetes Foundation Achievement Awards.

The awards are the focus and centerpiece of the evening, they are what the night is all about. Dina Merrill is the master of ceremonies, and she is elegant in style, serious in her devotion to the cause. Awards are bestowed with grace and even humor at times, and when Hillary Clinton receives the Media Awareness Award for her work for the cause—her private secretary's little girl died suddenly from undiagnosed diabetes earlier in the year, when the First Lady took up the awareness cause—the crowd goes crazy. There is a dazzling display of pyrotechnics with Roman candles, sparklers, firecrackers, and dragon dancers, celebrating the recipients. Then, to transport everyone to dinner in the Herbst Pavilion, rickshaws are available for $20 each, money going to JDF research, moving through the time gates once again. . . .

Jonelle and the travelers enter the Golden Gate Park of the 1960s where the essence of life is peace and love. Mama Cass sings of California Dreamin' while the guests are greeted by love children handing them love beads and flowers for their hair.

They sit at tables graced with lava lamps, tie-dyed tablecloths, on a floor of grass, feasting on the finest the Bay Area has to offer, under the protection of sheltering trees filled with psychedelic lights in the evening mist. A peaceful, calm atmosphere pervades where they have dinner and make good conversation.

Off camera, Jonelle talks to art patron and philanthropist Dodie Rosekrans, and Levi's Peter Haas. All agree this is a wonderful evening. She slips out to call MCI, checking both the cell phone and home, but still no word from Steven. She leaves him a message of love, appropriate for the setting she's in, and hopes that he's all right and that he's made sense of all this.

Through the time gates yet again, the camera follows the First Lady into the future, and everyone, including Jonelle, is astonished at the sheer wonder of the setting that M&K Design Group of Washington has designed for their pleasure. Part of the Golden Gate Bridge has been recreated in the ballroom to represent the Golden Age of the future, a time when automobiles are forbidden, pollution *has been conquered, and the bridge "leading halfway to the stars" has been turned into a block party under those stars, millions of tiny spotlights shining down on the dance floor. The music is hot, the energy wild, and everyone lets their hair down in this preview of tomorrow, a world awash with wonder. It's a party, Jonelle tells her audience, ending with a beginning. Then she says, "This is Jonelle Patterson reporting . . . from San Francisco." And she signs off.*

Then she starts dancing.

She lets her hair down. The music is so good and she's having so much fun that she almost puts from her mind the fears, the terror, the worry about Steven. When Clay comes up to her after working the room, and dancing his butt off as well, and he suggests they put a little more of this on tape, she is not cautious, she is not thinking. In retrospect, she should have seen it as a clue, a sign, but at the moment it passes over her.

Tape runs as Jonelle dances near Hillary and they start mocking each other's movements, laughing uproariously, feeling like sorority sisters back in college, doing the "twist" and "Watusi" and all those ridiculous dances. When someone brings out a plastic bar and holds it for the "limbo," Hillary draws the line, she is the First Lady after all and a certain decorum must be maintained. But she devilishly dares Jonelle, and it's when Jonelle attempts to dance under the bar that she looks up to the thousand stars overhead, the catwalk above the fake Golden Gate girders, and it's then she sees the hand of one of the stagehands—no, not a stagehand, someone else, but a hand she thinks she knows well, one she has seen again and again but never in person, a hand adorned with a gold band—

It happens too fast for her to know what she's really doing. She rises, knocking the limbo pole out of the hands of its holders, screams Hillary's name as she's waiting to go under the pole, becomes hysterical in one fast second, throwing herself on the First Lady the way the security guards did on Imelda, only there are no bullets coming from beyond them now, only the sky caving in, the roof falling, the millions of stars in the form of hot, searing, heavy lights dropping to the gathered below. In her last moment of consciousness, Jonelle saves the First Lady of the country. As the Secret

Service now dive into action to protect them both, she knows why Clay asked her to turn the cameras back on. And then Jonelle is hit, clobbered by steel and falling fixtures, knocked into unconsciousness, microphone buried in the rubble.

All on tape.

chapter 19

Steven heard what happened in San Francisco when he finally turned on the car radio, hours after he left Virginia Beach. Just outside of Richmond, he was switching stations, futilely looking for classical music, when he tuned into what sounded like NPR. They were broadcasting a report on a bombing; the newsperson was talking of a ceiling crashing down, light grids injuring more than seventy people, the panic it set off, etc. Only when the newscaster said they were going to switch to another reporter at a hospital to "check on the First Lady's condition" did Steven realize what he was listening to. Jonelle wasn't mentioned, and of course because of that he thought she was all right.

Had he tuned in only moments earlier, he would have heard that the First Lady suffered only minor bruises and scratches but that more serious injury—and quite possibly her life—had been saved by Jonelle Patterson, who pushed her out of the way apparently when she saw the roof giving in, and threw herself on top of Mrs. Clinton before the Secret Service even realized what was happening, so on and so forth.

He stopped at the first phone booth he could find. It was the first time in his life that he'd wished he'd taken a cue from his wife and leapt into the twenty-first century with a cellular phone. He put his quarter in, and then froze—who to dial? How would he find out if she was okay? He'd never get to talk to her, he knew she was probably on the air at that very moment. He didn't want to wake the kids—why bother them if Jonelle was fine? He stood for a moment, considering his options, and then had an idea.

He jumped back into the car and drove to the first place that was open. It was called the Roadhouse, and three or four pickup trucks were in the dusty parking lot. He pulled in, drove right to the door and parked it, telling himself every bar had to have a TV, and he'd explain what he needed to see, and they'd think him crazy but . . .

He didn't have to explain a thing. All the patrons, the bartender, the Mexican man who held a broom in his hand, and even a mangy dog were fixed on the TV screen over the bar. The jukebox was unplugged, the place silent, hushed. They were watching ABC, where Cynthia McFadden, who happened to be in San Francisco on another story, was reporting. Steven made his way to the bar and asked the bartender if they could switch to ONE. "I like this gal," the bartender said.

"My wife's reporting on ONE," Steven said.

"That so? Well, this gal up here," the bartender said, nodding to McFadden, "she's *my* girlfriend." Guffaws from the assorted regulars.

"My wife is Jonelle Patterson," Steven pressed.

Three heads turned. There was the usual reaction, the stardom thing, looks on faces he'd gotten used to years ago. He pleaded, "I want to see—I *need* to see her—want to hear what happened."

One of the men near him said, "You don't know?"

"Hey, buddy, you better sit down," the bartender said now in a less kidding tone. "Your wife's been hurt."

"What?" Steven felt his legs giving out. He slid his butt onto a stool. He suddenly knew why the phone was ringing at his parents' house as he was leaving; the reason his father was trying to flag him down was to tell him that Jonelle had been hurt. "What happened? Is she okay?"

A woman in cowgirl garb said, "I'm Connie Glover, Mr. Patterson. I'm a big fan. She's in bad shape, they said, but she's alive."

"Saved Hillary's life," another voice said.

"Republicans did it," Connie the cowgirl jokingly added. "Couldn't put Hillary in jail, figured maybe they'd drop the ceiling on her."

"What?" Steven gasped, astonished.

Then McFadden was getting a report from the hospital, but it was not a report on Hillary Clinton, it was a report on Jonelle Patterson. Steven heard that she was unconscious—in a coma?—and that the doctors had ruled her condition critical.

The customers filled Steven in on what they knew had happened at the gala in San Francisco, and he took the bartender up on the offer of a free telephone in the back room. Sitting on a case of Red Dog, he dialed first his home. He expected the kids to be asleep, expected Helen to pick up the phone, but Wyatt answered instead, and Steven could tell that he'd been crying. "Dad!" the boy called, then shouted in the other direction, "Sarah, it's Dad!" And he was back. "Dad, is Mom gonna be okay?"

"Wyatt, are you all right?"

"Yeah."

"Mom's gonna be fine. I promise you. How's Sarah taking it?"

"Hold on. Sarah, Dad wants you."

Sarah's unsteady voice said, "Daddy?"

"Honey, I'm so sorry. I wish I was there, I wish I'd never gone away, I wish I could do something. How did you find out?"

"Someone called wanting you. Woke us up. Auntie Helen told them you were at Grandfather Patterson's. They said what happened."

"I've got to go there," Steven said. "I'm almost in Richmond. What time is it?" He checked his watch. "One A.M. I'm going to the airport and taking the first plane in the morning."

"We want to go."

"Let me see how Mom's doing first, okay?"

"I said a prayer."

"Wyatt too?"

"Yes."

He heard her voice crack, and then his did as well, out of concern and fear and all the emotions that had been swimming around in him since he left his father's house. He talked to Helen, gave her instructions to protect the kids from the press, and promised he'd call her as soon as he got to the West Coast.

He didn't drive directly to the airport. Instead, he went to Kathleen Holm's house. He woke her from a sound sleep, and she greeted him on the porch in a Japanese kimono. "Steven!" she exclaimed, half in delight and half in surprise. She unlatched the screen door, a puzzled look on her face. "What brings you here this time of night?"

Steven told her what had happened.

She sat with him, passing the time till the airport opened, drinking strong coffee and eating cinnamon rolls she pulled from the freezer, constantly checking by phone with the hospital in San Francisco, but Jonelle's condition remained the same. Her doctor was too busy with other victims of the disaster, and Steven knew the only way to really talk to him was in person. TWA only had afternoon flights out of Richmond, so he booked the first plane in the morning, Delta through Atlanta at 6:00 A.M., which would put him in the San Francisco International Airport at 11:00 A.M. local time. With luck, he'd be with Jonelle by noon.

Kathleen was a wonderful hostess, offering him the support and comfort of a good friend. And when he left, she sent him on his way with Godspeed and all good wishes and prayers to Jonelle. "It's fall, good antique time. Tell her we'll do it as soon as she's ready to travel."

Steven promised. "Bless you," he said, getting into the car.

At 6:07 A.M. he was in the air.

At 10:40 A.M. San Francisco time, he landed on the West Coast and hurried directly to the hospital. There, he fought through the platoon of newspeople, many of whom he knew personally, and entered the doors at exactly 11:20 A.M. He was at Jonelle's side ten minutes later.

She looked battered and bruised, but calm and peaceful, a complete dichotomy, as if she was simply taking a nap. He held her hand, and sat there for one hour in loving silence before the doctor showed up and urged Steven to join him in his office.

There, he told Steven that this was pretty routine; Jonelle had suffered a crushing blow to the head, but she'd not lapsed into a coma as was initially feared. She had drifted in and out of consciousness all night, and the doctor found that a good sign. He fully expected her to recover, but indicated that it could be a while before she was "herself." He explained, "The brain is a tricky, yet resilient organ."

Steven wondered if that was supposed to make him feel better.

When he returned to Jonelle's room and sat in the straight-backed chair trying to run everything over in his mind, trying to make sense of it all, he remembered a movie he and the kids had recently seen on cable when Jonelle was in London. He remembered Sandra Bullock and the family of Peter Gallagher—he thought that was the actor's name—standing at the bedside while Peter was in a coma. Talking to him, playing music, laughing like on a normal day, keeping him feeling loved and part of them while he slept. Remembering *While You Were Sleeping* gave him a burst of enthusiasm. Jonelle was not in a coma, but drifting in and out of consciousness was the next closest thing. Steven wanted to do something to help her stay awake, alert, to keep her from drifting away forever. He knew now what he would do.

He rushed into the corridor, found a phone, and called his kids, assuring them Mom was going to be fine, and then made arrangements for them to fly out. They were a family, and they would remain one even while Jonelle was asleep. He told them to bring some of her favorite things, clothes, music, photographs, and lots of love.

When he hung up, he realized he had tears on his cheeks, and he brushed them away before he turned around. When he did, he found that he was facing Barney Keller, who'd just walked down the hall.

There was a moment of silence, a silence so filled with hate and anger that Steven actually felt his body trembling from the emotion.

Then he made a fist, and faster than could be seen with the human eye, he brought that fist into Keller's face with every ounce of strength in his 210-pound body, knocking him flat against the tile wall. A nurse screamed, another man came running, but Steven didn't have to be held back. He simply watched, with pleasure, as Keller slumped to the antiseptic floor, dazed. Then Steven bent down and said, loudly and firmly, "If anything happens to her, I'm going to kill you myself." He looked up at the people looking down at them. "I've got witnesses to that pledge," he told Keller.

And then he walked away.

At 3:00 P.M., as he was sitting with Jonelle in what was starting to look like a florist shop, talking to her inert body, telling her what had happened in Virginia Beach, what his father had said, telling her how he still couldn't quite believe it, how he felt he didn't know this man who was his father anymore, that he could see the evil in him and running from him was like running from the devil himself. "And now, they've done this to you . . ."

A Secret Service agent tapped lightly on the door, put his head inside, and asked Steven if he could spare a few minutes for the First Lady, she'd like to see him.

Hillary Clinton looked just like Jonelle, slightly battered, though alert and animated. Indeed, she'd been released; the President had shown up, interrupting a conference in Japan, and they were about to return to Washington. But before she would leave the hospital, she wanted to see Steven. To learn from him how Jonelle really was. "Anything the doctors aren't telling the rest of us?"

Steven shook his head. "She's going to be fine. She's loved, and she's got a lot of people praying for her."

Hillary smiled warmly, "When she comes to, after you tell her you love her, will you tell her I'll be grateful for the rest of my life?"

Steven nodded. "It will be an honor."

The First Lady hugged him and then accompanied him to Jonelle's room, where she took Jonelle's hand. Jonelle, almost sensing that Hillary was standing next to her, moaned, her eyes blinked, and a small smile creased her face as she seemed to recognize them. Hillary said, "We're praying for you. Rest now, be better," and then whispered, emotionally, "and thank you, dear friend."

After the First Lady left the hospital, a Secret Service agent lingered behind. "Mind if I ask you a few questions?" he asked Steven.

Do I tell him or don't I? The question reverberated through Steven's head the whole time he was speaking with the agent. The man was giving him the perfect chance to spill the beans, tell all, open up about the plot and who was behind it and why all those news events came to pass, why last night's disaster was no freak accident. Then it occurred to Steven that they'd goofed last night, they'd never meant for Jonelle to get hurt, they had probably only done it because the First Lady-in-jeopardy made for great news, and Jonelle would be right there at her side to report on it.

However, hadn't it worked even better than they'd hoped? He could see Barney looking at his overnights right now. Smiling, smug, proud, the way his father was proud. This was the clincher, this was the ultimate media boost. The sympathy for Jonelle was enormous, with the First Lady, no less, leading the supporters. Steven had to hand it to them, these Horsemen really were *good*.

The agent asked him if he had any idea if Jonelle might have suspected something, sensed something?

Christ, she knew it was bound to happen again, we both should have realized that! Steven said, "Why would you think that?" *Was this guy onto them? Did they already suspect, have a clue?*

"I ask it because in every situation like this we can't rule out foul play." The man rubbed his nose. "Course, anybody who'd try to assassinate the First Lady by dropping a ceiling on two hundred dancing guests is a little stupid."

Little stupid? It's too ridiculous for words. Nobody tried to assassinate anyone. It was just a good story to boost the ratings. "Why *did* the ceiling fall?" Steven asked.

"It was in the design, I'm told. Didn't anticipate the weight of the light grid. Pulled down the plaster and actual beams."

If you look closely, you'll find they were tampered with, just like the brakes on that bus. "Don't people check these things?"

"Old building," the man said, shrugging. "We are responsible, however. It's our job to check things like that."

"Didn't you?"

"Missed it, I guess."

No, you didn't. They set it up after you ran your check. "I'm very sorry you did."

"Hope your wife recovers fast. She's my favorite newsperson."

"Thanks."

"She looked up."

"Pardon me?"

"She looked up," the man repeated, "just before it happened. One of the Getty kids, dancing near her, said she had this momentary expression on her face. Like shock, or panic."

What did she see? "Looked up when? When the ceiling fell?"

"Before, split second before."

My God, who was up there? Did she see them doing it? Did she know? Is that why she was able to save Hillary? "Don't say," Steven said, curious. *Damn it! If I tell him, what am I unleashing? What does Jonelle know that I might not? What happened last night before the party? Who did she talk to? Is there more to this than I know at this point? If I tell this guy, am I risking too much?*

The Secret Service agent again pressed. "Anything more? Anything that comes to mind that might have a bearing, no matter how far off?"

Boy, could I tell you far off. "No," Steven said. "I don't know anything. I only care that my wife gets well."

"She's got the whole country rooting for her."

And voting for her in about eight years. "Can I go now?"

"Of course. And thank you, Mr. Patterson."

"What for?"

Wyatt played his current favorite album, the soundtrack from the recent big Disney musical *Sherlock Holmes*, over and over again, swearing that "Mom's secret" was that she liked it even more than he did. When Steven told him he was being selfish, he said, "Potomac's dad let him play Smashing Pumpkins when *his* mom was in a coma!"

"His mother was in a coma?"

"For *months.*"

"That's hopeful."

Wyatt got the message. "I'm sorry, Dad. I was wrong, Potomac's mom got better real fast. You can put on Mom's Julie Andrews disc if you want."

Steven smiled. Jonelle's favorite musical had been the one Jack Kennedy liked, one she'd acted in in high school: *Camelot.* Julie Andrews had always been one of her favorite singers. He put the CD on and let the music softly fill the hospital room.

Sarah sat on the edge of Jonelle's bed. She'd given her a spray of CKOne cologne, set a little needlework pillow—*Get The Story!* —that Larry King had sent her for Christmas one year next to her, and wrapped Jonelle's fingers around her cell phone. "That should really get through to her," Sarah said, and they all laughed.

Steven put his arms around both of them. "Come on, honey," he said to Jonelle, whose eyes opened almost on cue but did not register. "We're right here, just waiting . . ."

In suite 957, at the Mandarin Oriental Hotel in San Francisco, Clay Santangelo watched as an elated Barney Keller hung up the phone. "A thirty-seven share!" Barney yelled. "Jesus fucking Christ, that's incredible—we'll drive the election right off the airwaves. And it's showing no sign of abating, they're still glued to their sets like bloodsuckers."

"Gore and Quayle aren't pleased, I'm sure."

"Their first debate was overshadowed by reports on Jonelle."

"Did Hillary go home?" Clay asked.

"Who cares? It's Jonelle they're all wringing their hands about."

"She's becoming America's Eva Perón."

"And that putz Steven is her Juan. Listen, had Evita lived, she'd have kicked Perón out and run the country herself. Maybe there's hope."

"Sure there's hope. Evita would have been elected vice president."

"Don't cry for me, Atlanta, Georgia."

"More champagne?"

"I'm gonna get smashed, I'm so happy."

"This the one time that Findley's man's screw-up meets with your approval?"

"Christ, Clayton, pin a medal on our Saint Paul."

"By the way, are we through with him now?"

"Off into the sunset," Barney said with obvious pleasure. "Good riddance. Findley has to make his final payment and then he's taking an extended European vacation, I hear. This thing is finally over. And we did it. She'd win an election even if she were in a coma."

"Thank God she's not. Technically, there's still four years to go."

"She goes into political mode now. We did the show-biz sting. We're finished with her. That was the bargain." He kicked a table leg. "Damn, but I hate to lose those ratings."

"We still have a few problems."

"Party pooper."

"Damage control: Everyone's asking why Patterson decked you."

"I'll issue a statement saying he was so distraught about his wife . . . and I was talking about ratings, they'll believe that, huh?"

"That's for sure," Clay assured him. "How about Charles Patterson?"

"What about him?"

Clay looked surprised. "Didn't anyone tell you?"

"Tell me what?"

"Rex called with the jitters. Steven knows the whole story. His old man confessed. Course, after TWA's Perry Mason had figured it out."

Barney looked stricken. "Everything?"

"Everything."

"No wonder he decked me." Barney poured himself a drink and looked puzzled. "Why hasn't he gone to the authorities yet?"

"Maybe he has."

"Naw. They'd be talking to us. The media would sniff it out in a minute. He's said nothing."

Clay cautioned. "Yet."

Barney poured his drink down the bar sink. "Shit. This really ruins my celebration."

Clay gave him more bad news. "Another reason to ruin your fun: Rex is pretty pissed off."

"Pissed off? We just put her over the top! We just created more sympathy and love for this woman than the world had for Jackie O. when her husband croaked! Or when she croaked, for that matter."

"Dead Kennedys aren't the issue here," Clay reminded him. "We may have created an unbeatable candidate with this latest incident, but she got a good rap on the head, don't forget. She could have permanent damage."

"How so?"

Clay used his best news desk voice. "*After briefing Congress to-day, the President went back to the White House where she banged her head against the furnace for half an hour . . .*"

"Come on."

Clay was serious. "It could happen. Hell, she could even die."

"And what if she does?"

"Barney!"

"I mean it. I did what I contracted for. I fulfilled my part of the bargain. Life goes on. I've got a network to run."

"You're the coldest snake I've ever met in my life."

"And you're a shitty producer."

Barney poured himself another drink. Nothing was going to ruin his fun. He offered Clay one, who said it was too early. He drank from the Evian bottle near his chair. Barney was bothered, however, about Steven's knowledge of the real agenda. He wondered why Steven had remained silent. "It can't just be grief and worry. Do you think he's actually considering going along with it?"

"I doubt it. Always figured he'd be the hard sell. She'll be easier. She's the one who's craved power."

"Why has he stayed silent, then?" Barney said, looking out the window, more to himself than to Clay.

"Maybe he's waiting to talk to her first? She can't really speak yet, from what the doctors say."

"Then maybe I should talk to him first."

"And if he doesn't agree with you?"

Barney just smiled. "They'd lock him up if he told a story like this without corroboration."

Clay saw that he had a point. "Maybe that's why he's not spilled. He knows he'll be laughed out of the room." He finished his water. "So who is Rex going to run on the ticket with her?"

"Who the hell cares? I'm a Democrat anyhow, I don't much give a damn if she wins or loses."

c h a p t e r 20

"Daddy!" Sarah cried out to Steven from her usual perch on the side of Jonelle's hospital bed. "Dad, she's okay, Mom's okay!"

Steven, who was out in the hall helping Wyatt put new laces on his tennis shoes, jumped up. "What?"

"Look!" Sarah said, turning inside the door to look at Jonelle, "Mom's okay!"

Wyatt scooted in front of Steven. "Hey, Mom, can we go home now?"

"Jonelle, Jone?" Steven said as he approached the bed.

"Boy," Jonelle said with humor, "have I got a headache."

Steven kissed her. "I'll bet."

"What day is it?"

"November first. Election Day."

She attempted a smirk. "Quayle and Lott going to win?"

He smiled. "If my vote has anything to do with it."

"Mom, did you hear the CDs we brought you?" Wyatt asked, exuberantly.

"Mommy, we've been here since it happened. We knew you were

going to get better." Sarah waited for a reply, but none came. Jonelle's eyes closed again.

"Mom?" Wyatt said. "Don't go to sleep again."

Steven cautioned him to leave her be. "We don't want to wear her out. That was a good sign, she talked to us, she's going to be just fine."

They waited all afternoon for Jonelle to speak again, but she did not. The doctors told Steven that was one more good sign pointing toward recovery. Steven and his kids prayed all the harder.

Late that afternoon, in the furnished apartment Steven had rented for them on a week-by-week basis, he drank iced coffee in his undershorts, feet up on a window ledge, looking out at the rooftops of the Embarcadero, reassessing what to do. He'd decided to wait for Jonelle to make a decision with him, but he couldn't force her to be well, and he couldn't sleep nights. He'd gotten the answer to what the motive was behind this insane plot from his father, a man he'd not spoken to since leaving Virginia Beach, no matter how many times Charles called begging to be put through.

So he knew the Christian Alliance's plan, but what of Barney Keller and the things his father "washed his hands" of? He was dying inside, wondering what Barney would say—would he admit, deny, fudge, be cagey or forthcoming, devil be damned?

On impulse—and he did little on impulse—he picked up the phone. When the Network ONE operator answered in New York, he said, "I want Keller."

"Mr. Keller is at dinner, I'm afraid."

"You find him, page him, whatever. Tell him Steven Patterson is trying to reach him." He gave her the apartment number. "Tell him if I don't hear from him within one hour, I'm going to the authorities."

"Pardon me?"

"Authorities," he repeated, "as in the police, FBI, FCC, got it?"

"Yes, sir," the frightened voice answered.

The phone rang only four minutes later. "That was prompt," Steven said instead of hello.

"Intriguing message you left."

"I thought it was pretty clear."

"What do you want?"

"Lay our cards down on the table."

"Whose table?"

"Mine," Steven said. "I want you here tomorrow."

"Impossible."

"You want me to call Larry King?"

"He wouldn't believe you."

"He'd sure as hell be intrigued—your word—and I'll bet you anything that he'd investigate."

"Steve—"

"Steven."

Barney let out a deep breath. "I'd like to finish my dinner, if you don't mind. How about the same tomorrow night? Say eight o'clock, at, um . . . Charles Nob Hill. It's in the Clay-Jones apartment house, just ask anyone on the hill."

"Fine."

"Steven, how's Jonelle doing?"

"Go fuck yourself."

He picked up the *Examiner* and flipped through it. A lot about Gore and Feinstein. But he couldn't concentrate. He'd been at the hospital since five that morning, and he was dead tired. The kids were still there with Helen, who'd come to California with them. They'd be home soon, and he'd go back early in the morning. He usually read the paper to put himself out.

But something caught his eye. And there it was, for all eyes to behold, an editorial reprinted from the *Los Angeles Times* about a powerful woman named Jonelle written by another powerful woman named Arianna, the Pamela Harriman of the GOP. Arianna Huffington told the country what she could say publicly now that Dan Quayle and Trent Lott had been defeated, the same thing she'd been saying privately for years: that the GOP should dust off the cobwebs, take a good look that a female running for VP helped keep the Democrats in power, and to look to a woman as their standard bearer in 2008. But she now suggested a choice for that person: the most loved newswoman in America, Jonelle Patterson. It was a well-written piece, a terrific article, serious in tone—begging Jonelle to consider politics—and yet light enough to seem more a spirited plea for someone to awaken: *Look what's waiting for you!*

Steven cringed. He remembered the letter his father had shown him, Rex Heald seizing Arianna's innocent thought and twisting it to fit his own agenda. It was happening the way Rex hoped it would spin out: Articles like this would continue to appear, people would question Jonelle as to whether or not she would heed the call, Republican bigwigs would support her, campaign contributions would pour in, the tidal wave had begun to roll. And the tsunami would hit the beach called D.C. exactly eight years from now.

He fell into a troubled sleep. Tomorrow he'd face Barney Keller and force him to fit the last piece into the puzzle. And then he would decide how to expose him—them, all of them—and put them away forever.

chapter 21

Steven was already seated in the small, intimate back dining room of the restaurant Charles Nob Hill, just past a cozy wood-paneled bar, when Barney arrived fifteen minutes late. Steven acknowledged his appearance with a pronounced stare, which Barney ignored, greeting him cordially, as if they'd never had their phone conversation last night. After Barney ordered a Bloody Mary, he inquired if Steven didn't want something stronger than the water he was sipping. Steven did not answer. The waiter politely left the room. And Steven got right to it. "You know my father told me everything."

"Nice to see you too," Barney said. "Like this place? Was a private club, but it got overripe. The flowers make it inviting, don't you agree? Perfect place to share dinner with an intimate friend."

"The flowers are very nice," Steven said pointedly.

Barney shook out the folds of his linen napkin like a housekeeper beating a rug. Then he placed it on his lap. "Read Arianna Huffington's syndicated editorial yesterday?"

Steven nodded.

"Wasn't that interesting?" Barney was facetious. "I read that and said, what a marvelous idea."

"You're so goddamn smug."

"Anyway, it's a moot point if the candidate is unconscious, isn't it?"

"She's better." But Steven felt himself burning. "You have a lot of sympathy for someone who's made you millions."

"I paid her millions," Barney reminded. "You reaped a few rewards from those checks yourself. Dumped the station wagon for a new Jag I hear."

"I'm a pilot. I make good money myself."

"You're a loser next to Jonelle's numbers. And always in debt, I might add."

"I want to talk about the news."

"Specifically?"

"Those things that happened."

"What things?"

"News that Jone reported. News that just seemed to explode when she was on the scene. News that was—what's the word?—manipulated?"

"Pushed along," Barney offered. Then he nonchalantly broke a roll and dipped it in olive oil. "Just a little help. This is entertainment, remember, television. The carrot consommé is great, and there's a porcini-crusted lamb that's stuffed with pesto, my personal favorite."

The look of astonishment on Steven's face was not easy to contain. He was astounded at the gall, the ego of this man. They were talking about killing people and Barney dismissed it with a flourish and delved into the menu. "You *created* news!" Steven said, trying to wake him to reality.

"So what? It's not like it's the first time."

"What do you mean?"

Barney put his menu down. "Are you really this naive?"

"Yes, to something like this."

"Well, friend, time to pull your head out of the sand." He accepted his Bloody Mary from the waiter, lifted his glass toward Steven's disbelieving face, sipped, and continued. "Here, TV facts of life: Number one, this isn't something unique, as you perhaps have deluded yourself."

"What do you mean?"

"An example to illustrate: Nancy Kerrigan and Tonya Harding."

"I don't understand."

He leaned forward. "CBS had the highest overnights in the history of broadcasting the Olympics when those bitches took to the ice. And why?"

Steven shook his head. "Because of the personal drama that preceded it."

"Correct."

"And you're insinuating the whole thing was planned?"

"Simply brilliant, brilliantly simple. Hire a couple of morons, a couple of thugs who are willing to do some time—they're gonna spend most of their miserable lives in jail anyway, they know that —for a pot of money and you've just bought the notoriety to win in the ratings."

Steven laughed. "No, no, come on. CBS would never stoop that low. It's against the law, it's—" He stopped himself because he knew that, suddenly, he was sounding worse than naive, he was sounding downright silly. CBS was a huge conglomerate owned by another huge conglomerate. Who knew how many bad guys there were in the organization? One person—one Barney Keller—that's all it took, one guy with power who would "suggest" to someone else, who would whisper to yet another, who would pull money out of an account that could never be traced, who would pay the white-trash skater's greedy white-trash husband, who would then hire the team of fat white-trash hit men, who would do the job and botch it or whatever—at that point it didn't matter because it was already headline news.

Steven sat there, stunned.

"You don't want to believe it."

"That one's too easy. Kerrigan and Harding, it's too perfect. Tell me another."

"TWA 800."

That hit Steven in his heart; he'd lost seven friends on that plane, seven people he'd worked with and cared about. "What about 800?"

"Which new cable outfit went on the air just days before and no one was watching?"

"What?"

"Who cut their teeth on that story, who was broadcasting all night from the moment it happened?"

Steven dug back in his brain. "CNN?"

"Naw. They were ill prepared, like all of us. Think, who was new then, who got the praise in the papers? More to the point, who got an audience because of that crash?"

It hit him. "MSNBC."

"Now, you tell me Bill Gates doesn't have the money and the power to bring down a goddamned plane."

Steven was thunderstruck. He couldn't believe this man was even suggesting such a thing. "Come on."

"Answer my question," Barney said.

"I would imagine he's got the power to blow up the world if he wanted, but he wouldn't—" Steven's brain was swirling. "He wouldn't do something like that!"

"MSNBC would have sputtered along for months, maybe years, if they hadn't had an incident to launch them."

"You're crazy."

"Most visionaries have been called that."

"Visionary? You're a monster."

"Calling each other names is a puerile waste of time, don't you think?"

"The investigation into 800 would have found that!" Steven protested.

Barney lifted his menu again and muttered, "If a man has the money to blow a 747 out of the sky, he sure can pay off the FBI and the NTSB. Shall we order?"

Steven had the feeling that if he put anything in his stomach he would vomit. He took a drink of his water. Then he said, "Television may have lost its innocence with the death of Lee Harvey Oswald, and reached the lowest depths with you guys, but what you're trying to make me believe goes beyond all moral and ethical bounds. MSNBC—Bill Gates—murdering two hundred and thirty people, that's absurd."

"Just a theory, I could be wrong."

"You're just trying to justify your own crime."

"I said it is just a theory."

"To cover your own evil agenda."

"Think so?" Barney motioned for the waiter, who took his order. Steven said nothing, never even looked up. Barney ordered him the stuffed lamb loin.

When the waiter left, Steven said, "You had Imelda Marcos shot."

"Strong accusation. All I'll say is the incident involving Mrs. Marcos got Jonelle her place in the sun." Then he laughed. "Didn't hurt Imelda's career any either, come to think of it."

"The bus accident?"

"Bus mechanic could have been the guy who tapped Kerrigan, he was so stupid."

"But that writer who was killed, the one on the bus who was writing a book on the Christian cause. Why would you bump off someone on Rex Heald's side?"

"Pretend you and I are in a story session for a detective show. I'll say 'bumping him off'—as you put it—might be worth it to the bad guys to make it look like the anti-Christian element did it. You might say let's make this writer a turncoat, let's reveal that as he worked on his book it became less pro-Christian and more an exposé of the greed and corruption in the line of those clowns Jim and Tammy Faye. I'd say yeah, he was going to roast Rex and the Bible thumpers, and you'd say, great story point, he has to die!"

"Jesus. What kind of machine are you?"

"Creative. Next question?"

Steven said, "Tucker."

"Hopeless fag heroin addict. Had lots of enemies."

"Cardinal Riccio."

"Mighta become Pope. Had he lived. Probably made bigger news by dying."

Steven's head was swimming. "Molly Binenfeld."

"That was a personal favorite. What a story, so moving, all those Olympic dreams dying because of another girl's jealous mother."

"You did that one too!" Steven said with a raised voice. "I've got the proof on tape."

"You do? Then why haven't you taken it to the FBI?"

"I did, I gave it to Druey, I gave it to who I thought was the FBI, and he probably gave it to you. You know what I've got!"

Barney smiled. "The Gold Ring Collection. We could make money off those tapes, do an infomercial. Jonelle can say she was a second-rate reporter who was hungry for fame, and so she created her own news—and the tapes can show how you can do it too!"

"You miserable son of a bitch!" Steven wanted to kill him.

"Keep your voice down. This is a classy joint."

"The idea that you'd try to turn this back on her—"

"It would be believed faster than *your* story."

Steven knew he was right. Then he continued, "Regent University."

"Boom. Nice story, though. Conflict is good news."

"Was that kid, that Jake Hughes, was he a setup? He actually worked for Rex, didn't he? He was no more rebel than I am."

"You're naive, but you're clever. Why do you waste your time flying planes when you could open your own private dick shop?"

"Madeleine Albright? The bomb at her apartment house, way back that night Jonelle was in the car with her."

It shocked Barney. "Well, well, I'm impressed. Didn't think you'd figure that one out."

"And the abortion doctor story, when Jonelle was still with CNN. That too, right?"

Barney said nothing as he stuffed a piece of olive oil–drenched focaccia into his mouth.

"You look surprised. You look like you didn't think I knew that much."

"I must admit, you've been thorough."

"I have everything Alicia found out. I've got the documents on Saint Paul that got her killed. I've got tapes. I'm going to get more, and I'm going to see you rot."

"I'd speak to your wife first. Who knows? When she's well enough, she may want to go for it."

"For what?"

"The presidency."

Steven shook off the ludicrous notion. Then he asked, almost seeking a confidence, with no confrontation in his voice, "Why did you feel you had to do this? Jonelle was good enough on her own, in her own right. Why?"

Barney shrugged. "Truth is, she was okay. She's still okay, but she's really no great shakes as a reporter. Oh, she had a style, a charisma that was worth developing. But the fact is she never was, and never will be, Ed Murrow."

"She's the best reporter in the world today and you know it."

"She's certainly the most well known in the world, I'll grant you that. Ready for the next logical step. Look at Walters. Barbara's become the new Brooke Astor in the last few years, she's a social powerhouse in her own right these days, she'll play out her sunset years as the grande dame of New York society. That is the next logical plateau for someone her age. Someone of Jonelle's age goes into politics."

"Never."

Their dinners arrived. Barney ordered a glass of wine. Steven didn't look at his plate, while Barney dug in heartily. "Ah, great duck. Chinese five-spice powder, gives it a zing."

"What did you get from this?" Steven asked thoughtfully. "You don't care about the Christian Right any more than the agnostic left. What is this all about? Power? Money?"

Barney grinned. "I'm a greedy SOB, I'll admit. I've got a fortune already but I want more. Probably never be satisfied." He took a sip of the wine the waiter set on the table and smiled rapturously. "I like the game, the hit. Nothing makes my day like waking to terrific overnights." He looked lost for a moment as he pried duck flesh from the scrawny bones. "Tastes great, but it's a bitch to eat. Findley's the one doing this for money. He's dying of cancer, wants to take care of his big family. Gambled most of his earnings away over the years, now the asshole is desperate. He'll do anything for a buck. And has."

"Wait a minute," Steven said, it dawning on him. "He was at CBS . . . Tonya Harding!"

"Now you're wising up."

Steven pressed. "You need power. James needs money to die. What about Clay?"

A curious smile curled on Barney's face as the waiter poured him some Chianti. "Clay is doing this for fun."

"What do you mean?"

"He likes the challenge."

"Challenge? What, of not getting caught?"

"Naw, he's doing it for Rex."

"You're all doing it for Rex."

"Clay's got a thing for him."

"A what?"

"Thing. Interest, passion, desire. I think it's against your religion as well."

Steven gasped. "Rex Heald? My father's hero? The leader of the Christian Alliance that constantly preaches intolerance against gays?"

Barney put his fork down and rubbed his chin. "Good story, huh?"

"Rex is married," Steven protested.

"Steven, when are you going to learn that nothing is as it appears to be?" Barney leaned back in his chair and laughed. "Clayton Santangelo, video whiz boy, sucking the dick of the poster boy for the conservative right. I'll do the exposé one day, mark my words."

Steven said, "I thought Clay was your friend." Then he realized what a ridiculous notion it was that this man seated across from him, chewing on the duck bones in his fingers now, would be loyal to anyone. "Yeah, you know, you probably will."

"You don't want lamb? You should have said something. They have exceptional gnocchi, some old baba down in the basement shreds potatoes all day. They could make you a—"

"Jonelle's not going to run. We are going to expose you."

"That so?" He just laughed.

"You bastard." Steven was seething. "We will find someone who will listen. If not in the FBI, the Secret Service. The guy who questioned me yesterday would love to chew on this. We might even tell Hillary and Bill. Unlike you, they think Jonelle's a pretty good reporter. Barbara McMillan over at the FCC might really be interested. She's never been crazy about broadcasters."

"Don't waste your breath."

"I mean what I'm saying, I swear to God."

Barney's tone changed. "And I swear to God that if you do anything other than announce that Jonelle will accept the GOP's draft to serve her country, you won't live to hear the outcome of your investigation."

Steven wanted to tell the man not to threaten him, but no words came out. For at that moment he saw a look on Barney's face that frightened him to the core, shaking him more deeply than any manifestation of sinister evil he'd seen in the movies or read in a book. The man had just threatened his life, and he knew that he meant it. Look what he'd done already. Why did he think he and Jonelle would be immune to becoming notches on Saint Paul's belt as well?

"I think I know what you're thinking," Barney added, pulling a piece of duck skin through his teeth. "It would be the ultimate story, now, wouldn't it? Especially if it happened on camera."

"You wouldn't—"

"No, we wouldn't. If Jonelle runs for president like her country wants her to, we wouldn't even consider it."

Steven rose from his chair and started out.

"Damn good duck," Barney said, robustly.

Steven found himself walking on one of the piers near Fisherman's Wharf. He'd driven around aimlessly for a while, then parked at a space near the water, got out, and walked as far to the Bay as he could get without swimming in it. Ever since Barney had chilled him to the bone, he kept thinking about a book, one that he'd read years ago, *The Firm*. The proper law firm in the book turned out to be run by the mob. He had the same feeling running up his spine now because he felt he'd just faced the mob or worse. He'd seen the Tom Cruise movie they made from it. How did it end? Did the FBI help him or not? They had to do it on their own, didn't they? But didn't they also sail off into exile or something? He wanted justice, not a pot of gold on a Cayman island.

He went to a phone booth and dialed the hospital. What he heard from the nurse on duty on Jonelle's wing shocked and elated him. "Your wife has been chatting with the kids for over an hour now. We tried to reach you. She just seemed to come back."

Steven didn't even bother to go back to the car. He slid into a cab that was dropping people off at a fish restaurant and said, "San Fran General, fast!"

chapter 22

By the time Steven walked into the hospital room, he could see that a miracle had taken place. Jonelle's eyes were wide open, clear. Her lips were formed in a smile. Sarah sat on one side of her, Wyatt on the other, both eagerly filling her in on all that had happened—at least all that *they* knew—in the time she'd been "sleeping." The doctor stood beaming as well at the back of the room, and when he eyed Steven in the doorway, he nodded, said, "She's going to be fine, just don't tax her brain real hard right away, go easy on her," as he passed him, and left the family to their reunion.

Amidst shouts of, "Dad! Dad, Mom's okay and she remembers everything!" Steven walked to the bed and bent down, brushing Jonelle's hair with his hand before he kissed her, and whispered that he loved her.

"Are *you* okay?" she asked Steven.

He nodded.

"Are *we* okay?" she then voiced.

He nodded again, just to ease her worry.

"Mom, Potomac had his whole family and all his friends praying for you," Wyatt said.

Sarah rolled her eyes. "Oh, please."

"Did so!" Wyatt exclaimed.

"Thank him for me," Jonelle said with a grin to Sarah.

Sarah shook her head and turned to her brother. " 'Potomac' probably drove Mom's ambulance and gave her her MRI too."

"That's ridiculous," Wyatt said. "He's not that cool."

Sarah gave up.

Jonelle said, "What are you kids doing about school?"

Sarah laughed. "Not much."

Wyatt looked stricken. "If we go back home, do we have to go right back to school? Could you say you're sick for a little longer?" he asked his mother.

Steven sat down on the bed. "How much do you remember?"

"Most of it," she said, "at least I think I do. Mrs. Clinton came to see me. Or did I dream it?"

"She was here," Steven assured her. "And she's fine. You saved her life."

Jonelle said, "So the kids told me. But what's happened since? In the days I've been so out of it?"

"It can wait, honey," he said, indicating with a nod of his head that he didn't want to discuss it in front of the kids. "Doc told me to go easy on your brain."

"My brain's bursting with curiosity."

"Sounds more like fear," he pointed out. Then he assured her. "Don't worry. It's all going to work out. I promise you."

"Steven? Who won the election?"

"Who do you think?"

"Sorry."

"I know. But it was by a smaller margin than expected."

"The GOP should have run Chris Whitman with Quayle."

"Honey, you don't know the dangerous territory on which you're treading."

"Huh?"

"I'll explain later."

"Dad?" Sarah said.

"What, squirt?"

"Can we go back home now? I miss school."

Steven shook his head. "Sick kid." Then he hugged both kids and said, happily, "Yeah, let's go home."

Over their shoulders he looked at his wife, and he smiled an expression of confidence. But privately, inside his heart, he wondered, *But what happens then?*

She was released from the hospital two days later, but Steven obeyed the doctor and went easy on her, not wanting to upset or worry her by telling her of Barney Keller's threat. Or of the plot to make her president. Of the accident, she told him she'd seen a figure up on the catwalk above the dance floor, and on his hand was the gold ring. That's when she realized, that's when she dove for Hillary, that's when everything went black. He had surmised as much, and again assured her everything was going to be all right.

He went back to work by bidding for the flight that would take them back to D.C., and piloted the 767 from San Francisco to Saint Louis. The kids loved when Steven's voice over the loudspeaker said, "This is Captain Patterson, and on behalf of the cockpit and cabin crew, I'd like to welcome you, and thank you for choosing TWA today . . ."

Wyatt was always a little nervous about flying, and this was no exception. To take his mind off it, after lunch a wonderfully wacky flight attendant with flyaway hair named Georgeann took Wyatt and Sarah to the cockpit, where they watched Dad in action. Lenore, the other girl working the first-class cabin, delighted them with hot fudge sundaes heaped with whipped cream and toasted walnuts, but Wyatt devoured most of Sarah's. Touchdown in Saint Louis was flawless, and Wyatt proudly told everyone getting off the plane, "My dad did that."

In the Ambassador Club where they waited for their connecting flight, they met people Steven had talked about for years. Hostesses Jane, Cathy, and Mary—all fans of Jonelle's—kept Jonelle busy with questions about her trauma. Michael the bartender brought the kids sodas, James gave them pretzels, and Wyatt decided, after talking to them, he wanted to work for an airline, but not as a pilot. He liked it even better on the ground.

Steven and Jonelle sat together behind the kids on the flight to National, and he started filling her in on what had come to pass with his father. Jonelle had wondered why Charles and his wife hadn't come to San Francisco, and she now learned why. And now that she knew, she wouldn't have wanted them there anyway; she said she hoped she'd never see Charles Patterson again, for she felt more betrayed than ever in her life. "God," she remarked, "we're losing parents left and right." She didn't mean to be flip, for she knew how deeply wounded Steven was by the fact that his father was on the side of the enemy, and she could only give him her support and the few words that came to her. "He's a sick man, like so many of them," she said, by inference suggesting that one day he might get well.

In the terminal at National, Barbara Gordon again greeted Jonelle, as she had so many times in the past, with a new mystery. "I don't need it," Jonelle told her, "I'm living one myself right now."

In the Washington Flyer cab on the way home to 16th Street, Jonelle felt ready to burst with questions, but she knew she couldn't risk the kids hearing any of it. Charles and Alma Patterson were their grandparents, and she could not desecrate that bond. Her rage was kept inside.

Once home, however, after the kids went to bed, in the privacy of their room, they could finally talk openly and without reserve. And she was shocked. "President? President of the U.S.? Me?"

"You."

She laughed. "It's absurd."

"No, it's not. The idea of it isn't absurd at all. A woman was just elected V.P. Look at that article the other day. Arianna is right, it is a very good idea. You'd be great."

"It's crazy."

"What Rex and those other guys have done is crazy, but the end purpose—to get you to run—isn't crazy at all."

She tried to let it sink in. "President?" she repeated, almost stupefied. It just wouldn't penetrate her brain. Yet, at the same time, it was the perfect answer to what she'd been stumped over for so long now, the reason why they'd made her America's most trusted newsperson. "President," she again repeated, her voice vacant and dry. "My God."

It was a fairly warm night for November in D.C., but Jonelle felt frozen by the time Steven related Barney Keller's threat to them in San Francisco, so chilled to the bone that she had to put the winter-weight duvet on the bed. When she crawled under, Steven sat on top of it next to her, and saw in her eyes a vacant look that he knew was not a result of the blow to her head but rather of all that he'd just told her. Then she asked, "Am I any good at all?"

"What?" He didn't understand the question.

"It's all been a sham, my whole career . . . has been a lie. I didn't find those stories. Even the abortion clinic, they were already using me even then. Mrs. Marcos almost died to get me a lousy Emmy."

"Honey, you can't doubt yourself."

"How can I do anything but? They picked me, chose me, chose *us*, not for any ability on my part but for the fact that we're the perfect Christian couple to occupy 1600 Pennsylvania Avenue."

"Your skills had everything to do with it. When you add up the hundreds of stories you've done over the years, the ones they had a hand in are only a few."

"I feel that everything I believed is a mockery. I don't feel confident at all suddenly. It's like I'm a lie myself."

"I hate them for this more than anything. They have no right to do this to you."

She felt through the covers as he pulled her to him. She derived strength from the muscles of his body. He was her anchor now. Holding on to him, this independent powerhouse of a woman was sure she could get through anything. "Steven, what are we going to do? He's threatened our lives."

"I've spoken to that FBI agent, Jim Kallstrom, in Bangkok. He can't get back, but he gave me the name of a guy—Don Woolf— who is his partner."

She looked skeptical.

He rubbed her shoulder. "Honey, we have to trust someone."

"The kids, I'm afraid for the kids."

"I won't let anyone hurt them."

"Barney told you he'd kill us."

"What's the choice, Jone? You want to call Rex right now and sign up? Tell him you're in? Hold a news conference tomorrow and tell the world you're running? That's the alternative. Gear up for the primaries in a few years. You ready?"

"Steven, don't shout at me."

"Talk sense."

"It isn't sensible to risk death!"

"Honey, there's no alternative. Could you live with yourself knowing what we know and keeping it in? Even if you didn't do what they want, even if you didn't run?"

She closed her eyes. "No." It was simple, but it was the only answer. Then she seemed to recall something and said, "My fortune."

"Your what?"

"Fortune cookie. At the event in San Francisco, we all got a fortune cookie. I remember mine: *The offer may overwhelm, but only the fool answers in haste.*"

"Prophetic."

"Wise words."

He kissed her and she responded with a burst of emotion that erupted from deep within her. She kissed him back as though she was on fire, and that flame ignited passion that burned hot. She kicked off the covers so his body could find hers, and the goosebumps were back but now because of tingling pleasure, not the cold. He kissed her neck, her shoulders, her breasts. The nipples hardened and he took them into his lips lovingly, licking tenderly to stimulate her more. She did the same to him, burying her face against the rock solid hardness of his pectoral muscles, and heard him moan as she moved lower and lower on his body.

She took him with her mouth, warming him with pleasure that removed him from the danger, the fears, the problems, and put him somewhere on the outskirts of heaven. When he could stand it no longer, he pulled away, took her head in his hands, looked into her eyes, and whispered passionately, "I adore you." Then he pressed his body to hers, and entered her slowly and lovingly, joining them together as one.

What seemed like an eternity later, she nestled against his shoulder. "Good night," she whispered dreamily.

"You'd really make a heck of a president," he said. "I almost regret that it can't happen."

"Mmmmmm," was the response, and she fell asleep there with her head on his shoulder. But he didn't close his eyes all night.

At 8:00 A.M. on the 10th of November, 2000, Steven answered the front door in his sweats and a T-shirt. Standing there was a well-groomed delivery boy who was holding a letter from the White House. Steven took the letter up to Jonelle, to whom it was addressed, and watched her curiously as she read a handwritten note from the First Lady. When she finished, her eyes twinkled as she told Steven, "I'm being given the Presidential Medal of Freedom at a state dinner this Saturday. From the President himself. My God."

"My God, indeed."

"Congratulations," the voice said to Jonelle.

She looked up. Facing her was Barney Keller. She'd just bought herself two dresses for the state dinner, a slinky black Donna Karan and a deep green Calvin Klein, and was having lunch in Nordstrom's café at the Pentagon City Mall trying to decide which to wear. The last person she expected to see was Keller. The terrible surprise showed on her face.

"Don't be afraid," he said, "we're not enemies. May I?" He sat down even though she didn't answer. "When are you coming back to work?"

She wanted to answer *never* but she remembered what Steven had drilled into her: make them think we're playing along with it. "Soon."

"We may not have you for long," he said, "so we want to get as much bang for our buck while you're still ours."

She played along. "How is this supposed to go? What's the script?"

"Rex will be talking to you after your White House honor. He'll take over. First, though, I think you ought to respond to Arianna Huffington's article."

"How?"

"Call her and tell her you're interested. The GOP will jump at it. Everyone knows you'd win."

"Mrs. Huffington is under the illusion that I'm actually a good newsperson. She doesn't know what you did, she doesn't understand that I'm a fraud. She has no clue as to your hidden agenda."

"Jonelle."

"Go away. Please, just go away."

"Jonelle, this worries me. This attitude. There's still too much anger, too much—"

She had to set her fork down to keep from plunging it into his face. She'd reached her breaking point. "It *is* too much, you're damned right, too much for me to pretend, too much for me to act, too much for me to lie!" She felt everything Steven had ordered her to do going down the drain as her emotions took over. She wasn't a newsperson now, she was a woman who felt she had to say what she believed in her heart or she'd explode. "I won't do it. I can't do it." Women at every table were turning their heads in her direction. "You're the sickest man I've ever known and I'll destroy you and your insane, deceitful plan, everything you and those other monsters cooked up, we'll get you all. We'll see the Four Horsemen burn in hell!"

He just waited, saying nothing, until she realized she was making a spectacle of herself, and she sat back down. She hadn't even realized she'd gotten to her feet, she was so energized with hatred.

"Well," he finally said, softly, when the other heads had gone back to their quiche. "I thought for sure that, in the end, the allure of going down in the history books would prevail over a woman who has been so hell-bent on power and fame."

"They're not the most important things in my life."

"That so?"

"You underestimated me, Mr. Keller."

"How so?"

"Unlike Rex or my father-in-law, who call themselves such, I'm really the only Christian around. Funny, that was part of the criteria I had to meet, and now it turns out to be precisely the reason you can't have me. I'm just too good for you. I have honor, the way God meant Christians to be."

"Honor is every loser's middle name."

"God forgive you."

"Listen, you're upset, it's understandable. I'll give you a little time."

"Time won't help. There is something you need to know about me."

"And what is that?"

"I would rather die than lose my integrity."

Barney and Clay made their way through the bowels of Sloan-Kettering and finally found Findley's room. "Hey, Jim, you look better," Clay said, greeting the skeleton in the bed. Barney entered behind him and said nothing.

"I'm too mean to die. They're letting me out in the morning."

Clay said, "That means you can come to the White House with us tomorrow night."

James was perplexed. "White House? What for?"

Barney spoke up. "She's getting the Presidential Medal of Freedom."

"Jonelle? No shit!" Some color brightened up James's face. "Nobody tells me anything."

"Bill's pretty grateful she saved his wife," Clay explained. "Giving them an overnight in the Lincoln Bedroom on top of it."

"Shit," James said, "and they didn't even have to contribute a million bucks for it."

Barney nodded. "Those days are long gone."

Clay added, "It takes a scandal . . ." But no one laughed.

James eyed them for a moment, and then his tone turned suspicious. "Okay, fellas, what's wrong? I know you guys love me, but this ain't no picnic in the park, this place. This has got to be heavy or you'd have waited to meet me at the corner bar."

Barney was forthright. "She knows everything and she's refused."

James expected that. "Give her time."

"I said that," Barney assured him. "But last night I told myself to face facts. This isn't going to happen. Rex worried from the start. We picked the wrong girl."

"Jesus." He looked as sick again as when they'd walked in.

"I still think she may turn around," Clay said with hope. "They're in a no-win situation this way."

Barney's tone was ironic. "So are we."

James asked, "How so? Why are you so sure it's never going to happen?"

"They've talked with the FBI," Barney informed him.

James gasped, "No."

"Yes," Clay corrected him.

"Christ Almighty." James reached over and drank some water from his tray.

"We have a decision to make," Barney said.

James was swimming with fear. "Jesus. Jesus, Barney, what will Rex say? I mean, if we—"

"Leave Rex up to me," Clay said. "I can handle him."

Barney folded his arms. "We have to decide here and now, gentlemen."

James was getting angry. "Shit. After all that work!"

"You got paid," Barney reminded him.

James looked wistful suddenly. "I kinda wanted to see her run."

Barney reminded him, "You're not going to live that long."

"Doc says it's in remission."

"Congratulations." Then Clay took on a heavy tone once again. "Okay, guys, we know what we have to do."

James looked ambivalent, but finally gave in to reason. "You want Saint Paul to do it?"

Clay immediately said, "No. He's too old, couldn't get him in the White House gate the way I've arranged it."

James looked dazzled. "White House? You arranged it for the White House?"

Barney said, "Never underestimate the power of determination. Especially when your ass is on the line."

Clay nodded. "The same kid we used in Paris, we're turning him into a Marine by the time the party starts. He was down to the beach house yesterday. He'd do anything for Jesus. Or for Rex."

"This is asking a lot," James reminded him. "He'll get life. If he doesn't get shot himself."

"He's willing to die as a martyr for the cause."

Barney said, "I hope he does." Then he looked at James and explained. "He's kinda like the Palestinian kid whose mother straps a bomb to after breakfast and sends him off to blow up a bus in Jerusalem."

James got it. "Yeah, telling him he'll be a saint, the more Israelis he knocks off."

"Right," Clay agreed, "but this kid's no Palestinian, he's our own homegrown Christian variety."

Barney assured them, though, "Same kind of crazy."

James still looked worried. "Can we trust him? Those fucking Arabs actually believe that Allah shit. This kid that committed? I mean, in Paris he knew he'd get away."

Barney said, "If needed, we'll kill him ourselves before he talks."

Barney looked antsy suddenly. The smell of the place was getting to him, and they'd talked enough. "So, gentlemen, then it's done. Hell, one thing for sure, we're going to get the ratings of the century."

James was delighted. "On camera. In the East Room no less. Never heard a better pitch in my life."

Clay looked pumped. "I've got to get on it."

"See you at Bill and Hillary's, Jimmy."

chapter 23

"Steven? Should I wear pearls or the Elsa Peretti?"

"Who won the dress competition?"

"Donna."

"What color's the Peretti?" He stepped from the shower stall, drying off.

From the bedroom he heard her say, "Silver. I think she only does silver."

He called, "The pearls. Basic, you know."

She held them up to her ears in front of the mirror. He was right. Then she dropped one and bent to the floor to find it, which was no easy task on the Berber rug.

"You're a mess," Sarah said to her mother, watching all this while sprawled on Jonelle and Steven's bed.

"Thanks, that's just what I need." Jonelle's voice rose from somewhere out of Sarah's range of vision. "Found it."

"Mom, cool off."

Jonelle rose again and wiped her brow. "You're right, it's only the White House, it's only the President of the United States who is going to hand me the highest honor in the land, it's only the entire press corps I'll be in front of, and the queen of Norway and her entourage."

"Where's Norway?" Wyatt asked, just entering.

"Scandinavia," Steven answered, wrapped in a white towel, slicking his hair back with gel.

"Is that by Alba Kerkee?" Wyatt asked.

Steven stopped, mid-slick. "Don't you go to school?"

Sarah proudly said, "It's in Europe. Sort of. Above England. It's cold there."

"I was there once," Jonelle said, examining how the pearls looked on her ears. "Did a story on a guy who owned an antique shop in Oslo that the queen, come to think of it, frequented. I'll have to tell her that. Lars something."

"They're all named Lars," Steven added.

"Breda-Aas, that was it. He was a tour guide in his spare time, took tourists through Finland and Sweden and then on to the Soviet Union when it was still Soviet. Turned out he was really a Norwegian spy."

"I don't remember that," Steven said, slipping his undershorts up under the towel, then dropping it.

"He was so cute and sweet and unassuming," Jonelle said, "you'd never have guessed."

"He go to jail?" Wyatt asked, expecting by the tone of his voice to hear a juicy James Bond story.

"No. By the time it came out, the Iron Curtain had melted and no one much cared anymore. He still sells chandeliers. Okay, where are my shoes?"

While she looked everywhere for her new black pumps, Sarah said, "I wish we could go."

"They're going to tape it," Steven said, hoping that might be a consolation.

"It's our mom. We should be there."

"Sarah," Jonelle said, sitting up to slip her feet into the shoes, "I agree with you, but we don't make the rules. Maybe Sonja doesn't like kids."

"Who's Sonja?" Sarah asked.

"Queen of Norway."

Wyatt said, "*You're* getting the medal."

Jonelle shrugged. "Well, maybe she has a lot of guests she dragged along with her."

"You're not their mom," Sarah said.

"Honey," Jonelle explained, exasperated, "this was a dinner in her honor long before I had anything to do with it. They're just killing two birds with one stone."

"It would be so cool to sleep over there too," Wyatt said. "Why can't we?"

Sarah chirped, "We weren't invited there either."

"Lincoln only had one bed," Jonelle explained.

Wyatt asked, "You guys taking backpacks on your overnight?"

Steven laughed. Jonelle said, "I never really thought of overnights as anything but ratings. I've been in TV too long."

"You look good, Mom," Wyatt said.

She winked at him. "Sharp eye."

Steven slid into his tuxedo pants and pulled the already-attached suspenders up over his shoulders. "I don't understand how you can wear Jockey shorts under a tux," Jonelle complained.

Steven looked at the kids and rolled his eyes.

"I'd wear silk boxers," she said.

"Next time you wear a tux," he said, "you do that."

The kids laughed.

"I mean something classy," Jonelle added.

"Who's gonna be looking?" Steven said, and the kids laughed again.

"You do look pretty sexy with those suspenders and no shirt on," she admitted.

Wyatt made a farting noise with his mouth.

Steven let Jonelle help him put the studs into his shirt, and asked the kids, "Now you guys know we're going to leave before Auntie Helen gets here. She'll run over when she gets back from her bridge club."

"Dad," Sarah said, "Helen can barely walk."

"She's eighty," Wyatt said, making it sound ancient.

"She's sixty-seven," Jonelle corrected him, "and she's no slower than I am."

"Potomac's sitter is twenty-four and beautiful."

Jonelle said, "So go stay with him."

Then Sarah asked, "Mom? Why don't you ever talk about when you were our age?"

The room filled with silence. Steven decided not to help Jonelle out of it. He waited for her to answer. She finally said, "It's a time I don't like to remember."

"Why?"

"Yeah, why?" Wyatt added. "Didn't you like being a kid, Mom?"

Steven stared at Jonelle. She wanted him to say something, but he didn't. Finally, she said, "I had a lot of problems at that time."

Sarah's ears perked up. "I heard the bell."

"Lucky you," Steven said to Jonelle, "*saved* by the bell."

"The limo's early!" Jonelle said in a panic. "I've got to check my makeup and I never finished packing the things we'll need for morning—"

"Hey, baby," Steven said to Sarah in a movie-gangster voice, "go stall 'em awhile, okay?"

"Sure," Sarah said, giggling, and Wyatt followed her out.

When Steven started to tie his bow tie, he watched Jonelle packing the overnight bag. And that's when the reality that had never been far from the surface hit her. "They're going to be there. Barney, Clay, Findley, without their horses. It's not going to be easy."

"Rex won't be there," he added.

"That supposed to make me feel better?"

"Agent Woolf told us what to do: play it cool. This is a great honor for you and you can't let anything mar it."

She thought for a moment as he grabbed his jacket and slipped into it. "Steven, there's something—" But she stopped herself and zipped the small suitcase closed.

"Something what?"

"Nothing."

"Sure?"

"Yes."

He picked up the bag and offered his arm. "I'm going to be the proudest man in the world tonight."

She grinned. "I didn't think I'd feel so . . . well, I've got but-terflies."

"You are a butterfly. And I love you."

And they started down the stairs.

In the limousine, Steven held Jonelle's hand. It was a beautiful, crisp night in the District of Columbia, and Steven asked the driver to take them "the long way," around the monuments, so they wouldn't arrive too early. They drove down to the Lyndon B. John-son Memorial Grove to get his favorite view of the Washington Monument, past the Jefferson Memorial, and just viewing the lighted buildings made the journey even more thrilling. They basked in the knowledge of what an honor this was for her, and felt like kids who were experiencing something bigger than life for the first time in their life.

Until they were finally nearing the White House. That's when Jonelle suddenly said, "I can't keep it in any longer. I feel like I'm lying to you."

Steven had no idea what she was talking about. "What?"

"I started to tell you just before we left."

"Yes?" He stared at her a moment, then said, "Driver, would you put the partition up, please?"

The window rose.

Jonelle then told him of her run-in with Barney Keller at Nord-strom's café two days ago. She told him she'd done exactly what Steven had asked her not to do, what the FBI had expressly forbid-den her to do: She told him to take his plan and shove it.

"You really made him believe it?" Steven probed.

"I think so. I was very strong."

Steven looked sick. "But, honey, you know the danger you've put yourself in? You don't turn these guys down. Remember how he threatened me? Even Kallstrom initially told me to play along till they can get them."

They were almost under the portico. They were waiting for the car in front of them to unload its passengers. "Steven, I just snapped, I came apart. I couldn't take it, I wanted to kill him, wanted to murder him! I was outraged and crazy, I'm sorry."

He grasped her hand again. "It's okay, it's okay. I'm sure he didn't really believe you, these guys won't give up. We'll see how they act tonight, how they respond to you. We'll talk to them after the ceremony, after dinner, let them think we're still considering it, we haven't closed our minds to—"

"Excuse me? Sir?" It was the driver on the speaker. "We have arrived at the White House."

"Thank you."

Mrs. Gore was on her way out. She explained that she had a previous engagement but had stopped at the White House purposely to congratulate Jonelle.

"Congratulations to *you*," Jonelle returned.

"We won an election. You saved a life."

"It's a great honor," Jonelle said, modestly.

"The highest you can get," Tipper replied. "And well deserved." She asked how Jonelle was feeling, talked about the kids for a few minutes, and then mentioned the article pointing to Jonelle for a future run at the presidency. "Everyone's been talking about 2008. That's what happens when the ballots are counted, they suddenly jump to the future. You interested?"

"Never," Jonelle replied.

Tipper feigned relief. "Well, if you decide to do it, make sure it's after Al and Dianne have completed all eight years. Don't you dare run in '04."

Jonelle teased. "Scared, huh?"

"Honestly, I think you could win. Dianne's sort of paving the way, the big breakthrough. About time a woman became president, don't you think?"

Jonelle agreed with that. "Yes, but—"

"But nothing. I like it. The new issue of *Time* is going to say the same thing."

Steven blinked. "What?"

Tipper said, "An article on why you're the woman to watch. Your champion Arianna is interviewed."

Steven smiled because he thought the First Lady–elect would

think he was nuts not responding favorably to the exciting news. He wished he could tell her it scared them to death.

"Why not Congress in 2004?" Tipper suggested. "Senator, governor—"

"Mayor of D.C. maybe," Jonelle kidded, "so I can fix the potholes I keep wrecking tires in."

"Best idea yet!" Tipper exclaimed, and then was told by a White House aide that her car was waiting. "Gotta run. Again, congrats. Al's inside already, have a wonderful evening." And she was off.

"We'll try," Jonelle said to Steven in a deadpan voice.

But her spirits began to lift as they walked into the East Room. Her entrance was greeted by a smattering of applause, and the Marine Band was playing a beautiful lush waltz in the background as well-wishers offered her their best. Everyone was proud of her, beaming at her, starstruck, in awe of her.

Then, suddenly, the band struck up "Hail to the Chief," signaling the entrance of the President and First Lady, and Jonelle began to be filled with pride and wonder that this was, tonight, really all about her. . . .

Five hours later, after an attempted assassination had shocked the world and altered the evening and Jonelle's life forever, she and Steven emerged on the same steps from which they entered. The turn of events precluded any overnight in the Lincoln Bedroom. In the panic and chaos that had overshadowed the evening, all plans had gone out the window. The doorman politely apologized and asked if they needed a car. They said they had decided to walk home, they lived right up 16th Street, and it was a cool but beautiful night. They didn't even bother taking the time to have their overnight bag returned. They wanted to get out of there fast, while Barney, Clay, and James were still inside.

When they passed through the White House gates, they were attacked by a barrage of reporters clamoring for news of the shooting. Everyone wanted to know what had happened from an eyewitness POV, and Jonelle responded that she'd talk to them in a minute, she needed to make a call. With that, she jumped into the

front passenger seat of one of Network ONE's vans, pulled her cell
phone from her little clutch bag to use as a prop, making sure the
keys were in the ignition. When she nodded to Steven, he got into
the driver's seat, started the van, and took off, unplugging twenty
cables that dangled from the back of the vehicle like tin cans and
crepe paper after a wedding. The astonished reporters stood speech-
less.

And as the van moved past the glowing Jefferson Memorial and
over the 14th Street Bridge to Virginia, Jonelle knew they'd never
be able to return to Washington again—until they'd gotten the Four
Horsemen.

Trouble was, would the Four Horsemen get them first?

Part Three

chapter 24

"What are we going to do about the kids?" Steven said, nervously driving the Network ONE van.

Jonelle answered, "It's all I thought about while we were waiting down there. I think I know." She picked up her cell phone and asked information for the number of a Gallindo, Victor, on 16th Street in the District.

"Why?"

"The kids are in danger too, Steven! They'd be perfect, kidnap them, use them against us."

"I mean why the piano teacher?"

"Because he's a good man. Because we can trust him. The kids love him. Where else is Helen going to take them?" She paused while she listened to the recording giving her the number. "And because no one will look there." She dialed. "Besides, he adores them."

He answered on the first ring. "Victor? It's Jonelle Patterson. Yes, I know, that's why I'm calling. Victor, I'm in a lot of trouble. I can't tell you what it is, but you must trust me that it's very real. I need your help. I need you to go down to the house right now and help Helen, our sitter, get the kids to your place. I need you to keep

them there for a while, because that's the only place I know where
they'll be"—her voice cracked—"safe."

Steven said, "Tell him to be careful, protect them, tell them we
love them—"

Jonelle did all that. The piano teacher didn't ask for details on
what this was all about, he only assured them that he was there for
them and would do exactly as they asked. Jonelle explained she'd
call Helen and inform her of the plan before he got there.

Steven said, "Tell him about the money."

"Victor," Jonelle repeated, "there's cash in an envelope in the
third drawer down on the right in the bedroom armoire. Use whatever you need."

When he said, "How do I get in touch with you? How do the
kids reach you?" Jonelle shrugged and looked at Steven.

"We'll have to call you," Steven shouted.

"Where are you going?" Victor asked.

And it hit Jonelle: They didn't have a clue.

Before she hung up, Steven took the phone. "Victor, listen, when
you get to the house, go down to my workroom in the basement,
the stairs are off the kitchen. There is a locked file cabinet in the
corner, you can't miss it. The key—listen carefully—is on top of the
big insulated pipe above it and to the left. Inside are tapes and en-
velopes filled with photos and such. Dump them all in a trash bag
and drag them over to your place. Get Wyatt to help you, he'll love
the intrigue."

"Okay," Victor said. "What do you want me to do with the
stuff?"

"Get it to me. I'll have to think how."

"All right."

Steven said, "There's some danger in this, Victor. I want you to
know that."

"It's all right. I'm glad I can help."

Emphatically, Steven added, "Whatever you do, don't go back
to the house, or let the kids go near it, okay? Hurry now, you only
have an hour or so at most." Steven was judging from the time it
had taken the Secret Service to question them. Barney and the others
would be let loose any minute.

Jonelle took the phone again. "Victor, God bless you for this."

Then they called the house. Helen answered, distraught. "We have been so worried."

"Helen, I want you to listen to me closely," Jonelle said, her voice trembling. "I want you to do exactly as I say. Victor Gallindo, the kids' piano teacher, will be there any minute now. I want you to . . ."

They gave Helen the instructions and didn't dare risk taking the time to speak to the kids. The faster they got out of there the better. When they hung up, Steven felt emotion bursting and he knew Jonelle did as well, but there were practical matters to attend to. "We have to ditch this thing. Talk about what not to use as a getaway car. We're running from Network ONE in a van emblazoned with their logo."

"This was all I could think of. Couldn't very well ask a cab driver to take us on the run."

"Gotta get rid of it."

"What will we exchange it for?"

"I could manage stealing a plane. But a car's another story."

Then Jonelle got an idea. "National! We'll rent a car at the airport."

"We're at the Pentagon, we passed the airport. One thing I learned from cops-and-robber movies is that you don't turn back in the direction they're chasing you from. Besides, National's a ghost town this late. Car rentals won't be open."

She saw a sign for the Glebe Road exit. "I know!" she shouted. "Get off here, turn—"

He followed orders. "Where are we going?"

"There." She pointed. "Quaker Lane, the National Hospital Medical Center."

"Huh?"

"One thing people do is leave their keys in the car when they pull up to the emergency room."

"My God."

"I hate to do it to someone, but—"

"Trading them for a nice van equipped with about a hundred

thousand dollars' worth of broadcasting equipment isn't such a bad deal."

"I just hope they agree."

But he applied the brakes just as he was about to turn into the massive hospital's emergency entrance. "Jone!" He looked as though he'd just had a brilliant inspiration. "This van, it may come in handy."

"How?"

"Think about it, all the equipment."

It occurred to her too. "You're right. It's like having our own private editing room."

"With broadcast capabilities," Steven reiterated. And with that, he backed up and returned to the highway.

"Can we get to Richmond in this?" she asked.

He pondered it. "Think so. It's not like they're going to call the state police and put out an APB. They're going to be looking for us themselves."

"That's what I'm afraid of," she said.

Passing the Potomac Mills shopping complex made Steven more worried. "The ONE logo on this thing," he said about the van, "it's gotta go. I wish a paint store was open at this hour."

"Yeah, spray cans," she agreed.

"Where would we get them?"

"Aren't Wal-Marts open all night?"

"Where do you think we'd find one?"

"You kidding? The country's crawling with them."

He laughed, "Any coming up?" She looked at the East Coast and Vicinity map that was in the glove compartment. "Dale City sounds about right. We're almost there."

They found the Wal-Mart in Dumfries. A fat girl with teased hair had to open a caged display to allow Steven to purchase the paint. Before she turned the key, the dedicated salesgirl made him promise he wouldn't use it to "tag."

"Huh?"

"Scrawl graffiti."

He pulled on the lapel of his tux. "Do I *look* like I'm going to put gang slogans on an overpass?"

It went over her head. She was programmed to continue: "And we here at Wal-Mart highly recommend American Accents by Rust-Oleum because their colors are really great."

"I want gloss white, any brand you have."

"Yes, sir. How many?"

"Five cans."

It took him nearly twenty minutes to check out because only one lane was open, it was backed up with people—what were they all doing buying milk at this hour?—and every one of them seemed to need a price check or had a check-writing problem. In line, Steven loaded up with candy bars, Sun Chips, and Diet Rite from the sale displays to each side of him. He was suddenly feeling hungry, and just now realized they'd never gotten to eat dinner at the White House.

When he found Jonelle in the lot, cleaning off the lettering on the van with a towel in her evening dress, he laughed. "If Donna Karan could see you now."

She laughed right back. "And Joseph Abboud should know you're the only man ever to buy spray paint at a Wal-Mart at one-thirty A.M. in one of his tuxedos."

Then they set to work, shaking the cans, spraying out the lettering. The white covered well, closely matching the original paint. They didn't worry about the license plates, because they knew the police wouldn't be looking for them. It was the visibility of the news van they were concerned with.

Two stoned teenagers sitting in a car watched them in wonder.

Back on the highway, Jonelle told him she had been thinking while he was in the store. "About tomorrow. Or maybe not tomorrow, but surely in a few days."

"Hello?" He didn't have a clue as to what she was talking about.

"Me. Us. Being gone. The shooting will be the big news for a long time, but sometime soon the press is going to talk about us, they're going to want my version of what it was like to see the Marine draw the gun. Stuff like that."

"And that neither of us ever went home after the party."

She nodded. "And why you're not flying planes and I'm not in the newsroom."

"And that a van is missing."

"And our kids have vanished."

"We don't know how long we're going to be doing this—this running."

She nodded again, defiantly. "Damn them! They should be the ones on the run, they should be the hunted!"

He took her hand. "We need a cover. A story."

She said, "We don't want everyone in the world looking for us. That could be more dangerous."

He thought awhile. Then he said, "Betty Ford."

"What about her?"

"That's the story. Betty Ford. You're in Betty Ford."

"The clinic?" She gave an expression that was half gasp, half laugh. But she knew in an instant that he'd hit it right on the head, the perfect cover. "Wow, if we just tell the press I've gone to Betty Ford for—what, four weeks?"

"Six sounds like a better recovery time."

She was energized. "Everyone will be talking about whether it is pills or booze or both, and that'll take the onus off the truth."

"People will think the White House experience put you over the edge."

"It almost did."

"Great thing," he said, "is you're protected at Betty Ford. No one can find out you're not really a patient."

"God, Steven, it's brilliant."

He shrugged. "Too bad we *couldn't* go there. It would be the safest place we could possibly hide."

They pulled into a rest stop an hour later. They went to the bathroom, stretched, ate the junk food, took deep breaths. "I keep thinking, who was he?" Jonelle said. "I knew the face the minute I saw it. I swear the gold ring was under his glove."

"Good. They'll match it to the photos I've got, they'll see."

"It's the guy on the staircase in Paris, it has to be. That's how I know the face."

"We've got to tell the FBI to look at the Marine's hand, look at the ring. That's all the proof they'll need."

Steven pulled back onto 95 toward Richmond. "What I don't understand is how the Horsemen could use this guy and think they could get away with it. I mean, if Alicia Maris could learn his identity, the Secret Service sure should."

"There's something wrong with this picture still," she said.

"Nevertheless, the message is the same."

"What's that?"

"They're out to kill you."

She looked at him.

"And me too."

In a sumptuous suite at the Willard Hotel in Washington, three of the Horsemen gathered, sweating after their White House ordeal. James was nervously making himself a sandwich from a tray they'd had sent up, while Clay was talking intently on the phone in the bedroom. Barney was drinking.

Clay rushed in. "House is empty, looks like they made a fast getaway. Food on the counter, TV on, box of garbage bags all pulled apart in the kitchen. Looked ransacked. Someone dragged the kids out in a hurry."

"Any sign of them?"

"Negative."

Barney asked, "Check the old bag who sits for them?"

"She's gone too. Her landlady said she never came in last night." Clay added, "Oh, it looked like Sherlock's office and tape-editing room got cleared out. Big file cabinet empty, looted."

James cursed. "The tapes. The stuff they got from Maris." He looked like he was going to expire with fear.

"We know what's on them," Barney assured him, "no hard evidence."

James looked at the mute TV screen, where the coverage outside the White House was nonstop. "We got anything to worry about back there?"

Barney turned to Clay. "Clay?"

"Our little Marine fashions himself a saint tonight, and he didn't even have to die for it."

"Think he'll crack under investigation?" James asked.

"Not unless they torture him," Clay assured him.

Barney laughed. "You put that past them?"

James cackled, "They could sic Hillary on 'im. Hell, *I'd* talk."

"Not funny," Barney deadpanned. "I'm a Democrat. But don't worry."

Clay said, "Right now he's probably spouting his manifesto, and it'll hit the airwaves by morning. It's all going according to plan."

"I don't know." James nervously chewed his sandwich.

Clay said, "Don't look so worried, James. Our boy believes that Jesus has chosen his destiny—going to prison—so he can convert the anti-Christian element there."

"The anti-Christian element there is gonna cornhole him and kill him," James quipped.

Clay smirked. "So? Right now, he's happy as a pig in shit."

"To hell with him," James shouted. "She's the threat. She's gone and she's got tapes and we don't have an idea where to find her."

Clay reassured them. "I've got a platoon of people on it. Rex's people. These guys know from this kind of stuff."

James nodded. "Same guys who got him into the White House. Yeah, we can trust them."

Barney said, "I know you think I'd be the last to say this, but I think we need Saint Paul."

Clay turned to Findley. "James? Can we get him back from wherever it is you sent him?"

James looked at him funny. "He's across the river in an apartment in Arlington."

Barney blew up. "I thought he'd fled to Istanbul or something."

James bit into an olive. "Naw. Had dinner with him last night."

Barney went stiff. "You *what*?"

Clay said, "We ordered him to disappear."

James tried to justify it. "He's got other business, doesn't just work for us. Hell, we can't deprive the guy his living. And it's a goddamn good thing he's here. If anyone can get them, he can."

"But will we get them before they get us?"

Clay nodded "Sobering thought."

"We have to watch Agent Woolf's house, the roads to Quantico, their Bucks County place—called their neighbor up there, Janet Edwards, gave her a cock-and-bull story how worried I am about her, she promised she'd call if she saw them."

Clay added, "Alicia Maris's old lady in New York—where else?"

"Charles Patterson?" James offered.

"Two places you can count on them *not* to go to," Barney said assuredly, "are his parents and her mother. They won't be hiding in Virginia Beach or Atlanta."

Clay explained, "We're going to tap into her E-mail and hopefully her cell phone. Rex has got an FBI man on it. Oh, he thinks he can screw up their missives to Woolf if they try to get in touch with him."

"Good." Barney poured himself another Scotch.

"Baloney, good," James countered. "Forget all this shit. We meet with Saint Paul tonight and give him one simple order: find them. And shoot them."

Barney licked the Macallan off his lips. "Finally, James, we agree on something."

chapter 25

When Jonelle opened her eyes the next morning, she thought for a moment she was in their Bucks County house and that Steven was already downstairs cooking, for the scent of strong coffee and fresh-baked biscuits filled the air. She sat up in bed with a start, the pieces not quite fitting together, wondering if she'd dreamed the whole thing. Then she saw Steven next to her, a naked leg sticking out from under the unfamiliar comforter, the different configuration of the room, and she rubbed her eyes and knew it had been wonderful wishful thinking.

Kathleen had a feast of a breakfast ready for them when they came downstairs. She'd gotten up with the sun, hoping to ease their jitters, make them feel safe. "And I got you some clothes," she told Steven. "Old Mr. Darwin next door, big as a house, but his son, Brian, he's about your size. He's at college, but they had a few pairs of pants and a couple of shirts."

Steven looked at the pile of clothes. Pants were going to be a little snug, but they'd do. He rather liked the red University of Texas sweatshirt. "Great."

"Afraid you'll have to buy your own underwear," Kathleen said mischievously. "All he had were red bikini things."

"Kinky kid."

Jonelle had already been given some of Kathleen's clothing the night before, but she too needed undergarments and toiletries. She kicked herself for not making the White House aide give back their overnight bag. "We'll have to do a little shopping later."

Before they ate, Jonelle called to see that the kids were fine with Helen and Victor. Wyatt seemed to really be enjoying the adventure. "Mom," he said, "Potomac said you gotta infiltrate, that's the only way to get the bad guys!"

"Tell Potomac that's easier said than done."

Sarah, a little older and wiser, worried about them. "The newspaper is all about last night. Did that man really want to kill the President?"

"No, honey, he didn't," she said, and left it at that. She looked over to Steven. "Just thank God no one was hurt."

"Mom, the paper says—"

"We've got the TV on here," Jonelle said. "I pretty much know everything."

Kathleen handed Steven the local morning paper. The cover page was devoted to the story. It said little about Jonelle other than she was about to receive the medal when it happened. None of the papers nor anyone broadcasting yet knew the identity of the Marine who had fired the shots. No one had picked up on the fact that Jonelle and Steven were long gone in a Network ONE van.

"I'll get a *Post* later, honey," Jonelle said back to Sarah.

"Mom, it says no one knows where you are."

"That's right."

"Where are you? Grandmother and Grandfather Patterson's?"

Jonelle thought that would be ironic. "No, honey, it's best I don't tell you. That way it won't put you in a difficult position. If anyone asks you if you've heard from us, you say no. But I'd really like you not to go out for a few days, till this is all over."

"Will you come back before Thanksgiving?"

"Sure, honey. Of course."

"Mom, I'm scared for you."

It broke Jonelle's heart, and it was all she could do to keep her voice steady. "Daddy and I are fine and this will all be over soon."

Sarah didn't sound convinced, probably because Jonelle didn't sound convincing. "I hope so." She took a pause. "Mom? What about school?"

"Not even school. Who knows what these people might do?"

"What people?"

"The bad people, the guys who are making it hard for Dad and me to come home. Please, just stay inside Mr. Gallindo's apartment for a few days, okay?"

"I say 'Victor' now, Mom. I'm old enough. He said."

Jonelle grinned. "Okay, honey. That's fine. And one other thing. You're going to be reading in the paper that I've gone to the Betty Ford Center to seek treatment for medical and emotional problems. If anyone should ask you if it's true, you tell them yes. Understand me?"

"Sure, Mom. I see enough detective movies to know you gotta throw the bad guys off the track."

Jonelle smiled warmly. "I love you so much." In the background, she heard Wyatt again shout, "Infiltrate, Mom! Infiltrate, Dad!" She smiled.

Jonelle spoke to Helen. "I can't tell you how relieved I am to know you're with them."

"And I'm going to stay with them. My landlady says there are guys looking for me at the building, says someone's always watching your house."

"Don't go near it," Jonelle warned.

"Tell the truth," Helen said with some amusement, "Mr. Gallindo has a wonderful place here, very charming. We play cards, and he's giving me—"

"Piano lessons," Jonelle laughed.

Steven got on the phone with Victor and gave him instructions after Kathleen handed him an address he'd asked her for when they arrived last night. He told Victor to box up the tapes and stuff in two small cartons and send them to Museum Textile Cleaners—

Kathleen's brother's place—in Salt Lake City. "Send them *TWA Next Flight Out.*"

"Are you really in Utah?"

"I'd better not say where we are."

"Okay," Victor responded.

Jonelle took the phone. "Victor, thank you again. I can't tell you how—"

"You two just see this out, and take care of yourselves. These kids want you back in one piece. Hey, gotta go help Helen get the cookies out of the oven. This new life is fun." He hung up.

Steven explained to Jonelle that he would call a cargo handler named Bud, who'd recently transferred to Saint Louis from JFK, and alert him to the two packages. He'd pull them when they were to change planes in Missouri and reroute them to Richmond. Without changing the destination address. TWA would inform Steven when they were there. It would only take a day.

In the meantime they would sit tight and try to get their wits about them, and figure out just what they would do. The only thing they were sure of was they had to contact Agent Woolf.

To play it safe, Kathleen made the call for them from a phone booth two blocks away. Steven had no idea if the FBI's own phones could be tapped—*they* were the ones who did the tapping, weren't they?—and whether or not their voices might be recognized, but he was unwilling to take chances because if these monsters could arrange to get a man with a loaded gun into the White House itself, they were capable of anything.

Kathleen returned in ten minutes. "I spoke to him."

They both breathed easier.

"I used the name Connie Roderick as you told me to—"

"That's our code if we're in trouble," Jonelle explained.

"When I told whoever answered in his office that 'Connie' was calling, I was immediately connected. He talked about redecorating the house and how his wife said I was the best—meaning Connie —and how he wants to meet with the 'architect' and the 'landscaper' tomorrow morning."

Jonelle asked, "What time?"

Kathleen said, "Nine."

"Darn," Steven said. "I won't have the tapes yet."

"I think we're going to have to study those tapes ourselves, Steven. We know what we need. I don't trust anyone's eye but yours."

"We have to take him photos of the rings, clear ones, so he can compare them to the Marine's."

"God knows we have enough."

Steven turned back to Kathleen. "Where do we meet him?"

"Here, he gave me an address, directions. You'll take my car."

They went shopping on Monument Avenue that afternoon. Jonelle wore a kerchief and sunglasses. "I feel like Greta Garbo," she said, as a woman passed her looking strangely, for it was anything but sunny.

"Wish you were," Steven said, " 'cause all she had chasing her were fans."

They walked the charming streets for almost an hour, talking about the morning, how they'd leave early to be sure to meet with Don Woolf, on time, how they'd get his advice on where to go to remain safe, see if there wasn't a way he could arrest the men now, on some kind of suspicion charges. They went into antique stores, gift boutiques, potpourri stores—Steven called them "smelly bag" shops—in The Fan. They watched the early autumn leaves cascade from trees in the wind, and picked a bunch of mums from a pot someone had discarded in the street corner trash, wonderful reminders of what they were missing in their own house in New Hope.

"There's the papers," Steven said when they walked out of an ice cream store licking at two nut bars. They made their way to the stand in front of a small pharmacy, and after bending down for the *Post*, which was buried under a pile of *USA Today*s, Steven handed it to Jonelle and went inside to pay.

When he returned, he saw the most astonished look on her face. He turned to the paper in her hand. MARINE CHARGED IN ASSASSINATION ATTEMPT, the headline blared. Then he saw the name: *Jacob Hughes*. And he knew why she was so stunned.

Walking back to Kathleen's house, Jonelle tried to put it together. "That's why I wasn't sure, why I thought I knew him but yet couldn't place him." There was a photo of Jake Hughes at the bottom of the front page, which they'd lifted from his previous claim to fame, the firebombing of Regent University. "He probably wasn't even wearing a ring. It was Jake, not Saint Paul."

Steven was beside himself. "That's how you knew his face. But it makes no sense," he said, animatedly. "How can a guy go from fighting the Christian Right to giving up his freedom for them?"

Jonelle was reading the account as they walked. "Here's how: 'The accused told investigators he was angry with remarks President Clinton had recently made about the importance of Christian institutions and Christian doctrine on the American way of life.' They're keeping him true to form: anti-Christian guerrilla rebel all the way."

"But it's not true!" Steven was so energized and angry that he nearly walked into a tree. "He's their man, he's a setup like he was down at Regent. He was gunning for you at the White House. And then he would have shot me, I'm sure. Jesus, what a scheme."

"It's so sick," she said, "that it's almost brilliant."

"How did they ever manage to get him into a Marine uniform in the White House?"

"If they could get into the Vatican," Jonelle reminded him, "they can get into the White House."

They walked half a block in silence. She finished the paper and said, "It goes on about the incredible breach of security, how heads are going to roll, Congress is calling for a big investigation, the usual stuff. Only a mention of us, how odd that we had not spoken to the press, and a report of us leaving in a ONE van that was reported missing to the police by someone at ONE today. And so on."

But Steven was thinking only about Jake Hughes. "How does he think he'll get out of this? His life is over. It's John Hinkley. He'll be jailed forever, he had to have known that, there was no way to escape."

"Think about it," Jonelle reminded him. "These guys are fanatical. Martyrs for their cause."

"Okay, so Jake's a saint just like Paul. Now how do we prove he worked *for* the Christian Right. How do we prove Rex Heald did this?"

"I suggest," Jonelle said, "we leave that up to Woolf and the FBI."

The next morning, they set off south in Kathleen's car to meet with Don Woolf in Petersburg, Virginia. Arriving at the town's municipal airport at 8:45 A.M., they had coffee and stale Danish in a small diner, enthusiastically awaiting the arrival of his small private plane. They felt secure in the knowledge that the agent was soon to join them.

He never did.

At 9:40 they called Kathleen to be sure they'd understood the instructions perfectly, to be positive she'd written them down correctly. Kathleen called the FBI from the pay phone once more, and when Steven again dialed her at 10:00 A.M., she relayed the information that Mr. Woolf had indeed gone to meet with the "landscaper and architect," his small plane left Washington this morning at 8:45. Steven felt a queasy feeling creeping up his spine. Woolf should have been there by now.

They waited most of the morning, fear gradually engulfing them. At 11:00 A.M. they figured they had best get out of the little restaurant so they didn't look any more suspicious than they already did. They sat in the car until noon, and then decided they had to leave.

They drove back to Richmond in frightened silence.

It was not until they were back at Kathleen's that they heard what happened. She had an ashen look on her face as they entered the house, and she pointed to the TV. There was Tom Brokaw in a special report:

It is ironic that Agent Woolf, who with FBI Director James K. Kallstrom, worked on the investigation into the crash of TWA Flight 800 in 1996, would nearly die himself in a plane crash. Again, his private Cessna went down this morning in a wooded area south of Washington, D.C., near Fairview Beach on the Potomac. We'll have a report from the hospital as soon as—

Steven put his arm around Jonelle. There was no need to say anything, to exchange thoughts, words, questions. They both knew what had happened. And they felt cut off, overwhelmed, and sad.

The phone rang. Kathleen picked it up. It was the TWA baggage handler at the Richmond Airport. He was told to call to tell her two parcels had arrived, forwarded from Bud in Saint Louis. She asked that he have them sent over immediately.

But Steven said, "What for?" when she hung up the phone. "We have no one to give them to now."

chapter 26

"If they could get Woolf, they'll find us," Jonelle said. She and Steven were in bed in Kathleen's guest room, but neither could sleep.

"Someone intercepted the message at the FBI," Steven said, trying to figure out how Woolf was stopped.

"Or he talked to someone he shouldn't have."

"That means they've got someone inside."

"Lots of Christians there."

Steven shook his head. "It's only the extreme right, and just a few of the leaders, insane zealots. It's not all Christians. Most Christians are like us."

"All you need is one radical nut loyal to Rex Heald firmly planted in the FBI. Like there was one in the White House. And the Pentagon, the Marines."

"Real secure feeling, huh?"

She shivered. "The news said Woolf is going to be okay, but he's still in guarded condition."

"Which means he's in no shape to hear from us."

"Who else can we go to? I feel totally cut off."

"We are. And we can't trust anyone till we can walk into the Hoover Building and set down the proof that puts Barney and the rest of them away forever."

"You mean we're going to do it ourselves, don't you?"

"I don't think we have a choice."

The next morning, they put their words into action. Steven disappeared into the van inside the garage, where he could work on the tapes with better equipment than he'd had at home. Jonelle used Kathleen's laptop to begin a search for keywords:

PERE, ST. PERE, ST. PAUL, HUGHES, JAKE HUGHES, JACOB HUGHES.

She also instituted a search of the Web for information on less-known leaders of the Christian Right. Besides the usual suspects, a name popped up on the screen:

Reverend Steven Rovig.

She remembered him from dinner at the Pattersons and wondered for the first time if he too was involved in all this. Then, risking it, she checked her E-mail: forty-three messages. Moving through them took her a fair amount of time; most were from colleagues and friends wondering where she was. Judy Kresge, her assistant at ONE's studios in D.C., reminded her of appointments. Dale Harmon, her favorite cameraman, said he was positively bored without framing her in his lens. Stacy DeLano, her stage manager, sent her love, and added that Jay, Robin, and Melody all really missed her and hoped that she was okay. Jonelle felt a surge of emotion. All the good guys had responded, and she missed them too. So she wrote them:

E-mail:
Sub: My Absence
Date: 10-4 11:20:56 EST
From: jonepat@dci.com (Jonelle Patterson)
Reply to: jonepat@dci.com

Dear Judy & Dale & the Gang:

I suppose the way to do this is be blunt: I'm a patient at the Betty Ford Clinic in Rancho Mirage, CA. I want you to hold that news until you can't possibly keep a lid on it anymore. I will be here for 6 weeks and I ask only that no one worry, that I am left alone (Steven is nearby, thank God), so that I may make a speedy recovery. I know this comes as a big surprise to all of you, but trust me, it comes as an even bigger one to me. I love you all, and I'll be in touch soon. <Jonelle>

The next message, though from the same place, really stood out, and was not as warmly received:

Jonelle: Where are you? What happened? There is no danger. Let me help you! Barney.

She read the message to Steven and Kathleen, and then she hit Reply and typed a few words:

You won't get away with it. It's only a matter of time and you know it. Give yourself up while you still have a chance. J.

Without even asking what Steven thought, she pressed Send. But the final message in her mailbox was even more startling:

Architect and Landscaper, please contact me, I was in touch with The Developer on this, I want to aid you in your building plans. My name is Kevin Bass and my E-mail address is www.BassQuant.gvt.

"BassQuant? Quantico?" Jonelle asked.

"Seems to be," Kathleen said, "but can you trust it?"

"No." Steven was emphatic. "Don't reply. We've been through three agents already, it's ridiculous. Wait to see if we get more messages." He paused a moment. Then he took the computer from Jonelle and began typing something. "I just changed my mind," he whispered into it.

When he finished, he turned the machine around so they could read the screen:

Agent Bass: Barney Keller, Clay Santangelo, James Martin Findley and Rex Heald are behind the shooting at the White House. Jake Hughes works for them. The only help we need is for you to put them behind bars so we can go on with our lives. Give us a reason to trust you. We're praying for Mr. Woolf. The Architect.

"Should I send it?" Steven asked.

"What have you got to lose?" Kathleen said.

Jonelle didn't look convinced. "What if he's one of them?"

"Won't do more damage than what's been done. They know this already anyhow. Let's see what happens."

Jonelle nodded.

Steven hit Send.

And it was done.

He worked in the van until late that night and returned with a tape in his hand. "This," he said with some pride, "is the start of what's going to put them away, condensed onto one cassette."

"But?" Jonelle said, knowing there was one.

"But there's no conclusive proof."

"Did you check the E-mail?"

"No replies yet."

"What do you need to show the FBI?" Kathleen inquired.

Steven was clear. "Tie the man with the gold ring to the Horsemen. The ONE guys. Or Rex. We need tape of them together. Pictures. We need to connect Jake Hughes with some of them, one of them, it doesn't matter. Alicia's drawing lines between names won't do it. That's why we're hoping to find this Saint Paul's face with the men on tape."

"But you don't know what he looks like?" Kathleen asked to be certain.

"But we sure know the kind of ring he wears," Jonelle answered.

———

Jonelle checked the E-mail postings again before they went to bed. Nothing from the FBI. Nothing from Barney. But her Web query had come to fruition: no photos, but a family history, anecdotes, and a tree for the Pere clan of Ottawa, Canada. She printed it and brought it upstairs to Steven and read it to him while he soaked in the tub. The only interesting part of the lengthy list of Peres was the biography of LEOPOLD: *Born Ottawa, 1966, single, graduated University of Toronto, three unpublished novels, head writer CBC serial* Bloodlines *(canceled before airing), works in television development at CBS, NYC.*

"When was that entry made?" Steven asked.

Jonelle looked. "Last year. That means he's thirty-four, no, thirty-five now."

"CBS means Findley."

"Sounds like he wasn't too successful in the creative department."

"Makes a pretty creative assassin."

"Bet he really wants to direct." She looked at Steven for a reaction. He did not laugh. "Sorry," she said, "trying to make you smile."

Steven thought a moment. "Saint Pere is the family name, so Saint Paul would be a likely nickname. Think there might be a picture of him on the Web?"

"Could try."

"Do it." She was sitting on the edge of the old claw-footed tub. "Want your back washed first?"

He grinned and stretched out. "More than my back."

She reached down and touched his groin through the water. He looked up at her, then closed his eyes and rested his head on the back of the tub. She moved her fingers down into the wiry hair above his penis. He moaned in anticipation. Then with the other hand she flicked bubbles into his face and giggled.

"Hey, no fair!"

She pulled her hand from the water, laughing at how she tricked him, but the joke was on her, for he pulled her, clothes and all, into the water with him. She howled, splashing water all over the room.

He kissed her, she screamed in delight and shock, he kissed her again. "Shhhhh, we'll wake Kathleen! I'm soaked!"

"That means you'll have to take off your clothes."

She giggled, dropping the wet document on the floor as he unbuttoned the blouse she had on. "What about the search?"

"Search tomorrow. We have more fun things to do tonight."

"Jim."

A grumpy, sleepy voice. "Go to bed."

"Jim! I am in bed. The dogs."

"What about the dogs?"

"They're upset. Listen."

"Go feed 'em."

"Someone's at the door."

"Let Rosa get it."

"Rosa went out with her boyfriend."

"You're hearing things."

A loud knock echoing from the cold marble entry hall. "Jim, there's someone—"

"I hear it, I hear it." James Martin Findley sat up in his bed in East Hampton and switched on the light on the bedstand, knocking over several bottles of pills as he did so. He patted his wife's rump, slid into his slippers, and made his way to the darkened hallway of the Long Island mansion in his Saks Fifth Avenue silk pajamas, muttering, "All right, all right, all right!"

He approached the front door without even a thought that this might be dangerous. The street on which they lived on Georgica Pond was safe. Good security. He figured it was a neighbor who'd locked himself out. Billy Joel had done just that one night a few years before and came pounding at his door. They'd had a beer together. He'd heard Martha Stewart had had the same problem recently, but she lived too far from him to be rapping tonight. He swung the door wide open.

A ruddy man in a trench coat held up a badge. "FBI, Mr. Findley. Sorry it's late, but we need to ask you some important questions. May we come in?"

———

At his severely modern clapboard-and-glass house near Myrtle Beach, Rex Heald hung up after speaking to his wife and returned to the deck.

"How are the kids?" Clay Santangelo asked from the swirling hot-tub water.

"Asleep."

"The baby?"

"Awake. More wine?"

Clay laughed with a sexy undertone. "Any more and I'm not going to be responsible for my actions."

Rex filled Clay's glass with a devilish twinkle in his eye. "I seldom drink," he said, then poured himself one anyhow.

"I know," Clay said, giggling, "it's against your religion."

"This doesn't make me a hypocrite, does it?"

"Naw."

"I mean, this is a party, right?"

Clay's tone was unmistakably sensual. "If you want it to be."

Rex didn't react. He sipped the wine, dropped his towel, and slid back into the swirling hot water.

"Feels good, huh?"

"Great."

"Don't understand why you and Marjorie never used this."

"Too sybaritic."

"Well, now you know a few pleasures of the flesh, and God still hasn't struck you dead."

Rex met his gaze. "Not yet, anyhow."

Clay stared at him. "You know something? You have marvelous eyes. They're really deep—"

The phone on the deck near them buzzed.

"Forget it," Clay urged.

"It's the gate. Someone's out front."

"Visitors?" Clay reached out for his trunks and started slipping them on under the water as Rex answered the phone.

"Yes?"

"Mr. Heald?"

"Yes."

"Agent Carlucci from the Federal Bureau of Investigation." Rex gave Clay a look he didn't understand. "Is Mr. Santangelo inside with you? His car is parked out here."

Clay stared at the startled eyes, knowing something was wrong. He pulled himself out of the water. "Who is it? Who's here?" He started furiously wiping his body dry.

"Yes, he's here, we . . . he just dropped in to see my wife and me." Rex reached for the towel he'd dropped to cover his nakedness.

"Could we interrupt that meeting for a few minutes?"

"What do you want him for, if I may ask?"

"Actually, we want you both."

In a tone that had goose bumps, he said, "Both?"

"Routine questions, that's all."

Barney heard a hard rap on the door of his TriBeCa loft. He was wearing jogging pants and a polo shirt, holding a glass of Scotch, when he looked through the peephole. "Who are you?"

"FBI, Mr. Keller."

"FBI?"

The agent held his badge to the hole. "We'd like to ask you a few questions, if we may?"

"Hello?"

"Barney? James."

"Why are you calling at this hour?"

"The goddamned FBI was here! Goddamned grilled me for over three hours!"

"Yes, I know, but I'm very busy right now."

"Busy? What are you, nuts? I tell you the FBI paid me a visit and you say you're—"

"Sir, I'm sorry, but I just don't need any more life insurance."

"Life insurance? Oh, my God. They're *there*? Now? With you?"

"Yes. I can't talk. Thank you for the call."

"Jesus."

"Yes?"

"Rex?"

"Hello, Barney."

"Did they talk to you too?"

"Yes."

"Everything all right?"

"Big mistake, I told them so."

"They saw James too. He told them nothing, but he's pretty shaken. Heard from Clay?"

"Clay?" Rex watched Clay shake his head violently, crossing his hands in front of him, emphatically indicating he didn't want Barney to know he was there. Rex said, "No."

"I can't reach him, don't know where he is."

"Did you try California?"

"Malibu and West Hollywood both. Houseboy said he's on the East Coast. We have to meet. Tomorrow. Tell Clay if you speak to him."

"Where?"

"Someplace where the Federal Bureau of Investigation won't find us. I'll let you know."

"James, wake up. It's Barney."

"You think I can sleep after those gorillas come in and accost me?"

"No one accosted you."

"Accuse me."

"No one accused you. They asked you the same questions they asked me and Rex."

"Rex too? Jesus. How about Clay?"

"No one can find him."

"They got to him too, I'd lay money on it."

"Don't. That's how you got into trouble before."

"Gamblin' men don't stop."

"Meeting tomorrow. Regent U. Charles Patterson's office. Four P.M."

"Why there?"

"He's the only hope we have of finding them."

"I see. Yeah."

"James?"

"Bring Saint Paul down with you. Just in case."

"With pleasure. But Barney, I'm scared. I think this whole thing is gonna fall apart."

"James, pull it together! Nothing's gonna fall apart. You hear me? You hear me, James?"

"Sure, Barney. But I'm still scared."

"Okay, okay," Barney said to the other Horsemen gathered with him in Charles Patterson's office, "we've determined nobody told them a thing. But it's just buying time. She gets to them before we get her, we're cooked."

Charles gasped. "This is my daughter-in-law you're talking about! My son's wife. The mother of my grandchildren."

"Fuck your grandchildren," James said.

"How dare you?"

Clay tried to do it more diplomatically. "Charles, we're talking about our lives, our future here. Yours too. I swear, you don't help us, you're gonna get your ass dragged in on conspiracy charges."

Rex was more gentle. "Charles, no one wants to harm her. We must convince her she's got to go along with the plan. And stop these silly accusations."

Charles shook his head, paced. "I don't see how that can be accomplished at this point. I don't think she'll ever accept it." His voice broke. "My son, I thought he would, but he—"

James slammed his fist down on the desk. "Fuck this shit, this hearts-and-flowers crap, this talking nice here. Your goddamned kid wants to put all of us in prison, you included, you asshole!"

"He's got a point," Clay admitted.

Rex spoke with fervor. "And destroy the Christian movement, set it back a thousand years. He'll undo everything we've worked so hard to attain, he'll eradicate everything that this school stands for. All your work, Charles, everything we've done—Reed, Robertson, yourself—everything down the toilet. And the backlash will be like a tidal wave."

Clay added, "We may have waylaid Woolf, but they got some-one else in the FBI on this now. We know for a fact no agents have met with them yet, but it's only a matter of time. Help us, Charles."

Charles was suffering. These people, these men he valued, were asking him to turn in his own flesh and blood. "I don't know what I can do."

Rex pushed his Christian button. "Do what God needs you to do, Charles." James tried to keep from gagging. "Tell us where you think they might be."

Charles blurted, "I don't know!"

Barney gave him an order. "Think. Friends, places they love, names of someone they mentioned—"

Rex urged, "Anything, Charles, anything."

James couldn't find it in him to be nice. "Cough up, old man," he grumbled, "or I'll have Saint Paul chasing your ass as well."

Barney had enough of him. "James, will you shut up? We're all gentlemen here."

James snorted. "I'm never gentle when it comes to saving my butt."

Clay pointed out, "You're dying anyhow."

And James pointed out, "And I sure as hell don't want to help it along."

"Kathleen somebody."

They all heard Charles say that but none of them were sure just what he'd uttered. Barney said, "What? What did you say?"

Clay got the first name. "Kathleen Doyle? That sexy actress who's in all the ONE TV movies?"

Charles shrugged. "I don't know."

Clay shook his head. "Doyle seems unlikely to be Jonelle's buddy."

Charles explained. "The last time they were here, they were stop-ping on the way home to see someone named Kathleen, a friend they go antiquing with, I think Jonelle said."

Barney's blood was starting to pump again. "I think we're onto something. 'On the way home?' Meaning between here and D.C.?"

Charles looked as though he were being asked to slaughter his own newborn. "This is very difficult for me. I feel I'm betraying my own blood."

Rex really worked him. "You'd be betraying God himself if you didn't tell us this, Charles." They could tell he really believed what he was saying, however. "You'd be betraying all you stand for as a Christian."

There was a long pause in which Charles looked up at a framed photograph of himself and Alma, Steven and Jonelle and the kids, when Sarah was only two and Wyatt still a baby. Then he said, softly, without any emotion at all, "Kathleen lives in Richmond."

chapter 27

In the morning, they opened the laptop as Kathleen poured coffee, connected to the Net, and got into gear. They sent out three requests on a World Wide Web message board, posting it in several places on the Internet.

The first message said:

For a documentary on the interesting and successful owners of Network ONE, we are looking for tape or photographs of Barney Keller, Clayton Santangelo and James Martin Findley at various points in their careers. Banquets, awards ceremonies, any group shots showing them interacting with others are welcome.

The second message read:

Planning a retrospective on the life of Rex Heald and his rise to leadership of the Christian Alliance. Need tape of him interacting with friends, neighbors, family, etc.

Steven tried calling all the "St. Peres" he could find listed in the Quebec area, but none of them elicited anyone who admitted to having a photograph of Leo St. Pere. Calls to Leo's parents in Montreal went unanswered. Jonelle tried someone she knew at CBS, but there was no existing picture of the man on file. It made sense, for writers were seldom photographed.

Thus, the third message read:

Does anyone have a photo of Leopold St. Pere, a Canadian television writer?

They left an E-mail address with each message, creating a new mailbox to which the replies could be downloaded. They also left a post office box address in New York, which was really a lockbox at Kennedy Airport used by TWA pilots. Steven's friend Bud arranged that anything arriving there addressed to DOCUMENTARY would be held for Steven, or forwarded wherever he wanted it.

Jonelle went to the kitchen to get coffee, then she disappeared. Steven found her later in the tree house in the backyard, sitting alone, lost in thought. "Remember when Wyatt and Sarah gave that 'tea'?" she said when he climbed up to join her.

"Honey," he said softly, putting an arm around her, "I miss them more than I can say."

"It's different, you know." She sipped her coffee, trying to find the best words to make her point. "Balancing career and kids is difficult these days, and we have both tried hard. It's one thing when you have a flight and are gone three, four days. It's one thing when I've got to rush away on a story. Usually one of us is still at home—"

He nodded. "And it's by choice. This is painful, we're cut off, forced to abandon them."

He could hear the hurt deep inside her. "We didn't do anything to deserve this!"

"Just remember they're in good hands, and God's watching over them."

"I wonder about God sometime."

"Don't doubt your faith. God never gives us a mountain that we can't climb over."

She smiled a little. "This one's proving to be a real challenge, though, isn't it?" She rested her head on his shoulder.

They talked to the kids again, thinking they'd have to cheer them, but Wyatt and Sarah were both high on the fact that Mr. Gallindo had planned a week's holiday over Thanksgiving to see his parents in Indiana, and he'd decided to take them with him. Helen was going too, and she was relieved because she was afraid to even leave Victor's apartment for the market. "Don't you worry about a thing," Helen told them. When Victor got on the phone, he said, "Figured it would be safer. I always go home for holidays, so it wasn't a problem. We're leaving tomorrow. My mother and Helen will hit it off. The kids just have to get outside, this isn't fair to them."

Jonelle breathed easier. "I can't thank you enough," she said gratefully. She knew they'd be safer far away from D.C.

Victor gave them the necessary phone number and address and wished them well. Then Steven disappeared into the van, while Jonelle and Kathleen drove downtown to the First National Bank of Richmond, where they entered the office of Kathleen's good friend, Lori Flanders. They were there to use Lori's sophisticated computer, which interfaced with every banking institution in North America. It took three hours, time during which they talked about everything from the dilemma they were in to current movies to children—Lori had one of her own—to antiques. They went to a delightful restaurant for lunch, and Jonelle felt pleased that because the way Kathleen had done her up—little funky hat with a veil, almost no makeup, granny glasses, high collar—no one recognized her. Some took a second glance, but that was more because she looked so exotic—this was Richmond, Virginia, not Venice Beach, California, after all—than because they thought she might be someone famous. When they returned to the bank, they had the first part of what they wanted.

The records—based on what Alicia Maris had found, their jumping-off point—proved that money from the Christian Right had flowed directly into the coffers of Network ONE. That in itself did not prove anything, but it violated FCC rules of disclosure and surely would help their case. There was a paper trail from the Christian Broadcasting Company to Network ONE, and although it got laundered through two banks before it got there, the CBC records were clear as to what the money was for.

The second part of Jonelle's banking need was not realized: proving that "Saint Paul"—Leo St. Pere—had been paid large sums by the men for his work as a hit man. Jonelle had the records Alicia had dug up, the fact that ONE bought him plane tickets, paid for his hotel rooms, the stuff Findley stupidly ran right through the business. But where were the payments for killing Jared Tucker? Where was the reward for shooting Imelda? Who wrote the check for his portrayal as a priest in the Vatican, the good father who slipped the old cardinal his cyanide?

Lori said she would continue to search. "I could get used to this detective stuff," she said, and the gleam in her eye told them she meant it.

Steven was sitting in the living room, warming up with hot tea, when they returned to Kathleen's house. "Cold out in that garage," he said. "How'd it go?"

They told him.

"I have good news too. Got some E-mail replies. Two photographs downloaded, one of Clay and Findley at a golf meet out in Palm Springs last winter"—he handed them to her—"and one of Barney at the Emmy Awards, which isn't very useful."

Jonelle smiled. "No hands with gold rings, in other words?"

"No hands at all. Just faces. But look closely at the golf meet."

She stared at it. It was a picture someone had taken of the two men being congratulated on Clay's winning game, five fellows— including Gerald Ford—slapping him on the back, hands visible, faces very clear. She recognized no one but Clay and Findley and one other elderly man, whom she knew was a programming director at ONE. "Is it helpful?" she asked Steven.

"Can't really see hands," he admitted, "but one of the faces could come in handy. Now, want to see something?"

He took them out to the garage, where, in the back of the van, on the little video screen, he played some tape. They were all the way back at the swimmer's accident. Jonelle saw what she'd seen about a hundred times. "What's changed?"

Steven said, "Look carefully at the other custodian, the other maintenance man, the one in the BG, the younger one—"

The word "younger" did it for Jonelle, she knew already what he was about to show her. And sure enough, when Steven froze the tape and magnified the frame, it was clear that this was a face they now recognized. It was the radical student. It was the perfect Marine. It was Jake Hughes.

"He and Saint Paul have been working together all along?" Jonelle exclaimed. "That's how I knew the Marine's face."

"I haven't gotten to others. This took me all day. But we're onto something."

It was dark when they left the garage to return to the house. Kathleen was the first to enter, clicking on the back porch light. "No, don't! Kath, turn it off!" His voice was sharp, apprehensive.

"What's wrong?" Jonelle exclaimed.

"That car. I swear, same one went by when we were—" He stopped, peering between the house and the garage toward Monument Avenue. "Get inside."

Jonelle ducked inside. Steven followed her, but rushed through the kitchen, the dining room, to the front windows. He stood to one side, watching, waiting. "It was blue, dark blue metallic I'd say."

"You think—?" She didn't have to finish the thought.

"No. Just jumpy, I guess."

"I hope."

He worked in the van till midnight, with Jonelle at his side, scanning every other piece of tape they had. And they found Jake Hughes's face two more times: in the crowd after the bus accident, and again on the tape of the San Francisco gala. He was there in a tux, one of the party-goers, appearing briefly at one of the bars where he could be seen being handed orange juice, and again seated at dinner, but not on the Golden Gate dance floor. "Sure," Jonelle muttered, "he was probably up on the catwalk with Saint Paul, loosening the screws."

"We've got him, though, Jone," Steven said with accomplishment, "we've got him tied to them."

"Not really."

"Why not?"

"We've got him tied to the *incidents*, and to Saint Paul. But he doesn't tie to Barney or any of them yet."

"That's next."

"We don't have tape of any one of them with these men."

"I know who might have."

"You do?"

"Yeah. My father."

When they entered the house, they found Kathleen kneeling on the sofa in the dark, facing the front windows. "Don't turn on the light!" she warned.

Curious, they both moved closer to her. "What is it?" Jonelle asked.

"What's going on?" Steven said softly, tensely.

"That blue car. It's gone past three more times."

They left before daybreak. Kathleen helped them get away safely. At 5:00 A.M., she made a big production of carrying suitcases out to the car, which they'd parked out front, on Monument. It was clear she had more luggage than one person might ever travel with. She locked up the front doors, made a production of looking both ways, acting nervous, and then she started the car and drove off toward the airport. The blue car, which had been sitting in the dark one block away, waited a few moments, and followed her.

That's when Jonelle and Steven ran to the van, backed it out, and left Richmond for good.

Kathleen grabbed the phone on the first ring.

"Kath?"

"Hi, baby." She didn't want to say Jonelle's name.

"Things work out with your flight?"

"Canceled. Had to come back home. But someone had broken in."

"You were robbed?"

"No, just messed up. Can't imagine what they were looking for."

"Your computer is missing, if you haven't noticed. I needed it. Okay?"

"Don't tell me that. Insurance would have bought me a new one!"

"We made it to our destination."

"Listen, Lori called from the bank, got some more information on your checking account problem. You might want to check with Connie." They'd agreed to keep Connie Roderick as their code word. In this case, it meant she should check her electronic mail.

"Great."

"Good luck, honey." Kathleen hung up.

"Barney?"

"Yes, Clay."

"Where have you been?"

"I've got a network to run. What are we going to do next week? We've run out of Jonelle's taped shows."

"Play reruns, who cares? She's number one anyhow."

"*60 Minutes* is number one."

"You'd know. Anyhow, they're not in Richmond."

"You sure?"

"Saint Paul and Findley found the woman. Kathleen Holm is her name. Staked her out, she went to the airport early in the morning, thought maybe they were in the car already or something, I didn't quite understand what James was saying. When they realized she'd led them off on a goose chase, they checked the house and no go. But they were there. The van had been in the garage. Neighbor attested to the fact that he saw them drive away."

"Where to?"

"Search me."

"Where are you?"

"Virginia Beach still."

"Stay there. I got men on her on-line, they'll get her when she next signs on. We'll know where she's talking from."

"I was gonna go down to Myrtle."

"You can give Rex a blow job some other time. You stay at that goddamn hotel number and be available when they call to say they're tracing her. This cost me a fortune, make it worth it for me. Keep the two fuckups there with you. And warn them—James and his patron saint—not to screw it up again."

Charles Patterson, as usual, did not lock his office. There was nothing there anyone would want, and what was valuable was so well hidden that he felt it unnecessary. Besides, this was a Christian institution, and good Christian values were upheld. There'd never even been a theft on campus. Ever.

Fifteen minutes after he left the quadrangle for his home close by, the door on his office did lock, from the inside. Jonelle and Steven closed the blinds and turned on the light over his desk. Steven reached into the bottom drawer and pulled out the jar of peanuts. He dumped them onto the desk and fished around in them until he found the key. "Told you," he whispered to Jonelle.

When he opened the safe, he reached up with both hands to withdraw the documents and folders as carefully as possible, so they could put them back without any suspicion that someone had been visiting. He handed half to Jonelle, and he took the other half for himself. She took the easy chair near the window while Steven sat at the desk. And they began their work.

Jonelle found financial records. When she'd pulled Lori Flanders's E-mail earlier, she'd learned that James Findley had signed several large checks made out to *Bloodlines, Inc.* Did that mean anything to Jonelle? It did; that was the name of the failed TV show Leo St. Pere had written in Canada. Now Jonelle was looking at proof that *Bloodlines, Inc.* was Leo, and that he was the only stockholder of the California corporation. The checks were written from ONE's development account, which looked like a slush fund created simply to finance murder. To record what she was looking at, she needed a copying machine, but running down the hall was too risky. So she pulled her laptop from the briefcase she'd bought after leaving Richmond and plugged the modem into Charles's phone line.

"Got her," the voice said.

"She's on-line?" Clay asked.

"Yes, sir."

"Where from?" He cupped the receiver. "James, Leo, she's on-line, they've got her traced."

"Sir?"

"Yeah, go ahead." Clay then listened in astonishment. "It can't be," he said, "you've got to be wrong."

"No, sir," the technician replied, "that's the number and that's the location."

Clay hung up the phone. "She's here. She's at the university. She's on-line from Charles Patterson's office!"

Steven found something even more valuable. A photograph of the Rovig family on an outing with Charles and his wife, and Rex and Marjorie Heald. What was interesting was that all the names had been written in under each person, and the Rovigs seemed to have a son who looked college age, and he bore a striking resemblance to a face Steven was getting to know well. Being unsure, he continued looking but found no more photos in the safe.

There were, however, two Christmas cards in the file. Why in a safe? He opened the first one. Inside was a professional photograph of the Rovigs again, and this time the face was more recognizable, for the photo was more recent—he checked the date on the envelope, 1997—and he was more than sure. The second one was of the smiling Rovig clan once again, and this was even more like the boy he knew so well, sent for Christmas 1999—just a year ago. The boy in the photos, the Rovig's oldest son, was the young man they knew as Jacob Hughes.

"Drive, drive!" James told Leo.

"Which building?" Leo asked.

"To the right, administration building, two-story one there!" Clay barked from the backseat.

The car squealed tires as it rounded the drive in front of the building.

"Hurry, hurry!" James gasped, breathless, cocking the gun he was now putting in his jacket pocket.

"Steven."

"Huh?"

"You hear that?"

"Yes."

Alarm lit up their eyes. No one squealed tires on this goody two-shoes campus.

"The door's gonna be locked," Clay warned as they hurried down the corridor.

"Bust the fucker in." James was breathing hard, barely able to keep up. Students looked at them with curiosity.

Leo got to the door first, pressed his strong shoulder against it, withdrew his gun, and then gave it a mighty shove. It flew off its hinges.

The room was empty. Papers were everywhere. On top of Charles's desk was a pile of roasted peanuts. The safe hung open. The laptop was still on. On the screen, a message:

YOU WON'T WIN!

Outside the open the window, the one they'd jumped from, the men could see a white van pulling away from near where they had parked. "Shit!" Clay shouted.

James popped a peanut into his mouth. "Don't worry. We're right behind them now. It's just a matter of time."

"Where are you going?" Jonelle asked Steven in panic. "We've got to get out of here!"

"And lose the best chance yet?"

"How do you mean?"

"I know where they're going to go. It's obvious, isn't it?"

She got it. "Your dad's house."

He nodded. "And we'll be there too."

They crouched in the darkness amongst the bushes and foliage, and then Steven risked standing on the curled-up hose, which allowed him to peer into the den window. It was pitch black outside. He knew they'd not see him. He stared, surveying the room.

"What do you see?" Jonelle whispered.

"Clay, Dad, a glimpse of Findley—he's pouring himself something from a flask."

"Probably cursing that your father doesn't have booze in the house."

"Darn."

"What?" she asked, looking up.

"No Leo."

"Let me see."

He got down, held her hand to give her support, and she took his place on the perch. She saw the men talking animatedly. Steven was right, Leo St. Pere wasn't there—or was he? She suddenly saw a hand gesture out from the high wing chair whose back was to the window. "Give me the camera," she ordered.

"Here. Be careful."

She was. She taped the scene. She got them all, Clay, Charles Patterson, Findley, and the hand of Saint Paul—she got the gold ring on tape. "I got the ring," she whispered with the camera still going, "I got it, Steven."

"His face?"

"No."

Steven felt it was enough. It tied the same hand, the same man, the man they had on tape in all the incidents, to James Martin Findley, Clayton Santangelo, and even, unfortunately, Charles Patterson. "Let's go."

"I want to get more."

"What for?" He reached up and took the camera from her. "Jonelle, come on. Let's get out of here."

She stepped down from the hose viewing stand. And she walked behind him, though she did it reluctantly. "But we might be able to see his face. If he gets up, if he—"

"If he gets up, the meeting may be over, and we may not have enough time to get out of here."

"But we'd have the proof that—" Her voice shut down and she froze as the yard light suddenly clicked on.

Steven thought fast. "Means they're going to come out, the den light is off."

She glanced at the window they'd been peeking in. Black.

"Run!" he said.

She did.

But he dropped the camera.

It hit a pile of terra-cotta pots his mother had been emptying for the winter and cracked one of them in two. He froze for the second time.

Jonelle realized what had happened and stopped about three yards away from him, in the middle of the drive. She looked at the house. "They didn't hear it inside. It's okay."

Steven picked up the camera and hurried toward the back of the truck, hidden in the trees past the garage. Jonelle got into the passenger side. Steven opened the back doors, reached in to set the camera inside, and that's when the shot rang out.

The bullet first ricocheted against the inside wall of the van two times, *ping, ping*. Then Steven shouted in pain, and Jonelle, already in the passenger seat, turned to see his face, his eyes connecting with hers, as an explosion of blood burst from his shoulder. A hot searing pain instantly flowed through him, rendering him paralyzed for a moment, as another shot rang out, striking the back of the van. She could hear her father-in-law shouting into the night, "No, don't shoot them! Don't hurt them!" Then another shot. And another voice, Clay's she thought, but what did it matter?

It was happening so fast but it seemed like slow motion as she reached out toward Steven, but saw him say no—did she hear him or just read his lips?—because he was crawling into the van, blood gushing from his right shoulder, wetting his neck, his arm, telling her to drive, drive, drive.

She lifted herself across to the driver's seat as he pulled the doors closed in back, shielding himself from more bullets. She started the van and smashed her foot to the floor and they pealed away from the darkness of the shadows with stones and dirt flying behind them. There was only one way out, and she knew she'd have to risk it.

She rounded the garage and came over the yard, through the flower garden, through what was left of the summer vegetables, smashing several pumpkins, mashing the rest of the flowerpots, and nearly running down Charles Patterson as he dove to get out of the way. She wanted to hit him, wanted to run him over, adrenaline rushing through her like it had never done before, screaming, "You did this to him! He's your son! Your son!" Angry tears jumped from her eyes as she piloted the van to the street and headed away from this place forever.

Eight bleary-eyed hours later, the road was still as she remembered it. It was almost as if no one had touched it in all these years. Even in the early-morning twilight, she could see the same holes, same jagged rocks, same orange dust. She looked at Steven sleeping in the seat next to her, his arm in a sling she'd fashioned herself, shoulder wrapped as best she could to keep it from bleeding more. Was he really sleeping? Or was it the fever getting worse? Soon, she said to him silently, soon, we're almost there.

Chickens clucked and ran in circles as the van approached the creaking old farmhouse, and an old mangy cat looked up for a moment from her perch atop the rusting Sears washing machine, a wringer type, that had sat on the front porch for more years than Jonelle had been on this earth. It was all so familiar, yet distant and faded, and it frightened her so.

She knocked at the door. She could see the woman asleep in the chair inside the parlor, near the old pump organ. At first she thought the woman was drunk, and it was all she could do not to turn and run away. But she knocked again, and when the old lady had rubbed the sleep from her eyes and realized she had company, Jonelle felt her heart pounding and her knees knocking. The woman pulled open the door, then pushed on the screen door, to get a look at who or what had come barging into her place so late at night.

"Ma . . . Mama?" Jonelle said, trembling, when the woman's eyes registered astonished recognition of who was standing there. "Mama, I'm in . . . in a lot of trouble. And I need your help."

chapter 28

Esther Lighter rubbed the sleep from her eyes and stared at what she believed to be an apparition. "Jonelle?" she voiced, not even realizing she'd said the name out loud.

"Mama, please, let us in."

But the white-haired woman did not open the door. She was in shock, uncomprehending. "You come home for Thanksgiving . . . after all these years?"

"I'm in trouble, Mama, big trouble," Jonelle explained with urgency. "Steven's in the van. He needs help, a doctor. I know you don't want to see me, don't want to help me, but I beg you—"

"Nobody has to beg me, least of all my own kin," Esther said, lifting up the rusted hook to unlock the screen door. "Beggin's beneath the Lighters. I know. Did it enough when I needed you."

"Not now, Mama. We'll talk about it all later."

"Let me git a look atcha." The stocky woman stepped out onto the porch. She called out to hush the dogs. Then she looked Jonelle up and down. "You're too skinny."

"You've gained weight."

"Eat now instead of drinkin'."

"I'm proud of you. Mama, we need to help Steven."

"What's wrong with him?" Esther asked, starting to the van.

Jonelle followed her. "He's been shot."

Esther stopped dead, turned to her. "Shot?"

"Mama, four men want to kill us."

Esther Lighter put her hand on the passenger-side door handle and pulled. The interior light went on and emotion finally crossed her face, pain and shock. "Well, honey," she said, looking at Steven's pale face, "I'll be danged."

Jonelle's mother knew ol' Terk would be awake. The doctor lived only minutes away as the crow flies. Jonelle reminded her of the danger to all of them if anyone knew she and Steven were there, but Esther assured her the man could be trusted. "Why, 'cause he's a good Christian?" Jonelle asked with irony. She remembered her mother feeling anyone who was Christian was automatically a good person. Jonelle had grown up believing that too, until recently.

"No," her mother answered, surprising her. " 'Cause he's a good atheist." Her strength came in handy as she supported Steven's weight from under his arms. "Get his legs, we've gotta carry him . . ."

Jonelle did as instructed. "Then tell the doc to come over here. Steven's lost a lot of blood."

That's just what Doctor Terlecky said. The bullet hadn't exited his shoulder, and that was the problem with the excessive bleeding and also the fever that was now at 104. The doctor wanted Steven in the hospital, of course, but Esther had warned him on the phone that it was out of the question. So, like Doc on *Gunsmoke*, he did it at home. They boiled water, sterilized his instruments, and as the doctor gave Steven a hypo of morphine, they set up a makeshift operating room there in the kitchen. In an hour, the bullet was out of his body, the wound had been cleansed, he'd been sewed up, and it was over.

His fever remained high, but never went above what it was when the doctor arrived. The sun was up when they said good-bye to the doctor. "Happy Thanksgivin', Terk," Esther said, "and you be sure to tell the missus God bless as well."

"Obliged," the doctor responded, and left.

Jonelle stayed with Steven all day, bathing him with alcohol, cold water, keeping him warm when he shivered and his teeth chattered, loving him and believing that he would soon be better.

Her mother gave them privacy for most of the day, washing their clothes, cooking for them, praying for Steven. She hid the van in the barn and cleaned up the blood inside it in the back where Steven had sat until Jonelle felt safe enough to pull over and see to him.

His fever went down by evening, and while he felt pain, he didn't want anything to do with the three Demerol syringes that the doctor had left for them to administer. He took Tylenol and tried to grin and bear it. He felt his mind had to be sharp if anything happened.

He slept like a baby all night, but Jonelle drifted off only fitfully, afraid of what might happen if she were sleeping.

He was better in the morning. Esther brought him soup and crackers, and he swallowed her homemade chicken broth with delight. He and Jonelle sat that afternoon out on the hanging swing on the porch, where she'd first been kissed by a boy when she was sixteen. "He was a hayseed from over that hill," she said, remembering with the giggles. "Tommy Lee something or other."

"They're all Tommy Lee something or other," Steven whispered. "Or Billy Joe."

"He was gorgeous, though," she recalled.

"They're not all that."

"How are you?"

"Aching," he admitted. "Weak."

"Better than dead."

"I'll say."

There was a long pause. Then Steven said, "I had a dream. You were on the back of a train decorated in red, white, and blue bunting. People were clamoring for the touch of your hand, whistling, shouting. I was trying to catch the train, but I couldn't run fast enough."

"Steven," she said, soothingly, "don't—"

But he had to. "And then they shot me."

She winced, but he continued. "Then you and the kids were up on the podium."

"Podium?"

"The convention. There was a movie behind you with other White House hopefuls' kids, Eisenhower's children, the Nixon girls, Reagan's kids. They were applauding Wyatt and Sarah. Then huge drapes opened and four glorious horses pranced onto the stage, ridden by the Four Horsemen. The crowd went wild and then you told everyone you were accepting the nomination for the office of forty-fourth president of—"

"Steven, stop!" She didn't want to hear this lunacy.

But he didn't. "And then you said you had one regret, that your husband, Steven, had died before he could see this night of glory. . . ."

She held him, rocked her body with his, almost in tears. "Honey, honey, it's a nightmare. You're not leaving me, I'm not doing anything without you."

"If anything happens to me—"

"It already happened, and look at you! You're going to be fine." Then she kissed him. "What did you tell me about a mountain? God never gives us one we can't scale?"

And he felt reassured.

Then she had something to tell him. "I've been thinking. It could have been Jake Hughes—Rovig—who ran me down in Jared Tucker's building. I mean, if he was in on this from the start, that could be why the guy I saw seemed so physically different from what we think Saint Paul looks like."

"I'll bet you're right."

Jonelle changed the subject because she didn't want him obsessing on it again. She needed to help him get well. "Tomorrow's Thanksgiving."

Steven nodded. "I know."

"This will be the first time we won't be with the kids."

"We'll call them."

Her eyelids looked heavy with worry and lack of sleep. "Steven, what next?"

"Call Saint Louis and tell Bud to send anything that comes to Atlanta."

"We've got to get on a computer."

"Take it your mom doesn't have one?"

She looked around at the redneck yard, nodding to the lawn chairs with their straps missing, the washing machine on the porch, the tractor rusting in the sunshine, the chickens and the gravel. "Yeah, she just traded up from her Toshiba."

He laughed. It hurt. But it hurt good.

Jonelle and her mother said little to one another about anything other than Steven's condition and their predicament, even on Thanksgiving Day morning. Esther's initial astonishment at seeing her daughter on her porch after truly believing she might never set eyes on her again gave way to worry about Steven's wounds and what he and Jonelle were going through. But the tension that manifested itself in their first encounter on the porch never left its place just below the surface. They peeled potatoes together and ignored it.

Jonelle explained the story of the Four Horsemen to her mother while she helped ready the turkey stuffing. Steven napped while the two women broke cornmeal, toasted bread, hulled chestnuts, and fried pork sausage with broken leaves of fresh sage. Hearing the story, Esther at first thought her daughter had been drinking, for, as she said, "This sounds like somethin' I mighta made up when I was boozin'." She was incensed that a man calling himself a Christian leader would do something so evil. And that all of them had nearly gotten away with it. "Though, I got to admit, make a mother real proud seein' her kid in the White House."

"Forget it," Jonelle said flatly. "I had enough trouble redecorating Sixteenth Street."

"I heard that story about Betty Ford's place on TV. I was real worried when I heard that."

"That would be a lot simpler problem, Mama."

Esther stopped what she was doing. "No, baby. I know. You're wrong about that."

Jonelle nodded. "I suppose I am." She realized she probably had no idea how hard it was for this woman to stop drinking after a lifetime of doing it every day.

"Knowin' you ain't followin' in your mama's footsteps gives me a lot of relief."

Jonelle turned the gas off under the pan of sausage and tasted a piece of crispy sage, and swooned. This was the kind of stuff she never ate, but it tasted so good. "My dressing never turns out like yours."

"Here's the secret." Esther started melting one whole pound of butter.

"Here's instant death," Jonelle quipped, watching her.

Esther dumped all the ingredients into a big chipped ceramic mixing bowl that Jonelle recalled from childhood. She poured the melted butter over the top, mixed it with her bare hands, and added some of the same chicken broth she'd served Steven last night. Then she pulled the turkey from the refrigerator and really got to work.

Before dinner, they talked to the kids. Jonelle felt strangely jealous when they assured her not to worry, they were having the time of their lives. Apparently, they loved being part of Victor's big boisterous family. She and Steven were really glad for them, for if they'd been miserable, they certainly would have felt even worse than they did missing them. Wyatt and Sarah both wished their grandmother a Happy Thanksgiving and said they hoped they could see her at Christmas. "I'm extendin' the invitation right now," Esther said with an eye to Jonelle. "Santa's gonna bring all your gifts down here this year, so you're just gonna have to come down to git 'em."

Wyatt squealed with delight.

Steven nodded to Jonelle. "But watch, Potomac's been here before."

"But of course."

Esther made enough food to feed them for a month. Besides the turkey and dressing, she served mashed potatoes, steamed bitter greens, heaped on the cranberries, and whipped up a delicious thick gravy that she promised Steven would make him well faster than any pills.

"Or kill him off for good from all the fat," Jonelle interjected.

Esther laughed. "Didn't hurt you none growin' up."

The meal was delicious, but the tension that seemed to have dissipated when they were cooking was back. Something unsaid was thick in the air. It was like the moment Esther had opened the porch door. For Jonelle it was the fact that she and Steven were here with her mother, and the children belonged here too, should always have been coming here. But Esther had made that impossible.

For Esther, it was just the opposite, that her daughter had never brought her family there before. All these years, all these delicious turkeys and no one to eat them but Esther herself, and perhaps whatever man she was married to at the time. She resented Jonelle for it, but her guilt was getting to her as well.

For both of them, all that needed to be said was boiling under the emotional holiday surface, and it was tough. Jonelle tried to break through. "I'm grateful, Mama, for what you're doing for us."

"I'm doing it for Steven," Esther responded sharply, almost hating herself for saying it but finding it impossible to take back. She continued working on her turkey leg.

Steven gave Jonelle a "don't pursue this" look, but she paid no attention. "Mama, isn't there a way for us to make peace?"

"You make peace with the Lord," Esther said, not looking at her. "With people you make up."

"That's what I'm trying to do."

Esther set her knife and fork down. "You show up on my door in the middle of the night and it's 'Mama, you gotta help us.' And I did. And I am. What about when I needed you? Was that so different? I called and called. I wrote. I would have faxed if I knew how to do that. Steven would say to you, 'Please talk to her, honey.' But did you? Ever? I needed you and you weren't there."

Jonelle said not another word. Because she knew it was true.

For dessert, Esther had baked a heavy chocolate cake so gooey it didn't even need frosting. They ate it in the parlor, allowing Steven to sit in the easy chair so his arm would be propped up in its sling. Afterward, they watched TV until Esther started snoring, and Steven told Jonelle he'd like her help climbing the stairs tonight so he could sleep in a real bed, not the davenport they'd had him on last night.

But Esther woke when they were starting to get up.

"We gotta go to sleep, Mama."

"Let me show you to your room."

Jonelle knew that was completely unnecessary, and it made her feel more like a guest than one of the family, but she let it go. Esther walked up the stairs in front of them, pointing out that the only bedroom available was Jonelle's old room. Jonelle would have preferred the other bedroom, but Esther explained it had long ago been turned into an office for the recently divorced husband, who had left it filled with boxes and crates. "Called himself a salesman," her mother said, "only I never saw him sell nothin'."

They slept in the bed in which she'd spent so many nights dreaming of escape. Coming here hadn't been easy for Jonelle, even with the necessity of getting Steven medical attention; it was no less difficult facing her mother again after all these years, after all the silence, all the pain. But under the circumstances, she didn't know where else to go, and Steven certainly felt it would be safe, and that it was also time.

With Steven there next to her, even in his weakened condition, even in his physical pain, to fight off the demons, Jonelle hoped she'd get a good night's sleep despite the fact this was a place she would never have come to under any other circumstances.

"Don't be so hard on her," he whispered just after she'd gotten him comfortable, just before they turned the light out.

"She was hard on me."

"You deserved it."

She swallowed. "It's tough. It's so tough. There's so much stuff."

"Get it out then. Talk about the stuff. Yell a little, scream if you need to, let her do the same. Get it out."

"I st . . . start to think about it and I . . . I fe . . . feel like I'm right back—"

"Honey," he said, soothingly.

"See? It's happening."

"Come on, Jone. You licked it long ago. Don't fall back in that trap."

She closed her eyes and nodded.

Softly, he added, "She's a good woman, Jone. And she's trying mighty hard." And then he drifted off.

But Jonelle couldn't sleep at all. She worried about having to talk it out, having to confront her mother about the past, and that was something she'd run from for more than twenty years. How could they discuss it if she couldn't even talk? If the words tangled up in her mouth, if she couldn't get them out? The therapist had told her it was psychological, and it sure was—every time she tried to face her early life with her mother, it happened.

And she worried about Steven. Was he really going to be all right? She had terrible anxiety about missing the kids, she longed for her work, she didn't like running, hiding, she wanted to talk to the FBI and get them to do something about their situation. At 4:00 A.M. she walked down the well-worn runner on the rickety stairs to the kitchen to find something to eat. Her mother was sitting at the table, drinking what was left of the dinner coffee. "Should have known that caffeine'd keep me up."

"You were out cold at nine," Jonelle told her.

"Then I got a decent night's sleep already. Sun'll be up in no time anyway."

"Mama, got some milk?"

"Whole. You city folk like skim, I bet."

"That's fine." She found it and poured herself some.

"How is he?"

"Sleeping. I think he's going to be fine. Took his temp before we went to bed. Normal."

"He's a good man, Jonelle. I'm very fond of him."

"That's 'cause he's been nice to you."

The woman nodded. "He has."

Jonelle thought by inference she was saying, *And you're not.* The silence was tense. It hung in the air like the dew they'd find on the lawn in a few hours.

Esther finally broke through. "What I was tryin' to say at dinner was I needed strength and I couldn't get it from my own girl."

"I was carrying too much resentment, Mama."

"No support for your mother?"

"Where was your support when I was stuttering?" There. She'd said it. And she didn't even trip on her words.

Esther looked away. "I did my best."

"You were embarrassed."

"Wasn't so!"

"You treated me like a freak, hiding me, telling people lies."

"I don't lie. I live by the Good Book."

"Mama!"

"I got you help. In them days, nobody even believed in head doctors."

"You were so ashamed that you told everyone I had some kind of blood disease."

"And was seein' a specialist in the city, yes."

Jonelle felt all the anger rising. "But it wasn't to help me. It was so you wouldn't have to deal with a retarded daughter."

Esther gasped. "Nope. Not so."

"I heard you," Jonelle cried out, "heard you telling Daddy before he left that you were praying to Jesus to understand why God gave you a 'retarded' child."

"You could barely talk, honey. In those days— Heck, we were hill folk even though we lived in the shadow of Atlanta. We didn't know about treatin' things like that."

"I wasn't retarded, Mama. I stuttered. One of the reasons kids do that is because of childhood trauma. Like when their parents get drunk and fight and throw things at each other."

"Now it's my fault? Course it's my fault."

"You didn't help me!" Jonelle was nearly in tears. "I wanted help, I wanted to speak like everyone else. I wanted to communicate, just communicate my thoughts, ideas, dreams, instead of having to tap on the floor like a horse. You took me for help only 'cause you were ashamed of me."

"I didn't know, honey. I really didn't know."

Jonelle rinsed her glass. "Well, you do now. And you've had a big clue for a long time now."

"What's that?"

"My career."

"Your career what?"

"I've made communication my life's work. Talk about slaying the dragons!"

Esther put her head in her hands. Jonelle couldn't tell if she was ashamed herself, troubled, tired, crying. She just sat like that for a long time, until Jonelle gave up waiting for her to speak and started to leave the room. "I'm glad you came here," Esther finally said. "It means a lot to me."

"Steven felt it was the only thing to do."

"Baby, couldn't you say it's good for you too?"

Jonelle pulled out a chair and sat at the table. Okay, she was going to give it a try. Maybe it was time to stop blaming and attempt that communication she'd always longed for. "Mama, you know what?"

"No, baby."

"I'm not stuttering now."

"Well, course you're not. I see you on TV all the time. You wouldn't have that job if you did."

"I mean here, with you. I always felt it coming back. Whenever I even thought about confronting you, it would happen. It happened on the porch that first night."

"I done a lot of things wrong," Esther said.

"So did I, Mama." Jonelle's eyes caught hold of a jar on the counter and she remembered something else. "You still make pickles?"

"Pickles?"

"Yeah, you and Grandma made pickles when she was still alive. Big barrels full. Real briny, garlic and dill, bright green and crunchy. You sent me to pick cherry leaves for the top."

It came back to Esther. "Oh, sure. That's right. We'd put them on the surface and then put some birch pieces on that, and I think even my iron to weight it down." She looked pleased. "Hadn't thought about that in years."

"Still playing the piano?"

"Course."

"Wyatt's taking lessons as well as Sarah now."

"Steven told me."

Jonelle tried not to tense up, tried not to react at all, but she couldn't help it. And Esther caught it. "Baby, listen, I know you wouldn't be here if you didn't have to be. All I ask is that we be civil to each other and give respect. The Lord will work things out for us."

Jonelle said, "We were doing better than being civil to one another. We were talking."

"True." She seemed thoughtful for a moment. "I know what I was like, I know why you run away, I would have done the same thing. I made a lot of mistakes. See, baby, I'm not an old woman. Which means I was a much younger woman then, too young to be a mom. I had learnin' to do and I figure I'm catchin' up now. No, you don't have to say nothin' more if you don't want to."

Jonelle was shocked, and impressed. All the way down here she'd known there was no other place to go, but she also worried what the big confrontation would be like, would there be hysterics and recriminations, would they tear each other's hair out, would Steven have to referee? And now the woman was telling her, simply, without emotion, that they didn't even have to say a thing? She quite honestly couldn't believe it.

She sat there for a few minutes, finishing her milk, looking at her mother's long slender fingers, the hands of a pianist, but with telling cracks and calluses speaking of the wear and tear of a hard life. Yet they were expressive, tender hands, and they seemed to communicate a language all their own, almost saying *come to me and I'll hold you, I'll not let you go.* Jonelle felt herself reaching for her mother's hand across the table, almost as if some invisible force were compelling her to do it, and when her own fingertips touched Esther's, she felt connected again, as if a light that hadn't been lit in years had suddenly been switched on again and lo and behold, it still worked, it still burned as brightly as the last day it had been seen. Esther's fingers came around hers and clenched her tightly in what was at that moment more meaningful than an embrace.

"Yeah . . . hello?"
"Barney?"

"James?"

"Barney, they're closing in on us."

"James, it's three in the fucking morning."

"Barney, they were here. East Hampton."

"What are you doing in the Hamptons? You're supposed to be looking for her."

"Saint Paul is on it."

"Shit."

"Shit? What's shit is the fact that it won't matter about her because they're onto us already."

"Who?"

"FBI."

"Again?"

"Almost busted the door in. Were here since ten. Raked me over the coals, wanted to know everything, every detail about my having worked with Leo, about the incidents—"

"The incidents?"

"Named them—the diver, His Eminence the Fucking Cardinal, Tucker, all of them. Barney, they know. They know everything."

"Not enough. Not enough to do anything about it."

"Barney, I'm scared."

"James. James? Are you crying? James, pull yourself together."

"Should have never said yes to this. Should have stayed with CBS. Shit, Barney, you ruined my goddamned life."

"James, stop talking non—" Suddenly, Barney found himself speaking to a woman, a woman who was shouting at him. "This is Nina Findley, Barney. Get them to stop this, get them to leave us alone. Do you realize how ill Jim is? Don't you have any compassion? Whatever this is about, get them to stop. Please!"

"Nina, it's all a big mistake."

Man's terrified voice again. "Barn, do what she says, get them to stop."

"Only way to stop is to silence Jonelle. Find out where she is and kill her!" He slammed the phone down.

Steven awoke at nine feeling like a new man. He and Esther had cereal together, and then she dressed and rebandaged his arm while he called the kids at Victor's family's house. They were less apprehensive than they were on Thanksgiving Day to talk to Grandma Lighter. They continued to make plans for Christmas. Esther told them she was going to start baking cookies today, and looking for the prettiest tree they ever saw. Sarah told her dad it felt really nice to speak with her. But Wyatt was ticked. "Why do you guys get to go see Grandma down in Georgie and we can't?"

"Georgia. Not Georgie."

"Potomac says Georgie."

"Well, he's wrong."

"His dad *lets* him say it that way."

"I can't win with you, can I? Listen, squirt, I promise, you and your sister will get to come down here soon."

"When it's safe again?" Wyatt asked.

"Yes," Steven admitted.

"Okay." No advice, apparently, from Potomac.

Steven convinced Esther that he was just fine, but he could not convince her that he was capable of driving just yet, so she chauffeured him into Atlanta in her truck. He went into a Kinko's and used a computer to E-mail Carole Axline, a friend at the TWA Ambassador Club at LAX:

Carole: I need your help. Please E-mail someone at the FBI for me. I'm afraid of my location being tracked. Can you do it from the club computer so they think I might have been flying and did it as I was changing planes? Please send this:

E-MAIL ADDRESS: BassQuant.gvt

Agent Kevin Bass: The man they have in custody is not Jacob Hughes. His real name is Daniel Rovig and he's the son of Rev. Steven Rovig, friend of my father and undoubtedly in on this whole thing. The anti-Christian stuff is all facade; Rovig/Hughes is one of them. Leo St. Pere tried to kill us last week at my father's house. He was there with the Horsemen. But we don't know what he looks like. Are you on our side? Are you helping us? If so, show us! Give us a sign. The Landscaper.

pilotsp@twa.stl.com

"Lookit this," Esther said when Steven returned to the truck. She was holding *USA Today*. She read him a column: " 'What was the FBI doing paying late-nights visits to the three moguls of Network ONE? Is there some kind of FCC trouble no one knows about?' "

"So Bass did do something!" Steven said joyously. "That's the sign we needed!"

She continued. "It goes on to say something about some stations they were considering buying, boring stuff. Then it says, '. . . and speaking of ONE, an insider at the Betty Ford Clinic strongly suggested that Jonelle Patterson isn't there after all. If not, where is she? Do the FBI visits have anything to do with her?' Make me curious, if I was readin' this."

They went to Hartsfield, where Steven was thrilled to find a package waiting at the TWA cargo office. Yesterday, Jonelle had called Bud in Saint Louis and told him of the new destination. As Esther drove back to the country, Steven discovered that someone had sent him two tapes. He couldn't wait to get to the van to see them.

Jonelle waved her arms in slight panic as they drove up the hill. "Where did you go? Are you okay? I was worried sick!"

Steven assured her he was fine, they'd had a good morning, and if Jonelle hadn't been playing Sleeping Beauty, they would have invited her along. Then he showed her the tapes.

She was as eager to view them as he was. "This could be it, Steven, this could do it!"

They went to the barn, where a chicken had nested in the back of the van. Steven shooed her out and showed Jonelle the newspaper column, told her what he'd sent Bass, explaining how it was premature because it looked to him like the FBI was actually doing something this time. He would await a reply to the E-mail before attempting to contact them again. Then he put the first tape into the machine. "Who sent them?" she asked.

Steven handed her the note that had accompanied them. It read:

Hello. I'm an amateur video freak whose MTV obsession led me to start taping just about everything I do since I was fifteen. Saw your request on the Web and here's a copy of an Emmy Award

party hosted by Barney Keller in 1998, a reception at the Museum of Broadcasting in 1998 as well, again featuring Mr. Keller, but also Mr. Findley and Mr. Santangelo. On the second reel, is Mr. Findley shortly after he left his job at CBS for his new position at ONE, talking all about ONE, at a party thrown by Helen Hunt. I'm the interviewer and I think I ask him some good questions. It's exclusive, it hasn't run anywhere. My address and phone numbers are above, if you need more, just say so. I would love a job in TV some day, and if this helps, great!
Sincerely,
Todd Husted

PS: Will I get screen credit if this airs somewhere? I really hope this helps.

"Zealous lad, isn't he?" Steven commented as they started watching the first tape.

"I'll give him an Emmy myself if he's got something here."

It turned out that Todd Husted, video freak and TV hopeful, helped immensely. At the Museum of Broadcasting reception, Findley was seen chatting with several people Jonelle recognized to be with CBS. In the group in a few frames was a face that both she and Steven immediately recognized: the face of a young man that was in one of the photos they were recently sent of the men together.

But was he Saint Paul?

The same face appeared, though less clear, in the tape of Helen Hunt's party on the second reel. No CBS people this time, but that same young man, his hair longer and bushier, and what appeared to be, though they couldn't be sure, a gold ring on the finger they were looking for.

But was he Saint Paul?

"Mama?" Jonelle asked when Steven went upstairs to rest.

"Baby?"

"Know anyone with a computer?"

Her mother just laughed.

"We need to access the Web. But we're running out of money.

They can trace us through credit cards, so Kathleen gave us cash, but it's almost gone."

"Got six hundred in the pickle jar."

Jonelle smiled. "Thanks, but it won't do it. I need a little laptop that—"

"Little Paulie Tyburski!"

"Who?"

"Polish lady from church, her boy. He just got outta college, works on computers somewhere in the city. I'll give her a call."

"Little" Paul Tyburski, who turned out to be anything but, handed Jonelle a black CTX laptop. "It's a 586, not Pentium, but it'll do for what you need."

"As long as it has a modem, I don't care how slow it is."

"Twenty-eight point eight."

"Great. Don't happen to have a scanner lying around, do you?"

He smiled. "Think not, ma'am."

"Didn't imagine you would." She looked at Steven. "Need to send Jake Hughes—Rovig's—photos to Bass." She looked back at Paulie. "Really appreciate this."

"Ever do a show on computers, I'm available." Then he looked unsure if he should say what he was about to say.

"Go ahead."

"You look pretty good for someone who's supposed to be in Betty Ford."

"Miraculous recovery, but don't tell anyone I'm out yet."

He winked. "Wouldn't dream of it."

In the bedroom, she and Steven accessed his E-mail at TWA and learned that Agent Bass had indeed replied to them:

We had no prints on file anywhere for Jacob (Jake) Hughes. Kid led a clean life before the arrest down in Virginia Beach. Indeed, he's Rovig, proven by birth record prints which we accessed. Won't talk. Father is silent also. I feel you're onto something.

Steven laughed. "No kidding."

Questioned the people involved. Charles P. included. Denied knowledge of any shooting, but kept asking if his son was okay. Going after Findley; feel he will be easiest to crack. We are trying to get pictures of Leopold St. Pere, will transmit to you when we do, you can compare. Suggest meeting at that time to determine outcome. Please stay safe. Bass.

"Barney? Clay here."
"Where are you?"
"Rex's beach house."
"Anything?"
"Not about the girl, but there's other news."
"What?"
"Just learned that our pal James Martin Findley set up a meeting with Barbara McMillan."
"Barbara McMillan? Barbara D. McMillan of the FCC?"
"Don't think he knows any other."
Barney's voice went to steel. "What for?"
"Your guess is as good as mine."
"This isn't good, Clay."
"You're telling me. Rex is very upset."
"Tell him not to be. I'll check this out and get back to you."
"Barney, we can't let him spill."
"Clay, careful. He could be seeing her for a legit reason. Something to do with the network."
"I hope. Honestly, Barney, I really hope so."
"Me too."

chapter 29

Jonelle put three sweet potatoes into the oven, and when she turned to help her mother clean the greens for salad, she saw that Esther had sat down. There was a very serious look on her face, a troubled expression. Jonelle asked, "What is it, Mama?"

"What these people are doing." She reached out and lifted her worn Bible from where it sat near the magazines and receipts she had piled by the phone. "Lord give us this book to live by. These men—preachers some of them—are Satan, just as Matthew and Luke describe 'em."

"They're hypocrites, Mama."

"Did they 'spect you to give up your values? Everything you were taught? I may have been a lousy mother, but I taught you by the Good Book."

"Yes, Mama," Jonelle agreed softly, "you gave me moral fiber. I'm no saint—boy, do I hate that word right now—but I know right from wrong."

"These men are gonna roast in hell."

"I'll light the fire myself."

"They figured wrong with my Jonie. Figured you're like most of them celebrities you read about in the *Globe*, just trash. I'm very proud of you, baby. Turnin' down what they offered was the Christian thing to do."

"It wasn't hard, Mama," she explained. "There was no question about it." But she thought about it for a moment, for the first time really thought about what it would have been like. A woman in the White House. Her. "Had I not known that they'd had a hand in making news happen, however, I might have gone along with it." Then she felt apprehensive, ambivalent. "I don't know. I'm not sure. It would have been a difficult decision."

"Maybe you can run for president anyway."

Jonelle got up and turned on the water in the sink to clean the lettuce. "The White House holds very unpleasant memories for me at this point," she deadpanned. "Now, come peel this cucumber here."

Steven was in bed. Jonelle sat at the little table in the corner of the room, working on the laptop. She was reading the news headline:

SOUTHERN CHRISTIAN LEADER SHOCKED THAT SON IS IDENTIFIED AS MAN WHO SHOT AT PRESIDENT!

"Our buddy the elder Rovig says he's going to pray for his boy."

"Better add one for his own hide as well," Steven said. "Check your E-mail again."

She did. "Everyone at the studio is worried. Eight messages posted." She studied them. "Dale Harmon says you most certainly can use a computer while in the Betty Ford Clinic, and told me not to ask how he knows."

Steven laughed.

"Robin wants to know why am I not answering."

"Don't do it. Don't risk it."

She nodded. She wanted to write Kathleen too, but she still feared them tapping into Kathleen's computer or phone lines and learning where they were. So she brought up the still shots that Steven had isolated from the tapes sent to them by the video nut.

There was that same man in five of the shots, clear shots of his face, yet still missing one vital element: the ring on his hand. No matter how much Steven had magnified them, they didn't provide the conclusive evidence they needed so badly.

Jonelle sat moving back and forth between them on the screen, not so much studying them anymore as providing background music for her brain, which was clicking and clicking. Then it came to her. In the Museum of Broadcasting reception photo, in the crowd over what they thought to be Saint Paul's shoulder, stood a man in a dark sport coat over a T-shirt. He had close-cropped hair and he was holding a camera. "Oh, my," she said as it dawned on her.

"Oh my what?" Steven mumbled, half in dreamland.

"That's Larry Woldt."

"Who's he?"

"One of the paparazzi in New York. He's got the biggest collection of JFK Junior photos in the world."

"Jackie's son's own Ron Galella?"

"He's just wacko, fearless, he's the one who broke into the Gingrich-DeGeneres wedding last year."

"And almost went to jail for it?"

"That's him." She thought for a moment, studying the man in the photo she had on the screen. "You know, it looks as if he's about to shoot this same photo from the other angle."

Steven sat up in bed. "And the way Saint Paul is holding the glass, you'd see his ring from the other side."

"Exactly."

"Can we find this guy?"

Jonelle closed the lid of the computer. "We can't afford not to."

"James?"

"Barney, I'm busy."

"I told you to go down to Virginia! Clay learned they patched him up down in Petersburg. Someone told the cops they saw a woman driving a van tying a guy's arm in a sling in some parking lot. Blood everywhere, they said. That means they headed south."

"Saint Paul's down there with Clay and Rex. I can't go."

"Previous engagement?"

"Too sick."

"Not too sick to visit with Barbara McMillan."

"Who?"

"You heard me. Barbara D. McMillan, assistant director of the FCC."

"It's business, been scheduled forever."

"Yeah? What for?"

"HDTV."

"Selling like crazy, compatibility worked out, what more needs to be talked about?"

"Hell if I know. She didn't enlighten me."

"You called *her*. You asked for a meeting. Said it was 'vital.' "

"How do you know that?"

"Don't you dare try to fuck with me, Findley."

"You threatening me?"

"You talk to Barbara McMillan and I'll make sure you are buried right alongside America's favorite reporter."

"Rex, put Clay on."

A moment passed. "Clay here."

"It's Barney. They're using the Net."

"Can we get their E-mail? Confiscate what someone's sending them?"

"We can try. But it's not foolproof. It's a big Web out there."

"What do we know for sure?"

"They contacted a celebrity photographer in Manhattan."

"What for?"

"Beats me," Barney admitted. "Probably want a picture of something."

"Saint Paul."

"Could be."

"Can we monitor his E-mail?"

"No. He's all over the place, has a hundred different E-mail addresses."

"Clean out his archives."

"Can't clean out his computer, they're probably all in there."

"Technology," Clay muttered. "What a rotten age we live in."

"Did the FBI talk to Findley again?"

"No, but they had agents interrogating kids at the studio here."

"No shit."

"Tell Rex that all his Christian soldiers are being questioned as well—Robertson, Reed, Falwell, even Tammy Faye."

"She's in bad shape like James. Same cancer problem."

"If he talks to the FCC, it's not his cancer that's going to kill him."

"You tell him so?"

"I did. Clay, they know Hughes is Rovig."

"So what? Jake'll never talk. I'm sure of it."

"It ties to Patterson!"

"No, makes perfect sense: Jake is gonna tell them it's all in defiance of his father and his strict Bible-thumping upbringing."

"I wish I never heard of the Bible and this goddamned Christian movement. We Jews are just a lot more subtle about the way we do things."

"Yeah, like the Israeli army."

On the computer screen, Jonelle and Steven read the following:

Dear Jonelle,

Got your cryptic message. Found me in the Donnelly E-mail Yellow Pages? Glad to see it works. Yes I can access my photos of the MOB event in 1998. I have 434 of them. Since I can't be sure which one suits your purpose— the reverse shot of a photo you have of a man with a drink in his hand (everybody had drinks in their hand at that dull event)—I can do one of two things. A: Send you all 434 photos at $100 each and you find what you're looking for. B: You E-mail or fax me the pic you want the reverse of, and I'll fax or E-mail you what I think matches, for $1,000. You can see that 'B' is the better deal, but it's your money.

Larry Woldt Photography

Steven was aghast. "Forty thousand bucks for pictures of people drinking vodka and sticking carrot sticks into their mouths!"

"It's how he makes his money."

"We take the suggested option."

"Right. I'll attach the photo to the E-mail."

Steven worried. "But how will we pay him? A check will take time."

"Electronic banking," Jonelle said with confidence.

"Huh?"

"How do you think I do it at home? I can have a transfer of money—an electronic check—sent to anyone's account, anywhere, in seconds."

"Technology. Sometimes it really comes in handy."

A few hours later, when she opened the CTX, the screen flashed, the machine beeped, and she saw the notice indicating

YOU HAVE MAIL. CHECK MAILBOX.

"Is it Woldt already?" Steven asked with enthusiasm.

"Boy, that was fast," she said, finding the message.

"He must really be hungry."

But it wasn't from Larry Woldt. It was from the FBI. As Jonelle downloaded the attachment, she nearly jumped up and down. Steven watched a photo appear on the screen. They found themselves staring into a man's face, clearly the same man they'd just sent a photo of to Woldt. Only this one was closer, more detailed. He was younger, thinner than the man they believed to be Saint Paul, and his hair seemed a wild confection like black cotton candy atop his head. Jonelle knew from the features—the cheekbones, the slightly crazed eyes—that this was the man she slammed into on the staircase in Jared Tucker's Paris apartment building. The accompanying E-mail said:

In the hope of saving time, I'm sending this both to TWA and to Jonelle's personal E-mail. This is a photograph of Leopold St. Pere, Canadian, worked at CBS, etc. Is this your man? Reply immediately. Bass.

Jonelle typed:

Yes! But to positively link him to the incidents, we need photograph with his hands in the picture as well as his face. We are in process of obtaining that. A&L

She sent it by reply E-mail.
Then they waited for another.
Nothing came.

"Barney, it's Clay."

"What's up? Locate them?"

"Not yet. But our buddy Saint Paul just told me something very interesting."

"What's that?"

"Findley's wife knows about everything."

"He can't be that crazy."

"He is. Saint Paul's had dinner with them, she talks about everything as if she's in on it. And there's more. She keeps a diary."

"Jesus."

"Did you stop him from meeting with the FCC?"

"I hope so."

"What are you going to do now?"

"Put a tail on Nina Findley as well."

"What's the matter, baby?"

Jonelle looked up to see Esther standing over her. She had gone to the storage room after dinner, and was sitting on the floor when Esther surprised her. She was looking through a box of her report cards, photos when she was a child, mementos that Esther had saved all these years. "Nothing, Mama. Just traveling down memory lane."

Esther pulled up some floor and joined her. "Got all your clippings right over there," she said, pointing to a big cardboard tomato box. "Everything they ever wrote about you in the local paper, the *TV Guide*, and the papers you get in the food store."

"Oh, no."

"I don't believe that stuff. You havin' an affair with Brad Pitt, nonsense."

Jonelle gave her mom a conspiratorial look. "Don't tell anyone, Mama, but *that* one was true."

Esther laughed heartily. "Don't suppose he likes older women, do you?"

"I'm older than he is," Jonelle reminded her.

"I mean really older," Esther sang, and together they laughed again, and felt the walls tumbling down.

Jonelle proudly showed her mother her report card from the fifth grade. "Mrs. Rupp even wrote a personal note," she said, handing it to Esther, "see?"

Esther lifted up to her nose the reading glasses that hung on a chain around her neck. "Can't make it out—" She brought the yellowed paper closer to her face, then pulled it away.

"Need bifocals?" Jonelle inquired.

"These do me fine. Get 'em at the K mart, they're only nine dollars so you can sit on them all you want." Then the card came into focus and she read: " 'Jonelle continues to assert herself in all ways, despite her problem. She's a bright girl with a great curiosity and should be encouraged. Marge Rupp.' " Esther put the card down. Her expression changed. "Did you show me this to dig the knife a little deeper?"

"No. It was the 'asserting' myself line that I liked. I always was pushy, even then."

"Despite your 'problem.' "

"That's what they called it then."

Her mother softened. "Was it hard, honey? I mean, I don't really know, I was in a real state those days. Sometimes I don't remember your childhood. I was in a bad way."

"It was hard, yes. Mama, think of it this way. My brain is sharp and interested in everything, and I'm curious, like Mrs. Rupp says, about everything. I want to jabber about everything I think of. But the words don't come out."

"Sometimes you talked just fine."

"When I was relaxed, when I wasn't feeling frustration. Or pain."

"Pain?"

"You and Daddy."

Esther nodded. "We never belonged together. I think we loved each other. I loved him, I know that. But we were—this is a new term I learned—mutually dependent. On the booze and on each other. It was unhealthy for us, and even more so for you. But we didn't know that then."

Jonelle nodded. "We only recently learned the damage that gets done to kids. And it's insidious, like diabetes, you don't feel symptoms when you're young, even though you have high blood sugars, you don't hurt or feel bad so you don't think it's doing you any real harm. But the devastation comes when you're older, all those high sugars over the years directly lead to losing your eyesight, a limb, heart attacks, dialysis. Kids are resilient, they bounce back the next morning, and who'd have thought anyone was doing them long-term damage?"

Esther took Jonelle's hand. "Did it? I mean now, are you okay now. Is your marriage good, are you raisin' your kids good? Did I hurt you that bad?"

Jonelle patted her hand. "I'm okay, Mama. I've had years of therapy. Steven is the most understanding gift from God a woman could ask for. Wyatt and Sarah are cool kids. I think overcoming the stuttering left me with a feeling that I could walk on water, the conquering hero, which has helped make me successful. It's given me drive and ambition. It was the emotional damage that was the hardest."

"You mean blamin' your own ma?"

Jonelle nodded. "So many women I know have had happy, healthy relationships with their mothers. I have envied every one of them deeply."

Esther's eyes filled with emotion. "Is it too late?"

Jonelle smiled. "I don't think it's ever too late."

Esther nodded, "Appreciate that. Your forgiveness, it's what God teaches us is the hardest and best human thing to do. We missed a lot of talks 'cause you couldn't talk, you know? Maybe we can start now."

"Mama," Jonelle said, reaching up to kiss her on the cheek, "we just did."

———

The next morning, it all started to get to her. Jonelle awoke feeling anxious, stir-crazy. Even the calming talk with her mother—which had gone on into the late hours—didn't hold. She felt as if she were going to go out of her mind if she had to stay in hiding any longer. She tried to contain the feeling, but it slipped out in a strange way. "I checked the messages," she told Steven in the bathroom when he was brushing his teeth. "Jenny Flexner is coming to D.C. from Manhattan and wants to take me and her mom out to lunch."

"So?"

She burst out with emotion. "I want to go!"

Steven told her to be patient.

"Patient? I should be *patient*?" She was loud, nearly shouting. "I want to move around with freedom, Steven. I want to go to McDonald's with my kids and not worry someone's going to kidnap them. I want to play tennis with Lynne and not think I'm gonna get shot! Patient?" She turned and slammed out of the house.

"She's not comfortable here," Esther said when Steven came downstairs. "And she must miss the kids pretty bad."

"I do too," Steven reminded her, "but we just have to stay put until we hear something."

"Go talk to her," Esther said kindly. "Tell her you love her. She's hurting. She wants her life back."

Steven found Jonelle in the field behind the barn. It was a cool, gray, drizzly December day and he brought her a jacket. As he walked up behind her and placed it firmly on her shoulders, he said, "This might help."

She accepted it but said nothing. She looked away. He touched her shoulder and said he was sorry.

"Don't be sorry, it's not your fault."

"The frustration is getting to me too. Shall we do it without them?"

"Do what?"

"Tell the world? Get the help we need, get someone actually believing in us, force them to act."

She shrugged. She'd like nothing better. "How?"

He couldn't answer that. He took her hand and they walked a little. "I hated growing up here and I hate it now."

"She's a good person."

"Not Mama. This place, it seems so . . . out of touch. So primitive. Rather than feeling safe, I feel like we're in prison."

"We're loved here, protected."

She turned to him and shouted, "I miss my kids! Steven, I want our children back! I want—" She burst into tears and fell into his arms. "The kids want to spend Christmas here, but I don't want to stay here from now till then!"

"We won't, don't even think that."

"I can't have Christmas without Wyatt and Sarah," she cried.

"Honey, it's almost over." He meant it, but he was frustrated too.

"We've got to do something."

He took a stab. "Send everything to Katharine Graham? She printed *The Pentagon Papers*, Watergate—"

Through her tears, she said, "It's an idea."

He was on a roll. "Or put together a segment of your show exposing these guys."

She wiped her face and laughed. "That would be rich. Could you see me telling Barney I want to do the exposé on these guys who call themselves the Four Horsemen?"

Steven laughed and added, "And Clay can produce it!" For a moment he wished it were more than a fantasy, he'd give anything for it to be possible.

And then Jonelle said the magic words. "Wait a minute."

He looked at her. "What?"

She didn't answer, but the wheels in her head were turning so loud they could be heard over the next blue ridge.

"Jone?" He liked this. He'd seen this before, and this always meant something fascinating was coming. She'd had this look many times when she was thinking up a hot story idea. "Jonelle?"

Her voice was serious now. "Steven, what did Wyatt say?"

"When?"

"What did he say when he gave us advice? He told us to *infiltrate*."

"He said *Potomac* said to infiltrate."

"Potomac, Wyatt, it's the same person. *Infiltrate, Mom! Infiltrate, Dad!* Get the bad guys."

"What are you getting at?"

"I think Wyatt figured out how we're going to win this, Steven. I think he gave us the answer. Screw begging for the FBI's help!"

"What do you mean?"

"I mean we could do it, the segment—the fantasy could come true."

His wheels started clicking as well. "The van."

She quickly nodded. "Televise from the van."

"How?"

"Satellite?"

"We need to get into the network feed."

"So, let's."

"Not from here. D.C., maybe, New York for sure, but Atlanta, forget it."

"You just gave me an idea."

"How?"

"New York. Maybe my show isn't the place to do it. They're playing reruns I'm sure, the audience just won't be there."

"Advertise it."

"Are you nuts?"

He thought about it. "I see your point."

But he'd given her an idea. "We could, however, pull that off on somebody else's show."

"Larry King?"

"Chris," she said exuberantly.

"Chris? Who's Chris?"

"Christiane."

"Amanpour? She's on another network."

She nodded. "On the highest rated show in the world on that network. Perfect place to tell this story. Think of the publicity, *This week on* 60 Minutes, *a live interview with Jonelle Patterson!* Think of the overnights, that'll kill Barney Keller off without having to shoot him."

Steven laughed, but cautioned her. "We can't do a publicized live show, they'd get us at the studio. It's like saying come murder us."

"We won't be broadcasting from New York."

"You're going too fast for me."

"We'll do our part of the show from the best place I know."

Where she was going started to sink in. "Your studio."

She smiled. "I'm going to destroy Barney Keller from the inside, with his cameras, his equipment, the people on his payroll, from right under his nose."

"Revenge is sweet."

"Infiltrate!"

"Come on," she said, grabbing his hand as the rain started to fall, "we've got work to do. First of all, we have to think up a phony show format to advertise, something that's close to what we're going to do—"

"The Future!" Steven announced off the top of his head. "A Woman in the White House!"

Jonelle jumped over one of the dogs. "I love it!"

"Clay?"

"Barney, you've got that tone in your voice."

"James didn't meet with the FCC."

"Thank God."

"His wife did."

"What?"

"Nina Findley spent three hours in Barbara McMillan's office this morning."

"You sure? You positive?"

"Positive."

"What did she tell her?"

"Don't know, but I'm certain they didn't exchange recipes or discuss HDTV."

"Barney, we can't let this happen. We've got to stop them."

"I've already taken care of it, Clay. It's done."

While Steven worked on their presentation tape for the FBI in the van, inside the house Jonelle got an E-mail posting from Larry

Woldt telling her he had the photo she wanted, almost the exact reverse of the one she'd sent him. He gave her his Chase banking information and told her that as soon as the money was transferred, he'd send the photo.

Jonelle then carefully composed an E-mail message to Christiane Amanpour and sent it to her both through CNN and CBS. Then she crossed her fingers.

Only eighteen minutes later, as she sat talking to her mother, learning more about the woman she'd chosen not to know for so many years, and just when she was starting to believe how tough it had been on her and the courage it had taken to finally stop drinking, her E-mailbox clicked and flashed. She inputted the appropriate keystrokes, double-clicked, and there it was:

Jonelle. Message received. My cell phone is 500-887-8000. I'm waiting for your call. You can count on my help. Christiane.

Jonelle didn't even stop in the barn to tell Steven. Driving her mother's truck, she was so excited that she almost went off the road in the rain. The phone hanging on the wall outside the tavern offered no protection from the downpour, but she didn't mind. She called the number. Her old, dear friend answered.

They talked for one hour.

When Jonelle hung up, she turned on the TV. She hadn't looked at it in days and was curious what was on *Nightline*. And there was Ted Koppel, expanding on the day's top story, which she'd missed completely: *The shocking and curious deaths of James and Nina Findley.*

Clay stood in a phone booth in Virginia Beach. "They did a good job," he told Barney. "Everyone speculated he lost his mind with the cancer pain and couldn't bear leaving the world without her."

From his cell phone, Barney agreed. "Shot her and then turned the gun on himself. It's classic."

"Her diary?" Clay inquired.

"Quite a writer, the little woman. Got 'em all."

"Good work."

"How'd Saint Paul take it?"

"Sadly. He was fond of James, Nina too. But he understood. No tears."

"Sounds like he's got a real heart."

Clay threw it back at him. "Like you do."

Barney asked, "What about Barbara McMillan? It'll make her suspicious. I mean, Koppel said it was."

"No evidence. We'll weather it."

"You've gotta find them, Clay. I did what I had to do here. Now it's up to you guys down there."

"No sweat, Barn. They can't be far. Holed up somewhere waiting for Sherlock to get well."

"Make sure he doesn't."

chapter 30

The next morning was Friday. The rain had not let up all night. The ceiling was leaking just as Jonelle recalled from her childhood, despite the fact that her mother said it had been patched three times. The dogs seemed unfazed, but the cat was nowhere to be seen, and even the chickens were hiding. Steven sunk into the mud—as deep as his ankles—the night before as he attempted to hightail it back to the house from the barn, and today it was worse. They knew they should stay indoors. There was a lot of planning to do.

"But, baby," her mother said, "you're just setting yourself up for danger. Look what they did to that man."

"We don't know for sure, Mama."

"You said so yourself last night. You said you knew they killed him, his wife too."

"He wasn't the kind of person who commits suicide."

"Then I made my point."

"Got a better idea, Mama?"

"Why don't the FBI do somethin'? Isn't this their problem?"

"We asked for more help, for another photograph. We've heard nothing."

Steven added, "They haven't done much through this whole saga. I'm frustrated. I don't trust them. This will work if we can only make the logistics happen." He turned to Jonelle. "Did you get the people at the studio?"

"Yes. They're loyal, they hate Keller too. Chris knows somebody at ONE as well, a good producer, it'll make it even safer. I'm going to E-mail them individually tomorrow. That's the day before, just enough time. The publicity should hit today. Chris said they're taking full-page ads in the *Times*, *Washington Post*, *Chicago Tribune*, *USA Today*, *LA Times* all of them. Blanket the country."

"Cool," Steven said.

Her mother still looked worried. "You really trust this woman?"

"I'd trust Christiane with my life," Jonelle said.

"Well, you'd better," her mother replied, " 'cause that's just what you're puttin' into her hands."

At 11:00 A.M. they received the reply from Larry Woldt. He attached a color picture to his message:

Jonelle. Money transferred beautifully. I'm sending you a bonus, two for one, no extra charge. Came across yet another shot with the guy you are interested in. Hope it helps. Let's do business again sometime. Larry Woldt

The first photo was clearly the reverse, shot almost at the same moment, of the picture they had of Saint Paul at the Museum of Broadcasting event. There was Saint Paul—Leo St. Pere—holding the champagne glass in his hand, but this time the ring was visible. "I'll bet he used Velvia film," Steven commented, "it's crystal clear."

The second photo was darker, and a little grainy by comparison, but it was pay dirt. It was taken the same night, at the same event, and there was Leo, standing with a drunken leer on his face, between Nina and James Findley. His arms were flung around their shoulders—were they holding him up?—and the gold ring could clearly be seen on the hand resting just above Nina Findley's right breast.

They compared the new photos on the screen to the ones they had already printed, and it was irrefutable: This hand matched the hands in all the incidents, same stubby, thick fingers with the gold band, distinct striations, and this time there was a face attached to it, the exact same face with the cotton candy hair that Agent Bass had sent them. They E-mailed him:

Bass: Have proof positive now. Our man, face and ring, in a photo hugging Findley! Advise what to do.

Steven kissed Jonelle. "We're in the final stretch."

She finally felt it was true. "We are."

"I'm going to finish the tape," Steven said.

Jonelle said, "Remind me to send Larry flowers," and handed Steven the disk on which she'd downloaded the photos. "I've got to work the details of the format out with Chris." She went back to the computer.

"And I'm going to the barn," Steven said.

"Not until I get you some boots," Esther warned, and motioned him to the kitchen.

Passing the computer, Steven stopped and looked down, and Jonelle's eyes met his. Her heart soared. Then he kissed her hard and lovingly, expressively on the lips. "I think," he said softly, "this is finally over."

"Why'd you page me?" Barney asked into the telephone in Long Island's Islip Airport.

"You stupid fuck!" Clay shouted.

Barney ignored the greeting. "Clay? Where are you? Findley's stinking wake is tonight, the funeral is tomorrow, you've got to be here!"

"They're in Georgia!"

Barney blinked. "What did you say?"

"They're just where you said they would 'never go,' remember?

They went to both, first to his old man and then her old lady. You asshole."

Barney didn't retort; he had it coming. "Where are you now?"

"We're in a dive motel in Gainesville. Just got the report. I'm coming to New York. Saint Paul is going to get some sleep and continue on to Atlanta to pop 'em in the morning."

"Jesus, you're sure?"

"They're with Mama. They've been chatting up a storm with the FBI. They got some kind of tape made—"

"Get it," Barney ordered.

"With pleasure."

Then Barney urged, "Go with him. I'll cover for you at the funeral."

"What'll you say?"

"I'll tell them you got your dick stuck in Rex Heald."

If it was supposed to sound funny, Clay didn't take it that way. "You're a sick man."

"I'll say flu or something."

"It'll look suspicious. No, I've got to be there. I'm on my way. I'm sending Saint Paul to do it alone."

"You sure he can?"

"Positive. See, he's got more incentive now. He's real ticked at them for making him kill Findley."

chapter 31

At the garish funeral parlor on Long Island, Clay made his way over to Barney when he finally got a moment alone. "Doesn't look too bad for a guy who had a bullet through his skull," Barney sniffed, nodding toward the open caskets bedecked with roses.

"Nina looks miserable."

"Think about it. Poor bitch puts up with him for over fifty years, and just when she thinks she's gonna be rid of him, she joins him in heaven."

"I'd kill myself."

"An ironic notion."

Clay changed the subject. "I was just out in the lobby."

"So?"

Clay unfolded a newspaper. "I take it you haven't seen this."

Barney looked at the full-page ad for *60 Minutes* and gaped. And then read with interest: "Christiane Amanpour in a full hour on 'The Future: A Woman in the White House?' "

Clay quoted the ad. " 'Political power in the hands of women?

An interview with Vice President-Elect Dianne Feinstein! Secretary of State Madeleine Albright! New Jersey Governor Christine Whitman! Arianna Huffington on her belief that a female president is our destiny! And a live interview with Jonelle Patterson, who many say will be that candidate!' "

"They're wrong about one thing, it won't be a live interview." He stood there for a moment and then grinned. "It'll help."

"Help what?"

"Our chances."

"Barney, tomorrow sometime, somewhere down in a ditch in Georgia, Jonelle's gonna be in the same condition James is." He nodded again toward the casket.

"Our chances to get out of this, Jonelle's chances for sympathy. The way she'll be remembered. Look, she's been off the wall, Betty Ford and all that, drinking and drugs, now it's going to appear that she got in deep shit and someone iced her."

"Saint Paul's going to call the minute it's over."

"I'll be in my apartment," Barney said. "Make sure Saint Paul makes it look like a robbery if he has to kill all three of them. Maybe burn the house down. Where are you going to be so I know where to reach you?"

"I'm leaving right after the service in the morning."

"Back to Rex?"

"Told Saint Paul to call there. Hopefully, we'll know it's over by the time old James is six feet under."

"See you at the cemetery."

Clay started to move away, toward Findley's children, to give them a final word of consolation. "Clay, if I forget tomorrow, remember to watch."

"Watch what?"

"*60 Minutes.*"

"What for?"

"It's gonna do numbers."

"You really gonna risk getting on a plane?" Esther asked them with concern at the crack of dawn on Saturday.

"Air travel's still the safest way to go," Steven said.

Esther put her hands on her hips. "You know what I mean."

"Gotta be there today, Mama," Jonelle said. "We don't have a choice."

"It's dangerous. They'll recognize you."

"We talked about that last night," Jonelle said, glancing at Steven. "Steven thinks we can do it."

Steven dug into a pile of flapjacks adorned with melting apple butter. "A big hat and sunglasses and it'll be fine. I can bend the rules at TWA and get us on with false names. But, Mom, I think we'll have to take you up on your offer of the money in the pickle jar. We'll buy the tickets with cash."

"Worries me," Esther said, reaching for the money, which was wrapped securely in several rubber bands. She joined them at the table, handed it to Steven, and then lifted her orange-juice glass. "To a safe journey."

They clicked glasses together and ate breakfast. Halfway through, Jonelle said, "Thanks, Mama. You've been real good to us. God knows, better than I've been to you."

"Kin is what it's all about," Esther only said, but they could see that her heart was brimming with emotion, her face betraying the burst of feeling she was holding inside. "And I aim to get to know my grandkids real soon."

"You will," Steven said confidently. "You will. We're all coming back for Christmas, remember?"

It was still raining when they left the house. Steven got Esther's truck from the garage and drove it around to the back door, where there was a little porch to aid them in staying dry. The plan was to leave the van locked in the barn, while Esther would drive them to Hartsfield. She knew they would be rushed there, so she took a moment to say good-bye to them before they got into the truck. She pressed her hand on the sling still holding Steven's right arm. "Steven," she said with emotion, "I'm glad you're better. My Jonie's in good hands. I love you."

Steven closed his eyes and gave her a big hug with his free arm.

Then Jonelle faced the moment. "Mama, how do I ever thank

you? We have so much more to talk about, catch up on. So much more to do."

"Hush, now. You'll come back for that. We'll have plenty of time, plenty. The Lord's gonna see to that. Gonna make up for what we missed."

Jonelle felt rain on her cheeks, and then realized it wasn't rain at all but tears flooding down. "I . . . I love you, Mama," she said as she kissed her on the cheek. "I've never not loved you."

Esther brushed her own tears away. "Git now. We've got to put the pedal to the metal."

But they didn't get far. Esther's heavy foot hit the brakes when she saw the beat-up old white car sideways across the entrance to the farm. It was an Impala in its death throes, sitting half on the muddy road and half in Esther's driveway, between the gate posts. A man wearing a yellow rain slicker was standing behind the car, attempting to shove a piece of broken fence wood under the left rear wheel to give it traction. He got in, started it, put it in gear, only to send the piece of wood flying, and the wheel sinking deeper into the muck.

"Oh, would you lookit that idiot," Esther muttered, knowing it was a lost cause in that mud.

Steven opened the truck's passenger door and put his head out. "What happened?" he called to the man.

The stocky man replied with a hayseed accent. "Mornin', y'all. Just plum slid off the road. Lend a hand?"

As Steven and Jonelle got out to help—they had no choice, for there was no other way for them to get to the airport—Esther talked to herself. "What's he doin' on this road? Don't know nobody owns a car like that . . ."

As Steven and Jonelle walked closer to the disabled car, the man said, "Got some sand in here, might help," and lifted the trunk lid.

In the truck, Esther said, "Don't know this guy—" Her voice stopped because she now saw, as if in slow motion in her mind, the automatic rifle Yellow Slicker was lifting from the trunk. Steven was holding Jonelle's hand to help her walk on the slippery hill, and they were about five feet from the passenger side of the car. The man deftly lifted the rifle to his shoulder. Esther opened the door, and more deftly cocked her shotgun and fired.

The crack was loud, echoing through the trees. The front of the man's raincoat was suddenly spattered with red. When Steven realized what was happening, he threw himself over Jonelle, pushing her down to the mud, protecting her body with his. Yellow Slicker, still standing, gave a childlike moan in startled, shuddering pain. The rifle fell from his hands and sank into a puddle. He retched, one fast burst. And then tumbled into the mud himself.

"No one's messin' with my girl, hear?" Esther said, staring at the inert figure of the assassin.

Then she came back to earth and helped Jonelle from the ground while Steven hurried to the man. The gold ring on his chubby finger seemed to sparkle and gleam through the rain. He turned him over. He was gasping for breath, holding his hands over the bleeding hole in his stomach.

"We've got to get him help," Steven said as the women approached. "He's still alive."

"My God," Jonelle said, seeing his face as Steven lifted him from behind, under his arms, dragging him to the Impala, just now realizing, "it's Saint Paul."

"Open the back door," Steven ordered, and Esther did. "Help me get him inside."

Once he was safely in the gigantic rear seat, Esther said, "I'll get help, you leave this to me. You git on the road, git!" They knew she was right. They had to take off. There was no choice. "Take this," Esther said, handing Steven the shotgun. "Put it under the seat where it was. Never know when it'll come in handy."

"I'll say," he agreed with an ironic smile. He kissed her. Jonelle turned to her mother one last time. "What are you going to tell—?"

"Baby, I told some big fibs when I was drinkin'. I've had me lots of practice. This is gonna be a good yarn." Esther jumped into the driver's seat and started the Impala, backing it up to give them room to get out. Steven put the truck in gear and they were off.

———

They drove first to a post office, where they sent the tapes to the FBI in Quantico by Express Mail, guaranteeing Sunday delivery. Then they continued to Hartsfield, where Steven avoided the commercial terminal, passing TWA. Jonelle didn't understand. "Where are you going? I thought you—"

"I just said that. I didn't want you to freak if I had to steal a plane."

"Steal a plane?"

"Turns out I don't. There's this optometrist named Dr. Beuthe who built his own. We've got to find hangar number seven . . ."

"Whose optometrist?"

"Pilot I know. We're borrowing it."

"A plane some eye doctor built?"

"They'll recognize you on a commercial flight. I can't bypass security, it's an FAA regulation, I lied about that. It's this or we drive."

She shrugged. "We fly."

"Clay? You heard anything yet?"

"Barney, no, actually, nothing."

They nodded to some mourners on the cold, windswept hill in the overcrowded cemetery where they were waiting for the minister. "Why not?"

"Don't know."

"If Saint Paul fucked this up—"

"Barney, it's still early. Calm down. You're starting to sound like James."

"We're all going to end up like James if we don't hear from this bastard."

"Barney, he's gonna call." The minister arrived and everyone went silent. "Count ratings in your head or something," Clay said. "Have some respect for our late partner."

"We're going to have to send Dr. Beuthe money for the cleaning crew he's going to have to hire to clean up all the mud," Jonelle said somewhere over northern Georgia. They were filthy. They were shaken by what happened on the road just over two hours ago. They were flying six hundred miles in a tiny but sleek airplane that an eye doctor had built on weekends for fun and Jonelle wished she could be anywhere but there, anyone but herself today. Over Hoscoton, Steven patted the broadcast tape in the backpack near his feet and finally talked about it. "Close call."

"When I saw the gold ring," Jonelle said, "it was almost like an old friend we've been trying to find."

"Some friend."

"How'd Saint Paul locate us?"

"Don't know. But your mother was terrific."

"She's had practice. Chased my dad with a gun once, shot out all the car windows yelling and screaming in some jealous rage. And she wondered why I stuttered."

He checked the altitude and brought them down a hundred feet, as the flight plan Steven had filed had indicated. "There's a good side to what happened," he said.

"What's that?"

"Now there's only three of them after us."

"Barney, you leaving?"

"Hell yes. Funerals give me the willies. And it's too fucking cold out here. Saw you on the phone when that minister was blessing the old bastard. Anything?"

"Rex is a little worried. Me too. We should have heard by now."

"I'm going to be at Lincoln Center. Matinee. Page me the minute you hear something. Anything."

"Okay."

When Barney Keller got in the limo that would take him back to Manhattan, to the Metropolitan Opera House, he knew his mind was not going to be on Mephistopheles. He laughed. How ironic, going to see *Faust*. Jonelle had sold her soul to four devils, and now she wanted her money back, now she was out to destroy them. Well, she may have eluded Saint Paul, and driven Findley to suicide—well, sorta—and who knew what she'd do to Clay and that goddamn Rex? But Barney swore she wouldn't get him. She would never destroy him. He was a Horseman, he *was* the devil, and he was damned well going to win.

They landed at Potomac Air Field in Fort Washington, Maryland, at 6:00 P.M. They took a cab to National, where Jonelle's pal Barbara Gordon handed them keys to a car waiting for them in the parking lot. Steven had set it all up. They changed upstairs in the Ambassador Club. The hostesses there had made a shopping run to Macy's at Pentagon City. Kelley handed Steven a blue denim shirt, khaki pants, flannel boxers, socks, shoes, and a sweater he hated but was glad to wear. Nicole gave Jonelle exquisite undergarments, a blue skirt, silk blouse, soft blue sweater, shoes, and hose. Susan bought them overcoats, scarves, gloves and knit hats in case the weather required them. "My God," Steven said to his friends, "we could pack a steamer trunk."

"We'll have to," Jonelle joked, "if this doesn't work and we're run out of the country."

Changed, outfitted for the nasty weather, they drove Barbara's car to the Croydon Inn on Route 1 in Crystal City, a place so nondescript that Stephen figured they'd be safe. He registered them as Mr. and Mrs. Heald. It brought a little levity to the grim proceedings.

The room *was* grim. Blue florals and dark, cigarette-stained furniture. Shag rug and plastic vertical blinds. But their spirits were heightened. They'd made it back to Washington. Tomorrow everything would change. They had time now, tonight and most of the day tomorrow, to put the pieces in place. Jonelle spoke to the staff who worked with her, her support team, on whose secretiveness and impeccable planning rested the success of their plot. Judy Kresge had done her stuff, and everyone—Robin, Dale, Jay, Stacy—were excited about the fact that they were going to be able to help someone they believed in. They'd prepped the studio last night, when taping of another show ceased for the weekend. The set for *Jonelle Patterson Reporting* . . . had been pulled from storage and secretly carted to Studio B. Robin had worked all through the night setting the lights. Judy had changed the locks on the doors. Cables from the control booth were crossed, now set to broadcast into a different feed than usual, so the monitor from Studio B would appear blank. No one outside the group had a clue.

They went to a tired Denny's for dinner. Freezing rain blanketed the entire eastern portion of the country, and that's all anyone in the place talked about. No one paid any attention to Jonelle. She and Steven saw the ads for *60 Minutes* in a newspaper someone had left behind, and they were thrilled. It would attract a big audience. Driving back to the motel, Steven found the downpour so strong that he had to pull over and sit it out. He kissed Jonelle while they did, pretending to be teenagers at a drive-in movie in Dad's car, having their first make-out session. She laughed too hard for it to be sexy.

When they returned to the tawdry room, Jonelle made notes on what she would say, how she would present herself and the story. Steven E-mailed Agent Bass:

> Bass: Tomorrow, Sunday you will receive, at Quantico, the tape that proves the conspiracy and murders. In case you don't get to the office, watch 60 Minutes on CBS. Architect & Landscaper.

Jonelle called Chris Amanpour at her apartment in Manhattan to make sure that everything was a go. "You kidding? The producers are salivating. Mike Wallace is coming out of retirement to intro it. He's hated Keller for years. But it's your show, we just kick it off."

"The ads look great."

"I think they'll get viewers to tune in. Of course, they're not going to get what they think they're tuning in for."

"They'll get better," Jonelle said. "Chris, do you know if Barney is still in Manhattan?"

"I assume so. Told a reporter at the funeral that he was off to the Met this afternoon. He lives here, after all. I think you're completely safe."

"Barney Keller."

"Why didn't you get back to me when I paged you?"

"Shit, Clayton, it's only been ten minutes. I was watching Faust get fried."

"Saint Paul is in a hospital in Atlanta. Bad shape."

Barney's voice went cold. "What do you mean?"

"Shot in the gut."

"Shot in the—?"

"Old lady dumped him at the emergency room."

"They got away?"

"I guess."

"You guess?" Then Barney shouted, "Where'd they go?"

"My guess would be New York, to do the show."

Barney agreed. "Or Quantico first! The tape. We can't let them get that tape to the FBI."

"What can we do?"

"Get Rex to send some of his Jake Hughes–like Christian soldiers to cover Quantico, watch for them, head them off, fucking kill both of them."

"Okay."

"Get him on it, now. Same thing with CBS here."

"I said okay, Barn. What are you going to do?"

Barney thought for a moment as people hurried past him toward the line of cabs clogging the streets outside Lincoln Center. "I'm clearing out my files and booking a seat to Uruguay."

"Barney, no! You can't do this to Rex!"

"Fuck Rex and every Christian walking. I'm leaving this chaos forever."

"You thrive on chaos."

"Only when I'm not facing a jail term."

"Rex's men will get them."

"I gotta get my ass back to D.C. and the shredder, or we're both gonna cook like Faust. Taxi!"

Late at night, with the curtains drawn and no more calls to make or electronic mail to check, they showered, Steven shaved, and they made love, finding peace in the pleasure of one another's bodies on the eve of what they knew might be the most dangerous day of their lives, a respite from the horror of the situation just outside the chained door.

They slept late the next morning, and held one another for a long time before they got out of bed. Steven ran across the road to a coffee place, returned with gooey Danish and two cups of joe that tasted like it had been sitting on a burner all night. They put on the same clothes the Ambassador Club girls had bought them and drove into the District of Columbia. Jonelle's cell phone was working again because she was in her home area, and she used it to call everyone to synchronize watches and discuss last-minute concerns. There were none.

That done, she and Steven still had a couple of hours to kill, and it was well spent, for they drove up 16th Street, nearly to their house, to Foundry Baptist Church, where they attended a 4:00 P.M. prayer meeting and asked the Lord Jesus to help them through this evening, and to protect them in what they were about to do. Jonelle also prayed that justice finally be done.

Outside the church, a hefty black woman recognized Jonelle as she was trying to sneak past the parishioners. Jonelle froze, turned, trying to ignore her. But when the woman persisted, Jonelle looked at her. She knew her. Her name was Betty and she worked in the commissary at the studio. She was astonished to see Jonelle. "Everybody's worryin' 'bout you, girl," she said. "Folk say you was never in that rehab."

"I just got back to town," Jonelle offered. Then she took advantage of the moment. "Betty, tell me something. You hear when Mr. Keller is supposed to be back in town?"

"No, ma'am. Shame about Mr. Findley, ain't it?"

"The real shame," Jonelle said, "is that he was murdered."

Betty gasped. "Girlfriend!"

"He was, Betty, trust me."

"Murdered? That sick old man? Why?"

" 'Cause he was going to talk."

"About what? Girl, you got me real confused."

"Betty," Steven added, "watch *60 Minutes* later."

"That's the wrong channel for us, Mr. Patterson."

"Trust me," Steven added. "Tonight it's the right one. It might even tell you who killed Mr. Findley."

Agent Kevin Bass held out his identification, and Esther Lighter let him inside. He took a seat in the parlor and asked where Jonelle was. Esther said she'd not seen her daughter in twenty years. Agent Bass said if that was true, why was there a Network ONE van parked in her barn? Esther answered with a speech berating him again and again for not helping her baby, and told him he'd better save Jonelle's life or she'd shoot him as well.

"Did you fire the gun that almost killed Leo St. Pere?"

"Who?"

"The man you dumped outside the emergency room."

"You're hallucinatin'."

"Did you shoot him? Did Jonelle? Steven?"

"My girl never hurt nobody. Steven too."

"Then it was you."

She folded her arms. "Can't say I did, can't say I didn't."

It went on like that for almost an hour. Bass explained that they had witnesses who saw her pilot the big Impala that was left running at the ER entrance. Others saw her hurry from the hospital grounds, board a bus, etc.

"I don't know nothin'," Esther said firmly.

"The Impala has your prints all over it."

She blew. "I saved my little girl's life! He was gonna kill her! Steven too, me too I suppose." She jumped up, pulled the rifle that was now caked with dried mud from under the sofa on which they were sitting. "You're gonna find *his* prints all over *that*."

Bass examined the rifle.

"I shot that killer in self-defense and nobody's gonna say different."

He looked up at her. "I don't doubt you for a minute. But the danger isn't over. There are others still after them. Where did they go?"

"Airport. That's all I know." And she made it clear that was as much cooperation he'd get from her.

Bass located Esther Lighter's truck inside a private hangar at Hartsfield Airport. The shotgun was still under the front seat.

Checking, he learned that Steven had borrowed a private plane and filed a flight plan to a small airstrip in Maryland. "They went back to the Beltway," he said in astonishment. "Why?"

Jonelle and Steven drove past their house. Jonelle's heart suddenly went heavy, and she missed Wyatt and Sarah more than she could bear. "I want to call the kids one more time."

He pulled over almost in front of 1915 16th Street, Victor Gallindo's apartment building, where Jonelle dialed the cell phone. They told Victor where they were calling from when he answered in Indiana, assuring him they were in the final stretch. It would all be over after *60 Minutes* aired tonight. Jonelle admitted either this would save them or pass their death sentence, but they needed to take the risk—and it was too late to back out now. It depended on the FBI and the police and how seriously they took them and how fast they were able to make arrests. Hopeful, they told Victor that he and Helen should plan to bring the children back tomorrow. Then the anxious kids got on.

Sarah told Jonelle all about the new friends she was making there. Wyatt grabbed the receiver and blurted, "Sarah's got a boyfriend!"

Sarah said, "Do not!"

"Does too!" the smaller voice said again.

"Wyatt," Jonelle shouted, "let your sister talk!"

Steven laughed.

Sarah told her mother they missed them terribly, and she was thrilled when Jonelle said they could come back home tomorrow. "Can we still go down to Grandma Lighter's for Christmas?" she asked excitedly.

"Wouldn't miss it for the world," Jonelle replied. And she meant it.

Then Sarah admitted about the boyfriend. "Mom," Sarah said in a serious tone, "there's this boy across the street and he asked if I want to go steady."

"What's his name?" Jonelle asked.

"Damon Romine."

"Do you like him?"

"Yes."

"How old is he?"

"My age."

"Is that old enough to go steady?"

"Maybe." Sarah didn't sound certain.

Wyatt grabbed the phone again. "Mom! He's a creep."

"Is not!" Sarah yelled, and Jonelle heard a clunking sound that told her she'd struck him.

"Sarah, don't hit your brother. Listen, you're coming back tomorrow, if you miss Damian—"

"Damon."

"Damon. If you miss Damon, then you'll know if you really want to go steady." Jonelle looked at Steven and whispered, "She's growing up."

Wyatt got on the phone once more. "Mom?"

"Yes, Wyatt."

"You and Dad okay?"

"You'll see us on TV tonight. We told Victor, watch *60 Minutes.*"

"Okay."

"Wyatt, I just wanted to add, we took Potomac's advice. We infiltrated."

"Excellent!"

"Potomac had better be right," Steven said, taking the phone from Jonelle, "or he's gonna be in a lot of hot water."

There was a long pause. Then Wyatt, in a grown-up voice, said, "Dad, you may not realize this . . ." Wyatt hesitated, and Steven knew that whatever he was trying to say was hard for him. He gave him time. Wyatt finally got it out. "Dad, Potomac is made up."

Steven just smiled, and found that his eyes had filled with tears. "We know," he said softly, "and that's okay." He managed, "Bye, squirt," and clicked the off button on the phone.

They drove to the studio in silence.

At the same time, at the FBI headquarters in Quantico, Virginia, Agent Kevin Bass was placing a videotape into the machine in his office. He had been in Atlanta when his office called informing him of Jonelle's E-mail, that a tape was coming to him on Sunday—

today—and to watch *60 Minutes*, which he found puzzling. What for? He took the private jet back to Quantico, arriving at his office shortly after the Express Mail truck had left. Again, scrawled on a note accompanying the tape, was a message to watch the TV show. He was amused.

He was less amused, however, when he played the tape. It was, indeed, everything that Jonelle had promised: a complete accounting of the plot from start to finish, names, dates, sequences to back up every word, clear and unmistakable proof of an evil hidden agenda that four men had perpetrated in the name of God and country. He saw the shooter's ring in every picture from the incidents, the same hand with that ring sitting in Charles Patterson's living room talking to the Four Horsemen, the same hand lifting a drink near Findley at some kind of reception, the same hand nearly plunging down Nina Findley's cleavage in a photo of St. Pere between her and James. He could now go after them.

But it was 5:00 P.M. In one hour, Mike Wallace, Dan Rather, Morley Safer, Ed Bradley, and Christiane Amanpour would go on the air with a *60 Minutes* episode that had been heavily advertised as being, indirectly, about Jonelle Patterson. "The Future: A Woman in the White House?" was supposed to include Jonelle as simply one of its stories, but Bass feared what the country would be seeing tonight was what he just watched in the privacy of his office. Yes, he was sure of what they were planning to do. He picked up the phone and dialed the CBS Studios in New York City. He said he needed to speak to the producer, to the one person he was sure could stop it from airing.

They punched Jonelle's code into the ONE studio's door sentry at the side entrance off DeSales Street and gained access to the building. The security guard on duty was only a part-time worker on the quiet Sundays that Jonelle was seldom there, and he barely knew her. "Howdy," he said, looking up from a magazine. "Welcome back." No questions.

They made it upstairs without running into anyone else who was a problem, and then ducked into the writers' conference room on the second floor. They were greeted by applause. Her staff was waiting. "Oh, honey," Melody Clifford, her punky-looking makeup artist said, "you look like hell."

"Thanks."

"You ready, darling?" big, lovable Dale Harmon asked.

"I'd rather be dodging bombs in Bosnia," Jonelle frankly admitted.

"Oh, come on," her stage manager, Stacy DeLano, joked, "you know this is a lot more fun."

Jonelle laughed. But then her voice took on a serious tone. "Okay, everyone," the reporter in her now said, "let's get the show on the road."

At the same moment Jonelle was speaking to her staff upstairs, Barney Keller was parking his car in his reserved space in the parking structure right outside on DeSales Street. Beside himself with worry after last speaking with Clay at the cemetery, he'd decided to come to the studio directly from the airport and get to work. He had evidence to dispose of, a desk to clear out. He wasn't going to wait to hear from the Good Christian Soldiers Clay had promised would stop Jonelle and Steven near Quantico. He didn't honestly believe it would happen, for none of it had happened, it had been bungled and fucked from the start. The one thing he'd done was turn her into a star, and for that he was proud. The rest of it was shit. He cursed ever getting involved with Rex in the first place. You just couldn't trust non-TV people. They just didn't have a clue. You gotta be in the business. He put his key into the lock and entered his second-floor office, turned on the lights, the bank of monitors, and locked the door immediately behind him.

"This is Rex."

"Yes, Mr. Heald, sir?"

"You got the men outside the studio?"

"She can't get down West Fifty-seventh Street without being taken out, sir."

"How about inside?"

"There too. Couple of CBS pages we got them disguised as."

"Perfect."

"Not to worry, sir. God is on our side here."

"I hope so. I really hope so. God bless all of you, and let's hope this will be over in a little while."

Just down the corridor, as Melody transformed Jonelle from a hunted fugitive back into a glamorous TV personality, Judy Kresge assured her everything was ready. Jay Weinert reported that his sound check was done. Dale Harmon was ready to go with one camera if Steven didn't want to man the other.

"What?" Steven asked.

"Figured two would make it a little less static?" Dale quipped. "Three would be heaven, but this is amateur night in Dixie, after all, so let's not ask for the moon when we already have the stars."

"You've got to give me a fast lesson," Steven warned. "This equipment is more sophisticated than what I'm used to."

Dale said, "These cameras are junk. Network ONE, you know. With all that nice warm Christian money they got to kill people, you'd think there'd be a few bucks left to buy decent equipment."

Everyone laughed. It helped relieve the tension.

Steven handed the tape over to Idell Klatt when she entered, a stately, white-haired, no-nonsense producer who had worked with Christiane Amanpour in Europe and was her good friend, but knew Jonelle only in passing. She was already in earpiece contact with Amanpour at the CBS studio on West Fifty-seventh Street in New York, and she felt that they had about four minutes before it was time to go down to Studio B.

Stacy fastened her mouthpiece in place, grabbed her clipboard, and went over the stage plan for the show with Idell and Jonelle. It was last call for coffee, last time they could wish each other a good show. "Live television," Dale muttered, faking panting, "was it like this for Ed Sullivan?" They lifted their cups, savoring the moment, until a woman walked in looking terrified. "He's here," Robin Lyttle, the lighting designer, said.

"Who?" Idell asked.

"Barney."

"Barney Keller's in D.C.?" Jonelle blurted out, her face looking panicked.

"In the building. Snuck a cigarette, saw his car in the lot."

"That only means his automobile's here," Dale cautioned. "Let's not panic, gang."

"Yeah," Judy agreed, "could just be his car."

"He's never been here on a Sunday," Jay reminded everyone. "He's seldom in Washington."

"True," Stacy added. "He was at the funeral, with Clay, they're both there."

Judy backed that up. "They're both scheduled for a meeting in Manhattan tomorrow morning."

"If he's in town," Jonelle offered, "he'd be in his suite at the Willard, not here."

Idell was cool. "I would guess he's running a little scared by now."

"Probably shredding," Dale added jokingly.

But they realized it could be true, *that's* what he might be doing in the building.

"Studio doors all lock," Robin reminded them, "with new ones. We put them on last night. Even the guards don't have keys."

"The booth included," Jay added.

Dale said, "He won't be able to get in if he tries."

"Time," Stacy said with storm-trooper precision. "Places, every-one."

And they left for the cold, dark studio beneath them, being sure not to walk anywhere near Barney's office just down the corridor and around the bend.

Down that corridor and around the bend, Barney Keller sat at his desk, pouring himself a glass of Glenlivet, a double. No ice. He glanced at the bank of monitors. Unlike his office in the ONE head-quarters in Manhattan, this was a typical television producer's cu-bicle in an old building. Small, cramped, filled with tapes and papers and computers, and monitors covering all the major stations. He watched and listened for news of Findley, Clay, Rex, himself. He knew that Clay would be down at Rex's beach house by now, and he was hoping for a call telling him that Rex's men got them. But he didn't really expect it. He also feared Saint Paul talking.

Perhaps he should send someone down to finish him off before he could. Damn Jonelle's mother, why couldn't she have killed him?

Barney pulled open a file cabinet drawer and dumped the entire contents into the plug-in shredder he kept under his desk. He'd bought it himself a few years ago, from one of those Damark catalogs that seemed to arrive twice a week. Real cheap. In Manhattan, ONE had a big deluxe model in the copying room, but this cheesy place barely held a decent Xerox machine. So he got his own. And now he was glad. Because now, unfortunately, time had run out.

Jonelle entered Studio B. This was her second home, where she'd worked for years now, broadcasting her best stories. Imelda, Jared Tucker, Molly Binenfeld, The Reverend Hatfield, Cardinal Riccio, she'd reported them all from this space, and they suddenly raced through her mind. And her blood pumped hot. She felt that familiar surge of adrenaline she always experienced when she was onto a big story. This was the biggest one she'd ever done, and it was about her.

When she put her earpiece in, she first heard Idell, from the booth, and then Christiane, from the CBS studio in New York. "Well, shall we give it a go?" Chris said in a perky tone.

"Ready."

Robin adjusted a gel, shoved a screwdriver into her toolbelt, and then made sure all the doors were secured.

Judy double-checked them just to be positive.

"Lights," Stacy barked, and the bank flooded the stage.

Barney watched the CNN report on Findley's funeral, which they'd been running all day and which he, frankly, thought was tired. There was a small piece about a mysterious shooting just outside Atlanta, Georgia, about which the details were sketchy, but it seemed that someone had shot and critically injured a man who it was reported was a close friend of James Martin Findley. What was interesting was the speculation that a woman named Esther Lighter, mother of Jonelle Patterson, the famous reporter who'd been missing for almost two weeks now, had been the assailant.

That made Barney squirm. He figured the FBI knew more than they were saying, but what mattered to him right now was not finding Jonelle as much as saving his own ass. He had thought about this tape she supposedly had sent the FBI, this tape that the amateur detective pilot had pieced together, and he knew it would certainly implicate him, but never hold up. She couldn't have enough, wouldn't ever convince a court. It was ludicrous to even think that it presented any real danger. Jonelle and Steven Patterson, they were the only problem. Barney was powerful enough to come out of this unscathed, as long as they were eliminated. But if they weren't, then he'd better leave the country for a nice palatial spread down in South America, life in exile. He laughed. If Jonelle had become the country's Evita, he was turning out to be Juan Perón—running off to seek asylum in another land.

He got up to take a leak. He walked to the end of the hall, feeling the usual humiliation of not having his own private bathroom. That's why he hated this building and spent as little time there as possible. And the toilet was locked. He cursed Sundays and walked down the flight of stairs to the bathroom on the studio floor. And that's when he saw it.

ON AIR—TAPING. The red light underneath the sign on Studio B was flashing. He thought that very odd, for nothing ever taped here on a Sunday evening. He tried the door. Locked, as it should be. He'd report it.

He went into the bathroom, relieved himself, hiked back upstairs, and looked at the ONE network monitor. They were playing a rerun of that series about an angel that Rex had talked him into airing, one of those wholesome and idiotic dramas that spewed the ideals of the Christian Right in a more palatable way than the *700 Club*. Yawn. He switched on the Studio B camera feed and it was black. Of course nothing was taping down there. "Hey, you down there," he said, picking up the phone. "Wake up."

"Front desk."

"I know it's the front desk. Studio B's recording light is on. Shut it off." And he hung up.

At 6:54 P.M. EST, in Myrtle Beach, Rex Heald changed channels on the kitchen TV set because he never missed *60 Minutes*. And this episode, in particular, was one he wanted to watch. They were going to discuss what he'd known for years before the rest of them, that Jonelle Patterson was destined one day to be commander in chief. "I wonder if there's still a chance?" he said aimlessly. He returned to the stool at the island, and to the backrub that Clay was giving him.

At 6:55 P.M. EST, in Atlanta, Esther Lighter sat herself in front of her TV set and tried to calm her heart.

At 6:56 P.M. EST, in Indianapolis, Ramon and Eva Gallindo set pizza on TV tables in front of Sarah and Wyatt. Helen Prybilski served the salad. Victor brought the Cokes in. And turned on the TV set.

At 6:57 P.M. EST, in Richmond, Virginia, Kathleen Holm waited with Lori Flanders and her husband, Kent, eagerly anticipating what was coming after the commercial on CBS.

At 6:58 P.M. EST, in Quantico, West Virginia, FBI Agent Kevin Bass slammed the phone down in frustration because he couldn't get a straight answer out of anyone at CBS. He then reached out and punched the buttons on his remote to turn on that very channel.

At 6:59 P.M. EST, in Atlanta, Georgia, Leopold St. Pere, thirty-five, was pronounced dead of complications resulting from gunshot wounds.

At 7:00 P.M. EST, in New York City, Mike Wallace's voice, over the ticking clock, intoned: *The Future: A Woman in the White House? That was what you were supposed to see tonight on 60 Minutes. What you will see is not what you are expecting, but it is even better, and more provocative.* Then Mike's face was on camera, and he had the air of a serious journalist about him as he said, "*Our interviews with Vice President-Elect Dianne Feinstein, New Jersey Governor Christine Todd Whitman, Secretary of State Madeleine Albright, and Arianna Huffington will be seen at a later date. The live interview with Jonelle Patterson, however, has been expanded.*

"*Tonight's story is unlike anything we've ever done on 60 Minutes. This is an unusual, unprecedented, live broadcast. It is my personal feeling that we are making history here, and doing what the media must do when it can: enlighten besides entertain, seek justice rather than ratings. Here, then, is my esteemed colleague, Christiane Amanpour.*"

Christiane Amanpour looked no less serious. "Good evening. At the beginning of the Broadway musical play, *Irma la Douce*, a man introduces the evening by saying: *This is a story about passion, bloodshed, desire and death, everything in fact, that makes life worth living.*

"Our report tonight is about much the same things, but there is no humor in it. It talks of passion for money and passion for God. It is about bloodshed in the form of firebombs hailed through windows, ceilings collapsing onto the First Lady and hundreds of innocent heads, a bus purposely being rigged to crash, grease on a diving board causing a girl's dreams to die as if they'd been deliberately shot by a gunman. It has desire at its core, the desire of attaining power, all the way to the presidency of this country. And it is about murder, cold-blooded murder by shooting, bombing, lethal injection, poison, and the drowning of a brilliant television news producer. It covers territory from the Philippines to Vatican City, from a country road in Georgia to an apartment in Paris, from an Olympics training facility in California to your own places of worship and your voting booths. But this is no Broadway musical.

"Please, stay with us now as we go live to Washington, D.C., to the studios of Network ONE where Jonelle Patterson, who has been missing for the past thirteen days, and who has *not* been in the Betty Ford Clinic, has come forth tonight in the midst of great personal danger to tell you a story you will find hard to believe. Because it is all true. We call it *Hidden Agenda* and we take you now to our nation's capital. Jonelle?"

"Cue Jonelle," Idell said in the booth. "Here we go."

"Taping," Stacy barked. Then she realized that word was habit. "Live," she corrected herself, "transmitting live. Four, three, two, one—"

"Thank you, Christiane, and Mike, and everyone at CBS, for allowing me to do this tonight. Good evening, everyone. I'm Jonelle Patterson. When I first started reporting for Network ONE back in 1997, I felt I had the good fortune of finding top stories almost without seeking them. You might recall the piece I did in the Philippines on Imelda Marcos, or Olympic hopeful Molly Binenfeld, or Jared Tucker. Those stories, and others like them, it turns out, were not just 'my luck' in having been in the right place at the right time.

Those stories, and so many like them which I brought to you over the past four years, were manufactured, created for the express purpose of raising the ratings, and turning me into a 'star' . . ."

In Indianapolis, Wyatt shouted, "Way to go, Mom!"

In Atlanta, Esther, with tears running down her face, cried, "They made it, they did it!" She dabbed her eyes. "Bless you, girl. Jesus bless you."

In Richmond, Kathleen Holm called out, "Give 'em hell, honey. Go for broke."

In Chevy Chase, at Duca di Milano restaurant where they were waiting at the bar for a table to open up in the dining room after shopping together, Jenny Flexner glanced up at the TV set sitting atop a wrought-iron wine rack. "Mom," she said to Lynne, "isn't that Jonelle?"

"My goodness . . ."

In Quantico, Virginia, Agent Bass jumped up from his desk and ran down the hall, calling to several cohorts to follow him. "Asses in gear," he shouted, "we're going to North West. And tell the guys we got down in Virginia Beach to arrest Heald and Santangelo. Pick up Rovig and Patterson as well. This is it!"

In Myrtle Beach, Rex Heald, mixing a salad at the kitchen island, stopped listening to Clay, who was squatting down in front of the range, tasting the seafood casserole in the oven, still in his swim trunks, dripping wet from the pool. Rex thought he was seeing things. Jonelle was on the TV screen. "What is this? Tape?"

"I think it needs more Old Bay."

"Shut up," Rex barked. "Look."

Clay stood up and playfully said, "Wanna lick my finger?"

"Look, I said!" Rex was motioning toward the TV.

Clay looked. "Yeah, so?"

"What's she doing on the air?"

Clay recognized the set. "A rerun. It's her show."

"No it's not." Rex pressed Recall on the remote. "Her show is on Thursday." Channel 2 flashed. "It's *60 Minutes*."

Clay's heart sank. "Turn up the fucking sound!"

chapter 32

In Washington, Barney dumped more pages into the shredder and poured himself another tumbler of Scotch. Behind him, on the silent CBS monitor, Jonelle was saying: *When you look at the tape of the incident that started my husband and I questioning the rapidity and recurrence of incredible news events that fell into my lap, you see a hand with a gold ring. Take a look at this tape from the Philippines incident . . .*

Barney lifted his glass, slugged down some of the liquor, and then started packing things into his briefcase. As he did so, he punched one of the automatic dial buttons on his phone and got his travel agent at home. "Gary Ledwidge."

"Barney Keller. Find me a first-class seat to Uruguay."

"Pardon me?"

"Uruguay, down there by Brazil someplace."

"American doesn't fly nonstop—"

"I don't give a fuck if I have to fly Air Zambia," Barney barked, "just get me there."

"You always prefer American," Gary tactfully reminded him. "Hold on, I'll boot up the computer and check."

Barney came across a copy of Jonelle's ONE contract. He fed it into the shredder.

The tape that Steven had assembled for *60 Minutes* was riveting. It showed each incident, the same hand with the same ring, and then compared them to the photos of Leopold St. Pere, also known as "Saint Paul," the late television scriptwriter turned hit man. Jonelle talked about Alicia Maris, how she was drowned because she'd learned the man's identity. *Alicia was my producer and my friend, and she was killed not only because she knew that these men were creating news for me to report, but also because she was the first person outside the Four Horsemen—as they secretly referred to themselves—to get a glimpse of what this was really all about. Why "Four Horsemen"? It is biblical. And that is part of the Hidden Agenda. Part Two, after this break.*

Gary Ledwidge started to give Barney the particulars of the flights, times, seats he'd just reserved. "I don't need all that shit," Barney growled, "just the first one. I'm going back to Manhattan tonight, got a few things to do in my office there, and I can make that plane tomorrow morning at eight."

"Why Uruguay?"

"Because it's there. I'm busy now. Good-bye."

"Barney?"

"What?"

"I take it you're not watching *60 Minutes*."

Then he recalled. "A woman in the White House?" He scoffed. "What an ironic, fucking joke." And he hung up.

A moment later, he glanced up at the CBS monitor, curious. Three chipmunks were dancing on what looked like a laptop computer keyboard, singing silently—the sound was off on all of them —while SPRINT flashed like lightning behind them. He groaned, and went back to his files.

Welcome back. This is the year 2000, but back in 1996, shortly after the Republican candidate for president, Bob Dole, was defeated, the Christian Coalition, which was headed by Ralph Reed, lost direction and purpose. Many people felt that Reed had grown too liberal for them, and the lack of leadership in the Beltway was troubling for the Christians who wanted their agenda to influence the laws of this country.

Rex Heald took up the gauntlet that Reed had thrown down, naming his new group of followers the Christian Alliance, and swore that they would gain ultimate power by one day putting their candidate—their puppet—into the White House. But the Republican Party's chances for the future looked uncertain at best, and no one quite knew the way to make that happen.

At the same time, the radical element of the Christian Right, led by Heald, started a new network, my own Network ONE, funded secretly, but almost completely, by money from the Christian Alliance. I was hired, at an astounding salary, to report the news. They promised to make me a star. What I didn't know was the ultimate agenda I was to fulfill: I was to become, in the year 2008, the GOP candidate for the presidency of the United States. The puppet of the Christian Right.

The phone sitting on Rex's kitchen island rang. He looked at Clay. Absolutely paralyzed with fear, Rex picked it up. "Yes?"

"Rex?" The voice was calm. "Barney here. I'm pulling out of D.C. in a little while. Ask Clay if there's anything here I should take with me or destroy."

"Where are you?"

"I said, Washington."

"*Where* in Washington?"

"The studio. Rex, what's the matter? You sound sick."

"You don't know?"

"Know what?"

Clay grabbed the receiver. "Turn on CBS, Barney."

"What's happened? Why do you guys sound so—?"

"Turn on the fucking monitor!"

"I've got it on." Barney swiveled around to face the bank of screens. He was looking at a face he knew quite well on Monitor 8, CBS. "You knew she was going to be on, part of this female power thing. Probably taped it long ago."

"Barney, it's live!"

Cold sweat suddenly broke out, his heart raced, he felt like he was going to shit his pants.

"She's live, goddammit!" Clay shouted.

Barney tried to talk his heart out of an attack. "Naw, can't be."

"Barney, you moron, she's live!"

"All right, so she's live. How can I stop CBS in New York? Shit, I'm getting on that plane tonight."

"She's not in New York, Barney, that's what I'm trying to tell you. She's in the studio there, right underneath you! She's live feed to CBS from Washington!"

"That can't—" He looked at all the monitors. ONE's monitor showed the silly angel show. The other networks were airing their usual losing *60 Minutes* competition. But Jonelle was on her set, and she couldn't be live on her own set without being downstairs here.

He hit the sound button for Monitor 8 and heard her saying his name, Clay's name, James's name, and something about an insidious plot funded and hatched by the leader of the Christian Alliance, Rex Heald. He thought his heart would give out. Then he heard, through the phone, Rex Heald crying out like a wounded puppy.

He snapped on the monitor to his own Studio B, the one that had been dark just before the hour, to be sure this was not coming from downstairs. It was still black. He hit Studio A just for the hell of it. And there she was. Someone had reversed the cables, and it was tapped into the CBS network feed through his own Studio A feed, broadcasting to millions from under his own nose, just as Clay had said. Right downstairs where he'd taken a leak and seen the light on, they were ruining his life from behind his own locked Studio B doors.

"Stop her!" Clay shouted. "Fucking stop her!"

At a private dinner party at her mansion in Montecito, California, a startled and outraged Arianna Huffington spilled coffee into her beaded lap as she heard her name being credited as the inspiration behind Rex Heald's plot to put a Christian woman in the White House in 2008.

At 1600 Pennsylvania Avenue, at a happy tree-trimming party in the family quarters, Al Gore looked at Tipper, who looked at Hillary, who looked at Bill, who dropped an ornament as they all stared at the TV screen in shock.

In Virginia, just up the road from Regent University, Alma Patterson sat stiff and rigid in front of the TV set, her knitting needles frozen in her hands on the mitten suspended between them. All the years of standing politely in the background, deferring to her husband's cause, watching him use and betray his only son, came to an end as she ran to the kitchen, feeling she could take no more, and vomited into the sink. When Charles tried to comfort her, she pulled violently away from his grasp, and spit—vomit still in her saliva—into his face.

In Myrtle Beach, Clay stood barefoot, still in his swim trunks, trying to say something to comfort Rex, who had crumpled to the floor of the kitchen in his Christian Alliance T-shirt and was crying uncontrollably. The phone was ringing, the cell phone was beeping, the buzzer from the gate was sounding, but Clay only cared about Rex. "It's going to be all right, I promise," he said again and again, but Rex just kept on crying.

In the restaurant in Chevy Chase, a waiter told Lynne and Jenny Flexner that their table was ready. With eyes glued to the TV, they completely ignored him.

In Indianapolis, two children sat riveted to the screen, thrilled for their mother, and fascinated by what they were learning. *And then we remembered what our son, Wyatt, had said: Infiltrate! And we did. That's why I'm here tonight.* Wyatt beamed at his mother's words. And he was secretly glad she didn't mention Potomac.

In Atlanta, Esther stroked the cat who'd climbed up into her lap. "That's my daughter," she said, bursting with pride, "that's my kin, that there's my little girl."

Jonelle had only one segment to go. But as soon as the third break began, just as Melody started touching up her face, there was a terrible pounding on the main studio door. Steven looked at Jonelle, eyes locking. *It's him.* They had expected it. In fact, they were shocked that he'd not found out sooner.

"Don't worry," Robin assured them, "he can't get in. Had the locks changed."

"Can't fault a guy for trying," Dale muttered as they heard fists pounding on the metal door.

Barney tried his master key. No go. He then ran down the tunnel leading to the loading dock and tried to enter Studio B from the doors there. Locked tight. He kicked at them and cursed.

Inside, the sound was deafening. Idell Klatt whispered on the earpiece, "We've got trouble."

"He'll cut the cable," Robin worried aloud.

"Someone stop him!" Jay shouted.

Steven motioned to Dale on the other camera dolly. "It's all yours. I'm gonna go out there." He took his earphone off and got up from the seat. Dale switched the shot to Camera 2.

"Steven, don't!" Jonelle shouted.

"All we need is fifteen more minutes," Steven said as he hurried over to her. "I'll be fine." He kissed her on the cheek.

"Send him our regards," Dale sang as Steven hurried to one of the doors.

Robin let Steven out into the corridor, locking the door tightly right after he slipped through. "Good luck," she said.

"Yeah," Steven said, moving down the hall to find Keller and keep him from pulling the electricity.

Inside the studio, as the commercial time lessened, Jonelle worried about Steven. "I hate this."

Jay said, "He'll keep him away."

"He could get killed."

"Two minutes," Stacy bellowed. "Places."

Jonelle said a prayer for strength and returned to her desk on the set. Lights came up. Idell gave the green light. Judy, in the booth, gave a thumbs-up signal. Stacy said, "On air." They were broadcasting again.

Steven cautiously made his way around the perimeter of Studio B, checking all the doors, but there was no sign of Barney Keller.

He stepped out into the alley and immediately ducked as he saw Barney trying to lift a window that Steven assumed connected to the studio in which they were taping. But Barney could not make it budge. He pulled back and started walking directly toward Steven. Steven slid behind a flat that looked as though it had been leaning against the wall there for a good five years. Barney walked right by him and disappeared back inside the building, running.

Steven dashed in as well. No sign of Barney. Remembering his office was upstairs, he hurried up the steps leading to the conference room where they'd met before the broadcast, and listened. He could hear Jonelle's voice coming from a monitor down the hall someplace. He wasn't sure where Keller's office was, but he guessed that's where the voice was coming from. He carefully walked down to the bend in the corridor and rounded it.

He saw one open office door. His heart in his throat, he moved along the wall toward it. As he did so, he could hear a file cabinet drawer sliding open. Just outside it, he heard the sound of what he at first thought was an air conditioner running, but it was the motor of the shredder whirring away under the desk. Steven stepped into the room, ready to attack the guy, figuring it was perfect because he saw Barney reaching into a file cabinet, his back to the door. Steven brought his hands up, clenched his fists, planning to bring them down on Keller's shoulders to slam him against the cabinet and knock the wind out of him. What he wasn't prepared for was the fact that Keller was reaching into the cabinet for a gun, and when he turned, before Steven could grab him, he held that gun pointed at Steven's heart.

"Don't," Steven gasped, freezing his hands in the air between them.

"Well, well. Our Savior of the Skies," Barney mocked, holding the gun on him.

Steven was scared, but he tried to be clever. "You're mixing me up with another saint."

"Saint Paul botched it with you. But I won't. This time I've got better range." The gun was only a few feet from Steven's chest.

"It's over," Steven said in a controlled voice. "She's told the whole story." He nodded toward the monitor. "The world knows."

"Fucking ungrateful bitch," Barney said.

"Give yourself up."

"Like hell."

And then, in that instant, with the gun aimed at his heart, Steven knew—he didn't know how he knew but he knew—that Barney was going to pull the trigger. So he risked it all. He deftly and quickly brought his leg up and put his knee into Barney's crotch. The reaction gave him just enough space to knock the gun up and out of Barney's hand just as the finger pulled the trigger, just as the bullet shot out and exploded the glass in Monitor 8.

Jonelle's image and voice were gone. Barney, taken by surprise by the kick, fell sideways onto his desk, but as Steven lunged at him, he thought fast and brought his feet up, doing a reverse somersault. All those workouts at the Vertical Club had paid off. He was on the floor directly behind the desk, a good vantage point from which to counterattack.

Steven took the slug in the chin, which made his head spin. The man was fit. The adrenaline was pumping, making him even stronger. Steven struck back with a punch in the arm, one toward Barney's face that got deflected, and then a good one in the gut, which doubled Barney over. Steven jumped on top of him and grabbed the hand that was reaching out toward where the gun had fallen, shoving Barney's fingers, with all his might, into the blades of the shredder.

Barney screamed in pain as blood spattered the white plastic case. But he withdrew his cut-up hand and brought it to Steven's face, crushing his nose and eyes with his curled fingers, blood smearing everywhere, until Steven choked and Barney grabbed the bottle of Scotch with the other hand and smashed it on Steven's head. Glass shattered and Steven wobbled.

Barney picked up the gun and was about to shoot the dazed man when the security guard shouted down the hall, "What's going on? Mr. K?"

Barney jumped up, distracted for a split second.

Steven came to and thought fast, curling into a ball under the desk just as Barney shot again, missing his intended target, his head.

The guard was in the room now, facing Barney. "Mr. Keller, what—?"

His voice stopped as Barney shot the man. And ran.

Steven grabbed the wounded guard, breaking his fall, eased him into a chair as he dialed 911 on the desk phone. He saw immediately that the man was only hurt in the shoulder. "I've got experience in this line," Steven laughed, "trust me, you'll be fine" and he left him to pursue Barney.

But at the top of the stairs, Steven felt as if it were raining. His head was wet. Were the fire sprinklers on? He felt his head. Yes, it was wet, with blood. Then he saw the world starting to spin, and the stairway looked to him suddenly like a funhouse slide, one he was starting down even though he desperately didn't want to. Steven called out in pain as he tumbled down the cold, hard steps and crumpled in a heap at the bottom, unconscious.

Jonelle was halfway through the last segment when suddenly there was a sound above them, like metal being ripped open. Was it Steven? Barney? No one could investigate, because they were all needed to keep broadcasting. Jonelle, on camera, ignored it and kept going. In the booth, Idell told Judy, "I love it. The sound effects. This is unbelievable."

"Honey, Jonelle's in deep shit."

"Yes, I know," the producer said, smiling still. "This is great."

A moment later, everyone heard footsteps on the catwalk above the lights. "We've got company, children," Dale said.

Robin agreed. "Forgot the roof hatch."

Dale went in close on Jonelle in case anything happened that he didn't want to pick up.

Jonelle read from documents from Charles Patterson while Judy punched highlighted passages onto the screen in front of the eyes of twenty million viewers.

And then everything went dark.

In Indianapolis, Sarah screamed. Helen brought her napkin to her lips, her arm trembling. Wyatt stopped eating his pizza. Victor took his hand.

In Atlanta, Esther sucked in her breath so deep that the cat ran and hid. She prayed it was just her old TV set.

In Richmond, Kathleen felt her worst fears being realized. She had worried that this was the most dangerous thing Jonelle could possibly do. It looked like something awful had happened.

In Chevy Chase, Lynne Flexner felt her stomach turn. What happened to Jonelle? What did they do to her?

In Myrtle Beach, Clay said, "Yes, yes, yes!" as he ignored the ringing phones and the FBI bullhorn to open the door. Then he bent down and put a comforting arm around Rex and whispered, "Barney got her, she's off the air."

Far from it, Christiane Amanpour told the audience, continuing with the show, dismissing it as "technical difficulty" between ONE and CBS. She picked up where Jonelle left off, without missing a beat. She filled the audience in on the story of Daniel Rovig—aka Jake Hughes—and then presented a short interview she'd taped with Barbara D. McMillan of the FCC, who told the world what Nina Findley had shared with her—backing up everything Jonelle was reporting—and how she strongly suspected that James and Nina Findley were actually murdered by their partners to silence them. She was cool, sharp, and almost as compelling as Jonelle.

Jonelle had no idea what was happening. Pandemonium had broken out in the darkness as the sound of footsteps rushed above her. Dale called out that someone had cut the cable. Robin was trying to find the generator power line. Then there was silence. No one spoke. No one moved. A loudspeaker suddenly crackled, and Idell's voice said, "What's happening out there?" No one responded, waiting to hear what was coming next.

Suddenly, there was the crash of feet hitting the desk in front of Jonelle, cracking it in two, and then she felt a man's powerful hands grabbing her, shaking her, pulling her to her feet, pressing a gun to her head, shouting every expletive she'd ever heard—

Lights. Suddenly, again, the stage lights were up. They flickered and then went bright and stayed there. "Backup power is on," Robin shouted.

Idell joyously said into her mouthpiece, "We're back in business."

Christiane Amanpour was cut short by the feed from ONE's single camera, broadcasting an astonishing sight: Jonelle Patterson standing in front of her desk chair, a gun pressed to her forehead by the owner of her network, Barney Keller.

"No!" Jonelle shouted into Dale's camera. "It's too late now. You're on live TV. The country knows, the world knows. It's over."

Barney turned and shot right at the camera. Dale ducked, and the bullet hit the camera casing and ricocheted off the metal. Barney dragged Jonelle away from the collapsed desk. It was clear that he was taking her hostage.

"Get the shot, Dale, get the shot!" Idell ordered into her mouthpiece. The camera was recording the studio's darkened ceiling.

"That woman's fucking bonkers!" Dale muttered from the corner where he was hiding. He started crawling back toward the camera dolly. "This isn't a beauty pageant we're shooting here."

A trembling Dale again slid his ample butt back onto the dolly seat. He found Jonelle, gun at her head, with the lens. "Jesus, Mary, and Joseph," he whispered, panting for real now, "risking my life for art. Nobody said anything about *this* in *Chorus Line*."

Barney backed Jonelle to the loading-dock doors. "Steven," she begged him, "where is Steven? What did you do with Steven?"

"Fuck Steven," Barney said, "you're my insurance to get outta here."

"Steven!" Jonelle cried out as loud as she could.

"This is incredible," Idell said on the earphones, "incredible. Open up on her, Dale. Get it all."

Then there was a sound above them again, footsteps. Jonelle shouted Steven's name once more, hoping it was him. Everyone looked up, but they could see nothing. Barney dragged Jonelle closer to the door. She kicked and twitched violently in a futile effort to free herself from his grasp, but each time she did, he pressed the gun even deeper into her neck. The camera's eye recorded it all. *60 Minutes* had gone over its one-hour airtime. But it was still going. There had never been anything like this in the history of television.

Above them, a booming masculine voice called out, "Freeze. FBI." And a beam of light—not from Robin's lighting grid—splayed down on Jonelle and her abductor.

Everyone looked up to see who was holding the light, but it was too dark in the studio sky to tell. Jonelle breathed hope again because it was the FBI, but she worried even more because it was not Steven. "There are marksmen aimed at you, you can't possibly get away with this!" the voice shouted. "Give yourself up. Throw down your weapon and release the girl."

"Fuck you!" Barney Keller yelled back, a man not used to taking orders from anyone. He pressed his rear end against the loading-dock doors and pulled Jonelle harder against him, nearly choking her. But in that gesture, she had her chance, for his arm was now pressing on her chin. And she bit, as hard as she could, as if trying to tear through the skin on a salami. Barney Keller screamed in pain, and with that she was able to get free.

But he grabbed at her and managed to get hold of her sweater, pulling so hard she fell to the cement floor. He went down with her, and they grappled. FBI men hurried down the ladder at the back of the studio, but no one could get a shot for fear of hitting Jonelle. Dale, sweating like it was the middle of a humid summer, never let the camera miss a beat. Everyone else wanted to help, but no one dared move. They didn't want Jonelle to be hurt.

Jonelle hauled off and slugged Barney, then tried to run, but he grabbed her foot and she fell again. When she hit the ground, she found her hand resting on the bottom rung of a metal stool. She wrapped her fist around it and swung it, with all her might, to the side and behind her, slamming it squarely into Barney Keller's face.

The gun fell from his hand. Jonelle scurried away, running to Jay and Robin, who were closest to her. Barney reached out for the gun, but a bullet hit him, a muted shot fired from a gun with a silencer, which is all the FBI man had on him when Bass called him into action at Quantico. Barney's hand missed the gun because his bones were shattered by the expert marksmanship of the FBI shooter. Blood gushed. He looked up—directly into the camera lens that was still on him—and suddenly bashed his way backward. The loading-dock doors opened behind him. But instead of running to freedom, he found himself in the arms of more FBI agents than anyone could count.

It was, finally, over. Chris Amanpour went back on live and took over, promising that they would continue to broadcast as long as there was news to report. Mike Wallace joined her to discuss the astonishing event they'd all just witnessed, and the hidden agenda that had led to this.

A handsome man with dark hair and bright eyes touched Jonelle on the shoulder. "I'm Agent Bass," he said.

"Where's Steven?" she asked in fear, realizing he'd not come back. "What did he do to my husband?"

Agent Bass gave her a blank look. But another man said, "I think he's in the corridor, ma'am. He's all right, they're seeing to him now—"

Jonelle ran to the door, which Robin unlocked for her, and dashed out.

Everybody breathed a sigh of relief. Idell beamed, Judy closed her eyes, Melody started crying. Dale wiped sweat from his brow. "Tell the Academy I'd better get a fucking Emmy for that, that's all I've got to say."

Jonelle hurried to the stairway where there was a commotion. Paramedics were carrying a man down the stairs on a stretcher, and she at first thought it was Steven. She cried out, but then saw that it was the security guard. "Looking for me?" a voice said from her right.

She turned her head and saw, at the bottom of the stairs, Steven sitting, being attended to by two medics. One was wrapping his bloodied head with a bandage, the other taking his pulse. She gasped, "Thank God," and bent to her knees to throw her arms around him. "Thank God, thank God."

"Honey, you're okay?"

She nodded. "What did he do to you?"

"Cracked a bottle on my skull. I think I fell down the stairs." He started laughing. So did she. Then they kissed.

Later, back on the set in the studio, they dragged Barney past Jonelle and Steven in handcuffs. He looked directly at her. She returned the glare. Then she mustered up her most biting tone. "Look on the bright side," she said to him, "this'll get the highest overnights in the history of broadcasting."

He let out an ironic laugh. "And it's on goddamn CBS."

She gave him a look of both hatred and pity. Then they dragged him out.

Steven put his arm around her. Dale got one more shot on camera, during Christiane Amanpour's wrap-up: Steven resting his head on Jonelle's shoulder, as they hugged one another with joy that the audience could positively feel.

In Indianapolis, Wyatt jumped up and socked the air with his fist. "Way to go, Mom! Way to go, Dad! *Infiltrate!*"

Epilogue

ABC News Transcript

November 5, 2008, Election Night
Peter Jennings/Jonelle Patterson

JONELLE: Thanks, Peter. I'm here on the floor of the ballroom at the Washington Hilton where you have all just heard President-Elect Christine Whitman's gutsy and gracious victory speech. I've been trying to get to her, Peter, but she's being mauled by well-wishers.

PETER: Is that Arianna Huffington I see over there?

JONELLE: She's as happy as Chris is tonight, I'd say. And for good reason. She's very much responsible for this historic victory.

PETER: So, Jonelle, what's the wrap-up?

JONELLE: This has been one of the closest races in U.S. history, but it's been decided: Christine Todd Whitman, former governor of the state of New Jersey, has been elected the forty-fourth President of the United States of America, the first woman to hold that office ever.

PETER: This night must hold special emotion for *you.*

JONELLE: There but for the grace of God go I?

PETER: In a way, what happened to you led positively to tonight. I think the publicity of your ordeal eight years ago made the public think: *This is not a bad idea.* The men who went to jail certainly didn't poison the concept. Having a female vice president for the past eight years didn't hurt matters any either, even though she was a Democrat.

JONELLE: Vice President Feinstein was a trailblazer. But I think the real credit goes to Arianna. She championed the cause of a woman president all along and gave it honor after Network ONE fell apart, after the indictments.

PETER: Just as Ralph Reed regained control of a stronger, yet gentler, Christian Right after Rex Heald was convicted.

JONELLE: Precisely.

PETER: I take it you've ruled out politics forever?

JONELLE: I'm here to report it. That's what I love.

PETER: In all, an incredible campaign and an incredible night.

JONELLE: An incredibly *long* incredible night, Peter.

PETER: [*laughing*] It's almost six A.M. here on the East Coast.

JONELLE: I'm going home. My daughter is asleep in a chair in the corner over here, she's worked for the campaign since day one. My son is playing piano in an orchestra concert at the Kennedy Center tomorrow. And I've almost forgotten what my husband looks like. He's home watching our six-year-old and I think it's time I join them to do some of the spoiling as well.

PETER: See you tomorrow?

JONELLE: *Late* tomorrow.

PETER: Good night, then.

JONELLE: Good night, Peter. Good night, everyone. God bless. This is Jonelle Patterson Reporting . . . from Washington, D.C.